To Janice

SAVING
VERAKKO

THE CLECANIAN SERIES: BOOK THREE

Victoria Aveline

First paperback edition June 2021

Cover design by Mayhem Cover Creations

ISBN 978-1-7346788-2-6

www.victoriaaveline.com

Saving Verakko

The Clecanian Series: Book Three

Victoria Aveline

1

∽

*N*ope. *Nuh-uh. Nein. Nyet. No way.* There was only so much a girl could take. Lily watched as a large alien hefted Alice over his shoulder and sprinted away at an inhuman speed, leaving her and four other furious women screaming at his retreating back.

So far, these aliens had made a crappy first impression. Being snatched out of her own backyard by disgusting, bulbous, purple creatures had been bad enough, but then waking up in a cell and being ignored by even more aliens had been infuriating. What kind of ass-backward place was this where the men felt they could lock up a bunch of women like lab rats? Lily sure as shit didn't know, because they'd refused to answer any of her questions.

Luckily, she'd only been fuming in her cell for a couple of days before Alice's soft yet frantic voice had echoed through a speaker in her ceiling and outlined an escape. Lily and the four other women who Alice had freed had managed to find one another and run. They'd made it almost to the exit when their path had been blocked by their abductors.

That was when the crazy, black-eyed alien had appeared. The wild-looking man had helped them fight off their captors and had led them out of the underground prison they'd been trapped in. She'd give him credit for that at least. But then, just as Lily had begun to trust the guy, he'd hoisted Alice over his shoulder like a sack of potatoes and hauled ass. *The bastard.*

As soon as the man and Alice disappeared from sight, the women began to argue. Lily remained silent and listened, trying to let her reason overcome the icy fear prickling her senses.

"Should we go after her?"

"Are you kidding? Did you see how fast he was?"

"We should run before he comes back."

"Run where? Back into the bunker from hell? Or down into the forest of death?"

Lily's ears pricked at the word *forest.* She scanned the dark tree line to her left and quickly worked through the pros and cons of venturing into the wild. The night air was humid and warm. Hypothermia wouldn't be likely. Even if it took her longer than expected to start a fire.

It looks like any other forest, she reasoned. Sure, the leaves were a little odd and the colors weren't quite right and the dense canopy blocked out a surprising amount of the bright light cast by the *two* moons. But it was *basically* a forest. And if there was one thing Lily knew for certain, it was that she could survive in a forest. She'd spent a large portion of her life doing just that, after all. Albeit not of her own volition.

A tall woman with dark brown hair the same color as her intelligent eyes shouted, "It's better in there than it is out here!" She threw her hands up and looked at the other women as if they were crazy. "Are you suggesting we stay here and wait for that guy to come back or worse, more of the assholes who locked us up?" They all stayed silent for a moment, and she gestured to the opened hatch in the ground. "That isn't a random bunker. That thing was made to imprison people and be hidden. Do you really think we were able to get free without tripping *any* alarms? Reinforcements are probably on their way right now!"

The hair rose on Lily's arms, and she glanced around, searching for any evidence of an approaching cavalry. She agreed with the woman wholeheartedly.

Vanessa, a sarcastic raven-haired woman and the only one who'd taken the time to introduce herself during their escape, spoke up. "We're on an *alien* planet! You have no idea what kind of crap is waiting in the wild to eat you. You won't make it a day."

She might if I went with her.

"How do you know these aliens don't want to eat you?" the tall woman fired back. "I don't care what you guys do. I'm going."

"I'll go with you," Lily said calmly, drawing all eyes to her.

Vanessa raised her brows and looked Lily up and down, studying her manicured nails and small stature. "You? You think you can survive out there?"

Lily frowned. She was used to people underestimating her. It didn't bother her anymore. All that mattered was that she knew what she was capable of. "Probably. We're not going to thrive. It'll be tough, but I know enough to survive." She glanced back into the woods and spoke aloud, more to herself than to the group. "I'm not saying it won't be hell. We have no tools. No food. No water. We'd have to use primitive techniques, and we wouldn't even know if the resources we scrounge up are safe until we consume them and see what happens."

The tall brunette's eyes were alight with determination. "But…"

As if they shared a mind, both glanced in the direction the alien had disappeared with Alice. Lily muttered what they were each thinking. "But…it might be better than the alternative."

"We should go now, then. Anyone who wants to join is welcome."

Lily nodded, and they both began making their way toward the tree line.

"Wait!" An older woman rushed over to one of their captors, who was now bound and unconscious, thanks to the black-eyed alien. A small woman who'd been silent through this whole ordeal looked on with wide, terrified eyes as the older woman rifled through his pockets and then patted down his body. Nothing.

The small woman with deep brown corkscrew curls and wide amber eyes hurried over to a discarded metallic weapon. She rushed to Lily with the weapon outstretched as if she wanted her to take it.

Lily eyed the silver object, a cross between a cattle prod and a taser. She wanted to take it. Boy, did she ever. They could use it to protect themselves against predators, and if the crackling spark she'd seen before still worked, she could probably also use it to light a fire. Still, she hesitated. "I would love to take that, really, but…what if more men show up? You won't have any way to defend yourselves."

The amber-eyed woman frowned and tapped her own ear, then whispered, "They hurt my ears. I can't hear you."

Lily's mouth tightened. She was injured? Doubts about whether they should be separating gnawed at her but couldn't overcome the itch to leave. They were so exposed here, and who knew how angry the knocked-out guards would be when they came to. "Come with us," Lily said to the woman, making sure to exaggerate her words. She must've understood, because her eyes shot to the dark trees and she shook her head so vigorously that Lily assumed she too thought they were crazy for wanting to leave.

The white-haired woman joined them while both Vanessa and her soon-to-be travel companion looked on with sour expressions. The small curly-haired woman, only a little taller than Lily herself, shoved the zapper into Lily's arms and gave her a small terrified smile Lily assumed was meant to be reassuring.

"She's right," said the older woman. "You should take it. If more men come, a little shock won't stop them. You need it more than we do."

"Thank you," Lily whispered, eyeing each of the women with a grateful nod. She turned, gave a stubborn-looking Vanessa a nod as well, and jogged down toward the forest, where her new companion was already lingering.

"You guys are insane!" Vanessa called from behind them.

Lily caught up to her new brunette friend, who was currently darting nervous glances around the clearing, and they made their way toward the edge of the forest. Both of them came to an abrupt stop at the tree line as though the dark eeriness of the woods had turned their feet to lead.

Lily's heart slammed against her chest. *I can do this. I can get us through until we come up with another plan.* She let out a slow breath, worked to clear her mind, and straightened her spine. *I can do this.*

The brunette woman peered at her, her mouth curled in a crooked, uncomfortable smile. "I'm not backing out, but I gotta tell you, the extent of my wilderness prowess involves RV camping."

Lily glanced at the woman and saw barely masked fear peeking through her expression. Lily assumed her face looked the same. "I have some skills. Earth skills. But what I know might not matter in there. I think I can at least keep us alive until we figure out our next move."

She tried to remain humble about her wilderness training. Truth be told, she could hike into most jungles back home with a machete and elbow grease and live off the land without too much trouble. The miserable annual treks she took with her parents had ensured her skills remained relatively intact but…this was different. Being too cocky would do nothing but land them in hot water down the line if Lily found she couldn't be the self-sufficient badass she thought she was.

"Good enough for me." The woman held out her hand. "I'm Alejandra. You can call me Alex."

"Lily," she replied and gripped the outstretched hand. She turned back to the woods and stared into the darkness, limbs itching to move even as her mind urged her to turn back. *This is gonna be fucking awful.*

***

"Motherfu—" Lily stifled a curse as yet another thorn stabbed through the flimsy soles of her flats. They were bright red, snug, and had cute leather ankle straps that chafed. She glared down at them and decided against tearing off the straps. Although painful, they at least kept her shoes from flopping off. *The worst possible shoes for a daring escape. Well, maybe not the worst,* Lily thought, picturing her favorite pair of strappy, royal-blue stiletto sandals from her closet.

Their trek so far had reminded Lily why she now hated the great outdoors. City sidewalks never tore up her feet. Manicured window boxes didn't scratch at her face or pull at her hair like these twigs. If she were back in Portland, all she'd have to do to get where she wanted was call an Uber. She wiped the sweat off her forehead with her sleeve. *A nice, air-conditioned Uber.*

They'd been walking for what felt like hours through the increasingly dark forest, and Lily had begun to doubt herself more and more. Everything was so different. Where she'd expected thick undergrowth, there was only damp moss. It didn't make sense. The air was heavy and saturated, as it would be if she were cutting through a thick jungle, but their path was clear save for the trees. A crisp, astringent scent hung in the air, undercut with a sweet, minty aroma so unlike the deep, earthy scents of most forests on Earth.

What kind of canopies overlapped like this? Lily glared up at the large, round leaves of the trees blocking most of the light. She'd been in forests all over Earth, but she'd never encountered a place like this. All the survival skills in the world would be useless if she couldn't see what she was doing. *Is it time to call it quits?*

"Maybe we should stop for the night?" Alex panted behind her.

Lily placed her hand on her hips and turned back, breathing deeply. "I'm worried we're still too close. If more aliens arrive and the other women tell them where we went, they might come after us."

Alex leaned against a tree and clutched her side. "We've been walking nonstop for hours!"

"Yes, but we've been moving at a snail's pace. You saw how fast that guy ran." Lily let out a huff and took in their surroundings once again. Rustling from the treetops to her right drew her gaze, but she couldn't make out much in the dim light. Unease lifted the hair on the back of her neck. They'd need to find shelter soon. "You're right, though. We can't keep trying to hike like this. Let's just go a little farther. We need to gather dry branches and kindling anyway."

"Okay. Okay. Just give me a minute to catch my breath." Alex sank to the ground and tilted her head back against a tree. "Where are you from?"

That was always a difficult question for Lily to answer. Her upbringing had been...interesting, to say the least. She wasn't from anywhere, not really. "Right now, I live in Portland," she said without elaborating.

"Cool. I'm from SoCal."

Lily was relieved to see Alex's breathing slowly become more even. The rough days ahead would be a hundred times harder if she wasn't in shape. Lily took the pause to sit and catch her own breath. She squinted to her right at an odd vine that appeared frayed at the end.

"Do you think they did a West-Coast grab or something?"

"Could be," Lily answered, half paying attention. She forced herself not to reach out and inspect the vine until she could examine it in daylight. *Might not be a vine at all.* She cringed.

"What do you think they want with us?"

"No idea." To be honest, Lily hadn't spent too much time thinking about her abduction. Her parents had always trained

9

her to focus on one problem at a time when in a survival situation. Expending mental energy worrying about the past, when she should be keeping her mind focused on their safety, was dangerous. For now, it didn't matter how or why she'd been taken. What mattered was how they could make it until tomorrow.

In the dim light, Lily witnessed Alex roll her eyes then shift until they were facing each other. "Look, I get that you're not super chatty, but I'm *barely* keeping it together here. You realize we're on another planet, right? And we're breathing? Not crushed by a difference in this planet's gravitational pull? These are things I can't not discuss! If I'm gonna make it, I need someone to talk to."

Lily gave Alex what she hoped was a sympathetic smile. "Sorry." She caught the woman's exasperated look and continued, "Sorry! I just don't talk a lot. I get stuck in my head."

It wasn't that she didn't like people. She loved people. One of her favorite pastimes was plopping herself onto a picnic blanket and people-watching. She liked to observe, though, not participate. It was the one downside of her otherwise awesome job as a hairdresser. People expected to chat while they spent hours getting their hair done.

Alex let out a deep breath and studied Lily for a moment longer. "It's okay. I'm just being needy." She rose and brushed the dirt off her jeans. "Alright, Lily from Portland, what now?"

"Now we cover our tracks so anyone following will lose our trail."

***

"Here they are," Alex panted. "Another load of rocks for your perusal, madam."

Lily cracked a smile and paused her digging as Alex trudged toward her, arms full of stones. They'd been attempting to identify knappable rocks after finding a small stream yesterday and settling into their camp but had yet to find any that fractured well enough to use as a blade. While Lily had been in charge of digging a Dakota fire hole, Alex had been tasked with grunt work.

The stones tumbled from Alex's arms, and Lily bit her lip, recognizing a few gritty ones she'd already explained wouldn't work. Poor girl would get that frustrated, defeated look in her eyes again if Lily pointed out she'd hauled some of those heavy stones for no reason.

Alex had been working herself so hard. Harder than Lily had expected from a person unfamiliar with the physical requirements of primitive living. Normally, Lily would've never suggested a person expend massive amounts of energy transporting rocks from one place to another, but she needed to build this firepit, and digging in the compacted earth was about as tough as hauling rocks anyway.

The small fire she'd kept going to keep the lurking animals at bay, stave off the chill at night, and boil the water from the stream was great, but they had yet to find a type of wood that didn't burn incredibly fast. This type of firepit would help it last longer and reduce the amount of smoke rising from their camp, hopefully concealing their location from any aliens who may have attempted to follow them. The early stages of setting up a primitive camp were always tough, even tougher when she didn't know the materials she was working with. Her growling stomach urged her to move faster, knowing a search for food would be next on the agenda. The few charred alien minnows they'd managed to catch had been underwhelming, to say the least.

"Anything usable?" Alex asked, watching her sort through the collection of rocks. When Lily didn't immediately answer, Alex plopped down and pulled out a few rocks herself. "I think these ones might be good, yeah?"

Lily's brows rose in surprise as she examined the proffered rocks. She beamed up at Alex, marveling at how quickly the girl caught on to everything she'd taught her. They'd escaped the bunker two days ago, and during that first night alone together, Lily hadn't been sure of Alex. She tended to complain a lot, but Lily had soon learned her complaining was just something that made her feel better. A way for her to expel her negative energy and stay motivated. Alex attacked every challenge Lily threw at her with a determination to prove her worth that rivaled Lily's own.

Alex studied Lily's proud expression. "Yeah? I did good?"

Lily nodded. "I think you did good. Let's see." She raised her hammerstone and struck it against the smooth, lavender stone.

A razor-sharp flake separated from the rock, and Alex leapt up, pumping her fist and dancing around the fire. "Yes. Yes. Yes!" she howled before collapsing on the ground again. She shook her head at Lily. "I was getting really sick of lugging rocks up here."

Lily bared her teeth in an apologetic wince. "Now that we know what type of rock will work…"

Her grin faded, and she let out a groan. "You magic that into a knife, and I go back to the quarry." Alex bit the inside of her cheek, breathing deeply, then lifted back onto her feet.

Lily tried to contain her laughter as Alex shuffled away, grumbling and cursing under her breath.

***

"You can't be serious!" Lily wheezed and clutched her ribs.

Alex was laughing so hard, tears streamed down her face. "Why would I lie? It was terrible. I was in my room, and I thought Ray had come over and used his new key to surprise me, so I got completely naked, not one scrap of clothing, and I put a rose between my teeth like we'd joked about the night before, and…"

They both laughed harder. Lily's head was pounding.

"Then this big, oozing, purple thing with spikes coming out of its head appeared. And for just a second, I thought it was Ray dressed up like some weird sci-fi monster."

Lily sipped warm water from the piece of wood she'd hollowed into a bowl. "What did you do?" She handed the bowl to Alex.

"I took a beat and thought about whether I was into Ray enough to deal with his weird fetish, of course! That's when it sprayed me. Thank God the thing had enough sense to pick up my clothes from the floor after it knocked me out. I'm thinking it'd already gathered other humans and figured out that we normally wear clothes. Could you imagine me running through this place naked?"

Lily erupted in laughter again, reveling in how good it felt. For the past week, they'd been miserable. Using everything she knew, along with some educated guesses and a ton of luck, they'd managed to find a suitable shelter, build a stable fire, and disinfect enough water to not die of dehydration anytime soon. They'd also taken a big risk and started eating red fruits from a nearby tree. Lily had been against it at first, but after days of hiking through dense forest without any food and without any luck catching an animal using one of her snares, she'd conceded the reward outweighed the risk.

She'd been relieved and overjoyed when the fruit had not only proven safe to eat but had also given them a burst of energy, hinting they were much more nutrient dense than she'd initially assumed. They'd still need to find other sources of food at some point, but at least they wouldn't become malnourished in the meantime.

Eventually their laughter subsided and they sat in amicable silence, bellies full of the tart fruit. The cave alcove they'd set up camp in was warm and cozy from the crackling fire. Lily stared into the bright green flames as Alex used a small stone to etch something onto another perfectly round rock.

It seemed an eternity ago that she'd been relaxing in her own backyard in Portland, staring into another fire. Only, that fire had been normal and mundane compared to the flickering green flames of the one she'd grown used to building on this planet. *It must be some chemical in the wood that does it.*

After a good amount of trial and error, they'd finally found a type of wood that burned slowly, allowing the fire to need tending every few hours rather than every few minutes. And as an added bonus, the green fire also had an odd, crisp, minty scent to it. Both Lily and Alex's morale had been greatly boosted after they'd taken their first smoke baths and gone to sleep smelling fresh and clean.

There'd been a learning curve, but Lily was coming to realize this forest was quite bountiful. The frayed vines she'd noticed on her first night here had turned out to be trees, oddly enough. Instead of dropping seeds, it seemed these trees had saplings that grew downward, then sprouted roots and burrowed into the soil when they were low enough. Lily had marveled at the different stages of tree growth while hiking through the forest their whole first morning here.

Although still much sparser than she'd have expected, she saw in the light of day that there were in fact many types of odd-looking plants growing on the forest floor, but they tended to swarm the bases of the trees. Most plants, in fact, appeared to feed off the trees in some way.

It made sense the more she thought about it, considering the trees had the most access to sunlight. Vines with bright flowers, giant fuzzy fronds, and a plethora of other small greenery engulfed the trunks of the trees as if Mother Nature had gotten a little drunk and generous with her plant life Bedazzler. Even the young saplings, whose roots had not yet touched the ground, had small air plants and flowers attached to their lengths. Winged insects with fuzzy bellies and cheerful dispositions buzzed happily around the trees at all hours of the day and night. Lily enjoyed the lulling sound, while Alex groused about the noise nonstop, always swatting the creatures away, whether they were anywhere near her or not.

The large leaves that dominated the forest canopy were round and sturdy, almost the texture of leather. After examining a few decaying leaves, quickly being covered by bright green moss on the ground, Lily had used a thin sapling as a rope and inched to the canopy high above to gather more.

She pulled some of those leaves over to her now and stared at them, wondering how she could fashion them into shoe covers for her flats.

"I think it's time we talk about what comes next," Alex murmured, interrupting her thoughts. She peered at Lily over the crackling flames. "We've been hiding out here for a week now, and there's been no sign of anyone coming after us."

They'd avoided having this talk until now, and Lily understood why. She'd avoided thinking about it herself. After they'd traveled far enough into the forest to feel safe, and the adrenaline exacerbating her flight instincts had dwindled, she'd too wondered...*Now what?*

"You want to leave." Lily took another gulp of water, stalling. "Where would we go? And how do we know we wouldn't end up locked in a cell again?"

"Maybe we can find a small city on the outskirts of town that has non-psychopathic aliens."

Lily chuckled weakly and raised her head to study Alex. She'd been slim a week ago when they'd left. Now, the hollows under her high cheekbones looked more severe than she remembered.

Alex wasn't lying when she'd said she had no wilderness experience, but the girl was tough. Lily had tried to teach her as much as she could about surviving on her own, in case they got separated. After all, death in a place like this was only a small cut and infection away. Alex complained but never lost focus, not even when the sinister little bugs that nipped at her bare ankles drew blood, or each night while they listened to the sounds of unseen animals shuffling nearby.

"It's not like I *want* to spend the rest of my life like this. But at least out here, I'm in charge of my life." She crossed her arms, resting her elbows on her knees and settling her chin on her forearms. "I agree with you, but..."

Emotion expanded Lily's chest like a balloon waiting to pop.

Alex crossed over to her and sat down, tilting her head and resting it on Lily's shoulder. "I'm scared too."

They sat together like that for a long time, not speaking until finally Lily whispered, "We'll leave tomorrow."

***

The next morning, she and Alex groggily gathered their belongings. Lily had lain awake the whole night thinking about the days ahead and what they might find. Judging from the dark circles under her eyes, Alex had done the same.

They set off as the sun started shining light between the dense leaves and had been walking for a few hours when Lily heard the telltale signs of rushing water. She knew from watching the small minnows in the stream that, although odd-looking, fish did exist on this planet. She listened to the loud rush of water and deduced the river must be large enough to hold fully grown fish. She just had to weave a fish basket, and with any luck, they'd finally have some real protein.

"We need to keep heading downhill," Lily called, hefting a bag Alex had weaved that contained their foraged supplies. "If you want to find a town, following the water is probably our best bet."

They continued walking downhill and talking. Although she'd met Alex a week ago, she felt a strong kinship with the woman that she'd felt with only a few others in her life. They talked about Earth and the foods they wished they had at the moment. Both kept the conversation light and filled with humor to distract from the fear that at any moment they might come across a wandering alien.

They started discussing what a wild alien might look like, and Alex listed off fictional aliens from movies she'd seen.

Lily hadn't seen any of the movies she was describing, and a pestering voice in the back of her mind taunted that she'd likely never get the chance to see any of them now.

"I can't believe you never saw *Alien*! I have to be in the right mood to watch sci-fi, but honestly, if it has Sigourney Weaver...I'm in," Alex called over her shoulder.

A small twinge of annoyance shot through Lily again. Alex, as it turned out, was a movie buff; more than that, she'd been a movie reviewer back on Earth. Lily, on the other hand, hadn't started watching movies until well into her teens. Unsurprising, considering TVs—and electricity, for that matter—weren't commonly available in the middle of the jungle. "No, Alex. I haven't seen *Alien* or *The Shawshank Redemption* or *Titanic* or any of the millions of movies you've mentioned so far," she called back sarcastically.

"Alright. Alright. If we never make it back to Earth, just know I'll be starring in and directing live-action remakes of all of them so you can truly experience them," Alex vowed with a crooked grin.

Lily chuckled and slid down a slippery area of the hill before stopping herself. "I'm looking forward to your performances."

Gradually the "slope" turned into a muddy, rocky descent that required all of their focus to navigate. Lily's muscles burned, and she could feel the skin on her heels peeling and oozing as her one-size-too-small flats rubbed against the area over and over again. *But they'd been on sale and out of my size*, she mocked, annoyed with herself for being impulsive enough to have thought they'd be fine once broken in.

The next time they stopped, she'd need to fashion a pad or wrap to protect her heel. Until then, she'd have to ignore the annoying sting and focus on the distant sound of rushing water. The trees had thinned and the cloud-filtered sunlight illuminated their path, but the wet, mossy rock was still slippery and treacherous. One wrong foot placement, and you'd go tumbling down.

Although fit, Alex was obviously not used to traversing this type of terrain. Lily winced in sympathy when her poor friend's leg slipped and scraped against rock yet again.

"I think we should stop and take a break," she called down to Alex, who had paused while gripping a rock face in an awkward position.

"But the river sounds so close! No, I'm—" Alex lost her footing and slid the rest of the way down the rock to a patch of mud below. Blood trickled from an abrasion on her cheek.

Drops of water began to fall from the sky, and Lily had to stifle a laugh. From this position, Alex looked so pitiful sitting sprawled in muck and glaring at the sky through squinted eyes.

"Just stay there," Lily called through her grin. She made her way down the rock face.

When she finally reached the bottom, Alex was back on her feet and glaring. "How did you do that so easily? You aren't even wearing real shoes, and you're carrying the bag!"

Lily gave a quick shrug and grinned.

Alex attempted to wipe the dirt off her faded blue shirt but only succeeded in smearing the mud and coating her hands. She held her palms up toward the drizzling rain. The small droplets bounced off the thick clay. "Fucking alien mud," she cursed under her breath.

They continued forward, their soles growing heavy from the accumulating sticky mud clinging to their heels.

"It sounds like the river must be just up ahead," Alex said, following a patch of relatively dry ground around a large rock face.

Lily followed behind but stopped to inspect a path of trampled vegetation. *This could be a game trail.* Hope and anxiety made her pulse quicken. A game trail meant animals that could be trapped and eaten, but it also meant alien fauna. Lily scanned the damp ground, looking for tracks. She'd come across a few tracks over the past week but hadn't had any luck catching anything.

A piercing shriek rang through the silence, and Lily's body erupted in pins and needles. She sprinted around the corner to the source of the scream. Her stomach plummeted.

Alex was hanging over a ledge, scraping at the mud for purchase. Without any roots to cling to, she was slipping away quickly. Lily dove, gripping Alex's wrists just as she was about to fall. She held on with both hands and pulled, digging her elbows into the thick mud. Through gritted teeth, she said, "What the hell happened?"

"The ground gave out under me!" Alex kicked at the wall of dirt before her, trying to find a foothold, but she only managed to pull Lily through the mud until her head hung over the edge and Alex was dangling from her wrists. Tremors wracked Lily's body, and her mind blanked for an instant as if wanting to retreat.

She tried to lift Alex's weight, but the ground was too slippery. The earth below her torso sagged. They were going to fall. The weight of Alex was slowly dragging Lily over the edge, and she had nothing to brace against. She forced herself to calm and assess the situation like her mother had taught her.

Alex's eyes were wide and panicked. "Don't let go!"

Lily turned her focus to the river below and swallowed. *Rapids.* "Alex, look at me." Alex's wide eyes kept searching around her for something to grab onto. "Alex!" Lily shouted, drawing her attention. "I need you to listen carefully."

Alex nodded, and tears leaked from her brown eyes.

Lily tried to keep her voice even and calm, but it trembled all the same. "We're going in the river. There's no way out of it."

Alex released a quick sob but kept listening.

"When we hit the water, you need to flip on your back and float. Make sure your feet point downstream. Do you understand? If we get separated, don't wait for me. Remember what I taught you and find a town. Keep heading downriver." The ground below them dropped a few feet, and Lily yelled, "Don't try to stand up or swim! If you go under, try to float on your back until you surface again! I won't let go of you! Don't—"

Before she could finish, the ground gave out and they were falling.

After they hit the water, everything was a blur. The ice-cold rapids sucked them under and buffeted them around. Lily managed to keep hold of Alex's hand for longer than she'd have thought, but then they were rammed into a boulder and Alex was wrenched away from her. The sudden lightness on her shoulder told her she'd lost her bag as well. Lily stifled the urge to kick upward and instead rolled until her body was flat. Eventually she felt air on her face and gulped in a deep breath before being sucked under again. Each time she surfaced, she tried to tilt her head and look for Alex.

At last she spotted her a little farther upstream, floating on her back. Relief made Lily cry out just as she was sucked back under. When she emerged again, she lifted her head a fraction and spotted a large downed tree jutting into the river about half a mile downstream right after a relatively calm stretch of river.

Each time her face emerged above water, she screamed and pointed at the tree, hoping Alex would understand. Once the menacing undertow of the rapids lessened, she turned on her belly and swam across the current, positioning her body in the path of the tree. Chancing a glance over her shoulder, she saw Alex was doing the same. They might make it through this, after all.

As the tree drew near and the current picked up speed again, she braced for impact. Her feet hit first, sending shockwaves through her ankles and shins. Instead of being caught by the trunk, her body was dragged underneath it. She thrashed her arms, reaching out for any limbs she could grasp before the current swept her away, and clutched a sapling vine. She pulled on the vine until she surfaced again, then flipped onto her stomach and dragged her body halfway out of the water and onto a tangle of branches still clinging to the trunk.

She turned her head just in time to see Alex coming toward her. "Grab anything you can!" she screamed over the roaring sound of the rapids.

Lily's stomach flipped when she realized Alex hadn't swum far enough over to catch the tree. She scrambled as fast as she could up onto the trunk itself and shimmied toward the jagged edge sticking out into the river.

Alex managed to grab a single branch hanging from the tip of the tree, but the current was dragging her back toward the middle of the river. Lily crawled up the trunk as fast as she could; the broken nubs of lost branches cut into her inner thighs, but she barely felt the sting. All she could think about was the despair and sheer terror in Alex's eyes. When Lily reached the edge of the trunk, she stretched her arm toward Alex as far as it would go. Alex kicked and thrashed against the current, trying to get closer, but it was no use.

The branch cracked near the base. Lily stretched, cantilevering herself over the rushing water toward the branch, just out of reach. She saw the moment Alex understood. Her eyes hardened like they had on the first night at the edge of the forest. Just before the branch broke off completely, she rolled onto her back.

"No!" Lily's scream rose above the roar of the river as Alex's dark brown hair disappeared under a swell.

2

One Week Later

Verakko's gaze raced over the multitude of screens in front of him, unbelieving. He knew of the Insurgents and their plan to abduct and experiment on humans. He'd even heard first-person accounts of their treachery from the humans themselves, but a small part of him had clung to the unreasonable hope that no member of their supposedly advanced society would stoop so low as to cage sentient beings in such a vile way.

Here, in front of his very eyes, was irrefutable evidence that his people were no better than any other. Feeds of miserable human females and a solitary male were being broadcast to his screen from over five different facilities across Clecania.

"Fuck," Luka croaked from behind him.

Verakko shot a sympathetic wince over his shoulder at the glaring male and saw his face had paled and his eyes were searching the screen with an undercurrent of rage.

Was the anger glimmering in his eyes for himself or his mate, Alice? Both Luka and Alice had been held captive in a different facility identical to the ones covering the screen. They, and a small group of females—two of whom were still missing—had escaped a little over two weeks ago.

Arguably, Luka had received the worse treatment while prisoner. He'd been beaten and drugged, but as Verakko studied Luka, he felt as though this male didn't care about his own experience at all. Bright blue mating marks, only the second to be seen on a Clecanian in centuries, ran over the large male's wrists and hands, and as Luka's gaze darted from the facility feeds to the exit of the small cabin they were currently in, he continued to absently run his fingers over the marks.

Verakko returned his attention to the task at hand and attempted to clear his mind of the unwanted pangs of curiosity nibbling at his senses. It wouldn't do to start daydreaming about someday finding a mate for himself.

His nimble fingers flew over the holographic control panel to his right. *Almost ready.*

To his relief, there were only about two or three guards manning each facility. For the past few minutes, Verakko had been trapping them as quietly as he could. Most had been easy to lock up as they sat in their facility's control room and didn't notice the sound of their door locking. But others had been wandering the halls. He'd lured them into vacant cells by broadcasting the sound of static. When the guards had investigated the faulty equipment, he'd sealed the door behind them. Only one guard remained.

Verakko felt his fangs pulse in anger. The last of the guards was currently in a room with a female. She was strapped to a chair, facing away from the camera, and he was seated on a stool next to her. At present, they were only speaking, but Goddess knew what the abhorrent male had planned.

The idea the Queen had devised to free the captured humans was imperfect, to say the least. Remotely opening the facility exits and releasing humans into the wild with no idea of how to survive seemed idiotic at first glance. But the alternatives were worse. The Insurgents, otherwise known as PRIC, were not yet aware they'd been found out.

If the Queen and her army spent resources attempting to find each secret facility, word might get back to the Insurgents, and they may decide to discard the evidence—namely the humans themselves—before being revealed as the traitors they were.

The strategy they'd settled on to free these humans had been more disheartening than hopeful, but they couldn't allow them to be locked up any longer. Verakko shuddered to think what may have already been done to them. It boiled his blood that he couldn't figure out a way to access the locations of the facilities.

"I'm almost ready for Alice to come in," Verakko said as he tripped an alarm down the hall and watched the last of the guards leave to investigate. When the guard was a safe distance away, in an unused corridor, Verakko sealed the only exit and inspected his work. Many of the trapped guards were banging on their doors, and some, those in the control rooms, hadn't noticed they'd been trapped at all. Verakko sensed no movement behind him, so he repeated himself. "You need to retrieve Alice now."

Luka's frown matched his own. He said nothing. It was clear he was very unhappy about Alice being here at all, but the persuasive female seemed to have a hold over this stubborn male that was quite impressive.

If I had a mate, I'd never allow her to be this close to danger. Never.

When Luka still made no move to leave, Verakko debated whether to *sway* the male. Normally, *swaying* was frowned upon, but he imagined that in this situation, a small nudge wouldn't be too bad. Whether Luka's mind would accept the *sway* was another matter. The ability of his people, the Swadaeth, to use their minds to influence the thoughts of others was unique and, like most unique things, often feared by those who didn't understand the practice.

Verakko shrugged off the idea. Although Luka was distracted and likely stressed, which were perfect conditions for a successful *sway*, it'd be...bad if Luka realized what Verakko was attempting to do.

"I'm ready now. Call her in. She needs to speak with the females and explain how to escape—"

Shouting from outside made both their heads spin to the exit. Luka flashed a worried glance toward the feeds then back to the door.

"Go!" Verakko barked, instinctually infusing the command with *sway*, but Luka was already dashing out of the small cabin.

Dread laced itself around his throat as he began to secure access to the communication system in the first facility. *How much time do I have?* The echoes of pummeling fists and pained cries boomed through the doorway, and Verakko stiffened. There wasn't time to talk to each human individually as they'd planned.

Someone or something was thrown into the side of the building with a heavy thud, just as Verakko focused himself on the task at hand.

Originally, they'd planned for Alice to speak to the humans, judging Verakko's voice and word usage to be too alien and thus untrustworthy, plus there was no guarantee all the humans had been implanted with a language translator. If there was ever a time to use his gift, this was it. He quickly programmed the comm systems to link and spent precious minutes making sure only the speakers in the humans' cells would produce sound.

A thundering bellow outside was followed by a loud crack. "They have Yulo gloves!" shouted a male from outside.

He forced his eyes closed and took a calming breath, willing his mind to focus. "Hello, humans. I am a friend." A flash of annoyance speared through him as almost all of the twenty or so prisoners flinched or jumped at his words.

He forced calm to leak into his voice as he *swayed*. "Listen. In a moment, your doors will open. You need to run. Look for a spinning stairway and run to the top floor, then out through the front doors. Once outside, you'll want to get as far away from this place as possible. Try to find a city and gather as much attention to yourself as you can. You'll tell them you wish to speak to the Queen of Tremanta."

A booming, anguished roar shook the house. That could only mean one thing—Alice must be in danger. He needed to help.

Mustering all the command he could manage into his *sway*, he said, "They're open. Leave now!"

He watched with bated breath as they rose and moved to their now-ajar cell doors.

Verakko spun and bolted to the cabin door, wrenched it open, and bared his teeth. He felt the sting through the roof of his mouth as his fangs filled with deadly venom. With one last glance to the screens, he slunk silently into the night.

He managed not to attract any attention as he assessed the scene, clinging to the shadows around the building. His secondary eyelid slid into place and disguised his glowing eyes. A Strigi male was soaring underneath the dense canopy, readying to shoot using an incredibly illegal Yulo glove. The other two-winged Strigi males were grappling with Luka and Kadion.

Three against three? Please. Verakko chuckled low and moved soundlessly until he was poised behind one of the males aiming a glove at Luka's head.

31

Strigi were notoriously hard to kill because of their lethal wings and ability to fly out of reach. Although their wings were their greatest strength, they were also their greatest weakness. The massive wingspan created blind spots while fighting, and the inability to bend their wings behind them made their backs particularly vulnerable.

The Strigi male stiffened, sensing Verakko behind him a moment too late. With one hand, Verakko gripped the male's chin from behind, and with the other, he wrenched the top of his head down until he heard a sickening crack.

Luka peered over his shoulder at Verakko and gave a quick nod before dashing into the dark forest near where Alice must've been standing only minutes ago.

Verakko kept his eyes trained on the two remaining Strigi, now circling overhead. He hefted the substantial weight of the male whose neck he'd just broken and shielded Kadion and himself from the Yulo glove blasts.

"Did they make it out?" Kadion rasped while attempting to strip the Yulo glove off the Strigi's limp hand.

Frustration made his fangs ache, and he grimaced. "I did what I could under the circumstances." A bolt of green light sizzled through the dead male's wing and whizzed past Verakko's ear. The acrid scent of burnt feather, mixed with the pools of blood at their feet, invaded his nostrils. "What's your plan, General?"

Kadion finished strapping the glove on and shot Verakko a lopsided, dimpled grin. "My plan is to shoot stuff."

How elegant. Verakko rolled his eyes and readied to toss the winged male aside. "Just get them close, and I'll do the rest."

In a moment, the boyish grin on Kadion's face vanished and was replaced by the hard, cold indifference the male was known for in battle. The swift and abrupt change in demeanor even had Verakko itching to scoot away.

Kadion crouched, and rivulets of blood ran down his upturned face from a nasty headwound. "We're aiming to incapacitate, not kill, so keep those bites to yourself unless we're about to die."

"Understood."

At Kadion's quick nod, Verakko used all of his considerable strength to launch the Strigi corpse into the air, giving their attackers a moment of shock that would last long enough for the Yulo glove to do some damage.

These males were smarter than the others, however. They kept to the air rather than fighting on the ground, as their deceased counterparts had done. Verakko searched the area, seeking any means to attack or delay. If he could give the females enough time to escape by preventing any of these Strigi from getting to the control center inside the cabin, at least this night wouldn't have been for nothing.

A furious growling hiss tore from his throat. There was nothing that could be used as a weapon and no way to reach the airborne assailants unless he climbed a tree and leapt. There were many reasons why that idea would never work, though. What he wouldn't give for a shade spear right now.

The males dove away from each other suddenly. Verakko kept his gaze trained on the Strigi hovering above him. When the male opened fire, he vaulted into the shadow of a nearby copse of trees. He felt the slice of a Yulo beam tear through his hip and stifled a shout. He crawled across the dark ground, allowing his skin tone to deepen even more and camouflage him as it was designed to do.

The shots ceased, and he peered out into the clearing. To his horror, a third male, who'd been lurking in the woods, was now silently sneaking up behind Kadion, long blade in hand. Had he not joined the fight before because he didn't have a Yulo glove?

The male gripped the handle, and rage roared through Verakko at the dishonorable position. The lingering venom in his fangs ached to be released. Chancing a quick glance above him, he saw the Strigi had sped toward Kadion, an attempt to distract him.

Verakko dashed toward the attacker at Kadion's back, making sure to keep his footfalls light. Just as he came within a few feet, the large Strigi turned and clumsily jabbed with his sword before trying to sweep Verakko's legs with his wing.

Verakko ducked and rolled, then sprung up and trapped the male's left wing between his forearm and ribcage. He used his other hand to grip the thick but hollow bone that ran from his shoulder to the apex of his wing and wrenched it downward, cracking the bone in half.

The male screamed and swung his blade wildly in Verakko's direction. He jumped out of reach and squared off with the Strigi. Verakko hissed a laugh between his teeth. "You can't fly away now, can you?"

The Strigi male was larger than most and had the furious and slightly vacant glare of an overeager warrior. One who rushed into battle with little regard for honor or loyalty. Only looking to kill and prove themselves powerful. The male's eyes flashed to Verakko's side, where blood still poured from the open wound at his hip. If they didn't win this fight soon and he kept exerting himself like this, he knew he'd succumb to blood loss. Verakko studied the male and let his limbs relax. He shifted his weight left to right in a fluid motion, drawing the male's confused gaze. "Your wing is broken, but you could still get a lucky shot in if you rushed me right now."

Verakko could see the *sway* take hold. The male's eyes glossed and narrowed. The corner of his mouth lifted in a smirk, as though he'd had a grand idea about how to dispose of Verakko.

The poor idiot had no idea what he was in for. Verakko clutched at his wound weakly to aid the *sway,* and as he expected, the male let out a loud howl and rushed toward him. When he was within a foot and confidence was etched into his features, Verakko dodged, grabbing the male's sword arm as he went. Before the Strigi could right himself, Verakko had sunk his fangs into the flesh just below his elbow and released a few small drops of venom.

He stood back as the massive male shuddered and dropped to his knees, eyes wide with terror. Verakko crouched before him, put a single finger on his chest, and watched as he tipped and then sprawled on the ground. "You were going to stab him in the back like a coward. Now you'll die like a coward."

The male made a gurgling sound in his throat, and his eyes glossed over. Verakko clenched his jaw. *Fuck.* He deserved to die, but unlike some of his people, Verakko didn't revel in the suffering his victims experienced.

A stray tear leaked from the male's eye. His limbs shook as though he were trying with everything he had to lift them. Verakko couldn't stand the sight anymore.

Leaning forward a fraction, he whispered, "Sleep now. And feel no pain."

Immediately, the tension left the male's body and his lids grew heavy. The blood lust Verakko had felt a moment ago ebbed as the life faded from the Strigi's eyes, and as always, a sliver of regret knotted in him. His mother would've been ashamed if she'd seen him grant that small mercy.

A booming voice echoed through the clearing. "We need one of them alive for questioning."

Before Verakko could regain his composure and jump back into the fray, a sizzling thud hit the back of his head, and then everything went black.

***

Shards of ice pelted Verakko's face, rousing him. His head was pounding furiously, but his body felt weightless. He peered below himself and froze. Fear coursed through his veins, dissolving all of his pain and leaving terror in its place.

One of the Strigi was holding him by the arms and flying, its wings buffeting the chilled air around them.

Being this high up was Verakko's worst nightmare come to life. His heartbeat banged out of control in his chest, and his breaths grew shallow.

He needed to find a way down. Now.

Closing his eyes, he forced his mind to calm, the way he always did whenever he had to deal with heights. *You aren't afraid of the height, you're afraid of the fall and the ground. All you need to do is get closer to the ground.*

Below him was the Sauven Forest. It had to be. He couldn't possibly have been unconscious for that long.

He glared up toward the Strigi holding him. Cuts and fresh bruises marred the male's face, and a wince was permanently etched in his expression. How could he *sway* the male? What might he have already been thinking? A communicator strapped to his left bicep caught Verakko's eye. He shot a glance to his own bicep and found his communicator missing. *Shit!*

As they passed through a particularly dense, low-hanging cloud, shards of ice stung their skin again. The male cursed under his breath, and Verakko had his answer.

"It would be much easier to fly lower. Out of the path of these clouds." Verakko kept his voice low yet audible.

Without glancing to Verakko, the male suddenly scanned the ground, eyes searching for any signs of life.

Verakko *swayed* again. "There are only trees down there. No one to see if you don't follow orders."

The male dipped, heading out of the clouds and down into warmer air. He leveled out into a glide several hundred feet above the forest.

Still too high.

"Your wings are so sore from all this extra weight. Maybe you should find a spot to rest for a moment."

The male dipped until the treetops were only a few feet away but then squinted and shook his head. The *sway* wasn't holding. Verakko glanced down again, and his insides twisted. He might survive a fall from this height, but…the pain. Memories of cracked bones and limbs twisted at odd angles assailed him.

One more try.

"Your throat is dry. There's a river up ahead. A perfect place for a drink."

The male's eyes narrowed on the river in question, but then they widened, and Verakko knew he'd shucked off the *sway* entirely.

Mustering all the strength he had left, Verakko shot his legs up and wrapped them around one of the male's large wings. They banked sharply, spinning and diving into the dense trees below. The male flapped but couldn't dislodge the tight grip of Verakko's legs while also holding him by the arms. Wrenching one arm loose, Verakko grappled to pull the communicator free, but the device slipped between his fingers and tumbled into the rushing river below. Verakko cursed and clutched the male's forearms, lunging and snapping his teeth at any bit of flesh he got close to.

He managed to inject the few remaining drops of venom he had left as his fangs scraped across the male's upper arm. It might not kill the Strigi, but it would do damage.

The male looked at his oozing cut, aghast. As Verakko had feared and hoped, the male let go.

For a moment, Verakko hung in midair. Then, he was falling. He tried to make his body go limp, knowing a stiff form would only cause more damage. The navy-blue sky disappeared a moment before his shoulder crashed into a branch, sending stars dancing across his vision.

He tried to grab onto the small sticks and twigs that tore at his skin, but every time he caught sight of a suitable limb or sapling in the darkness, it was too late. The trees continued to batter his body until one particularly dense, low-hanging limb cracked his head. His vision wavered. Soft ground could be felt underneath him. He was no longer falling. As the world went dark once again, he recalled lying in a ditch in a similar position. Broken and wondering if he'd ever be found.

3

∞

Pink juice from the fruit Lily bit into squirted onto her dingy yet clean white shirt, and she ground her teeth. *Already?* Only that afternoon had she taken precious hours to wash and dry her clothes. Why had she even bothered?

For about a week now, Lily had been hiking alone through this alien forest, and it was wearing on her. The constant hunger and thirst, incessant bug bites, and perpetual state of hyperawareness were all things she'd never enjoyed on Earth and now despised. To top it all off, she'd lost a good ten pounds from her already slender frame.

Throwing the small fruit into her woven grass bag, Lily glared at the flickering flames of her bright fire, no longer concealed in a pit, and became lost in her own thoughts. The small clearing she'd found two days ago was one of the more comfortable spots she'd camped while searching for Alex. The patch of soft, moss-covered earth was within walking distance to the river and protected by trees on three sides.

She regretted having to leave, but tomorrow she'd need to move down the river yet again.

After she and Alex had been separated, she'd dragged herself onto the bank, then sprinted as fast as she could along the shore. She'd run until her legs had given out but hadn't found a shred of evidence. She hadn't even found any supplies washed up from the bag she'd lost in the river. Then a nasty rainstorm five days ago had flooded the whole area, forcing Lily to retreat to higher ground. Any evidence of Alex, or her lost supplies from her broken bag, would've been washed even farther downriver.

The chirping of insects she could never find, no matter how hard she looked, pulsed through her ears. She wrapped her arms around her waist and frowned. What she wouldn't give for Alex to be here right now. A small smile tugged at her lips. The woman had talked enough to drown out the bug's noises. Alex had always been great at that. Lily hadn't realized how much her friend had done to keep her spirits lifted. She now wondered if Alex really talked that much normally or if she'd chatted nonstop because she'd somehow sensed Lily needed lightness to combat the nagging pressure she always put on herself. Either way, the loneliness was wearing on Lily.

Why had she told Alex to keep going? She should've told her to stay put! *No,* Lily argued. *What if I hadn't made it?* It would've been selfish to force Alex to wait.

As she picked at her nails, now devoid of the bright pink polish she'd applied mere days before her abduction, she ran through her plan once more. The first few days on her own, Lily hadn't been smart. She'd pushed her body too far in pursuit of her friend. Only sleeping a few hours of the night and only eating what little she found along her way. If she really stopped to think about it, she should be dead right now. Poisoned from the random foods she'd eaten without first testing.

Though she hadn't died, she'd become incredibly ill. Lily didn't know if it was the food or unpurified water, but her stomach pains had halted her in her tracks. The rainstorm had turned out to be a blessing in disguise, as it had forced her to take shelter until it'd passed and had provided water that was reasonably safer to drink than river water. She'd crawled into a dark, empty crevasse between some boulders high on the hill and had ridden out the worst of her illness while praying no wild animals came to take advantage.

After two days of misery, she'd regained her sense and had decided she'd need to work smarter if she was ever going to learn what had happened to her friend.

Lily felt the balloon in her chest expand, threatening to burst at the thought of Alex. She pushed it down. *She's a smart girl. She made it to shore and started walking along the river just like we planned.* Lily kept carrying out the one-sided conversation in her mind, the only activity that prevented her from falling apart. *I'll find signs of her any day now; they were just washed farther down by the rain.*

She vehemently silenced the voice in the back of her brain wondering if there was any evidence left to find.

A loud snap from the fire drew her eyes, a welcome distraction. She reached over to her pile to throw on more wood and cursed. She'd left all the wood she'd gathered today by the riverbank.

After spending the morning chopping and hefting a heavy load of firewood, Lily hadn't been able to resist the crystal-clear water. She'd been dirty for long enough, hadn't she? She deserved to have a few hours of frivolity where, instead of toiling, she washed herself and her clothes and sunbathed on a nice, big rock. Well, that was exactly what she'd done. Lily cursed and stared at her stained shirt again. She'd felt clean and rejuvenated for all of two hours, and now she'd have to drag herself back to the river in the dark to maintain this damn fire.

She grimaced and rose. Her muscles, stiff from the hard work of the morning, groaned in protest. She grabbed a stick from the fire and held the flaming end ahead of her. The trees were thinner here along the river, and the two moons, only one of which was visible from her vantage point, lit the area in soft light. Lily told herself the fire was needed to ward off animals, but really it was more for her own comfort than anything else.

Although she hadn't been attacked by any of the animals lurking nearby, she heard them watching her throughout the days and nights. The longer she spent in this place, the more convinced she became that the creatures who stalked her were intelligent and were biding their time until she was either too weak or injured before making their move.

A rustling sounded from the trees, and Lily spun in place, holding her torch high. She crouched, ready to run or fight, whatever the situation called for. The rustling grew louder, and she peered into the dark forest, trying to make out any signs of movement. She saw nothing. The crack of snapping branches hit her ears, and she realized the sound wasn't coming from in front of her but from above.

What the fuck?

A loud crashing sounded overhead. She dove out of the way, sliding to a halt and scratching the hell out of her side as her pants dragged down over her thin hips. The weight of whatever had fallen hit the ground hard enough to make the earth under her vibrate. She scrambled onto her back and scuttled away, attempting to keep the dark, shapeless mass that'd fallen from the sky in view. She reached her still-burning torch and was about to bolt, when a deep groan emanated from the lump.

Lily sat frozen, her pulse racing and her breathing labored. It'd sounded like a person, a man. She was torn. Her limbs itched with adrenaline, urging her to flee, but she held her ground. On the one hand, she hadn't seen another person since Alex, and she desperately wanted help for her. On the other, she had no way of knowing if this…thing…was even a man at all. And even if it were, was she in more danger with him than she was on her own?

Am I so miserable that I don't even care anymore?

Lily shut down the thought as soon as it came to her. She might no longer care about her own well-being, but she still needed to discover evidence of Alex, whatever that may be. She wouldn't be able to live with herself knowing she hadn't done everything she could to find her friend.

The shape in front of her remained still. *Oh, shit. Did it die?* She hurried forward.

As she got close, she slowed and examined the creature. Raising her torch, she made out the shape of a large, muscled back, clad in a black long-sleeved shirt and pants. Lily swallowed. Definitely a man. The shallow rise and fall of his back confirmed he was still breathing, at least.

Maybe he'd come from a nearby village and could lead her there. She eyed his broad shoulders. But how had he gotten here? He didn't have wings. One of the men who'd held her captive in the bunker had had wings. Lily shuddered, renewed caution tempering her excitement at seeing another person.

She swept the ground with her hand and found a small rock. She lobbed it at his back and held her breath. Nothing. Next, she moved in with a long stick and prodded. He remained motionless.

This is just ridiculous. The one person who might have answers as to where Alex could've gone might be slowly dying because she was too scared to get close. Lily took a deep breath, gathering her courage, and inched toward the man. She knelt next to his large figure and, with a heave, rolled him to his back. He released another low groan of pain but remained otherwise unmoving. The soft glow from the torch illuminated his features, and she lost her breath. He was an alien, indisputably, but he wasn't like any of the aliens she'd already seen.

His skin was a deep navy blue but flickered to a lighter green in some areas where small cuts and scratches appeared. His ears were long and pointed, with faint punctures as though he usually wore earrings. Lily tilted her head and took in his defined square jaw, straight regal nose and high cheekbones. Had she ever seen such a perfectly sculpted face? His dark brows were furrowed upward in worry, and his full lips twitched. Her hands ached to smooth his brow.

And his scent… His clothes smelled of crisp air and nutty wood, but there was an underlying smell she couldn't quite place. The more she tried to identify it, the further away she got. Like chasing the memory of a dream.

She shook her head. *Get a hold of yourself.*

Scanning the rest of his body, Lily searched for injuries. When he continued to lay still, she became bolder in her search. His shoulder had been dislocated, likely during that fall. She winced in sympathy. It was going to hurt like a son of a bitch to pop it back into place. Venturing lower, she found the side of his shirt was damp. Upon lifting it, a deep gash in his hip came into view. Blood, red like hers, oozed out of a pale-green wound. The flow was slow enough that she didn't believe he was in danger of bleeding out anytime soon.

Lily sat back on her heels. She needed to make a decision. Either leave him here and take off in the night, or drag him back to camp and help him.

What if he's one of the men who likes locking up women? her mind prodded.

"What if he's not?" she shot back in a whisper. Suddenly she recalled Alex's comment about the aliens caging them as food, and her stomach turned.

Wedging her torch in the dirt near his head, she crawled over the man and carefully lifted his top lip. His canines were sharp, more like fangs. All the blood seemed to rush to her head, and her ears buzzed. Maybe they *were* raising humans as a delicacy for alien consumption. Only predators had teeth like that.

A rattling growl rumbled through his chest. All of her breath seemed to catch in her chest as her gaze shot up and met glowing green eyes. Eyes that were alert and angry and very much focused on her. Before she could dash away, he gripped her hand, still hovering over his mouth, and flipped her onto her back. He brought her other wrist above her head and loomed over her.

His sharp fangs were bared, glinting in the firelight. Lily bucked, attempting to force his center of gravity forward and throw him off balance, but he was too heavy and her energy was just too depleted to put enough power into any of the moves she knew.

"Where am I?" he rasped, his eyes growing unfocused.

"Get off me, and I'll tell you," she shrieked, writhing under him with every ounce of strength she had left.

A pained expression crossed his face, and he winced. He released her and raised his torso. Her hips were still trapped under his massive thighs, but her hands were now free. She stretched toward the spot she'd left her torch. As she swept her hands around blindly, she kept her eyes trained on the alien above her. He rubbed at his dislocated shoulder, then his features hardened. His resolute eerie gaze returned to her, pinning her in place.

She watched in horror and awe as in one quick movement, he wrenched the wrist of his injured arm out and forward. She heard the resounding crunch of bone sliding into socket, and her skin crawled. Not because of the disgusting way in which he'd fixed his joint but because his eyes had been glued to her the whole time and he'd barely flinched.

Her body seemed to catch up with her mind, and she strained harder toward the torch. He descended on her, fangs bared, and she cried out just as she felt the wood beneath her palm. The faintest brush of his teeth traveled along her collar bone, but he refrained from biting her. She pulled on the torch, trying to loosen it from the odd angle as he sniffed at her hair, then raised his head only a few inches above hers and studied her. His mouth opened, about to say something, but she never heard what it was. She brought the heavy torch down on his skull with a resounding crack.

He crumpled on top of her. Lily wheezed and gulped fruitlessly, attempting to draw air while crushed under his weight. She squirmed and wiggled until she was out from underneath him, then breathed deeply.

He lay unmoving again, and her torchlight revealed a large wound gushing blood on the back of his head. She winced in sympathy. The gash was much too large to have been caused by her meager attack. It must've happened during his fall. Lily cursed again, her fear giving way to anger and exasperation. She glared up into the trees. *Where the hell did you come from?*

Lily stared at the man and then back toward her camp. She didn't regret knocking him out, though a small squirm in her belly argued differently. He'd pinned her down, after all. And it was clear he hadn't been completely with it yet. Yes, knocking him out had been the right move. But guilt still pulled at her as she stared at his head wound. She hadn't been the one to cause it, but she'd most assuredly made it worse.

What was she supposed to do now? What if a scavenging animal came by and he wasn't able to wake up? No, she couldn't leave him, no matter how badly her logical brain urged her to. He could've easily hurt her, but he hadn't. Maybe if she helped him, he'd help her. Tell her where the nearest town was. He'd spoken English.

Lily's heart picked up speed again, and her eyes widened. How had he spoken English? The aliens in the bunker had as well. Did he know them?

She couldn't tell him about Alex until she knew she could trust him. She needed some answers. A stray thought came to her, and she explored it. *I could tie him up. Make sure he doesn't die, and then ask him questions when he comes to.* Lily glanced in the direction of her camp, where all her gathered cordage sat waiting. She'd never be able to drag him that far. He weighed a ton. She'd have to bring the rope to him.

Lily assessed the area. A large tree limb hung overhead. Not the safest place to build a fire, but it'd have to do.

She took a moment to catch her breath then stood. Glancing down at her body, she saw she was filthy, stained everywhere with blood and dirt. She stretched the material forward and huffed out an annoyed breath. *So much for that!*

***

Verakko's head was pounding. Not the normal dull ache he felt when dealing with people. More like the butt of a knife being rammed into the base of his skull. It was difficult to think, but Verakko could feel that he was sitting up. A spurt of venom shot to his fangs when he perceived tight rope binding his hands and…a sling around his right arm.

His eyes flashed open and took in the shape of a fire. He blinked, trying to clear his vision, and ground his teeth against an onslaught of pain shooting through his skull.

"You should keep still."

Verakko froze at the sound of a soft voice. A female voice. Scanning the area, his gaze landing on the blurry shape of a person sitting on the opposite side of the fire. Slowly, the world around him came into focus. "Who are you?" he growled, tugging on his hands experimentally. The rope was strong and the knots were tied with expertise, but whoever had tied them had underestimated his strength. He could break out if he wanted.

Verakko recalled falling through the trees and landing. There'd been something else, though, some event. His heart picked up a fraction as the female's narrowed eyes came into focus. She'd been there, touching him and checking him over. But then she'd touched his fangs, and he'd known he needed to stop her before she accidentally cut herself. If there was even a drop of venom left, his gentle savior would be dead in a matter of minutes.

He'd flipped her, meaning only to hold her in place while he explained, but her scent had distracted him, and then... Verakko frowned, anger and embarrassment coursing through him. Then she'd knocked him over the head and tied him up.

His vision cleared, and the pounding in his head reduced. He stared at the small female crouching with a large piece of wood in hand as though ready for a fight. She had dark brown hair that framed her oval face and shimmered gold near the tips. The color distribution was odd but not unpleasant. He imagined her eyes were brown, but it was difficult to know for sure with the green fire reflected in them.

"Where did you come from?" she demanded.

The Strigi, he recalled with a start. His eyes shot to the trees above. Would the male return for him?

Verakko relaxed a fraction. *Not anytime soon.* Even if the small amount of venom he'd been able to inject into the male hadn't killed him, it would've certainly put him out of commission for a few days. Still, he could've landed close by to recover. It'd be better if he and this mysterious female got out of here sooner rather than later. Unless she, too, was an Insurgent. She'd tied him up, after all.

"Hey, alien! Answer me."

Verakko felt a flare of annoyance for a moment before her use of words settled over him. *Alien?* He stiffened. Sitting up straighter, he ran his gaze over the female again. His eyes locked back on hers. "You're human."

A small pink tongue darted across her full lower lip, distracting him, and she gulped but said nothing.

Did this mean their plan had worked? He studied her worn clothing and pile of handcrafted supplies. "How long have I been unconscious?"

"You'll answer my questions first," she said, shooting him a glare.

Verakko tilted his head at the small human, and his mouth quirked upward despite himself. She was brave, to say the least. "I was dropped here by some pishot Strigi. Does that answer your questions?"

Her frown deepened at his tone. "How can we understand each other?"

"You were implanted with a translator, it seems." Allowing his body to calm, he *swayed* her. "It would make sense to tell me where you came from. What would be the harm?"

Her irises dilated, and she swiftly replied, "I came from…" She paused and blinked at him. After a moment, she shook her head as if to clear it. "What was that?"

Verakko couldn't stop his mouth from falling open.

She narrowed her eyes at his surprised expression. "Did you try and do something to my head?"

Never in his life had his *sway* been so easily rejected. He was regarded as one of the more powerful of his kind, and although his *sway* often didn't hold for long stretches of time, it usually required more effort to shake off than *that*. He shifted in his seat, his pride injured by the tiny Earthling, and decided his weakened state was obviously the cause of his malfunctioning gift.

"How about you untie me, and then we can talk?" he offered. Breaking out of these ropes would be easy, but he suspected the only reason this human was sitting so close to him at the moment was because she assumed he'd been rendered immobile. If he revealed his strength, she'd likely run or attack, and he was not in the mood to subject his abused body to any more physical exertion at the moment.

She grinned, displaying small white teeth, and his cock gave an unwelcomed twitch of interest. "Not a chance. How do you know what humans are?"

"How about a drink of water, then? At least give me that." Truth be told, he didn't really need water. His people were most comfortable in the dry Dakuun desert, their bodies adapted to survive on minimal resources. What he *did* need was to see her more closely. The urge to leap over the fire, just to get a clear view of her eye color, was like a living entity clawing inside him.

She stared at him hard, and he could almost see her weighing his request. Her gaze strayed to a primitive wooden bowl filled with water, and she nibbled her pink lower lip. His blood heated, and his cock gave another involuntary twitch.

Recently, he'd witnessed quite an odd practice from a few of the humans and their mates, and he'd not been able to get the image out of his mind since. It'd been odd and unpleasant, their mouths locked together like they were trying to inhale each other's air. So why couldn't he stop thinking about taking that lip between his own teeth?

Goddess help me. What'd gotten into him? He peered down at his wrists, holding his breath, then exhaled. *No marks.*

"Answer one of my questions first, then I'll give you a drink of water," she said finally.

He lifted his chin, mirroring her own stubborn posture. "Have my eyes changed? Have the irises and whites both turned completely black or possibly yellow?"

She pursed her lips.

Verakko stifled a hiss. How to get her to answer him? "It's important. It...it's indicative of...my health. Please."

Her eyes widened a fraction. "No. They haven't changed."

"Promise to tell me if they do, and I'll answer your questions."

She studied him for a moment and then gave a tight nod. "How do you know what I am?" Her stoic countenance held strong, but he saw the briefest flash of fear in her eyes. What had the Insurgents done to her?

He took a deep breath to allow the bubbling snarl building in him to abate before answering. "I've met a few of your kind. Two, to be exact. I was with one of them, Alice, only hours ago. We released you from the facility you were being held in. Do you not recognize my voice?"

"Alice?" she shot forward before realizing it and then halted. "You know Alice?"

"*You* know Alice?" Verakko searched his mind for an explanation. There was no way this female could know Alice unless… He took in the sight of her weathered clothes and handcrafted supplies once more. "You're one of the females who ran off into the forest weeks ago, aren't you?"

She opened her mouth then closed it again.

Relief, worry, and annoyance all exploded in Verakko and, failing to contain himself, he blurted, "That was such a *stupid* idea. How could you have run off like that? Do you know how many people have been trying to find you? The other humans have been worried sick."

Her head snapped back, and her cheeks flushed bright red. "Hey! You don't get to judge me. You have no idea what I went through and no idea what I've been through since. So I'd appreciate it if you kept your opinions to yourself," she spat.

She moved away before Verakko had time to decide on an apology or a retort. The humans who'd escaped with Alice two weeks ago had taken to their new lives in Tremanta relatively well. All except for the two impulsive females who'd decided they'd prefer the wilds and who hadn't been found, until now. Like most, he'd assumed they'd perished.

Anxiety warred with relief once more. He'd been so satisfied to see that his attempts to free the humans from the rest of the facilities had been a success. Now he realized he was still in the dark as to what had happened to them. He needed to get back to civilization—and fast. If Kadion and the others hadn't survived the attack, someone would need to report back to the Queen. Leaders around the world had to know that humans may be roaming aimlessly, looking for a safe haven.

But first he'd need to convince this stubborn female to return with him.

Muttering, she snatched the water bowl and fished a few rocks from the liquid.

"Why are there rocks in your water?" he questioned harshly, his frustration seeping into his words. How had this slip of a female managed to survive in the Sauven Forest this long?

"Another *stupid* idea, is it?" She slowly lifted her head and raised a delicate brow. "Do you know of a better way to purify water without a pot? I heated them in the fire, then dropped them in to boil the water. If you know of an easier way, I'm all ears." She held his stare and waited.

Verakko clamped his mouth shut. He didn't know of another way without tools, and he hated the smug smile that spread over her face at his silence.

She knelt in front of him, and some of his annoyance faded. Brown. Her eyes were indeed brown. And beautiful. Her scent toyed with him as well. It was buried by smoke, dirt, and blood, but he could just make out a sweetness underneath the grime.

She lifted the bowl to his mouth and waited. When he continued to stare, she cleared her throat. "Do you want the water or not?"

He drank a few sips of the warm water, not wanting to take all of the precious liquid she'd spent so long disinfecting. He licked his lips and was pleased to see her eyes tracked the movement of his tongue.

Her gaze lingered for a moment longer, then she abruptly stood and put distance between them.

He scowled. "Aren't you going to untie me now?" he called, wiggling his hands.

"No," she said simply, piling wood onto the fire. She moved farther away from the camp, and Verakko had to fight the instinct to break his measly bonds and drag her back to the safety of the fire. He hadn't spent much time in forests, but he knew fire equaled safety no matter the environment.

"Where are you going?"

"To bed." She took hold of a hanging sapling and began to climb.

"Do you always sleep in trees?" he complained, angling his neck to keep her in view, muscles taut. *What if she falls?*

She swung to the limb of a tree nearby, as agile as a teuy, and settled herself there, over the fire. Did she somehow know that her position high above was the last place he'd follow her? He would if he had to, of course, but his recent fall from the sky had been enough to keep him firmly planted on the ground for the next few years.

"I could come up there and get you just as easily as if you were down here," he bluffed.

"Not with that tender shoulder and bleeding side," she countered. "Also, I believe the words you were looking for were *thank you.*"

His chest puffed. Did she really think him so weak that he couldn't climb a few feet into the air after an injury? He flexed his side experimentally and felt fabric circling his hips. Then he realized the sleeves of his shirt had been torn and utilized as a makeshift bandage and a sling. The itch of a forming scab scraped against the fabric. His wounds were nearly mended. She must not have known his kind could heal quickly. Should he throw that piece of information in her face or allow her to sleep secure in the knowledge that he was a weak, incapacitated male?

He scowled. For tonight, he'd let her sleep, but his pride wouldn't allow him to be viewed as an invalid for much longer. He reclined as much as his bindings would allow and glanced up to where she lay.

She stared back, watching him.

"What's your name, human? I'm Verakko."

She turned away, and Verakko assumed she'd decided not to answer. But then she said, "It's Lily."

Verakko grinned even through his foul mood. "Sleep well, Lily."

4

Lily cracked her eyes open, and the flush of anger and embarrassment from the night before returned. That alien, Verakko, had called her stupid. Had implied she'd been reckless. Well, what the hell did he know? She'd dragged him to safety, cleaned his wounds, and made sure he didn't die. How had he repaid her? By being a self-important bastard.

What now, Lily? What do we do now?

No matter how badly she wanted to, she couldn't just leave him. He didn't even know how to get clean water on his own. He may be useful in identifying edible plants, but how much did he know about what plants were edible to humans?

Was it stupid for her to be so worried about this alien? Probably. He'd said he knew Alice, but why should she believe him? For all she knew, he could've been part of a group who'd recaptured Alice and then tortured information out of her. Lily tried to cling to the image of him as a villain but couldn't. He just didn't seem the type.

She inwardly groaned. No, she couldn't leave him behind, but she also couldn't free him, which meant she'd have to tow a large bound man through the forest. Emotion welled in her throat. Would she ever find Alex moving at that pace? *All I can do is try.*

She stretched her arms in front of her and winced. At the time, sleeping in the tree far away from that infuriating man had seemed like a grand idea. All through the night, she'd felt less and less proud of her decision. Although the limb itself was soft, lined with moss and small flowers, it was still a limb, dozens of feet from the ground. She'd barely slept a wink, worrying she'd roll in her sleep, the rope binding her to the limb would snap, and she'd tumble off the tree into the fire. It'd also been chilly so far away from said fire, and small bugs that thrived among the tree plants had nipped at her exposed flesh all night, redoubling their efforts as the fire died out.

She'd argued with herself to simply climb down, feed the fire, and sleep near the warmth of the flames, but her pride wouldn't allow it. He'd already treated her like a child, and she had no intention of letting him see how wrong she'd been.

She lifted her head and peered down to where he slept, only...he was gone. She shot upright, almost losing her balance in the process, and scanned the ground for any sign of him.

He was nowhere in sight. Had he left? Been eaten? Was he on his way back with reinforcements even now?

Lily untied herself, scrambled over to her makeshift rope, and slid down to the forest floor. Dashing around the camp, she stuffed her meager belongings into her woven bag.

"Going somewhere?" came a deep silken voice from behind her.

She turned, keeping her legs tensed to run.

Lily had to contain her shock. He was standing a few feet away and watching her, but he looked different. His skin was no longer dark blue but a pleasing combination of teal and seafoam green. Could he change color? His sling was also gone, yet his shoulder seemed to be working perfectly.

His vivid peridot eyes traveled down her figure, leaving her skin heated in their wake. She silently scolded her traitorous body. Even last night while fuming and flushed with embarrassment, he'd elicited much the same reaction. His deep voice was smooth and velvety, and images of darkened bedrooms had manifested in her mind whenever he'd spoken. She'd only been able to shake off the continual goosebumps at hearing him when he'd begun to berate her choices.

"How did you get free?" she demanded, attempting to focus on her dislike for the arrogant man and not the way the sun highlighted light-blue streaks throughout his hair. Had he colored it that way on purpose, or was it natural?

"Without much difficulty." He nodded toward the snapped remnants of his bindings.

He sauntered over to the cold remnants of the fire, and her insides burned with frustration. *That was strong rope, dammit!* And her knots had been tight. Curse her bleeding heart. If she'd just hog-tied him like she'd wanted, he may not have gotten free so easily. But no, she'd felt bad about manipulating his injured shoulder in that way.

Sitting, he pulled a bright red fruit from his pocket and tossed it to her. She fumbled, then caught it. The corners of his eyes crinkled. "I say we eat and then start heading back up the river."

"Wha—I—" Lily's mind stuttered along with her words. The impertinence of this guy. "Who do you think you are? I'm not going up the river. I need to head downriver."

He frowned, his full lips pulling into a devastating pout. He spoke slowly as if she were an idiot, ratcheting her anger. "Upriver is where my people are. We're going that way."

Lily's chin dropped. "I'm not going anywhere with you. I need to head downriver, so I'm going to head downriver. You can do whatever you want."

"Why?" he demanded, slicing a piece of fruit with…a knife.

Her gaze zeroed in on the small silver blade, locking in place. *He has a knife.*

Lily eyed the tool covetously. She'd been making do with sharp rocks. What she wouldn't give for a knife. It'd make everything so much easier.

He waved the blade in front of his face, recapturing her attention. "Why do you need to go downriver?"

"That's none of your business." She glared, not yet trusting him enough to reveal that Alex might still be alive.

Not at all cowed by her death stare, he studied her, taking another bite of fruit from the tip of his blade. Dammit, she always loved when men did that. "Fine. I'm coming with you."

"What? Why?" Lily tried to keep the annoyance in her voice, but a small part of her rejoiced at the thought. She'd been alone for so long, and life had been difficult. And he had a knife.

"Because you're my responsibility now." He gestured around the forest with a superior air that made her head start to pound. "I need to make sure you don't make any more rash decisions and get yourself killed."

A disgruntled heat crept over her limbs. "I've been doing just fine, thank you very much."

He snorted. "Oh yeah? Well, I was under the impression that there were two of you. If you're doing so well, then where's your friend?"

The air whooshed out of her chest, and she took a step back, as if someone had punched her in the gut. "Go. To. Hell," she said, masking sudden tightness in her throat.

Swiping her bag from the ground, she turned and marched away. *Screw him. He has no idea what he's talking about.* The balloon in her chest welled again, and a stray tear leaked down her cheek. He wasn't right. What had happened to Alex wasn't her fault.

Pounding footfall sounded behind her. She refused to face him and give him the satisfaction of seeing her tears.

"Hey, you forgot your...this."

She whirled, and her heart sunk into her stomach. Her bow drill. She'd forgotten the one tool she had to make fire. The tool she'd spent days perfecting.

Lily wanted to shriek. She needed to get a hold of her emotions. Her parents would be so disappointed if they could see her now. Letting some man work her up into a frenzy. It was life or death out here. She couldn't let this alien make her doubt herself.

She reached for the drill, but he hoisted it into the air and out of reach. His brows furrowed, and he scanned her face, likely seeing the evidence of her tears.

Her cheeks heated with embarrassment, and she focused on the ground. "Can I have my drill back, please?" she said, biting out the last word.

He stepped forward, crowding her, but she refused to back away. Her whole life, she'd made sure she was a self-sufficient woman. She could survive in the wild as well as she could survive in a city. She knew how to defend herself, but this situation wasn't fair. She'd studied both Brazilian Jiu-Jitsu and aikido, yet something told her if Verakko wanted to hurt her, she'd have no way of stopping him. Not in her current, malnourished state anyway. "I'm coming with you whether you like it or not. Get used to it. I won't leave you alone out here. It wouldn't be honorable." He held the drill out for her, and she shoved it into her pack.

She closed her eyes and took a calming breath in and out, trying to wash away all her emotion and assess the situation.

He'd gotten free, probably could've gotten free last night too, but he hadn't. A flicker of hope bloomed in her chest. If what he'd said was true, that meant there were good aliens on this planet. Ones who didn't want to abduct women. And he was one of them. He'd claimed he was honorable, and so far he'd done nothing too concerning, other than proving himself to be a twat. It didn't matter if she didn't like him, though; the question was could she use him to help her find Alex and safety? Could he be trusted?

She caught his determined stare, then eyed his body, attempting to keep her perusal professional and failing. The biceps she'd uncovered last night after removing his sleeves were well defined and seemed even larger in the light of day. He was strong. Very strong. That strength would be useful for gathering firewood and carrying extra supplies. Having someone else to feed the fire at night would be helpful too. And God knew she could use a break from the bow drill. It depleted almost all of her energy reserves to start a fire each night.

"Can you hunt?"

"Better than you, I'm sure."

Lily let the insult slide off her decidedly slippery emotional shield. She would not let him get to her anymore. Instead she eyed him, making it clear she was waiting for him to elaborate.

A muscle ticked in his jaw. "I haven't done much hunting in the forest, but I could give it a shot."

"Can you identify edible plants?" she pressed.

His frown deepened, and he crossed his arms over his large chest. "More easily than you."

She smirked. "So, you can't hunt, you can't gather, you don't know how to purify water, and you don't know what a bow drill is. What I'm hearing is that I'm now going to have to provide for not only myself but a six-foot-something, two-hundred-fifty-pound man."

His eyes seemed to glow brighter, and a vein bulged in his neck. Good. He needed to be taken down a peg.

"I'll make you a deal." She crossed her arms, mirroring his stance. "You answer all of my questions, and I'll let you come with me. I'll even make sure you don't starve or freeze to death. How's that?" Fury flared in his eyes, and she had to stop herself from scrambling away on instinct.

He shot his hand out and gripped her crossed forearms, binding them together. Lily pulled at her arms, attempting to wrench them down to break his hold, but it was no use. His one massive palm was an immovable iron band. Why had she taunted him? Had she lost her mind?

Pulling her in close with a quick tug, he growled, "Watch yourself, female. If I wanted to, I could haul you over my shoulder and take you in whichever direction I please. Don't push me."

Lily tried to scan her memory banks for all the techniques she'd learned in her self-defense classes, but his damn scent kept distracting her. *I can knee him in the balls—Wood smoke? Was that it? But if I knee him, he might crumple on top of me and break—No, cedar! Burning cedar? Focus, woman!*

His gaze strayed to her mouth, and the glowing bright green of his eyes darkened. The hand trapping her wrists together squeezed, dragging her forward another inch.

The intoxicating scent of cedar wood smoke intensified, and her breathing hitched. She felt almost dizzy. Lily had always loved that smell.

A memory from the night before played through her mind. "Are you doing something to my head again?" she murmured, eyes locking on his mouth.

"No," he said simply, meeting her gaze. "Maybe you just don't want me to leave as much as you claim." Heat suffused her core, making her cheeks heat in embarrassment. His eyes widened, almost as if he could tell.

He released her, stepping away. Lily had to stop herself from inching closer to him.

Outrage suddenly flared in her. He obviously had some kind of alien mind-control gift that was making her lose all reason. "Just stay away from me. And keep that weird smell-lure thing to yourself."

A slow, predatory grin spread across his face. "I told you, I wasn't doing anything. You must just like the way I smell."

Her face flamed. So much for controlling her emotions. "Keep dreaming."

***

Oh, he would keep dreaming. The sudden luscious scent of her arousal had surprised him and sent an answering rush of blood to his shaft. There was something more about this human, though. Something that had his hands burning to pull her close again. It didn't matter that they'd done nothing but argue. Everything about her called to his baser instincts. Was that just how it was with humans?

He thought back to Alice. She was attractive, to be sure, but he'd never felt anything near the unquenchable thirst he felt for this female. If he didn't know better, he'd assume she was his mate. But the fact that his eyes hadn't changed and his hands were still mark-free invalidated that thought.

Wouldn't he know if she were his? A small part of his heart pinched at the idea she could be, but he ignored it. He was already intended for marriage in less than three weeks. His betrothed, whom his mother had selected only a month ago, was a sensible choice. Still, if the human was his mate, he'd have a valid reason to deny the betrothal.

Lily turned and walked along the river, muttering under her breath. His translator was only able to decipher some of it, inserting its closest approximation to unfamiliar words. Something about a creature that drinks human blood to survive. Verakko grimaced and trailed behind her along the soft riverbank. He tried to force his gaze to remain on her head and not on her perfect ass, the outline visible underneath her thin pants.

"Tell me more about how you know Alice," she said, shooting a suspicious glance over her shoulder.

He couldn't blame her for not trusting him yet, but her distrust still rankled. "A few weeks ago, she and three other females were rescued from an Insurgent facility and brought to Tremanta, the city in which I currently live." *Not for much longer, though.* Once he was married, he'd be expected to return to his home city. He'd have to leave his job as Head Technologist to the Queen of Tremanta and settle into a dull role in the much less forward-thinking city of Mithrandir. One of the reasons he'd sought to leave in the first place was their sluggish acceptance of emerging technological innovations.

With a pointed click of his tongue, he continued, "Two others escaped and should've been rescued, but they chose to slink into the woods and somehow avoid all rescue personnel assigned to find them."

Lily raised a smug brow in his direction. "You think that was accidental? Please."

So, this female also knew how to cover her tracks. Interesting.

"There are more humans here? How many facilities are there? What are Insurgents?"

Verakko took a deep breath then told her everything he could about the rescued humans and the Insurgents. He glossed over certain details he wasn't at liberty to share, such as the human Jade's pregnancy.

He'd also made the decision not to explain mating or mating marks. Her eyes had grown wide and anxious when he'd explained the current ratio of males to females was twenty to one, and he feared that explaining the intensity of a Clecanian looking for a mate might push her over the edge. The female before him seemed fiercely independent. If she knew how relentlessly males would pursue her in order to call forth mating marks, she may never want to leave the forest again.

Before he explained the significance of humans to their slowly dying species, he needed to ease her worry. Make her understand that not all Clecanians were evil. He wondered how the males of Earth might've handled a sparse female population. If her continual nervous glances in his direction were any indication, not well. Winning her trust would be a battle hard fought.

Although he still wanted to return to Tremanta and report to the Queen as soon as possible, the urgency didn't seem quite as desperate in the light of day. After he'd been carried off, Kadion would've only had to bring down one other Strigi. Verakko was certain the general could've done it even without a Yulo glove. It was unlikely Verakko had been the only one to survive.

His current mission was to see this human to safety. It had absolutely nothing to do with her wide, sparkling-brown eyes or the way her quick comebacks lit a curious fire in his belly he refused to acknowledge as anything other than ire.

As the sun made its way across the sky and the day grew hot and damp, they continued farther along the river. For the most part she remained quiet, processing what he'd told her, then surprising him with insightful questions. All of the other humans had asked about things related to returning to Earth and had argued endlessly when they'd learned it was against the law for Clecanians to interact with their Class 4 planet. But not Lily. She'd seemed…thoughtful, as though she didn't fully believe him, or maybe she didn't accept it. She hadn't argued; instead, she'd asked thoughtful questions about how the law had come to be in the first place. He hadn't rightly known the answer.

"We're the same species?" she asked, eyeing his fangs and pointed ears.

"Yes. And we're a very old one too. I'm assuming humans are descended from the first Clecanians, before our ancestors started experimenting with genetic engineering." He ran a hand through his hair, marveling at how unique Lily was.

"They wanted to upgrade themselves, did they? Normally I'd advise against screwing with Mother Nature, but what do I know?"

"I don't recall the specifics, but I believe they isolated traits from other creatures living in similar environments on our old planet. My people became better suited for hot, dry climates, while others were altered so they could live in cliffsides or on islands far out to sea. Although the scientists of that time made miraculous progress, they also caused the extinction of many native species on Clecania in the scramble for advancement. Genetic engineering was outlawed before we ever left our old planet. Many believe the experimentation done long ago is in part a cause of our infertility, so maybe you're right about 'screwing with Mother Nature.'"

"So you and that winged guy from the underground bunker are really the same species?"

"Me, that winged guy, and you are all the same species."

Lily pondered this for a long while, her dark brown brows knit in concentration.

As they walked and she asked more questions, he only continued to feel inept.

"Who makes the laws? How many planets are in the Alliance? How many representatives from each species are there? What constitutes each Class?"

As a person who'd never been very interested in politics, he answered as best he could.

Despite himself, Verakko found he enjoyed watching her mind work. She nibbled her bottom lip and furrowed her brows in such an intriguing way. When her features were clear of suspicion or annoyance, he was able to witness her intelligent eyes dart as she worked through the information she was receiving. He recounted the battle at the cabin and their plan to release the trapped humans, casually playing up his role in the rescue in an attempt to win her approval and rebuild his ego. After he'd finished, she remained silent, and a twinge of annoyance ran through him.

"What happened to that crazy guy who carried Alice off? He was obviously unwell, judging by his black eyes."

"Black...?" Verakko suddenly recalled his lie and realized what Lily must've seen. Luka's eyes black from recognizing Alice. "Yes, he was quite unwell when we found him."

Not a lie. He'd been unwell at the time, after all, Verakko argued with himself, feeling a twinge of guilt.

"Was he punished for doing that?"

"More like rewarded. They're now mated." Verakko chuckled and leapt over a large boulder, landing gracefully at her side. She failed to appear impressed.

She lifted a brow in confusion. "You mean, like, married?"

They'd come to a rocky area of the river, and she kept her head down and concentrated on traversing the slippery boulders. Though impressed by her sure, calculated steps, he still had to fight the urge not to offer her an arm. He hadn't known her long, but he felt certain she wouldn't appreciate the gesture.

"Married for life, I suppose," he hedged, careful not to go into too much detail on the mating bond.

She appeared satisfied with his answer, and he recalled that humans thought of marriage differently than Clecanians, yet he couldn't remember exactly why. He'd been focused on working through a way to free Insurgent prisoners for the last few months and hadn't felt it necessary to waste his time researching human customs that didn't relate to his work. As he watched Lily skip from one rock to the next, a small smile tugging at her mouth, he suddenly wished he had.

"I guess he wasn't going to eat her, then." She laughed.

The sound sent a pleasant surge of electricity through his shoulder blades, but then Verakko halted in his tracks and cocked his head. "Eat her?"

Lily slid over a large boulder and began walking along a smooth, moss-lined path. He rushed to catch up with her. "Yeah, some of us guessed that maybe that's why you guys took us. As a delicacy or something." She glanced at his mouth sidelong.

Was that why she'd been studying his fangs last night?

He scowled. "We aren't barbarians. We don't eat sentient beings."

"Oh. My apologies. Your kind is okay with stealing defenseless humans and locking them up for God knows what, but they draw the line at eating sentient beings." She turned to look at him and pulled a long, rounded object, the same length as her forearm, from her bag.

Verakko balled his fists. "Those aren't my kind. Those were a group of traitors who broke the law."

Lily pursed her lips and rolled her eyes. She pulled at a round stopper in the top of the object, and he realized she'd somehow crafted a traveling water container. He was torn between praising her ingenuity and throttling her for continued suspicion. How did she know so much about surviving in a place like this? Even if she'd been an expert back home, was Clecania really so similar that her skills translated to this environment? Or was she so resourceful that she'd adapted?

She took a long draw, then handed the makeshift canteen to him. "Water?"

He glared. Had she not been listening to a word he'd said about his role in the rescue mission? "You have to acknowledge that I'm not the same as the cretin who took you."

When he still made no move to take the proffered water, she released an exhale and returned the canteen to her bag.

"I don't have to acknowledge anything. You're not human, and I'm just getting to know you. For all I know, you could be lying about everything. I'm not saying you are, but I'm not going to blindly believe a man I've known for all of a day. So far, you've tossed me around, forced me to fight you off, insulted me, excreted some kind of hypnotizing spell, and tried to use crazy mind powers on me. I trust you enough not to eat me, at least. Does that make you feel better?"

She turned away, and Verakko felt as if his whole body was flushing indigo.

For the next few hours, he trailed well behind her. She appeared not to care. Didn't even attempt to ask him any more questions. The little tishti had a way of heating every part of him to a boil.

After his temper had cooled to a simmering indignance, he focused on her comment about his smell, and his mind wandered to devious places. He hadn't lied when he'd said he'd done nothing, but he'd failed to mention his scent's ability to change, like his skin.

It was a predatory response, one he couldn't control even if he wanted to. The scent his body produced was a luring aroma unique to whoever was near. While a person might smell a sweet confection from their hometown or another scent that made them feel relaxed, an animal might smell a particular flower or plant they liked to eat. Occasionally, when hunting or with heightened emotions, the scent became stronger. The adaptation was used in the old times to lure prey. The only way to control it was to control his emotions, which he seemed unable to do around her.

The image of her docile and heavy-lidded after he'd pulled her close re-formed in his mind. Maybe he could finally get some use out of the ability.

Their progress was slow. Although she moved at a reasonable pace, considering her short frame and scrawny build, he knew they could cover ground much faster if she'd just let him carry her.

When the sun began to make its descent, she turned back to him. The soft orange light lit her eyes, revealing flecks of gold in the brown depths. Averting his gaze so as not to be drawn in by her beauty, he glanced down her body and had to stifle a groan.

Verakko's people didn't lose much water through perspiration like many Clecanian races, but he could see that humans did. The dampened material of her white shirt clung to her curves just enough for Verakko to make out the swell of her breasts and an odd covering. The faintest hint of black fabric molded to her small breasts teased his eyes.

Blood flowed to his shaft, and his palms itched to tear away the damp material and inspect the covering more thoroughly.

"I think we should start moving through the forest. We can try to find some food along the way if possible, and we can also look for a place to camp."

Thankfully, his focus returned at her words. "Already?" he said with a sharpness he hadn't intended.

The amiable smile she'd plastered on her face, in what he assumed was an attempt to be cordial, fell. She placed her hands on her hips with an annoyed glare. "If we wait too long, then we'll be searching for supplies and building a fire in the dark. If you want to make yourself useful, you can use those muscles of yours to gather firewood on our way."

He straightened, a masculine spike of pleasure pulsing through him at her acknowledgment of his strength. The anger and frustration he'd been carrying all day seemed to melt in the light of her compliment, and Verakko found himself wondering, could she *sway* him too?

5

The hungry look Verakko leveled on her was almost as destructive as his intoxicating smell. It was unsettling how quickly she flipped between annoyance and curiosity for this man.

Lily lifted a slim branch from the ground and held it up in the air. "This is the kind of wood we're looking for."

He nodded, scanning the ground, so she walked away from the river and into the forest, knowing he'd follow, though she still didn't understand why. He'd made it clear that women were a commodity on this planet, but it seemed like humans in particular were even more valuable. Why else would he be subjecting himself to a wilderness trip for an unknown amount of time, with a woman who so clearly disliked him? There had to be more he wasn't telling her. She could sense it.

There was some hole he was explaining around, but she didn't know enough to decide how to question to it. His mere presence had also made it difficult to focus. She'd felt his stare on her like a brand all day, and she couldn't for the life of her decipher what it meant.

It appeared to Lily as if he couldn't decide whether to wring her neck or tear her clothes off. More disturbing still, she couldn't decide which fate she'd prefer.

A loud crack sounded behind her, and she turned to find Verakko breaking a sturdy downed limb in two over his thick thigh. He eyed her as though knowing the display of unreasonable strength would force the primitive part of her lady brain into overdrive.

"Are you ready to tell me why we're heading downriver?" he asked with a raised brow.

What to say? It wasn't that she didn't want to tell him. She just didn't think she could talk about Alex without breaking down. Lily wasn't ready to show a complete stranger that weakness, and with her nerves already frayed to their breaking point, there was a good chance she would. She walked around the area, keeping half her mind occupied in a search for food, and answered, "The girl I was with, Alex, we got separated. We fell into the river, and I was able to make it to shore before her."

She chanced a glance in Verakko's direction, bracing for the sneer, and was surprised to find that he didn't look self-satisfied but rather thoughtful. "How long ago were you separated?" he asked while bringing down another large branch over his thigh.

A mix of irritation and awe briefly swept through her. It would've taken her days and heaps of precious energy to break up that much usable firewood. "A little over a week ago."

He paused in the act of breaking another branch and stared at her with widened eyes. "You've been living in the woods by yourself for a week? Why didn't you go back?"

Lily studied Verakko's face. His tone was more curious than accusatory. Her hackles, which had been primed to rise at any moment, calmed. "We'd planned to follow the river until we reached a city. Alex is smart and resourceful. I told her to stick to that plan." She picked up some fallen nut-like spheres she'd been gathering but thus far had been too nervous to eat and muttered, "I couldn't just leave her."

Verakko tucked the large bundle of firewood under his arm and stared thoughtfully into the depths of the darkening forest.

The silent moment dragged on until Lily felt like she was going to burst. "What, no comment about how stupid and impulsive my choice was?" she groused. In all honestly, there was a grain of truth to what he'd said before, and that was what upset her the most. She found she cared what he thought of her decisions.

"No. I understand now. You've given me hope, actually, for the freed humans. If they feel a fraction of the loyalty you do and are anywhere near as brave, they might stand a chance."

Lily's knees quivered, and her eyes stung with tears at the unexpected and wholeheartedly sincere remark. It hadn't been a compliment exactly, more of a statement of fact, but to Lily, that was even better. A knot seemed to loosen deep in her gut. She murmured a quick thank you and retreated farther into the forest.

He gave a small grunt behind her and followed. "However, I only saw one human male, so unless all the females have your survival skills, they still may not make it."

And just like that, Lily's irritation returned. She held her tongue, stewing, attempting to convince herself that his comment hadn't been meant to undermine the female sex as a whole. Her restraint only lasted for a short time before she spun on him. "And why would the amount of men dictate how easily the women can survive? I've survived out here for weeks without a man helping me."

Surprise at the sudden reply to his comment registered on his face for a moment before his eyes narrowed. "You, little female, are an enigma. I just assumed the male of your species would have learned how to fight in school as our males do and would therefore be helpful in this circumstance."

"Guys here are taught how to fight in school?"

He shrugged and tromped past her, taking the lead. "Depends on where you're from. I had to learn when I was in husbandry school, but not all cities require it."

Lily scanned her memory. She'd never attended a real school, but she was pretty certain fighting wasn't part of most curriculums. "So, you're a farmer?"

"A farmer?" He studied the area, not really paying attention to her, and gestured to a clear patch of earth. "Will this spot do?"

"Not unless you want to be impaled by that widow-maker," she said quickly, pointing up to a dead limb near the top of the tree that hovered precariously above the clearing. "Husbandry school. That's for farmers, right? Animal farmers."

Verakko scowled up at the branch as if willing it to fall. Then, her words seeming to register, his brows knit and he faced her. "It must be an odd translation. There may not be a direct equivalent in your language, so sometimes the translator will use an approximation or an outdated usage. We learn to manage a wife and household in husbandry school, not livestock."

Lily watched his retreating back as he moved farther into the forest and had to prevent herself from recoiling. *Manage a wife?* No wonder this guy had a low opinion of women; they trained misogyny into boys at an early age.

She shuffled behind him. *Keep it to yourself. Not your planet, not your culture. You don't have enough information to judge. And who are you to judge anyway?*

"What about here?"

Lily scanned the spot with a clenched jaw. A few feet away, she spotted puddles of stagnant water. "If mosquitos don't exist on this planet, then sure." Her tone came out a little more curt than she'd meant.

He frowned at her. "Do you have something you'd like to say to me?"

Before she could stop them, words burst from her lips. "*Manage* a wife? How do the women feel about being managed like a bank account? What do they even teach? How to calm a wife's inevitable hysteria, or how to guide her in making you the perfect meal?"

To her utter disbelief, a wide grin spread across Verakko's face, and he barked out a laugh then gave his head a little shake of disbelief. "You don't even understand how far off the mark you are." He resumed his search for a camp location but over his shoulder added, "And for the record, out of all the females I've ever met, you are by far the most likely to dissolve into hysterics."

Lily snatched a small brown nut from her sack and pelted him in his broad back.

Stiffening, he eyed the fallen nut. He stooped while managing to hold the firewood and scooped up the small orb. Holding her furious gaze, he cracked the dried husk with his molars, then popped the bright yellow nut into his mouth. "You just made my point."

Steam must surely be whistling out of her ears. Crossing her arms, she closed her eyes and breathed. *In. Out. In. Out.* Lily tried to focus on her father and all the ways he'd taught her to be master of her emotions, a lesson she'd never truly exceled at. When she opened her eyes again, she saw Verakko waiting impatiently.

"Can you help me find a camp now, since you seem to have a problem with every one I choose?"

She donned a smug grin. "That's because you've made terrible choices."

The vein in his neck pulsed again, and she felt a modicum of satisfaction.

She strolled past him, ignoring the enticing whiff of cedar as she did, and forced her mind to focus on the task at hand. After a few minutes of silence, she spotted a clearing set among a grouping of large boulders and, without saying a word, began setting up camp.

Verakko dropped the logs nearby. Lily could feel his eyes on her but didn't want to lose her newfound calm by acknowledging him. What he'd said was true in some ways. She'd never been closer to hysteria since being in these woods. Not even when she'd woken up in a cell.

The hardships of the last month finally seemed to be catching up with her, and this man did nothing but heighten all the emotion she'd been suppressing. In a situation like this, that was dangerous. Lily distracted herself by wondering what Alex would think of Verakko. She grinned and imagined all the random movie comparisons she'd make to the handsome teal guy.

Her grin fell; Verakko would probably like Alex more than her. He could take care of her, and she'd allow it. That had always been a problem in Lily's relationships. Too independent to make men feel comfortable. Why did they always want her to need them? Wasn't it better if she didn't?

Lily sighed and retrieved her bow drill kit and a tinder nest from her pack.

"What can I do?" he asked from behind her.

She peered over her shoulder and nearly chuckled. The look of pure male frustration was almost enough to make up for his earlier comments. If he truly was a misogynist, this whole ordeal would be just as frustrating for him. Lily knew exactly how it felt to let your pride get the better of you—her insect bites from last night proved as much. *It must be killing him that he has to rely on a woman.*

Or maybe she had it all wrong. She'd let him rile her up to such a degree that she hadn't actually bothered to learn anything about him. Lily let out a defeated sigh. "You can explain what I'm missing about husbandry school while I start a fire."

"If you tell me how, I can start it instead."

He looked so…earnest. "Just watch while I do it, alright? I'll let you give it a go tomorrow."

He plopped down, seeming frustrated but resigned.

"So, what *do* you learn in school?" The wooden bow ate into her newly healed calluses as she began to use the drill.

"Cooking, childcare, sexual health and proficiency, pampering, self and family defense, finance management…those kinds of things. Things a wife might look for in a husband. I learned more about how to fight while serving in our infantry for a few years after finishing school, but they taught the basics in school. My curriculum wasn't nearly as rigorous as the husbandry school of my current city, Tremanta, but I learned enough."

Lily's hand rested atop the bearing block, her task forgotten at the words *cooking* and *childcare*.

Verakko smirked. "I told you, you were far off."

"Why is the schooling in Tremanta more difficult?"

He blinked at her, perplexed. "You never ask the questions I think you will." He shook his head. "Well, in Tremanta, the males are expected to use their grades from school to attract a wife, whereas in Mithrandir, the matriarch of the family organizes our marriages. Our grades are still taken into account, but if a female head is able to negotiate well, males with subpar grades can still find a wife."

"Are women's grades taken into account too?"

Verakko tipped his head from side to side. "Yes, but they bear less weight on marriage negotiations and more on their chosen professions."

Lily returned to her task, making sure not to meet his eyes. "And are you married?" *Why do I care?*

In the periphery of her vision, she saw Verakko shift in his seat. "Not yet. My mother will choose for me when the time comes."

"Subpar grades?"

"The majority of my grades were excellent," he hissed.

She took in his bunched shoulders and the thin set of his mouth. "I didn't mean to offend. I only meant..." *He doesn't deserve a compliment.* "It doesn't make sense that you wouldn't be married otherwise."

"Because I'm attractive?"

She kept her gaze averted but could hear the smile in his voice. "For an alien," she evaded. "But your crappy attitude drops you a few notches on the hotness scale."

He sighed. "Yes, my grades reflect the same. All high or acceptable marks, except for communication."

"I'm glad it isn't just me." Lily chuckled. "I hope you and your mom are close." A small curl of smoke rose from the base of the thin wooden spindle she was spinning with the bow. *Almost there.*

"Close in what way?"

Lily chanced a glance to Verakko. Over the last few hours, she'd noticed his coloring darken to an inky blue again. Maybe the change happened every night? He appeared confused. "You know, close. Your relationship. I hope you guys talk a lot and she knows what kind of women you like." When his brows remained furrowed, she huffed, "So she'll pick someone good for you."

He blinked at her, the corner of his mouth lifting into a comic display of confusion. "Whoever my mother chooses will be a match based more on what she thinks is important in a pairing and who she believes will produce ideal offspring. A male's feelings on the matter are taken into consideration but not by much. My mother is...powerful. She'll want to make sure my wife is a strong female so our children will be strong."

A muted guilt suffused her. She'd misjudged Verakko. He may be rude, pushy, and stubborn, but he was no misogynist.

"So, what? You're supposed to spend your whole life with a woman your mom picks out, and you have no say?"

His glowing green eyes remained intent on her actions. "No. Our marriages don't last that long. A typical contract would last anywhere from a few months to a few years, depending on what the females have negotiated."

Lily set the bow drill aside and gently transferred the small burning coal she'd created to her tinder nest, then softly blew, feeding the small ember with oxygen. Before long, a flame crackled to life within the bundle. Gathering kindling from her bag along with the logs Verakko had collected, she built the fire.

When she was done and the flames snapped and sizzled happily, she sat back, thinking. "I have to say, from an outside alien perspective with no real right to comment on the customs of another culture, that sounds...unpleasant."

A low, rumbling chuckle emanated from him, causing goosebumps to break out over her forearms. "I suppose to a human it may seem that way."

"What about being mated? You said Alice was. Does that mean she's with that guy for only a few months?"

Verakko's lips thinned, and he stared at her as if he were trying to decide something. "No, mating is forever. It's different than marriage. Marriage is a contract. Mating is what would be considered a love pairing. Something unbreakable. They'll be together forever."

"Forever?" Lily asked, unease bubbling under her skin at the finality in his words. "What if she wants to leave him later?"

"That isn't how mating works. Our people view it as sacred. Marriage is more of a duty."

"No offense, but neither sounds very appealing to me. It's either a business arrangement or promise your life to someone without any kind of safety net. I'm surprised Alice agreed to that. I don't know her well, but…no chance of divorce? Yikes."

Verakko stared at the flames and rested his elbows on his knees.

Shit, did I offend him again? Gotta stop doing that. Keep your opinions to yourself, Lily!

"Must mean you're a good cook, though," she said brightly, trying to lighten the mood. Reaching into her bag, she pulled out the last two red fruits and tossed one to him. "Think you can do anything with these?"

"Alas, my skills lie in a real kitchen with appliances and seasoning."

"Hmm." Lily crossed to the other side of the fire and sat with her back against a broad purple rock. "Can I ask you a serious question without you biting my head off?" she said, nibbling at the tart fruit she'd once loved but had grown to despise.

"Odd choice of words for the alien you thought ate human flesh." A spark of humor twinkled in his eyes, and she stifled a grin.

"If you were raised in what I can only assume is a female-run society, and trained on how to make a wife happy, then why have you been so bossy with me?"

The glint in his gaze faded. He opened his mouth to speak then closed it again. Finally, he said, "You aren't my wife."

Lily took a gulp of water, choosing not to tug at the thread of disappointment that statement made her feel. Instead, she held the water canteen out to him and frowned when he refused it. "You have to eat and drink. I did my best to clean that wound while you were unconscious, but your body needs calories and water to fight off an infection."

"You forget. I'm not human. I don't need as much as you."

"Fine, but you need to drink soon." A wave of exhaustion hit her, dissolving her urge to argue. "We'll gather more supplies tomorrow." Stifling a yawn, she continued, "I only have one full canteen of water left, and these were the last two pieces of fruit. All that's left are those nuts, and I still don't know if I can eat them."

"They're a common food, guren. You can eat them." Verakko gathered the pile of wood and dragged it closer. "Sleep. You barely got any rest last night. I'll keep the fire fed. Tomorrow I'll hunt and find us some real food."

She narrowed her eyes at him but stretched out on the ground anyway. "How do you know whether I slept or not?"

"Do you really think I was able to rest with you teetering on a branch like you were? I spent the night making sure I was prepared in case you fell."

Lily's brief flare of annoyance at his distrust of her judgment was quickly quelled. The image of an aggravated Verakko, pacing under her tree and wringing his hands, made warmth spread through her chest and shoot all the way down to her toes.

"No sneaking up and cuddling with me while I'm asleep," she commanded out of good sense, ignoring the larger part of her that wanted to use the big guy as a blanket.

He settled onto a large boulder. "Males and females don't often cuddle on this planet."

She forced her lids to remain open. Was it smart to be defenseless in front of this stranger? Why was she having so much trouble staying awake anyway? Every other night, she'd been exhausted around this time, yet still alert. Lily's ears suddenly pricked and she listened to the sounds around her, but it was oddly quiet.

The gentle buzzing of the fuzzy insects could still be heard, but the scratching and snuffling of the animals that nosed around her camp each night were gone.

Lily studied Verakko and wondered if he had something to do with it. Did the creatures of the forest recognize that a threat had joined her? Were they keeping their distance from *him*? A flutter started in her stomach, and she nibbled her lip. Why did that possibility only make her feel safe and not terrified? If she had any sense, she'd be scared of what other animals were scared of, after all.

"I can trust you, right?" she whispered, her eyelids becoming too heavy to fight any longer.

"With your life."

***

Verakko watched as Lily's breathing became deep and even. She'd fallen asleep almost immediately. In the green light of the fire, he could make out the dark circles under her eyes. Her clothing was stained and bloody. His blood.

Lifting his shirt, he examined his injury again. Only a purple scab remained. Verakko hadn't thought much of it. He'd healed from worse. But the knowledge that she'd used her precious water to clean his wound, in an attempt to keep him alive, made his chest ache. He wasn't used to being cared for in that way.

Verakko shook off the feeling. Reaching for a long branch he'd found, he began carving a spear tip with his knife. His gaze kept returning to Lily.

Her skin was dirty and scratched. Her clothes hung off her in a way that indicated she'd lost weight. Even so, she was beautiful…and terrifying. If she was this enchanting to him now, he could only imagine how much more so she'd be when not surviving on wanget fruit.

Would the weight she put on fill out her delectable hips and ass? Would her pale, chapped lips become pink or red?

He heard a crack and looked down to find a pile of shavings under a broken spear tip.

He let out a long sigh. There was no use in fantasizing about this female. He couldn't have her. He was meant for another, and Lily wasn't his mate.

When she'd asked him why he hadn't doted on her as he would with any other female, he'd lied. In truth, he'd never been so unguarded around a female. Maybe it was the fact she didn't know their culture, or maybe it was that Lily gave as good as she got, a trait he'd never experienced from the emotionally distant females of Mithrandir.

He refocused his efforts on whittling a spear tip. If husbandry school had done anything, it'd given him the instinct to care for a female. Make sure they were content. Although he'd always considered this urge tiresome and annoying, the instinct to provide for Lily in every way didn't feel like a chore. It felt like a need. An unyielding need for her happiness to be brought about by his actions alone.

Maybe that was why her continual ability to care for herself left him so cantankerous. She may not need him for much, but he knew if he set a large piece of delectable meat down in front of her, she'd smile at him and thank him. She might even kiss him. As if on cue, his cock pulsed.

He'd seen a couple of the human females kiss each other on the cheek in greeting. Was kissing on the mouth only reserved for romantic partners? Or would he be able to experience the act in a platonic way that wouldn't dishonor his betrothed?

Verakko clenched his jaw. He'd lied about that too. When Lily had asked whether he was married, he should've admitted that in a few weeks he would be, but he hadn't.

The tip of the spear began taking form as he whittled in irritation. It wasn't as if he even knew his future wife. He knew of Ziritha, of course, but he'd never so much as spoken to her. From what he gathered, she preferred not to interact with her husbands outside of her ovulation cycles. The rumor was she had a favored male of her own who wasn't eligible for marriage, but Verakko had no way of knowing whether the rumor was true.

Ziritha was close to his mother, though, and he knew she wanted Ziritha to take her place in Mithrandir one day. Negotiating a contract for her son with a female she thought of as queen material made sense.

There was no need to tell Lily. Why was he even worrying about it? It wasn't as if she'd care about whether he was unattached. Would she?

The ghost of the scent of her arousal flitted through his memory. She was attracted to him, a dangerous prospect.

6

∽

By the time the morning came, Verakko was prepared to stab any animal that moved with his small knife. Losing a night of sleep was one thing. Being left for dead, beaten and bloodied in the jungle, was another. But Verakko had learned something insidious last night.

Lily made noises in her sleep.

Some were breathy sounds of fear that made him want to rush over and pull her close. Others were small gasps and pants that caused her breasts to quiver and his fangs to ache. Worst of all, a few times during the dead of night, she'd moaned, and the faintest trace of arousal had lingered in her scent.

The sounds had been soft and short-lived, but the feminine exhalations and scent had had his shaft hardening and his mind wandering to dark places. He'd tried to focus on their current predicament instead.

They'd need to cover more ground today. Verakko didn't know exactly how much venom the Strigi male who'd dropped him had been dosed with, but if he'd only received a scratch, he may be close to recovered by now. Would the male return for him? Strigi were notorious for their single-minded pursuit of their goal, and if capturing him for questioning had been the goal, then he had to assume the Strigi would be on the hunt as soon as he was able. It was at least a possibility he had to take seriously. Not just for his sake, but for Lily's.

Verakko estimated they had another day of hiking out in the open before the threat would force them to travel in the forest, ensuring cover from overhead.

He didn't know how Lily would react to his suggestion that they move through the forest rather than along the river. So far, he had let her take the lead, had traveled in the way she wanted, but if there was a threat to her safety, he'd need to insist, and he didn't look forward to that inevitable argument.

How long was she expecting to stay out here anyway? Her friend was gone. Verakko sensed she may believe the same but wasn't ready to admit it. He worried about what would happen when she finally did. She was so strong, so competent. But she was also caring. To a level he didn't understand. The way her eyes had shone with tears yesterday morning. The pain on her face had just about floored him.

He hoped that when she finally gave up searching, she'd let him be there for her. Hold her while she cried and whisper reassurances into her mop of tangled, gorgeous brown hair.

Verakko's mind latched onto his thoughts, and his head jerked back. What was happening to him? He hated it when people cried. A few weeks ago, he'd tried to calm Alice, who'd been on the cusp of tears. But the only reason he'd done it was because he'd been literally trapped underwater in a meeting room with nowhere to escape to. He glanced at his hands for the hundredth time this morning and let out an irritated hiss to find them unmarked.

From the stories he'd heard, most of the mates from his family line had recognized each other fairly quickly upon meeting. Even his great aunts, who'd been legendary for not getting their marks until a year after they'd met, had recognized each other as potential mates from the first moment they'd locked eyes.

But if Lily was to be believed, his eyes hadn't changed.

Was it because she was human? Maybe if he got her out of the forest and they were both safe and comfortable, their souls would relax and recognize each other. It was a long shot, yet the odd jumble of feelings he was experiencing for her after such a short time begged to be explored.

He might not know exactly where he was, but he knew of this river and knew it would eventually lead to two cities. They'd need to travel to one of them. At this point, they were both closer in distance than Tremanta by a long shot. The prospect of visiting either city sat heavy in his gut. Staying out here and letting Lily suffer was not an option, though. He'd need to decide which city to move toward soon.

She began to stir, and like an overeager male fresh from husbandry school, he nervously smoothed his hair. Realizing what he'd done, he promptly mussed it again. He cracked his neck and rolled his shoulders. At least he'd be able to burn off some of this inner turmoil during their hike. At present, his mood was beyond foul.

Why in the name of the Goddess had he been dropped into the presence of this tormenter? If he'd only recognized her, this whole situation would be different. He'd be over-joyed, attempting to woo her at every turn. Instead, he had to now watch her stretch her arms above her head in the dap-pled morning sunlight and pretend the slice of skin exposed below her top didn't make his mouth water.

She rubbed her eyes and then squinted over at him. The gold flecks in her irises were bright, and the dark smudges underneath were gone. "Wow. Thank you for keeping watch. I haven't slept for a full night in...well, I can't remember how long." She studied him. "You should've woken me up so we could take turns, though. You look like crap."

"Why would I care about how I look to you?" he snapped, caring very much about how he looked to her.

She raised her hands in surrender. "I get it. You're not a morning person. Noted." She rolled her eyes and rummaged in her bag, mumbling, "So, even aliens need coffee."

"Are you ready to go?"

She shot him an exasperated look. "I just woke up. Would you cool it? I want to brush my teeth and take a trip to the woods, then we can go." She pulled a small, frayed twig and wooden bowl from her bag, then swept her gaze around the camp. "Can you hand me that rock?" she asked, pointing to a small stone near his knee.

Lily pushed the ashes of the long-dead fire around with a stick and tentatively grabbed a piece of charcoal. Verakko watched in fascination.

She crushed the charcoal into a fine powder, mixed a few drops of water in until a paste formed, and used the substance along with her twig to clean her teeth. Damn. Why did she have to be so impressive?

"Wha…?" she said around a mouth full of black charcoal. She'd caught him staring.

"I can go get whatever it is you need in the woods while you finish." He didn't have the experience she did to survive in the wild, but he could take direction. Make himself useful by fetching her things and carrying their load. He'd wanted to carry the bag for her all day yesterday, but a weak part of him had desired to hear her request his help. It had struck him as both vexing and endearing when he'd realized she never would. Especially since the woven green bag was wider than she was and looked moderately heavy.

She raised a brow and flushed her mouth out with water. "That's okay. I can do it."

Heat rose on his neck. "I insist."

She stood and dusted off her clothing. "It's fine. I'll only be a minute."

Frustration, mingled with his long, sleepless night, forced him to his feet. "Lily, I need to help in some way. You stay here, and I'll go get whatever it is you need." He advanced. She backed away, eyes wide. She'd slept soundly three feet away from him all night, and he'd just destroyed all that trust in a moment. "Why do you have to be so…so…difficult?"

Her look of worry instantly transformed, lips pulling tight and eyes narrowing. She shoved her hands on her hips. "Okay, you really want to help?"

"Yes!"

"Then let me pee in peace!" Without another word, she stomped away.

Way to go.

***

Just when she was beginning to feel like she understood him, he had to go and get all pushy again. She used some of her water to clean herself up and then made her way back toward camp, being sure to take her time.

It makes sense he's grumpy, she admitted. He hadn't slept all night, after all. Had he stayed awake because it was clear she'd needed a good night's sleep more than him? Or had he done it out of some misguided sense of male duty to sacrifice his own needs and protect her while she slept?

Either way, she'd have to force him to take a turn sleeping tonight. If this was his mood after two nights of no sleep, she couldn't imagine how much worse he'd be in a few days.

When she reached the camp, she froze in place. "What are you doing? That's my toothbrush!"

Verakko was cleaning his teeth the same way she had, using *her* toothbrush. He shrugged and reached for the water container she'd brought with her. When she didn't hand it over but instead glared at him, he crossed to her and plucked the canteen out of her hand.

Lily seethed. She didn't share toothbrushes. It'd taken her countless tries to find the type of tree that would have sticks fibrous enough to create a brush and soft enough not to tear up her gums. Now she'd have to do it all over again.

She made short work of gathering her belongings—apparently *their* belongings now—and slung the bag over her shoulder. She hadn't made it two steps before the weight was gone.

"Hey!" She spun, and her breath caught. He was only a few inches away. Her eyes focused on his broad chest first, then traveled upward to meet his gaze. He smirked.

Reaching forward, he brushed a hand across her cheek and into her hair. She had to stop herself from leaning into his touch. "You asked me to put my muscle to good use." She felt a tug, and his hand reemerged, pinching a bright yellow leaf. "Remember?"

She cleared her throat. "Fine. I need to find a new toothbrush anyway. The bag will slow me down." Traipsing past him, she kept her breaths even and her chin high.

They emerged onto the riverbank, and Lily frowned. It was only morning and the air was already thick and hot, the last of the early morning sunshine blocked out by a sheet of gray clouds. *Gloomy day, gloomy companion, gloomy me.*

"We'll have to stop earlier than normal today. We need time to boil more water, scavenge for food, and find you a few water containers of your own." Lily said, halting at the edge of a particularly hazardous hillside.

The steep descent was covered in slippery bedrock and about fifteen feet high. She wiggled her toes and winced in anticipation. The soles of her once-bright-red flats were wearing thin. Thanks to the ankle straps, she'd managed not to lose the shoes in her rapids ride, but the cheap metal buckles of the ankle straps had cracked four days ago. Although her feet were quickly becoming calloused, no longer hurting as much during her daily hike, rocks were always painful.

Before she even heard Verakko move, he was next to her. "I could carry you today. We'd cover more ground faster, and then we'd have more time to hunt and find some real food."

Carry me? "I know you're a strong guy and all, but seriously? That's crazy. You can't car—" She gasped as Verakko swept her up, one arm under her knees and the other around her waist. She threw her arms around his neck on instinct. "Put me down!" Lily eyed the steep, rocky pass.

She glanced back to him and saw he was grinning. "Hold on tight."

Before she could blurt out her rejection of his request, he'd jumped.

She screamed and buried her head against his chest. *This is how I'm gonna die. A stupid man comes and takes stupid risks. Trying to show off. This is it. No more soda. No more French onion soup. No mo—*

Hot breath near her ear brought her mind to the present. "Lily, you're safe."

The way he said her name in that velvety voice, like he was savoring it, sent a flutter through her stomach. She was still clutching his neck, her face buried against the warmth of his shoulder. His scent toyed with her again, making her relax despite herself.

Cautiously, she peered around and her lips parted. His leap had cleared the rocky outcrop. She focused on him. "How did you do that?"

His eyes were a deeper shade of emerald green, and from this close, she could see they were almost translucent, like the inside of a gem. Hypnotizing.

Lily knew she should let go of him, but he was so damn warm and firm and he smelled so good. She was used to the bad smells that came from extended camping trips; it was one of the reasons she loved her assortment of scented candles so much. It felt nice to be held by her own personal scented candle. A stray thought concerning the amount of sex she'd have to have with this giant in order for his smell to rub off on her danced through her mind.

He was staring at her mouth hungrily. Would he kiss her? Then his gaze traveled lower and settled on her neck. He ran a pointed tongue over his fang.

Fuck no!

"Put me down." She squirmed. No way in hell was she letting some super-hot alien gnaw on her carotid. A surprising jolt of electricity shot directly to her clit as she imagined his fangs brushing against the sensitive skin.

He set her back on her feet, but the arm around her waist stayed locked in place. "It's easier this way. It would've taken you ages to climb down."

Lily balled her fists and glared up at him. It was true. She couldn't move as fast as he did, and she hated feeling less than. Hated feeling like she was holding someone back or slowing them down. "No one's stopping you from going on ahead. I can take care of myself. Don't let me hold you back."

She could've sworn a look of hurt flashed over his face. "The only reason I'm out here at all is because of you. Why would I decide to leave you behind now?"

Gah! She wasn't some charity case. "Because I don't want you here!" The lie settled in her gut, cold and heavy.

He scowled, remaining silent, and his scent intensified.

Lily's eyes drooped before she snapped them open. "Stop that! Whatever that whole smell thing is, turn it to zero." Lily tried to move away, but he pulled her in closer.

"I told you, I'm not doing it on purpose. You smell whatever your brain wants you to. It just happens. And my scent should only be pleasing to you, not intoxicating." A wicked grin spread over his face. He wrapped his other arm around her waist and pressed her into his body. Her heartbeat picked up speed. "Are you sure it isn't just that you find me sexy?"

She sputtered. "No I don't!" Hell yeah she did.

He frowned again, and a low, rattling growl escaped him. It almost sounded like a ragged, resonant hiss. Although she'd never heard a sound quite like it before, the intention was clear. She'd been warned. "Look, little female. I can't control it, so stop complaining about it." His hand shot up to grip the back of her neck, dragging it forward until his mouth was a breath away from her ear. "You don't hear me complaining every time the scent of arousal floods your cunt."

Lily choked on her retort as her sex grew wet. His warm breath on her ear, paired with the firm grip on her nape and the massive bulge pressing into her belly, had already muddled her thoughts. Now, hearing those dirty words uttered in a sexy-as-sin voice? If she hadn't been so shocked by the idea that he could actually smell her arousal, she might've melted into him right there.

His grip tightened for a second before he jerked away, putting space between them.

He let out a sound of frustration. "Yes, that smell. You think it doesn't drive me up a wall?"

Lily was left cold and weak. She'd been just about ready to throw caution to the wind and twine her arms around his neck.

"But I don't constantly attack you for your smell. I know you can't help it. It's a natural physical response." He stalked past her. "Stop pestering me about mine."

Lily's cheeks flamed. Was all that sexiness a ploy to seduce her into making a point? *The nerve!*

She sped after him. "I haven't seen any men in a month. At this point, an old, hobbled Davy Crockett would garner the same response. Don't flatter yourself."

Lie. Lie. Lie.

Verakko aimed a death glare at her, then stalked forward at a pace she couldn't match without jogging. Lily let out a pent-up huff and followed.

Forget about him. The sooner you find Alex, the sooner you can get out of here and ditch that overgrown chameleon for good.

The reminder of Alex served to cool some of her anger. The subdued dread she'd felt for days on end before Verakko had arrived replaced it. Maybe it was better to think about Verakko and her anger. Maybe then, the hollow guilt and worry wouldn't claw at her insides, demanding to be acknowledged.

Lily continued on, taking her time to scan the water and land for any signs of Alex. How realistic was it that she would've floated this far? The river had a few spurts of calm, long enough for a floating person to swim to shore at least. Why hadn't she found any evidence yet? Had it all really been washed away, like she kept trying to convince herself?

Lily swallowed a lump in her throat and tears burned in her eyes. She was grateful Verakko's back was to her.

There was a possible answer as to where Alex had gone, but she didn't think she could stomach it at the moment. *If she got caught by a boulder or log and it pulled her under...* Nausea roiled in her gut, and Lily had to stop. *Alex is alive. She was tired and couldn't make it, so she kept floating, and then the storm washed all signs of her away.* That was all there was to it.

Just breathe. In. Out. In. Out.

"Do you need a break already? Water?" Verakko called from in front of her, his tone edged with irritation.

A spark of indignation flared, and she let it overtake her. "No, I'm fine!"

He crossed his arms over his chest and scanned her body in a way that made her skin tingle. "We've only been walking for an hour or so. Are you *already* tired?"

"I said I'm fine. I just had a pebble in my shoe."

Verakko turned, grumbling about something under his breath, likely her.

They resumed their silent hike, him in front and her trailing behind. He slowed a few times, probably giving her the opportunity to catch up, but she made sure to slow her pace when he did. Sending a clear message that she wanted to walk alone.

Lily replayed what he'd said earlier about his scent. Could he really not control it? He'd compared it to the smell she put off when aroused. If that was the case, then did that mean she was smelling his arousal too? How could that be? She hadn't even known that was something people *could* smell. He wasn't exactly "people," though, was he.

He'd said *her* brain was choosing what he smelled like. Could that be true? Her mind wandered back to a memory she'd thought about often over the years, and she knew why her subconscious had chosen crisp, burning cedar.

She'd been fifteen or maybe sixteen and camping in Turkey. Her parents had decided they'd wanted to hike the Carian Trail, and as always, they'd brought her along. Unlike many of their trips, this one was like a vacation for Lily. They'd followed a cleared path, slept in a tent, and packed food. They'd even brought a lighter with them that time. A real lighter, not a fire starter or a bow drill, but an easy-to-use one-click lighter.

Looking back, she suspected they'd done it because of her incessant whining. When you've been dragged around the world practicing primitive bushcraft survival techniques and hunting for all your food and water, even a bag of trail mix seems luxurious. There was another reason that trip had been so special to Lily too. There'd been people.

One handsome, tall teenage boy in particular.

His family and hers had both been headed in the same direction and had decided to hike together. The family was from New Zealand, and the boy's parents had been fascinated by her parents' descriptions of truly living and thriving in the wilderness. To her utter embarrassment, her parents had forced Lily to demonstrate flint knapping and point out all the edible plants she saw as they'd walked, claiming the education she'd received from them was far better than any she could've gotten from traditional schools.

When she'd gutted and fileted a fish without batting a lash, the boy had given her such a bewildered look. As if she'd had two heads. Looking back, she understood she hadn't been a normal teenage girl.

She was so wrapped up in the past that she wasn't paying attention to her surroundings and walked directly into

Verakko, who stood staring at her with an odd expression. Just like the boy had.

Panic swamped her, and she glanced up to see the sun was shining high in the sky, peeking through the surrounding dark clouds. How long had they been walking for? "We need to go back!" she yelled, already heading in the opposite direction on the verge of tears. "I was thinking about something else, and I didn't watch for signs of Alex. I could've missed her."

Verakko wrapped a large palm around her arm and swung her around. "Calm down. I kept watch. There was no sign of her."

Lily could still hear the blood rushing in her ears, but there was something else. Verakko's voice echoed in her head again, trying to find somewhere to stick. Instead of pushing his words out like before, she listened and, despite herself, she calmed. "Really?"

"Really." He ran his palms down her arms and gave her a lopsided grin. "I want to find her as much as you do."

How could she have been so careless?

She eyed Verakko, and the last of her panic faded. He'd done something to calm her down with his voice. She knew that for sure, even if she was unclear as to how he'd done it. But he looked sincere, and regardless of their constant bickering, she trusted him not to lie about something as important as a missing person.

"Here, drink some water." He held the canteen out to her expectantly.

"You first." An anxious edge still lingered in her tone, and she amended, "I mean, you need to drink too. You haven't had anything for almost two days."

Verakko took a long breath and ran a hand through his somehow flawless hair. "How long can a human survive without water?"

Lily shrugged. "About three days, but it depends on myriad other things."

Verakko's eyes widened and concern creased his brow. "Goddess...three days? You only have two canteens. Why didn't you..." He paused at the warning look Lily gave him and held the canteen back out to her with raised brows. "I can go two weeks."

Two whole weeks with no water? "How?"

He shook the canteen at her when she didn't move to take it. "I'm not a doctor. Do you know how you can go one day with no water?"

"Yes," she said instantly, earning her a frown. Her parents had made it a point to teach her exactly how her body worked. If she were on her way to death, she'd know specifically which organs were failing and why. *Lucky me.* So far, her two butternut-squash-sized canteens had managed to stave off the warning signs of dehydration.

"Well, I don't. We don't have as many sweat glands as some of the other Clecanian races. Or humans." He eyed her damp forehead and her lower chest, where she was sure a lovely line of underboob sweat was present. "That has a lot to do with it, I think. Our kidneys are different too. And our skin helps regulate temperature."

Lily took a large gulp of water. She'd been holding back, wanting to make sure they both had enough, but now she felt okay about truly quenching her thirst. "At least you know *some* stuff, I guess. They don't teach you about your own anatomy in husbandry school?"

Verakko pinned her with a dark look. "I can assure you, we were all more interested in learning the ins and outs of female anatomy to waste time on studying our kidneys." He let his gaze roam down her body again, and she stifled a shiver.

"We're probably very different. I mean, human women and your women."

"As I explained before, we're the same species." He held her gaze. "You're similar enough. I bet I could find my way around."

Butterflies flapped around in her stomach, and her heart pounded furiously.

Verakko's brows furrowed in thought as he looked at her. He gave his head a small shake and replaced the water canteen in the pack.

Lily was burning to know what he'd been wondering just then, but she clamped her mouth shut.

Verakko peered into the sky, and to her shock, a dark, translucent second lid slid down over his bright green eyes. Without thinking, she grabbed his face and wrenched it down to her own. "You have a second lid! How cool. You have no idea how many times I wished I had something like this. You go on a three-week trip into the Australian outback and lose your sunglasses the first day—trust me, constant squinting messes with your sanity, not to mention the wrinkles I must've accumulated. It's like you have built-in sunglasses! This would've come in so handy if only for the flies. My God, they're terrible there. You wouldn't eve—"

A low, rattling vibration, more melodic than the growl he'd directed at her before, sounded from his chest, and she jumped away.

"Oh my gosh, I'm so sorry. I just got excited. I shouldn't have grabbed you like that. What was that sound?"

"It was nothing." Verakko straightened, clearing his throat.

Lily stared at the spot on his chest where the sound had come from, then back to his face. She held back a wide smile at what she found.

Verakko, the sour, proud, strong alien, appeared…ruffled.

"As I was saying." His gaze darted, and a deeper cerulean tinted his high cheeks. He glanced around again. "What was I saying?"

Lily bit her lip to keep from grinning. "Do you mean, what were you saying before you started blushing?"

His blush deepened. "I am not blushing," he said, then stomped away. Something in the trees caught his attention, and he stopped again. He motioned triumphantly toward the tree line. "Ah! I was going to ask when you were planning to stop. There's a guren tree here."

"We can stop now."

Without looking at her, he nodded and made his way over to the tree. Lily studied his six-and-a-half-foot frame as he plucked the guren nuts from limbs higher than she could reach while jumping, and smiled again.

What was that sound, and how can I get him to make it again?

7

∞

"Confusing female. Grabbing my face," Verakko griped under his breath as he hauled the last load of firewood to the small camp they'd set up.

Lily sat under a beautiful sprawling tree heavily laden with delicate yellow flowers. The small blossoms floated down around her as she focused on cracking nuts open against a smooth rock. She looked like some kind of forest goddess come to life. Verakko scowled. And he couldn't have her. Couldn't even try.

He dropped the wood pile, and she started at the loud cracks of dry wood hitting dry wood. For a moment, she stared up at him quizzically then returned to her task.

Verakko settled himself with another long stick and began carving a new spear tip. The one he'd started on yesterday hadn't made it through Lily's first dead-of-night moan. He'd be prepared for the sound tonight, though.

"Do you know what these flowers are?" She asked, examining one of the small yellow blossoms.

He scraped a large flake of wood from his spear and ground his teeth in frustration. "No."

"Hmm. Too bad. It'd be nice if it could be made into a medicine or tea." She returned to shucking the nuts.

The need to explain why his knowledge was so lacking bubbled in him. "They don't grow in the desert where I'm from."

"Tell me about your hometown," she said, never taking her eyes from her work.

"Mithrandir? What do you want to know?"

"Everything."

"Well," he began, leaning back against the soft bark of a tree, "it's a desert city. Fairly large. Surrounded by black sand as far as the eye can see. The old city is situated in the Well, an enormous pit formed by my ancestors centuries ago. But most people have moved into the new city, and now the old city is used primarily for recreation. There are shops and restaurants and spas."

"Spas?" Lily interrupted, her head snapping up.

Why was she so excited? "What are spas where you're from?"

"People go there for beauty treatments. Hair, massages, facials. Things like that. Are those the kind of spas you have?"

He gave a tight nod. "I didn't take you for the type to frequent such establishments."

"Just because I don't complain about being dirty and gross doesn't mean I like looking this way." Her chest puffed a little, and her eyes returned to the ever-shrinking pile of unshucked nuts. "I'll have you know, I was a hairstylist back home. I worked at a spa, and I loved it."

"You could work at one again now."

Lily paused and grew thoughtful. "I'd like to. I wonder how long it'd take to work through beauty school again. I can't imagine the products are the same. Or the hair, for that matter." She studied Verakko's hair, and he quelled the urge to smooth it. "What steps did they take to put those streaks in your hair?"

"I haven't colored my hair. I only get it cut on occasion." His comment seemed to irk her, and she returned to shucking the last few nuts.

"Do hairstylists get paid well in your city?"

Was Mithrandir *his* city anymore? He loved his town, and his people, but he loved them as an outsider would. He fit in much better in Tremanta, where technology and innovation were revered, rather than luxury and tradition. Verakko supposed he'd have to give up those things now. If he managed to have a child with Ziritha, he'd need to remain in Mithrandir indefinitely. "Yes. A trip to the spas and the basins is a regular occurrence and held dear among my people."

Lily cracked her last guren with a dreamy smile.

"What is it?"

Her eyes focused on his. "Oh, nothing. I was just thinking about some treatments I'd like right about now. A massage, a hot-oil scalp treatment, a manicure." She frowned at her small, somewhat dirty nails.

"I received high scores in my massage classes." Verakko's voice came out a little huskier than he'd intended, a small, rattling hiss punctuating his words.

Verakko couldn't believe it, but for a moment, Lily appeared to be considering his offer. His fingers twitched in anticipation.

She shook her head. "No, that's okay. I'll wait."

Verakko had to stop himself from breaking his newly sharpened spear in half.

***

"Are you ready to learn how to make a fire?"

To Lily's surprise, Verakko didn't argue or hesitate. Instead, he sat quietly and listened as she showed him how to use the bow drill and explained what to do after he managed to get an ember in the soft bundle of tinder.

"Got it?"

"I think so," he replied, brows drawn in concentration.

At least he didn't mind being taught by a woman, she thought, her estimation of him rising a fraction. Lily stood. "Good. Then I'm going to refill our canteens so we can purify the water before it gets too dark." She neglected to mention that she was also going to bathe. Better he didn't know.

He stood suddenly, and she had to take a step back. He peered around the clearing, then up to the sky just visible through the large leaves, worry evident in his eyes. "Maybe I should go with you."

Placing a hand on his arm, she tried to not sound too eager when she said, "No, it's fine. Someone needs to start a fire, and I want you to learn how to do it."

The muscle beneath her palm tensed, and his eyes traveled to where she touched him. His skin was warm and smooth. Awareness of his large, solid frame washed over her. How much better would she sleep curled against his warm chest after he'd used his strong hands to massage her stress away? Lily had been a breath away from agreeing to the massage before his dark tone had registered.

She jerked her hand back and awkwardly continued. "Okay, so…uh…you just stay right here and start a fire, and I'll be back before you know it." Lily gathered her water container and bowl, avoiding his intense stare that had darkened at her touch. "See you soon," she called, scurrying toward the river.

When she'd ventured far enough away and the frustratingly pleasant scent of cedar no longer hung in the air, she allowed herself a moment to breathe. It was funny how she'd been so lonely for so long, and now all she wanted was to be alone so she could gather her thoughts in peace.

Peering up at the sky, she estimated she had an hour or so before she'd need to head back. She picked up her pace and gave herself permission to finally think through what she'd learned. So much.

This planet wasn't at all what she'd thought. Her heart sank. If Verakko was to be believed, she'd have to get used to it, though. She'd never be allowed to return to Earth. Lily shook her head and dismissed the idea. Laws could be changed, and laws could be broken. Figuring out how to get back to Earth was a winnable fight, she was convinced of it, but it was a fight for another day. Besides, what was the rush? It wasn't like she'd have anybody waiting for her on Earth.

Lily's upbringing had instilled an unrest in her that she'd never been able to shake. As far back as she could remember, her family had constantly traveled. Even as an adult, she tended not to live anywhere for more than a few years.

A couple of friends she didn't stay in contact with and her globe-trekking parents were the only people who'd even notice she was gone. They'd probably assume she'd moved again.

Her parents would be okay; she didn't have any doubts. Her chest swelled. That thought hurt more than anything else. Sure, they'd miss her and wonder what had happened, but over time, she'd learned her mother and father didn't feel or express emotion in the same way most people did. They thought of themselves more as guides and teachers than parents. At sixteen, when she'd asked to emancipate herself from their care, they'd been thrilled. Overjoyed that she'd felt confident enough in what they'd taught her to venture out on her own. Although she'd never mentioned it, she'd been crushed at how easily they'd agreed.

The river came into view, and Lily let out a low breath. She had to hand it to them. Without their endless camping and survival training, she might not have made it out here. She supposed she owed them a thank you.

The river was curved here, creating a wide, sandy beach with shallow, calm water on one side and a sharp cliff on the far side, where the water rushed past. When she reached the sandy bank, she paused and took a second to admire the tranquil scene.

The sun was just setting behind the towering trees in the distance, turning the surface of the water gold. A cool breeze blew, carrying the crisp scent of the forest. Lily slid her eyes shut and inhaled. She bent, unbuckling her ankle straps, and toed off her flats. The wet sand between her curling toes was still gritty, yet a bit more velvety than most sand on Earth.

Lily waded into the water without thinking. Halfway in, she froze and glanced down at her wet shirt. Every other time she'd bathed, she'd made sure to clean her clothing as well as her body. She'd dive into the water then take off her clothes, scrubbing them as best she could. She'd lay them out to dry while cleaning the rest of herself.

Putting on wet clothes wasn't the most comfortable, but the warm air of most nights and the thin fabric ensured they dried quickly. Now, thanks to her distracted state of mind, all brought on by that confusing male, she'd forgotten to take her new travel companion into account.

Was it really wise to walk back into camp with a wet, white T-shirt? If his heated looks at her touch were any indication, no. She tore off her clothing and scrubbed away the blood and grime.

Her thorough laundering a few days ago made it so the clothes rinsed clean, or what could be considered clean these days, without too much effort. Peering around, she found a few dry boulders near a shallow area of river and moved toward them, squatting awkwardly to keep her shoulders below the surface of the water.

After her clothes were laid out and drying, she ducked back into the river and began to relax. It would take him ages to start a fire, anyway, her clothes should be partially dry by then. The water here was warm and soft and slightly aerated from the rapids upstream. As the sun dipped below the tree line, she enjoyed the last of the sunset. One of the moons was already visible in the cornflower-blue sky.

She thought about Verakko and grinned while paddling closer to shore to retrieve some sand. Learning how to use a bow drill was hard work. It took years of practice to master. Verakko would likely be fireless and livid upon her return, just as she'd been the first time she'd tried to use one on her own.

Lily ran the sand over her body as an exfoliant, trying to get as clean as possible without soap. She hadn't yet gotten lucky enough to catch an animal, but if she ever did, one of the first things she'd do would be to render the fat and make soap. She frowned, knowing that dream was just that—a dream. Even if she managed to get her hands on some fat, it'd take ages to convert into soap. Time she didn't have.

Noise behind her had her ducking into the water and spinning in place.

How? Is that...? There on the bank, looking pleased as punch, stood Verakko. And to make everything even more bothersome, he was holding a torch.

He'd made fire.

"You said you were only retrieving water," he called, crossing to her drying clothing and hooking a finger under her black panties. A wide grin spread over his face as he held them high in the air.

"Put them down," she grated.

He rocked back on his heels, dropping her underwear and lifting her matching black mesh bra. "I've never seen undergarments quite like this."

Her cheeks heated. "Well, now you have. Please leave and let me finish bathing in peace."

Verakko stuck the torch deep in the sand and stood. "You aren't the only one who deserves to get clean."

Pins and needles broke out over her skin as Verakko swung his shirt over his head, then stooped to remove his boots. Lily had to stop herself from squinting. Instead, she turned and walked deeper into the water. *It's okay. It's a big river. We both need to get clean, after all. I'm being selfish. He still has a wound in his side.*

She silently berated herself for not checking on the injury again sooner. If she had to nurse an infection...she'd never find Alex. Not to mention it'd be life threatening to him, and that made her insides twist for more reasons than just common human decency. Even through their bickering, she was beginning to like Verakko more and more.

The sound of a splash made her whirl around. Ripples near the shore showed her where he'd entered, but he was nowhere in sight. Confused, she scanned the area for a moment before cursing and covering her breasts and sex with her hands. Glaring, she searched the surface of the water. Where was that bastard? And how good was his eyesight under water?

"What are you looking for?"

The voice behind her made her shriek and almost skip across the surface. Her heart was still pounding in her ears when she spun to find Verakko standing halfway out of the water and laughing a full-bellied laugh.

The sound was infectious. She bit her lip to stifle the grin threatening to undermine her anger. "That wasn't funny."

He let out that odd sound again. Almost like a purr but sharper. "It was funny for me."

Suddenly, Verakko's naked torso caught her eye. Rivulets of water trailed over his large pecs and chiseled stomach and collected in the fabric of the bandage circling his hips. His skin was smooth and darker than it'd been when she'd left. "You can change color. Can you do it on purpose?"

"If needed." He ducked into the water, wetting his hair. Raising his hands to his pointed ears, he began to massage his scalp; the muscles of his large biceps bulging.

Lily bit the inside of her cheek and tried to keep her eyes focused on his face. His small smirk showed her he'd noticed her fascination with his body.

Her cheeks heated again, so she distracted herself by lifting her arms and raking her nails across her own scalp. As his gaze roamed over her shoulders and arms in the same way hers had, she was thankful she'd volunteered to be a guinea pig for a coworker looking to practice her laser hair removal. It was vain, but on her yearly trips into the wild with her family, the lack of body hair had always made her feel a little more human and a little less yeti. An unforeseen bonus of her months of hair removal procedures…she now felt more confident bathing next to the seemingly perfect specimen that was Verakko.

"I can't change to any color. Only the ones you've already seen. But if I needed to blend into a darker background on a bright night or during the day, I could make my skin change. Otherwise, it happens naturally throughout the course of the day."

Lily attempted to tilt her head back into the water without lifting her chest too close to the surface. Her awkward attempt made Verakko chuckle again.

"I can help you if you'd like."

Scrunching her mouth to the side, she shot him a look that said "Not a chance."

He shrugged and began rubbing his skin. The muscles of his torso jumped as he ran his hands over them. To combat her sudden and unwelcome desire to offer to wash his back,

Lily ducked her whole body under the water and shook out her hair. After a moment's hesitation, she opened her eyes and attempted to sneak a peek. *Fair's fair.*

To her disappointment, the water was too dark to make out much of anything. When she resurfaced, she met Verakko's eyes, only inches from her own. He was bent at the hip, rubbing clean his lower half.

Her breath stuttered as she stared into their glowing green depths.

"Did you get a good look?" he asked.

***

This female was going to drive him mad. After she'd run away from him, he'd been frantic, trying to recall her instructions and build a fire so he could go after her and make sure she was alright. It'd been obvious she didn't think he'd be able to build a fire quickly. A fair assumption. The bow drill was difficult to operate, and he'd had a renewed sense of appreciation for the ease with which she handled it.

When he'd finally succeeded in using the strange but effective tool, he'd sprinted to the river to boast untruthfully about how simple the task had been and force that pretty pink flush to spread over her cheeks, only to find a vision bathing in the river.

He'd nearly tripped over his own feet at the sight of her naked, glistening back and dripping wet hair. She'd left her clothes lying so far away, as if taunting him. For the first time in a very long time, he'd felt giddy, playful even. He couldn't remember ever feeling like that with a female.

But now, the heated looks she was giving him were enough to crumble any resolve he had. He'd refrained from looking at her naked form under the water, although his second lid would've made it easy. The way she blushed at his accusation told him she hadn't been as courteous.

"I didn't look!" she argued, sweeping the dark mass of hair over her shoulder and baring her neck.

His fangs gave a throb in time with his cock. He'd never felt the urge to mark so profoundly before. To bite a female was as intimate an act as any and was traditionally reserved for mates—and now for wives.

"Let me see your wound," she said, nodding toward his side.

He grinned and unfastened the tight knot on his hip.

When his side was revealed, she gasped and rushed forward. Her hand reached for him, and he readied himself, a cascade of anticipation stealing his breath. *Don't grab her if she touches you. You're set to be wed.*

Her fingers stopped an inch away from his smooth, unmarred side, and he hissed out a low curse.

"Sorry." She backed away, mistaking his disappointment for anger. "How is that possible? Whatever got you tore a hole in your side. It went through and through and looked pretty clean, but it can't possibly be healed already."

"My people heal quickly."

"What do you mean by 'your people'? Is it one of those genetically engineered traits you told me about?" she asked with of a tilt of her head. The act elongated the bare side of her neck even more. He stifled a groan.

"I'll tell you on our way back to camp."

"*Our?*" she questioned. "You go first, and I'll follow you later."

He let out a growl and, without meaning to, infused his words with *sway*. "I won't look, Lily. You can trust me."

Immediately, she clapped her hands over her ears. The action made the swell of her breasts, peeking out of the water, jiggle. Verakko ground his jaw and turned to retreat.

"Stop doing that!" she called from behind him.

"I can't always help it!" he barked. When he reached his clothes, he dragged his pants on. The damp, cool fabric chafed against his shaft, but it helped to cool his lust. He turned and frowned. Lily's back was to him. "I'm clothed," he called.

"Go on. I'll follow after you're gone."

Verakko threw his hands up. "Do you really think I couldn't hide in the trees and watch if I wanted to? I'll stand here with my back turned."

"If you turn around, I swear you'll regret it."

Verakko showed her his back and muttered, "I'll regret it either way, mivassi."

Muscles shooting tight in an instant, he froze. *Mivassi?* Where in this world or the last had that come from? He'd never even thought to use the endearment before. With any-one.

"Let's go." Her soft voice invaded his senses. How long had he been rooted in place?

With the slowly dying torch in hand, she headed off toward their camp. Her clothing was still as damp as his, and he thanked the Goddess he hadn't seen her from the front. The white material of her shirt was almost transparent. After shoving his boots back on, he trudged after her.

When they arrived back at camp, Lily gazed at the small fire he'd built. "Good job. Really, I'm impressed. It took me days to make a fire with a bow drill the first time I tried."

The compliment was meager, but he flushed with pride all the same. "You made it seem like it was going to be so…"

She turned with raised brows, ready to attack him for his insolent remark, but his words caught in his throat. The odd black scrap of material he'd seen by the river was clearly visible through her damp top. He scrubbed a hand over his jaw.

She sighed. "Yeah, I know. It's just my luck I was abducted wearing this shirt. There isn't anything I can do about it, though, so you're gonna have to deal with it. I'm not going to stay dirty and dry just because it's awkward for you to see me in a bra. Let's be adults about this."

Verakko met her eyes. "I'm going to go hunt," he blurted.

"What? Now? It'll be dark soon."

He gave her a forced smile then backed away. "That's when I do my best hunting." He gestured to his chest, now fully indigo. "Camouflage, remember?" And without waiting for her to utter another word, he took off.

8

~

Two hours later, and Verakko still hadn't returned. Lily peered through the leaves to the sky and silently promised if he wasn't back by the time *beta moon*—as she'd started calling the smaller of the two moons—disappeared from sight, she'd go search for him herself.

Lily topped off her last canteen with the water she'd spent hours purifying and huddled closer to the fire. The morning and afternoon had been hot, but the gray clouds from earlier had brought in a cold front and what she expected was the warning sign of a storm.

Where are you, Alex? Lily hated to think about it, but maybe it was time to give up her solo search. She should at least talk to Verakko about it.

Guilt swamped her again. She drew her knees into her chest and shivered in her damp clothes. The mere thought of giving up on Alex sat like a leaden weight in her gut. How could she even consider it? What if Alex was waiting and injured only a day's hike away and Verakko convinced her to turn back and head toward the people he'd mentioned before?

Tears leaked down her cheeks. Her chest expanded and the pressure begged to be released with a sob, but she held it in. Shudders wracked her body despite the warmth of the fire. No matter what she chose, it'd end up being the wrong decision.

She should send Verakko away. That way, one of them could continue on while the other went for help. Lily thought back to her week alone and wondered if she had the courage to do it again. *I'm such a coward.*

The sound of rustling echoed behind her, and she quickly wiped away her tears. She kept her eyes trained on the fire and worked to compose herself. *In. Out. In. Out.*

Verakko stood in front of her for a moment, then lowered his spear in front of her eyeline. She just about burst into tears again. Meat.

A huge chunk of rust-colored meat, already skinned and cleaned, was skewered on his spear. She shot to standing and took in the devastating grin on his face. His chest puffed out with pride. Then his keen eyes scanned her face, and his grin fell.

She tried to look away and inject her words with a lightness she didn't feel. "This is amazing. Thank you! I—"

He propped the spear on a nearby tree and took her face in his hands, forcing her gaze to his. Her chest tightened, and she cursed how close she was to crying again.

Choking back a sob, she plastered on a smile. "I'm fine. Really. Just had some smoke in my eyes. Sitting too close to the fire." Another tear leaked out. His thumb brushed it away.

Verakko's forehead creased as though he were the one in pain. "I can help if you allow it."

Lily sighed and held on to his wrists. Half of her wanted to tug his hands away. The other half ached to accept the comfort his warm palms on her cheek provided. "What do you mean?"

"I can *sway* you. Use my voice to help. If you open yourself up to it, I can convince you to let this guilt go."

She recalled the way he'd calmed her with his words earlier in the day. How much easier would it be to simply not care anymore? Lily shook her head as much as she could between his large palms and sniffed. "That isn't the answer. It'd be wrong."

His lips thinned. Just when she felt he would argue, he pulled her in close and wrapped his arms around her, enveloping her in his warmth. She remained stiff for only a breath before relaxing into his embrace. The low, rattling purr she'd heard that morning vibrated through his chest again, but he didn't try to quell it. The rumble against her cheek and the soft crackle of the fire soothed her.

They stood there in silence for a while before Lily finally pulled away. Verakko's arms tightened around her, and for a moment she thought he might not let her go. But then he did.

"What did you catch?" she asked, her voice strong once more.

His eyes tracked her as she examined the meat. "A hougap."

Plastering a smile on her face, she clapped her hands together. "Hougap feast it is."

Before long, they'd built a rudimentary stone stove top over the fire and were waiting for their thin strips of meat to brown. Lily's stomach would not stop rumbling.

"It smells great," she said inanely.

Verakko nodded. He'd been watching her in a way that heated her to the core despite the chilled night air. "I've had hougap a few times before. Mostly on trips to Sauven."

"Sauven?"

"A town downriver."

He now had her full attention. "Is it close? Do you think Alex might've made it there?"

Verakko casually flipped the pieces of meat on the stone before answering. "If we are where I think we are, the river will split in two before too long. One branch leads to Sauven, deep in the forest, and the other leads to another city."

Ice slid down her spine. Two cities. Two options. *What if I choose wrong?* "I'll have to see which direction seems like the one Alex would've picked when we get there." She drew her knees to her chin and gazed at the sizzling pieces of meat again.

"Who is Davy Crockett?"

Davy Crockett? Lily blinked at Verakko's thinned lips and tight jaw. Then realization dawned on her. She hid a smirk. "King of the wild frontier. Why do you ask?"

A muscle ticked in his jaw. "His name came to your lips so readily. I was curious." The corner of his mouth lifted. "Maybe he's the one you dream about at night?"

"Excuse me?" Lily *had* been having crazy dreams lately. Did Verakko somehow know?

"You make noises in your sleep, and you put off scents. Sometimes fear, other times"—his eyes glowed brighter in the darkness—"other smells."

Her entire body heated with embarrassment. "We were having a nice night. Why do you have to say stuff like that? Do you like to make me uncomfortable?"

Verakko shrugged and fiddled with the strips of meat, now brick red. "I prefer your face flushed, not pallid."

Warm coals glowed in her belly. Was he trying to distract her from her worry?

She swallowed. "Davy Crockett is an old folk hero. His was the first name that popped into my head. That's all."

"Folk hero?"

"Yeah. A person who existed a while ago, and their life has become something of a legend. Usually super-exaggerated. Davy Crockett was a frontiersman. I think there's a story about him fighting off a bear when he was three." At Verakko's confused look, she explained, "An enormous animal very unlikely to be fought off by a grown man, let alone a three-year-old."

Verakko gave a grunt, then replaced the cooked meat with raw and held out a leaf to Lily. She took the green plate and peered down at the arrangement with a raised brow. Thin slices of wanget fruit were fanned out around a pile of guren nuts and neatly arranged strips of meat. If she focused on only her plate, she might've been able to pretend she was in a trendy restaurant in Portland.

Lily lifted a piece of meat to her lips and hesitated.

"What's the matter?" She found Verakko's eyes on her again, a twinge of annoyance lacing his voice.

"Nothing. I just haven't eaten meat for a while. I'm normally vegetarian. I mean, I love meat. I've hunted for most of my life, but when I hunt, I make sure the animal has a good death and no part of it is wasted. You can't be sure of those things in the city, so vegetarian it is. I also feel a little bad that the animal is so large. I'm worried the meat will go bad before we can eat it all," she rambled.

The muscle twitched in Verakko's jaw again, and Lily inwardly cursed. She didn't want him to think she was ungrateful.

"I killed it quickly. It felt no pain." Verakko loaded his leaf with a pile of cooked meat, a little more raw than she would've liked. "And as for the quantity, I assure you, I'll finish whatever you don't eat."

Lily eyed his large exposed biceps. He must eat a ton to keep up that physique.

Without another word, she popped the piece of bright red meat in her mouth and failed to stifle a moan. The texture was warm and buttery, and the flavor was mildly salty. *God, I missed steak.*

Her stomach gave a painful clench, and all at once, her hunger hit her. Not caring that she likely looked like a starving dog, she shoveled the meat into her mouth, chewing so quickly she grew dizzy from lack of breath.

When her stomach was full of the delicious meat, fruit, and nuts, which tasted surprisingly similar to a bitter chocolate, Lily reclined onto the soft fallen leaves and stretched. The protein was like a shock to her system, lifting her mental fog and raising her spirits.

She closed her eyes and listened to the humming of the forest. The sounds were so similar yet so different from the white noise playlist that put her to sleep every night on Earth. The chorus of buzzing and chirping from unfamiliar creatures, mixed with the soft rustling of the leaves in the wind, had been her lullaby for as long as she could remember. As an adult, it was the only remnant of her bone-deep ties to nature.

"And you were worried about having too much left over?" came Verakko's satin voice from across the fire. He was still working on his food, eating it slowly rather than inhaling it, and had a curiously satisfied look on his face.

She wondered with a passing thought how unattractive she must appear but then promptly decided not to care. There may be grease on her chin and stains on her white shirt, but she was full and relaxed for the first time in weeks. And it was all because of him.

A slimy feeling of guilt that had been wriggling around her mind all day returned. "Verakko, I need to say something."

He shot her a curious look and nodded.

"What I said before...when I said I didn't want you here... I'm sorry. I didn't mean that. I'm grateful you're here, and not just because you caught us some food. It was..." Lily's voice caught in her throat, and she swallowed before continuing. "It was really hard being alone." She held his gaze, hoping he could see her sincerity. "I've been struggling with a lot, and I didn't mean to take it out on you."

Verakko silently held her gaze for a moment. "I know. You don't need to apologize." He said with a crooked smile. "I was trying to rile you up anyway. I shouldn't have."

Relief washed over her, and she let out a chuckle, shaking her head. "Well, you succeeded. When you told me you could smell my..." Lily's face flamed as she realized what she was saying. Why would she bring up the fact that she'd gotten aroused and that he'd smelled it? *Not the time, Lily!*

Verakko's gaze on her darkened, nostrils flaring. His tongue, slightly more pointed than a human tongue, ran across his full lower lip. Lily's heart picked up speed, and she darted her gaze around the camp, looking for any way to redirect the conversation.

"Let's play a game," she blurted, hastily clearing the leaves in front of her. With a stick, she drew a rudimentary checker board.

Verakko popped some meat into his mouth and followed the progress of the stick skeptically. "What game?"

Lily rolled her eyes at his suspicious tone. "It's not like I'm asking you to play Russian roulette. It's just checkers. It's a board game I used to play with my dad when we had free time."

She collected a pile of husks she'd discarded after cracking the guren and instructed Verakko to break up a twig into twelve small pieces.

Lily explained the rules of the game to a comically serious Verakko. Then made the first move. He stared at the hand-drawn board like it was a the most complex strategy game he'd ever encountered. She bit her lip to keep from laughing. *Someone is competitive.*

"My mom hated checkers," Lily mused while Verakko continued to concentrate on the board. "She said it was the poor man's chess." He reached out to move a piece, but then froze and pulled his hand back. "It's not like we could've found chess pieces in the forest, though, right?"

Verakko glanced up at her briefly, irritation clear in his glowing eyes. "You're trying to distract me."

Lily cocked her head and pursed her lips at him. "No, I'm making small talk while I lose a year of my life waiting for you to make a move."

The corner of Verakko's mouth twitched upward, and he moved a piece. "Do you miss your parents?"

"In a way I do. But we weren't very close." They took their turns as they talked, a pleasant ease settling between them. "Despite what you've told me, I'm still holding out hope I'll be able to see them again one day."

Verakko stilled while placing a stick segment in an unwise square and leveled a somewhat confused look at her. He frowned, and his eyes glimmered with pity.

Lily chuckled. "You're so quick to assume things will never change, I see. You said a Class 4 planet is labeled Class 4 because they haven't traveled far enough into space yet. Well—" she looked down at herself pointedly, "—I'd argue that if enough human women are found on your planet, that means a good many of us have traveled into space. And even if that isn't enough, who knows…" Lily shrugged. "I mean, if me sitting on this planet playing—" she moved her piece hopping over two of Verakko's, "—and winning checkers against a blue alien I'm somehow the same species as isn't proof that anything is possible, I don't know what is. Also, if we *are* the same species, then shouldn't we technically be classified the same?"

Verakko's furrowed brows softened a tad, and a thoughtful smile curled his lips. He stared at her like he was admiring a beguiling painting, the meaning behind which he couldn't quite articulate.

Lily's face heated, and she glanced away. She moved a piece into place, forcing Verakko to jump it and leaving her goal spot open for the taking. "King me!"

Verakko muttered something under his breath and topped her bit of husk with another.

"What about your family? Do you see them much now that you live in another city?"

"I used to see my father often, but he died a few years ago, and my mother is very busy."

Lily's heart clenched at the brief wince she saw on his face. "I'm so sorry. How did he die, if you don't mind my asking?"

"He chose it, in a way. Most Clecanians take a medication known as the elixir. It extends our lives many years past what's otherwise natural, but a few people choose not to take it. He wanted to live in the way he believed the Goddess intended and let nature take its course."

Lily remained silent, not sure what to say. Although her heart ached for him, Verakko seemed more or less at peace with it.

"Queen me!" he exclaimed, grinning and revealing his even white teeth and fangs.

"It's '*king* me,'" Lily corrected, laying another small stick next to his piece.

"Not in my city." He shook his head and stared at her again, his playful gaze settling on her lips.

She focused on her next move and attempted to quell the butterflies in her belly.

"We have a figure like your Crockett," he said suddenly.

Lily glanced up and found him still watching her. "Oh yeah?"

"Daera." He nodded. "When the city was first settled, she explored the desert, taking note of the plants and animals she found. There are many tales about her, but at the end of her life, it's said she wandered so far that she found the crystal mountains at the edge of the desert. The sight was so beautiful that she knew she wanted to rest there forever. She begged the Goddess to protect her body so she could always see the mountains, then she covered herself in a shroud and laid down to sleep. When a Swadaeth finally found her, he said it looked as if a thousand lightning bolts had hit, burning the sand and encasing her in glass, perfectly preserved forever, facing the mountains."

"Wow," Lily remarked, resting her head in her hand. "Have you ever been there?"

"Like you said, she was a real person yet most of her story was embellished. I've been there, though. Many times." Verakko chewed on the last pieces of meat while they sat and took their turns before continuing. "That place is where we bury our citizens. Of course, they're not buried in glass like Daera, but once a year during the storm season, we visit the graves of all those who've died and use metal rods to attract lightning. It's said that if the soul of the person has moved on, lightning will hit and create a glass grave marker. If not, we try again the following year. My father's grave was struck last year."

"He's moved on?"

Verakko smiled and shrugged. "If you believe the legend." His gaze turned serious, and he pointed down to the board. "I think you're letting me win, and I won't have it."

Lily's face broke out into a grin. "I assure you, I'm only letting you think you're going to win." She moved her piece. "And when I win," she said, watching him fall into her trap, "I have a question for you."

"Another question?" He sighed sarcastically.

Lily used her king to jump Verakko's remaining pieces and smothered a cocky grin while he scowled. "Yes. Another question."

Verakko crossed his arms over his chest and leaned back against a tree. He popped a few nuts in his mouth and leveled his annoyed gaze at her, waving impatiently to indicate she should ask her question.

"What is *sway*?"

Verakko's eyes darted, and his jaw began to work slower than it had before.

Is he trying to think of a lie?

"It's what I do when you say I'm messing with your head," he said finally, after swallowing.

Lily rolled her eyes. "Yeah, I figured as much, but how does it work? Mind control is just so…alien."

"It's not mind control. It's difficult to explain, but I can't make you think anything I want. I can only push you to think of something you already have."

"That doesn't make any sense."

Verakko let out a sound of exasperation and peered up at the sky in thought. After a moment, he said, "I can't, for example, *sway* you to take off all your clothes right now because that's likely not a thought that crossed your mind. If I tried to *sway* you to do that, it would ring untrue, and you'd discard it. But if I *swayed* you to go to sleep, it might work, because you're tired and may have already thought about going to sleep."

Lily wondered if there wasn't a small part of her that wanted to take off all her clothes. Verakko was incredibly sexy. She couldn't deny it. And although he was a bit temperamental and irritating beyond compare, he'd held her when she'd cried and tried his best to take care of her. He'd made her a delicious meal, done all the heavy lifting, built the fire and, most importantly, she realized, he hadn't complained about what they were doing. He hadn't tried to convince her to go back or to give up on Alex. He'd supported her, as if knowing this was something she needed to do.

Lily recalled the feeling she'd had when she'd allowed his *sway* in earlier that day, and warmth dripped down her scalp, making her shiver and grow hot at the same time. "Why don't you try now?" She had to stop herself from making her voice a purr.

He stared at her, and the bright peridot of his eyes darkened a touch. The veins in his corded forearms bulged. "Try what?"

For a moment she considered asking him to try to get her clothes off, but then her senses returned to her. "To *sway* me. I'm curious about it. I want to know how it feels so I know how to shake it off." Not a complete lie.

"It doesn't work on everyone. The calmer you are, the harder it is. It's easiest when a person is emotional or distressed. When their mind is distracted. The more intelligent a person is, the harder it is to *sway* them as well."

"I bet you could do it."

"You, my little anomaly, have been able to brush off my *sway* every time I've attempted it." Verakko snorted. "I think it may have something to do with the fact that you're human." He shot her a sidelong glance. "Or possibly your stubbornness."

Lily chose to ignore his jab. "You were able to *sway* me earlier today, though."

"I'm pretty sure you let me, and you were very upset at the time." Verakko held her gaze, sincerity shining in his eyes. "I meant what I said before. Sometimes I can't help it. It just comes out."

Lily considered that. "I believe you," she said slowly.

Verakko's tense shoulders relaxed a fraction.

"But I still want to try it." Lily shifted onto her knees and inched through the checkerboard before settling in front of him. "Give it your best shot."

9

∞

Verakko had to keep his mouth from hanging open. The object of his every waking thought for the past two days was kneeling in front of him, asking him to *sway* her. Goddess, did he want to take advantage of the situation.

"What do you want me to do?" His voice sounded shaky to his ears. It didn't surprise him. He felt shaky. And weak. He didn't trust himself with this task but wasn't strong enough to deny her.

Lily shrugged, eyes bright and trusting. So trusting. "Uh, just say anything, and I'll see if I can shake it off."

Verakko swallowed. *Anything?* He internally cuffed himself. *She'll be able ignore whatever the* sway *is anyway.* "Okay." Verakko sat up straighter. "It's quite chilly out here tonight. You feel cold," he lightly *swayed*.

Lily frowned and slapped him playfully on the knee. "Come on, that wasn't even a real try!"

Verakko grunted and scooted closer, mimicking her stance and sitting back on his ankles. "Fine, I'll give it my best shot, but I don't want to hear any complaining about it tomorrow. You asked for this. Agreed?"

A spark of fear and something that looked incredibly similar to excitement flashed in her eyes. Would he ever understand this female? "Deal." She reached her hand toward him and held it in place as though expecting something. After a moment, she dropped it. "Never mind. Okay, go. Are you going to try to make me feel cold again? I didn't even feel a little cold."

Verakko stiffened at the challenge in her voice and repressed a grin. "Oh, I'll make you cold. Just wait." He rolled his shoulders and gave his neck a satisfying crack, then focused on Lily's warm brown eyes.

Her lush lips pulled into a smile. "Bring it on."

Verakko felt himself growing hard, his instincts screaming to make her feel things other than just cold.

He rocked slowly from side to side, not much at first, just enough to make her eyes flick back and forth. He didn't always have the time for it, but the added motion often boosted the effect of his *sway*. "Lily." He grinned when her pupils reacted. She wasn't immune to his gift after all. "It's been warm all day. The night is oddly cold." Her eyelids drooped, and her smile faltered. He imagined all the things he wanted to do to her, letting his scent grow stronger to boost the effect of the *sway*. "The fire isn't nearly warm enough tonight. The wind is too chilled." He leaned in closer and wanted to hiss in triumph when her nostrils flared. Her smile relaxed, and she crossed her arms around her waist.

"It's cold tonight," she whispered, her eyes trailing his small movements side to side.

Verakko let out a low chuckle. He'd done it. "Yes, it is. Your whole body feels cold."

On cue, she shivered. Verakko's gaze traveled down her body, and his face fell. Shelved on top of her crossed arms were her breasts, her puckered nipples visible beneath her thin top.

"My whole body is cold," she repeated, shivering again.

His hands itched to touch her. He needed to stop this. He was engaged, and she was under his full *sway*. He wanted her, Goddess knew, but not like this.

"Verakko," she said softly while scooting toward him.

His muscles shot tight, blood rushing to his shaft. Now that he thought back, he couldn't recall her ever having said his name aloud before. The sound of it uttered on her lips did things to him. Things he needed to ignore.

Before he could find his voice or dash away, she huddled against his chest. He kept his arms locked at his sides and gazed up in bewilderment at the sky. *Why did I do this?*

"Lily, wake up." The words escaped him, but he failed to inject them with *sway*, the uncaring baser side of him roaring to let this scene play out.

She rose to her knees and wrapped her arms around his neck, pressing her body into his.

"You're warm now," he choked out. "Mivassi—"

Her head raised, her brown eyes bore into his, pleading. "Verakko, please, I'm cold."

All of his resistance shattered. In an instant, he had his arms wrapped around her, pulling her more firmly against his body. He forced *sway* into his voice. "You're warm now. Lily."

She sighed in relief, and her body melted against his. He buried his head in the crook of her neck and inhaled deeply before begrudgingly muttering, "Wake up."

She stiffened in his grip, but he held on for a moment longer, memorizing the feel of her body against his. He lifted his head, keeping his arms wrapped around her waist, and peered into what would surely be angry eyes. What he saw instead made his heart pick up speed.

Lily smiled up at him. "Wow, that was crazy. I felt like I could've shaken it off if I wanted to, but it made me a little nauseated to try."

She wasn't mad? He remained in place with bated breath, waiting for the realization that she was being held to sink in. Her hands, still resting on his shoulders, twitched, then her palms slid down his arms.

"You're really warm, you know." Lily leaned into his touch a little more, and her eyes strayed to his mouth. And then he smelled it, her arousal.

Lust flared, making his already rigid shaft swollen. She wanted him. Lily wasn't mad about him touching her or using his *sway*. If her heated looks at his mouth were any indication, she wanted to kiss him.

Verakko needed to play this right. He needed time to think. If he had a taste of her, he'd want more, and he couldn't have more. He was under contract, for Goddess's sake. And Lily didn't know about it.

Moving his hands to grasp her hips, he pushed her away. Every inch away she moved was like a rib cracking inside. There was something more with Lily. If he hadn't been sure of it before, he was now. She was his, recognition or not, marks or not, and he had to figure out a way to keep her.

Her pretty cheeks tinged with pink, and confusion creased the corners of her eyes.

"Told you I could do it," Verakko said, feigning a triumphant smugness.

The hurt that shone in her eyes felt like a punch to the gut and stung more than the flashes of disappointment and anger that followed.

She didn't rail at him or pepper him with questions about the *sway*. In a tight voice, she said, "Yep. You win," and moved back to her side of the fire.

Verakko sat back, ensuring his bent knee concealed his unrelenting erection. "Would you like to sleep in my shirt? It'll be cold tonight, and I don't need it."

"No, I'll be fine. Thank you, though." She turned her back to him and stretched out on her side near the fire. "Get some sleep tonight, okay? Goodnight."

***

I'm such an idiot. Lily continued to chant this to herself long into the night until she finally drifted off to sleep. As soon as her lids creaked open the following morning, the chant resurged. She'd never been so blatantly rejected by a man before, and it stung. To make the situation a hundred times more uncomfortable, she now had to spend all of her time with Verakko. Unlike on Earth, she didn't even have the option of retreating to her house to lick her wounds in private.

She lay curled on her side with her back to lukewarm remnants of their fire and listened to the sound of Verakko moving about, cleaning and gathering their supplies. *How awkward is this gonna be?*

Closing her eyes, she inhaled deeply and sat up. The sounds of movement behind her paused, then resumed. Steeling her features, she turned. "Good morning."

"Good morning."

Lily chanced the briefest of glances at Verakko and wanted to die of mortification. The look on his face told her he was worried about the mood she'd be in. She mumbled a sorry excuse about using the bathroom and scurried into the forest, face flaming.

While heading away from their camp, her nerves started to sing, and she could feel annoyance at random, innocuous things creeping in. Everything about this morning was beginning to aggravate, from the cheerful chirping of birds to the glistening early morning mist hovering around the forest floor. A rock underfoot made her stumble, and she glared at her own feet. It was the kind of bad mood that would permeate her day and affect those around her, innocent or not. It'd be better if she didn't hang too close to Verakko during their hike. A gust of wind tousling his hair to perfection might be enough to make her snap at him, and he didn't deserve her ire.

Lily finished her morning ablutions and headed back to camp, intent on acting like an adult while also allowing herself to be in a sour mood.

When she entered the cleared area, she forced herself to look at Verakko. He was standing, looking as gorgeous as always, and extending a leaf to her. A mound of the charcoal toothpaste she'd been creating every morning sat in a small pile on the leaf. The thoughtfulness of the gesture made her want to petulantly slap the leaf out of his hand, but instead she thanked him as politely as she could and took it, along with the canteen.

Lily washed her hands, then used her finger to mix the powder into a paste and scrubbed it onto her teeth, ignoring the flare of annoyance that surfaced when she recalled why she had to use her finger and not her toothbrush.

Verakko continued to stare at her with curiosity. He didn't even have the decency to pretend like everything was normal. The air seemed to be too thick, weighed down with awkward unsaid thoughts and embarrassment.

Time to put on your big-girl panties. Lily rinsed out her mouth and forced her gaze to remain on Verakko's. "Why don't we say what's on our minds, okay?"

Verakko lifted a dark brow. "I'm sorry about—"

Lily cut him off with an upheld hand and an awkward smile. "No, don't apologize. You did nothing wrong. I was comfortable and full for the first time in weeks, and we were having a nice time, and I misread the situation. That's all." She crossed her arms around her waist, then uncrossed them. Why was she so embarrassed about this? "I made a move, you weren't interested. It's done." Her face must be turning crimson at this point. "I hope you don't take offense, but I'm going to want to walk alone today. I need to stew by myself."

Verakko stood in silence, a tendon in his jaw working furiously. It seemed like he wanted to say something but couldn't decide if he should.

Please say I was wrong. Say you pushed me away for some other reason.

He remained quiet. Lily began walking toward the river, but a firm hand on her arm stopped her. "Lily, I..." He let out a low breath. "Last night..."

Her breath seemed trapped in her throat. *What?*

Verakko's shoulders slumped, and in a resigned tone, he said, "You didn't misread anything. I just...can't."

"You can't?" Lily's embarrassment ebbed, replaced with curiosity. He hadn't said he didn't want to or that he wouldn't; he'd said *can't.*

He took a step back and ran his tongue over a fang, gaze darting. "You aren't an option for me. You remember how relationships work with my people? How marriages work?"

Of course! Lily felt like an idiot for not thinking of it sooner. His culture was so different. Although he wasn't married now, that didn't mean he could start anything with her. He'd told her his mother had to arrange a contract for marriage. Did his people not engage in casual relationships? No dating?

"Your mom probably has other ladies in mind, huh?"

Verakko's lips thinned, and he shrugged in agreement.

"I don't want to get married or anything." She thought this assurance would help to ease his mind, but he only seemed more uneasy. "I just meant, once we find Alex and all...this could be casual. What happens out here doesn't have to mean anything in the real world."

Why was she saying this? Was she so infatuated with Verakko that she felt she could have a meaningless relationship with him? Not likely.

A small, sad smile curled the corner of his mouth. He lifted his hand as if to reach out to her, then curled his fingers into a fist and dropped it back to his side. "It would mean something to me."

Lily's heart thumped in her chest, and heat spread in her belly. She tried to work through the little he'd told her and came to a rotten conclusion. His mother would arrange his marriage. Verakko had said she was powerful. She'd pick a woman she respected and who she believed was worthy of her son. Why in the universe would she pick Lily? An alien who didn't own a clean pair of clothes. Was she even eligible for a contract as a human?

"I see," she whispered. Lily absently smoothed her stained, thin shirt. She wanted to argue, to explain how awful

153

it was that he couldn't choose who he wanted to be with, but if she'd learned anything from her travels with her parents, it was that a person's culture and traditions should be respected, even if she didn't agree with them.

She burned to ask more questions, but what was the point? She wasn't interested in marriage anyway, and if that was all Verakko was looking for, they'd be doomed from the start.

This was probably for the best. Her life had become difficult enough as it was. Throwing a complicated forbidden love into the mix seemed like a bad idea.

Moving on, she told herself dully, an ache already seeping into her heart. It was dumb—she had only just met Verakko—but something about him, about them, made her think they could've had something spectacular. Knowing nothing could ever happen made her feel like she'd lost someone she'd never had in the first place.

She looked to Verakko and saw a pained expression that must have mirrored her own.

Her heart pinched. *This is ridiculous! Two days. I've known him for two days! Get a hold of yourself.*

"Ready to go?" she asked in a tone riddled with phony alacrity.

He nodded, then cleared his throat. "We need to travel through the woods today."

"No, we can't! Why?" she blurted. Guilt swamped her when she realized she was spending all of her mental energy grieving the death of a nonexistent relationship with a man she'd done nothing but argue with and not on finding Alex.

"The Strigi who dropped me…I managed to incapacitate him, but he could be recovered by now. If so, we need to stay undercover."

"We can't do that, Verakko." Lily shook her head firmly. "I understand the risks, but we can't see the river from here. I refuse to stop looking."

"I refuse to allow you to be in danger." Verakko crossed his arms over his chest and scowled.

Lily almost smiled at the familiar stance, a sense of normalcy returning to their relationship. She mirrored his stance. "I'm going to follow that river until I either find my friend or find a city. You can't stop me."

He raised a brow. "I *could* stop you."

Lily narrowed her eyes. "I wouldn't recommend trying."

Verakko stared at her silently for a moment, tension radiating from every muscle.

He had every advantage. They both knew it. She might be able to do some damage to him if he tried to carry her off, but when push came to shove, she would tire long before he did, to say nothing of his *sway*. There was no chance of her winning a physical fight, so she played the only card she had left, hoping the lingering longing she'd seen in his eyes had been authentic.

"I'd never forgive you."

10

∞

"Stay near the trees! We talked about this," Verakko barked.

Lily frowned and sidled back toward the tree line. This female was going to send him to an early grave. He'd decided to let them hike along the river again today. Well, *decided* may be the wrong word. More like he'd surrendered at the mere idea she may never speak to him again.

Luckily, he'd convinced her to stay under reasonable cover at the edge of the forest while he walked in the open, searching for signs of Alex. For the last few hours, his attention had been so divided and his emotions in such upheaval, a Swadaeth child might've managed to *sway* him without trouble.

Search for Alex, watch out for the Strigi, make sure Lily stays safe, argue with Lily when she doesn't stay safe, think about Lily, work through how to be with Lily, remember to search for Alex. And on and on the day went.

He should've kept his mouth shut this morning, should've allowed her to believe he was uninterested in her. But he couldn't stand the idea. Instead, he'd omitted information and told a partial truth, surmountable to a full lie.

There'd been so many opportunities to push her away. He could've told her he was already under contract. That would've shut down all questions as to whether they could be together. Or he could've told her he was uninterested. Or that he wanted to be with her after his marriage to Ziritha was over, and would she kindly wait for him for an unknown period of time? If he understood Lily as well as he thought he did, she would've halted any budding relationship that may have formed then and there. But he just couldn't bring himself to tell her the truth. It would have meant permanently closing the door on the possibility of being with her, and, ashamedly, he was too selfish to do that. Not yet. Not before he'd thought through every possibility.

Crouching, he scooped up a bright blue item half buried in the sand of the river bed.

Lily rushed toward him.

Scanning the sky, he yelled, "It's nothing but a rock. Go back."

Shoulders slumped in defeat, she returned to the safety of the tree line. Verakko tossed the rock into the river and continued along the shore. Lily was loyal, annoyingly so. How might that translate into a relationship? From what he knew already, humans tended to prefer long-term monogamous relationships, but he had to take that knowledge with a grain of salt. For one thing, Jade and Alice, the two humans he knew who had relationships like that, were mated. For another, it was only two humans. He couldn't assume they all thought the same. Lily herself had told him she didn't want to get married. Where did that leave him? Marriage was all he had to offer, and he couldn't even offer that at the moment.

His mind kept revolving around the same problem, always leading back to the same disheartening conclusion. He couldn't have her. At least not for a long while.

He'd signed a marriage contract. If he backed out, he'd be punished. Sent away to work on a Clecanian space barge, transporting goods to and fro. The length of his off-world assignment would be dictated by the spurned female and local authorities.

How severe would Ziritha be? She was a reasonable female, but she was also in the public eye, and it'd color Mithrandirian's perception of her if she were slighted by a male and then went easy on him during sentencing. He'd likely be sent away for years.

Aside from his off-world service, the real issue arose from city laws surrounding a breached marriage contract. If he broke his agreement without cause, he would never be eligible for marriage again. The Tremantian Queen had been kind to the humans, allowing them to not participate in the marriage ceremony unless they chose to, but he wasn't so sure his people would feel the same. And he was only eligible for marriage with a citizen of his own city. If he led Lily to anywhere but Mithrandir, she would be out of his reach entirely.

But was taking her to his home too risky? Lily didn't want to get married, yet they had the right to force her to participate. The question was, would they? And if they did, would he be able to handle watching her with another male? The throb of his fangs said no.

Maybe he could convince his city to give her enough time to acclimate to the planet before negotiating a marriage. That way, he'd be done with his marriage by the time she chose someone, and she could choose him.

He peered over to her. Her gaze was trained on the river and surrounding land, and her eyes were squinted so tightly he could barely make out any white or iris at all. It wouldn't surprise him to learn she'd expect her unwavering loyalty to be returned in a relationship. He ground his jaw and scanned the clear blue sky again. *She won't wait.*

There was one other possibility, but it was out of his control. If he recognized her as his mate, everything else would work out. Even a change of his eyes indicating a recognition of a *potential* mate was enough to be released from a marriage contract with no consequences. He sighed, trying to stifle the hope that slithered into his chest. To have a mate? To never have to enter into temporary marriages? It'd been a fantasy out of reach to Clecanians for centuries before the humans had appeared and turned their world upside down.

He glanced toward her again, and his heart constricted, as it had begun to do whenever he looked at her. He needed to learn more about her life and human courting in general, then go from there.

Lily's eyes widened a moment before she sprinted away from the tree line. Verakko's gaze shot to the sky and he bolted after her. "Lily, that's it! We are traveling in the forest. That was my last warn—"

She halted at the edge of the river and removed her shoes. She began to lift the corner of her top over her head, but he reached her just in time, halting her movements. Hints of her flesh were enough. Seeing her clothed only in her thin undergarments in the daylight might be his undoing.

"Let go," she said, struggling in his grip. Her eyes never strayed from a spot across the river. Verakko followed her gaze, and to his utter shock saw what looked unmistakably like a small, torn piece of fabric, waving in the wind like a flag.

He *swayed* without thinking. "Let me go across." The current seemed to be calmer here, as the land had leveled out, but he didn't want to take any chances.

She blinked up at him, unaffected, but nodded. "Hurry."

Undressing fully, he held out his clothes to Lily and smirked at her turned head and crossed arms. He pulled at her hands, drawing her attention, and dropped the clothing into her arms. Her unblinking stare stayed glued to his face. "I don't mind you looking." He grinned.

She bit her lip to keep from smiling. "Just hurry, please."

He let out a noncommittal grunt, then waded into the water. When he reached the other side, he examined the small flag propped into the crevice of a tree, amazed.

"What is it?" Lily called from across the river; the hope in her voice was like a living thing.

He hadn't done anything at all to cause it, but the fact that he'd be the one to deliver such good news to her made him happier than he could remember. "Someone made it, and there's writing."

Lily sank to her knees, tears of relief springing from her eyes. Her smile was wider than he'd ever seen it, and she let out a sob, then another. He grabbed the flag and the flat log with the foreign, carved writing, also wedged into the tree, and waded back over to her.

He couldn't seem to cut through the chest-high water fast enough. When he finally reached the shore, he plopped down next to her, uncaring about his current state of dress, and pulled her into his arms. She dropped his clothes onto his lap, then reached over to the log and read the jagged, carved symbols silently.

"What does it say?"

"It says, 'Alive. Hit my head. This sucks. Alex.'" She grinned at the writing, her eyes scanning and rescanning the text.

She beamed at him and wiped her tears away, then wrapped her arms around his neck. Goddess, this felt right. His purr started in his chest again. And as he had the night before, he let it rumble through him. Lily didn't seem to mind it the way he feared she would.

Pulling away, she said, "We should cross to the other side, right? Walk along the forest on that side."

In an instant, he recalled the Strigi threat. Shooting tense, he nodded. "Hold my clothes. I'll carry you across on my shoulders."

She sprung to her feet, snatching his clothes as she went. "Ready."

Verakko was slower to move, surprised by the lack of argument she gave concerning being carried. She scooped the woven bag from the ground and waited. He knelt before her so she could perch on his shoulders, but she paused.

"Are you sure? It feels so silly for you to carry me when I'm perfectly capable of swimming."

He craned his neck to grin at her. "By all means, take off all your clothes and swim with me, then."

She stifled a smirk and draped her legs over his shoulders without another word. He rose, clenching every muscle, not because carrying her was difficult but to prevent himself from thinking too hard about her supple thighs cushioning his ears. He crossed the river, moving a little slower than needed. When the shadow of a large bird passed over the sky, he reluctantly picked up his pace. Rather than letting her go on the shore, he strode to the edge of the forest, stealing any extra moments he could.

When he knelt again and she got back on her feet, she held out his clothes and boots.

"Thanks." She lifted to her toes and pressed a kiss to his cheek.

His only thoughts were of the soft feel of her lips against his skin. Unable to stop himself, he clutched her neck gently, holding her in place. Lily stilled.

What now? Verakko was lost, his instinct to keep her close warring with the knowledge that he couldn't be her male right now. Not in the way she deserved. *Let her go, you pishot.*

It was a battle, but gradually he removed his hand, letting it fall at his side. She lowered until she was standing on the ground again and peered up at him through dark lashes. Her lips twisted into a knowing smile. Resting her hands on his shoulders, she stretched toward his other cheek and planted a soft, lingering kiss there.

Verakko's lids slid closed and his rattling purr, so foreign to his ears, vibrated through him. He felt the whisper of a smile against her lips. Then, she moved away again, leaving him cold.

"We should keep going," she said softly.

They gazed at each other for a moment, understanding passing between them. She began walking downriver once again, and Verakko quickly dressed.

I'll find a way for us, mivassi. I promise.

***

Lily couldn't wipe the smile from her face. It felt like a fifty-pound weight had been lifted from her shoulders. Alex had survived, and they were on their way to find her. Suddenly, all of her problems seemed surmountable.

She took in the sight of Verakko walking along the river, as alert and thoughtful as he'd been all morning. She'd had a while to think through their predicament on the long walk and had decided two things. One, she wanted to get to know the real Verakko. Initially, he'd held himself with an air of irritating superiority, but Lily could see it was just a superficial layer. Underneath it all, he was caring and attentive and honorable.

He also had a carefree, flirtatious side that had reared its head a few times now. Like her, he seemed to reveal more of himself the more comfortable he became with a person. This led to thought two—a far more involved and difficult thought, to say the least. Despite his claims that morning, Lily wanted to work things out with Verakko. If she needed to become an established member of his society to qualify for consideration by his mother, then she'd do just that.

Back on Earth, when she'd wanted to emancipate herself from her parents, she'd done it. When she'd wanted to get a diploma without ever having stepped foot in a classroom, she'd done it. Lily always accomplished her goals, no matter how seemingly impossible they appeared. And now on this new planet, she had new goals. Help Alex. Make a life. And give a whirlwind, out-of-the-blue relationship with a literal alien a try.

Finding that note from Alex had restored her confidence, her drive, and a small portion of her happiness. Verakko's fleeting moment of vulnerability earlier proved to Lily that he was just like any other creature. He wanted love and comfort, and even if she could only give it to him for a short while, she would.

There was no question about what her primary concern continued to be. Alex, of course. She still wanted to make sure they were both safe. But, in the meantime, she'd learn as much as she could.

Back on Earth, there hadn't been many things she'd missed about the wilderness. At night, she'd missed the sounds. When the litter and smog from the city had been too much for her, she'd missed the tranquil scenery. But most of all, what she'd missed was the honesty. Something about being alone with another human in nature cuts through all of the facades people wear. There was never enough energy left to be disingenuous.

Lily ducked under a low branch and marveled at the scenery anew. They'd been heading steadily downhill for the past few days until today, where the elevation had leveled out. The forest was more crowded here. Bushes and saplings battled for resources, making it almost impossible to walk through the brush itself.

The ever-evolving scenery made sense to her, though. What didn't make sense was the temperature. Higher altitudes always equaled colder temperatures, so why was it becoming chillier the farther downriver they traveled? It had to be a cold snap of some kind.

A small gust of wind blew, punctuating her thoughts, and she shivered. How much farther were they from the fork Verakko had mentioned?

"Look down there on the right!" he called, pointing into the distance.

Lily squinted and saw what looked to be another make-shift flag on the opposite side of the river. Had she decided the other side was better for some reason?

Come on, Alex. Give a girl a break. She suppressed a guilty grin. *Although, being carried by a naked Verakko again might not be so bad.* She snickered to herself like a schoolgirl, recalling her stealthy glances down to Verakko's glorious chest as he'd carried her.

She surveyed the scenery in front of her and waved Verakko over. "I vote we cross down there." She pointed to a stretch of river nearer to where Alex's leaf flag fluttered. "I'm also going to climb that tree and get a lay of the land. See if I spot any more flags or maybe the fork in the river." Lily gestured to a towering olive-green tree a few yards away.

Verakko eyed the tree in question, and she could've sworn his face became a lighter shade of teal. "That isn't necessary. I'm sure the fork isn't too much farther."

"It'll only take a few minutes and will give me peace of mind. I mean, what if she changed her mind again, and we're planning to cross for nothing?" Lily canted her head and studied him. "Are you worried about me climbing the tree? It looks sturdy."

His gaze shifted away, and he strode forward. "I just don't think we should be taking any unnecessary risks. You could fall."

Lily thought for a moment before following him. "Are...are you afraid of heights?"

The instant bunching of his shoulders told her she must be right. To be fair, he had fallen out of the sky only a few days ago. That would leave anyone with a lingering concern about being high up.

"I'm not *afraid* of heights," he hissed. "I just prefer to stay on the ground."

She reached out and gripped his hand; the tight corners of his eyes relaxed, and his vivid green irises locked on the connection. "It's nothing to be ashamed of. I don't do well in small spaces myself."

In a softer tone, he explained, "The height isn't the issue. I'm wary of the pain that follows a fall from a great height."

Something in Lily told her he was speaking from past experience, and not only from the tumble he'd recently taken. His thumb trailed over the back of her hand before he released it and continued forward.

"It sounds like you know what you're talking about," she urged, trying to sound casual.

"I do," he said simply.

Lily rolled her eyes, trailing behind him. *Subtlety isn't working.* "Will you tell me about it? I promise I won't climb the tree if you do."

He gave her a perplexed look over his shoulder. "Why do you care?"

She shrugged. "Can't I want to know more about you? We've been walking for days, and I don't know anything about your personal life."

He ran the tip of his tongue over a fang in thought. "Alright. When I was a boy, I had a nasty fall."

When he didn't continue, Lily huffed out an annoyed, "And?"

"Are you sure you want to hear this?" He peered down at her curiously and shifted the woven bag on his shoulder. "It isn't pleasant."

"As long as you're okay talking about it, I want to hear it."

The corner of his mouth twitched as though he'd almost smiled. "When I was young, I loved to build things. Tinker with electronics. My father didn't like me using my inventions in the house, so I'd go out to the empty towers in the new city."

Lily listened intently and watched as Verakko spoke while scanning the shore and sky.

"They'd begun building the towers as a way to bring increased sustainability and housing to the people of my city, but Swadaeth aren't very welcoming of change." He snorted as if that was an understatement. "Most of the citizens have now moved into the housing, but early on, a lot of the buildings were deserted. The perfect place for me to be alone. I would tell my father I was going to the desert, but really I'd override the security systems and work in one of the towers.

"One day I was testing out a new flying gadget. It had a hidden compartment on the underside with a programmable fingerprint scan."

Lily smiled, picturing a small Verakko quiet and stoic among a pile of springs and cogs. "What were you trying to hide?"

A wide grin transformed his features. Lily attempted to regulate the sigh building in her at the sight.

"Sweets from the kitchen."

Lily laughed out loud. "You built a flying machine from scratch when you were a kid to sneak candy?"

"I was told I couldn't have them." He shrugged. "And I love sweets."

Lily shook her head. *The priorities of a kid are the same every-where.*

The shore along the river had narrowed and risen until the space between the forest and water was barely wide enough for one person. Verakko motioned her ahead, and she shuffled forward, grabbing branches and vines along the way to keep herself steady. The small, slick patch of grassy earth rose a few feet above the water. It wasn't particularly dangerous, but she'd already fallen into a river once this month, and that had been enough.

Warmth spread through her belly at the sight of Verakko's large hand, outstretched and ready to snatch her back if she slipped.

"I had intended to transport a piece of candy from the top floor to the ground on its first test flight, but something went wrong and it stopped responding a few floors up," he continued from behind her. "When I found it, it was hovering just outside a window on the third story. I reached for it and slipped."

Lily veered her upper body around. "You fell from three stories up?"

Verakko's hand was on her waist in an instant, holding her in place. When he was sure she wasn't in danger of falling, he released her and grimaced. "I broke fifteen bones, most of them in my legs. The worst part was no one knew where I'd gone, and I couldn't move. It took them hours to find me."

"That's horrible!"

"Now whenever I have to deal with heights, I always remember that pain." Verakko let out a low chuckle, relieving some of Lily's sympathetic distress. "My father said it ended up being a blessing in disguise because I never snuck off to those buildings again."

The path widened once more, and a bend came into view around the corner. "Too bad you never got to sneak those sweets though," she teased, knocking her elbow against his.

He flashed her a smile that displayed even, white teeth and a set of oddly alluring fangs. "I'll have you know the Super Bandit version two was my preferred candy-smuggling device during my formative years. That is, until my father caught on and cleansed the house of treats."

In an instant, Verakko's body became rigid and his pointed ears twitched. His hand shot out, wrapping firmly around her bicep and wrenching her against him a moment before a shrill, piercing whine like nails on a chalkboard echoed behind her. The ground began to vibrate as if something were running toward them—something large.

Without a word, Verakko lifted her into his arms and leapt. Her breath caught on a scream as they became weightless. They slammed into icy water, knocking the air from her lungs. Once they surfaced, Verakko loosened his hold but didn't let go.

She shoved the tangle of hair from her face and sputtered, "What was that?"

Verakko's eyes were still trained on the shore they'd just come from. Rather than let her go, he slowly maneuvered her until she faced the shore as well, then he pulled her tight against his chest and paddled backward toward the opposite shoreline.

Lily's heart stopped. A creature…no, a predator prowled on the far bank in the exact area they'd been standing. Black shimmering plates lined a thick, four-legged body, as tall as a horse. Its massive head and squashed face were wide and displayed a gaping, perfectly round mouth filled with rows upon rows of needle-like teeth. Around its neck, a glowing frill of yellow flesh flared in a display of aggression. Three large black eyes curved over its cavernous mouth.

The muscles in Lily's legs tensed to sprint or kick or swim. Her grip on Verakko's forearms, locked around her waist, was so tight that her knuckles were white.

"We must be closer to Sauven than I thought. It's a sefa," Verakko rumbled into her ear. "It won't cross the water."

The creature widened its mouth even more and let out another ear-splitting shriek, making every one of Lily's hairs stand on end. The sudden feeling of ground under her feet made her jump. Verakko released her and clapped his hands over her ears.

She couldn't tear her eyes away from the screeching creature. Despite Verakko's solid hands, the noise thrummed through her, making her insides roil. The noise emanated from its yawning black maw. Was it shooting some kind of pulsing sound wave at them?

Verakko let out a thunderous sound, overpowering the high pitch of the sefa. The volume and depth of the throaty rattling was almost as terrifying as the sefa's shriek. She'd never heard anything quite like it before. The closest sound she could think of was the unsettling bellow territorial alligators made, except this was much louder and harsher. Although she felt safe with Verakko, the deafening percussion made her want to cower.

The sefa seemed to feel the same. Flaps of skin surrounding its face, which she'd taken for deep wrinkles, narrowed over its wide mouth and teeth, the opening shrinking until it looked like a smooth charcoal surface. The sefa's glowing yellow collar of skin folded and flattened against its neck and back. Two of its shining obsidian eyes blinked at them, while the third stayed trained in their direction.

Verakko let out another terrifying roar. The sefa crouched low and scuttled into the dense forest.

Heat pooled in her core. It was a completely inappropriate and unwelcomed reaction, but she couldn't help it. That creature had obviously judged Verakko to be the apex predator, and something about having him at her back, protectively covering her ears while scaring a literal monster into retreating did things to her she couldn't suppress.

She felt him still behind her, and the scent of cedar wafted through the air. Lily faced him. The muscles in his arms and shoulders were bunched, and a tendon ticked in his jaw again. His glowing gaze, now a darker shade of emerald, hungrily slid over her body. Her sopping clothing clung to her figure, doing nothing to preserve any remaining modesty she may have had. Lily shivered.

His rapt gaze lingered on her neck before returning to her eyes, the heated air between them crackling in the silence.

"You're cold." His tone was low and firm, almost as if he were convincing them both of the fact, even as they understood she'd shivered for an entirely different reason.

Lily swallowed. Verakko's gaze snapped back to her neck, and a quiet, softer version of his roar rattled through him.

"We should make camp early so we can get your clothes dry before night."

They walked without speaking, the silence between them dominating her senses. When they reached the small flag, she found another carved message left by Alex.

"'This side looked easier,'" she read. Her brows knit. "Do you think one of those things, the sefa, might've gotten her?"

Verakko shook his head. "Not if she was over here." The second lid slid over his eyes, and he searched the skies while motioning her to continue forward. "They live deep in the Sauven Forest and hate water. They'd never cross the river. I'm surprised we saw one this far out in the open, actually. It must've been struggling to find food."

"So, we're safe over here?"

He glanced at her out of the corner of his eye. "From them, at least."

11

∽

"Do you enjoy sweets as well?" Verakko turned around and slid his eyes shut in mortification.

An hour thinking of the best thing to ask to learn about her life, and that's what comes out of your mouth? He piled the firewood he'd gathered into a corner and faced her again.

Lily gave him a curious half smile but answered, "Yeah. I have a huge sweet tooth."

"Sweet tooth," Verakko repeated, rolling the odd phrase over in his mind and finding he liked it.

She scattered piles of large leaves around the dirt. Verakko's breathing deepened, and he became all too aware of the rough, wet fabric against his shaft. They both knew what was coming next. They'd need to remove their clothes in order to dry them, and the air would be too cold for her unclothed. She was making a bed. A bed wide enough to make it obvious it was for them both.

The more time he spent with Lily, the clearer to him it was how difficult it would be to be parted from her when they finally reached a city. It'd taken more strength than he knew he had to let her go after the sefa attack. Even thinking about how close she'd come to being hurt made a cold sweat break out over his skin.

He'd thought stopping anything physical from happening between them would keep him from becoming too attached to Lily, but he found that just being around her was enough to be drawn in—in a way he never had before. When she cried, he felt like a spike was being jabbed in his lungs. When she was happy, he had to actively try to keep himself from grinning.

Lily's eyes were unfocused, and a smile played at her lips. "I was never allowed to have any sweets either." She rolled her eyes. "Sugar, I mean. If I could find something sweet in the forest, I could have it." She laid a few large, smooth leaves over the top of her cushioning base piles. "Whenever my aunt Cindy joined one of our trips, though, she would sneak me candy. I still remember the first time I ever tried a peanut butter cup." Lily smiled over to him. "I think that's the day I decided I wanted to emancipate myself. That small piece of candy made me wonder what other things I was missing out on." Her eyes widened in exasperation. "A lot, as it turned out."

He should've been working, building the fire or retrieving water, but he kept still. Was there anything he enjoyed more than just being with her? Listening to her talk or watching her move around?

"Emancipate yourself?" The word usage was unfamiliar to him.

Now done with the bed, she reached for the bow drill. He snatched it away before she could grab it. She pursed her lips at him. "You've done it for the past two days. It's my turn."

Verakko ignored her comment and began to work on the fire. "*Emancipate* is translating as set free. You set yourself free?"

She looked like she wanted to argue but instead let it go. "In a way. Where I'm from, parents are legally responsible for their children until the child turns eighteen. If a child petitions for emancipation before the age of eighteen, it means they become responsible for themselves."

"Did your parents treat you poorly?"

"Not at all! I just didn't want to live the type of life they lived anymore." Lily hiked her shoulders. "They wanted to live in the forests. Making their own tools and connecting with nature. I wanted to be around people and technology and processed foods. I wanted to wear impractical clothing and sleep in a real bed I didn't have to carry on my back during the day."

"How demanding of you." He smirked.

She grinned back. "You might not know from looking at me now, but I love the luxuries of civilization. I've actually become kind of a snob."

"I doubt that." Verakko had barely heard her complain, aside from her complaints about him those first few days.

Lily piled wood onto the small fire he'd started. "Trust me. As soon as we find Alex and I have some money to burn, I'm going to need you to take me to a spa, then to a bed." Her cheeks flushed pink, and she worried her bottom lip. "I mean, show me where I can find a bed."

He knew exactly which bed he'd like to direct her toward. "I'd be happy to pay for a spa trip. It's the least I can do."

"Well, I'd like to turn you down, being the independent woman I claim to be, but seeing as I'm in a situation where I don't have anything but the clothes on my back and a winning personality, who am I to refuse a little help from friend?" Her smile faltered, and her eyes grew worried. "Verakko, what will happen to me? Are there homeless shelters or somewhere I'll be able to stay while I get on my feet?"

The anxious curl of her brows set his nerves on edge. He wanted to explain to her that he'd be seeing to all of her needs and that never in her life would she find herself struggling to survive, but he couldn't rightly promise her anything at the moment. "You won't have to worry about that. Citizens in most of the cities on this planet are supplied free housing, food, clothing, and medical care. If you marry—" Verakko glanced away, hiding his scowl and the snarl rising in his throat, "—your husband will make sure you have everything you want for however long you remain with him."

Lily remained quiet, thoughtful.

"Do you think you'd ever want to marry?" Could she hear the pathetically concealed interest in his voice?

"On Earth, no. My last boyfriend proposed, but I turned him down. You said it's different here, though, right? Only lasts for a few months. What's the point of it? It sounds more like dating to me."

A fiery mix of jealous rage and bitter approval roared through Verakko upon hearing she'd turned down her male. He made sure his voice was even when he answered, "The main goal of marriage is often pregnancy. Like I said, our people are going extinct. Females enter into short marriages to decide whether they want to have a child with their husbands, and then they can either extend the marriage from there and try to become pregnant or they can marry someone else."

"What happens if a woman gets married but decides not to try for children?"

"If it's clear she's actively attempting to not become pregnant, it'll be assumed she didn't deem the male worthy. Nothing will happen specifically, but the male will have a harder time negotiating his next contract."

Lily's lips thinned. "Well then, definitely no marriage for me, at least not right now. I'm not even sure I want to have children."

"Is that why you turned down your *boyfriend*?" Verakko questioned, stumbling over the odd phrase for the male she'd been interested in. He was intent not to make the same mistakes her last male had.

"No. On Earth, marriage is different. It's meant to be for life, and ideally two people should marry because they're in love and want to be together forever. Nathan was nice, but I just didn't feel that thing."

"Thing?"

Lily lifted her hands to the fire. "You know. That thing. That spark. The feeling that you can't go another minute without seeing the other person." Shrugging, she continued, "I'm not sure I believe in marriage long-term, anyway. Fifty percent of them end in divorce." Lily scowled in disgust. "You know how many of my married male clients at the salon have hit on me? It's like they don't even care about the person they're married to anymore. Such assholes. And don't even get me started on guys I've met who have girlfriends they somehow forgot to mention."

Fuck. Would she consider Ziritha my girlfriend? He didn't understand all the phrases she'd used, but the thought was clear. He wasn't technically married, but in his culture, he was as good as married, and he'd venture a guess that was how Lily would see it as well.

Should I tell her about Ziritha now? No, Verakko decided. *I won't be marrying Ziritha. I'll find a loophole in the contract and somehow get Lily to agree to stay with me. There isn't anything to reveal.*

Lily continued, unaware of Verakko's inner turmoil. "My parents were married my whole life, but they were more like companions than anything else. Friends who worked really well together. If they ever had a spark, it was long dead by the time I grew up. I don't want to end up like that."

Verakko shoved a hand through his hair, itching to throw something. Lily didn't want a Clecanian marriage or an Earth marriage, and she may not even want children. He'd never particularly rejoiced at the idea of having children, but he'd also never thought about it much. A child would be a blessing, and it was his duty to do whatever he could to have one. Whether he actually wanted a child had never entered the equation. Verakko pondered this for a moment. When the image of Lily cradling a small girl with brown eyes popped into his mind and longing spread through his chest like warm liquid, he cursed.

She raised a brow and peered at him. "Do you want to get married?"

As was the case in the question of children, no one had ever asked him that before. Did he? It was an honor to be chosen for marriage, something all males strived for. He'd never considered any alternative. If he knew anything for certain, he knew he didn't want a temporary marriage. He wanted a mate—Lily—for life. But this conversation had only made the situation more complicated. If he told her the truth and admitted he wanted to be with her, he might scare her off.

"It depends on who I'm marrying," he replied at length.

"And that's up to your mother? You can't pick yourself?"

Tell her the truth. "I'll be obligated to marry who my mother chooses," he said instead.

"And that's why you 'can't.'"

Verakko stilled, realizing what she was referring to. Goddess, his mivassi was confusing. "If you don't believe in marriages of any kind, then why do you care?"

Lily chuckled. "Is that how it is here? Marriage or nothing?" She sighed. "I'm not saying marriage is completely off the table—Earth-style marriage, that is," she quickly corrected. "I just think it would have to be a pretty spectacular relationship for me to consider it. That's why I like dating. You're saying you can't date?"

It took Verakko a moment to realize his mouth was hanging open. He'd learned a little about dating from the human named Alice and knew he'd love nothing more than to date Lily and convince her to stay with him forever. But that would take time, and time wasn't an option for him right now. What could he say?

He could only manage a shake of his head.

Lily gazed into the fire, her brows knit in thought. Verakko wanted to shout. She'd been asking him the same types of questions he'd wanted to ask her. Were her questions meant to be asked for the same reason? Was she trying to figure out how to be with him?

Verakko didn't know how he should act with her. He couldn't sleep with her. It'd be a breach of contract and result in him being drafted off-world, but he couldn't push her away either. If he somehow managed to figure out a way out of his contract, he'd need her to like him. He had to keep her interested in him without crossing any of the lines he desperately wanted to cross.

Lily shivered again, and he cursed. The sun had almost set, and the night was only going to get colder; he couldn't put this off any longer. "We need to get our clothes dry."

Her gaze became heated, making him want to flee. "I agree."

They'd eaten a small meal of nuts and fruit while setting up camp and had both agreed Verakko should wait until the following day to hunt. There was nothing left to do. No other distractions.

Silently, he rose and undressed, hanging his clothes on a nearby branch. He kept his eyes averted as he listened to her do the same.

Don't look. Don't look. Don't look.

He laid on his side on the bed of leaves, leaving a sizable spot for Lily to lay in front of him. She'd be warm here, nestled between his considerable body heat and the fire. Out of the corner of his eye, he saw her delicate feet walking toward him, and he slid his lids closed.

Her scent hit him first. Clean from the river but tinged with a light smoky scent, courtesy of their fire. Then the brush of her hair swept over his arm as she settled in front of him. Verakko kept his eyes squeezed tightly shut and tried to block out all thoughts of her naked body so close to his. She rested her head on his outstretched forearm, facing away from him and shattering the last bits of his control. What would be the harm? He'd only see her back, after all.

As soon as his eyes opened, he regretted it. She'd tucked her arms and legs into her body, and goosebumps had broken out on her bare arm, only a breath away. His hand rose of its own volition and hovered above her shoulder, not touching but close enough to feel the meager heat from her skin. With a defeated sigh, he allowed his hand to ghost over her rib cage and narrow waist, then up and along the flair of her hip. Her hips were thin, but the bone structure underneath hinted that they'd be lush once she regained the weight she'd lost during these past few weeks. They were the perfect shape to hold her steady while burying himself in her. His fingers flexed, and his shaft hardened.

Then he scented it. Her arousal. He couldn't do this, wasn't strong enough. In a hoarse whisper, he *swayed*, "Roll onto your back."

***

The command rang through her mind, sticking like glue to the forefront of her thoughts, but she discarded the *sway*. She could feel heat from his palm as it glided over her curves, hovering maddeningly close. Her breath was coming in pants. She clenched her legs together tightly, trying to hide the smell of her arousal.

Verakko had said he couldn't be with her even though he wanted to. Being naked together must be torture for him. She piled her hair underneath her and peered over her shoulder at him.

"Why?" she asked in a breathy voice.

His head dipped to her now-bare shoulder. A low, rattling growl emanated from somewhere deep inside him. "Because I want to see you."

Her sex clenched, and she stifled a whimper. "Is that allowed?"

He propped himself on his elbow, and his heated gaze bore into her. "Looking is allowed."

Lily bit her lip, releasing a shaky breath through her nose. Keeping her arms banded around her chest and her legs pressed firmly together, she rolled onto her back. The movement brought her even closer to Verakko, the left side of her body brushing against the front of his.

A hot, rigid bulge prodded her thigh, and she sucked in a breath. Verakko hissed at the touch.

Lily rested her head on Verakko's forearm and watched him. His glowing emerald eyes trailed down her body hungrily. The tense hollows and valleys of his torso glimmered in the green firelight, and his chest rose and fell quickly. When his gaze stopped at the vee of her thighs, he licked a sharp fang. She felt the length of him pulse against her side.

A flush broke out all over her body. To know she was causing this reaction in a man like Verakko made her feel powerful. Lily wanted him to see all of her. She lowered her arms, exposing her breasts.

Verakko groaned. His large, warm palm hovered above her chest but didn't touch, making her want to arch her back into his hands. The heat radiating off his palm as he swept it above her skin left a scorched trail in its wake. Her breathing became erratic, making her breasts quiver with every shaky exhalation.

"So beautiful, Lily," he rasped. He dipped his head and blew hot air on her nipple. It pebbled instantly, and he grinned, then moved to excite the other nipple.

"You can't touch me at all?" Another wave of smoky cedar hit her, and she felt like she was going to burst. Her sex was throbbing now, needing release.

"Not the way I want to. There would be consequences." He ghosted his knuckles over her trembling belly then lower. "Open," he commanded, hovering above the apex of her thighs.

This man is gonna kill me.

She spread her bent knees apart a few inches.

"Wider," he growled.

Lily let her knees fall open, resting her leg on Verakko's hip.

He inhaled deeply, and a rattling purr reverberated through his exhale. "Goddess, Lily. Your scent is enough to push any male over the edge." His palm curled just over her mound, making more liquid heat pool in her core.

"No one would have to know," she urged, past the embarrassment. *I'm practically begging him!*

His hand raised to her cheek, and he stared down at her. "If I touched you, I wouldn't ever be able to stop. I won't risk giving you up later for a few minutes of pleasure now." He licked a fang and stared at her neck. "No matter how much I may want to."

Lily's heart stuttered. *Screw this!* "Does it work both ways?"

"Does what work both ways?" He leaned down and breathed a line of scalding air against her ear and neck.

Her mind took a moment to come back to the present. "Can…can I touch you?"

Verakko froze, his breathing becoming labored. She took his silence as an opening and slid her hand between them and around his shaft.

His body jerked, and he hissed out a curse she couldn't understand. He was large and hot in her palm. The silky skin felt delicate, yet the hardness and sheer size of him was anything but. She began to slide her palm farther down, but he caught her hand, circling it with his own.

His gaze was furious, the muscles in his neck corded in anger, but she didn't sense it was directed at her. After a few breaths passed, he removed her palm from his cock and silently shook his head.

Lily glared back at him, frustrated beyond belief before finally trailing her fingers down her own stomach. His attention snapped to the movement of her hand as it traveled lower, and his brows lifted as though he were in pain.

When she slid her index and middle fingers through her slick folds, he exhaled a miserable groan. "Show me what you like."

Lily slipped two fingers inside her sheath, then removed them and ran the wet tips over her clit. Her hips twitched at the contact.

Verakko narrowed his eyes. "Let me see."

She tilted her hips toward Verakko's dark, intent stare and applied more pressure to the small circles she was drawing around her clit. He let out an appreciative hiss.

Lily watched breathlessly as his hand trailed down and he gripped his own shaft. She whimpered aloud, and her core clenched again. *This isn't enough!* She was empty, hollow. She needed him inside her.

She pressed a finger of her other hand inside her core to combat the ache. The hard muscles of Verakko's bicep bulged as he ran his hand up and down his length in slow, fluid motions. She couldn't look away. She'd never done anything like this with another man, certainly not in front of a man.

"Lily, look at me."

She met Verakko's serious gaze. The quick movements of her fingers became more frantic. She moaned, and his eyes locked onto her mouth.

"Let me *sway* you," he rumbled. His forearm rose a fraction, making her head to rest in the crook of his elbow. He lifted his forearm more, pinning her head against his bicep and forcing her to remain focused on his face.

Her rhythm faltered, and she peered up at him in confusion.

He ran a pointed tongue over his lips. "Please trust me. Open yourself up to it."

Tentatively, she nodded, readying to let his *sway* through. Heat flooded her core anew, wondering what he might try to do.

Deep, velvety soft words echoed through her mind. "Imagine my shaft filling you, reaching all the places inside you can't reach."

Suddenly, Lily's fingers felt larger, the sensation of being filled more intense. She arched her back, and her eyes slid closed.

"Keep your eyes on me. You want me to see you come."

Lily's eyes flashed open. Verakko hovered only a few inches above her, staring down into her eyes. Low moans and sighs poured out of her now. An electric current flashed between her clit and her inner walls with every swipe of her fingers. She could feel his fist pumping faster behind her thigh, the mere brush of his knuckles enough to make her tingle all over.

Lily's hips started to jerk erratically.

"Come hard, mivassi."

The *sway* echoed through her mind a split second before she broke apart. Her gaze, still focused dutifully on Verakko's, grew watery. Suddenly he roared, and his body stiffened. Then, without warning, his lips were on hers.

She moaned into his mouth, shuddering as the last of her climax sizzled through her. For a moment, he remained still, just holding his lips in place.

Fearing he'd get ahold of his senses and pull away, she coaxed his lips open with her tongue. When they did, she deepened the kiss, sweeping her tongue against his until he gradually responded. Verakko drew her bottom lip into his mouth. She felt the faintest brush of fang and sighed, letting her lids drift closed. The sound seemed to spur him on. His chest rumbled with a resonant purr that traveled all the way to his tongue. He tilted his head, taking charge of the kiss.

His pointed, strong tongue flicked against hers, making heat pool in her belly once again. She ran her tongue along one of his fangs, marveling at how they scared her and turned her on at the same time.

Verakko pulled away, breathing hard, and stared down into her eyes. "Careful. You might cut yourself."

"Has that ever happened before?" Lily exhaled, unable to keep a grin from spreading across her face. "Have you ever accidentally bitten someone while kissing?"

His hand reached up, brushing her hair from her damp forehead. "I've never kissed anyone like that before," he said quietly.

Lily stilled and pressed her cheek to his bicep, the muscles jumping at her touch. "Never? You didn't even learn about it in that school?"

"Kissing on the mouth isn't often done on this planet." Verakko smirked, then pulled a section of leaf from between them, forcing her to lie on her side once again. She felt heat rise on her cheeks. He was cleaning up after himself, she realized.

He wrapped an arm around her waist from behind and tugged her snuggly against his chest. She stretched, curling into him, and just about melted. His warmth enveloped her, and the odd purr still rumbling through his chest soothed her even more. The scent of cedar smoke clung to their bodies.

Verakko swept the hair from her neck and inhaled deeply. She felt the slightest trace of his fangs over the sensitive flesh. "Do you ever... Never mind."

"Do I ever what?" he crooned, gripping her more firmly around the waist.

Lily bit her lip. Did she really want to know? "Do you ever bite people?"

She felt a chuckle rumble through him. "Still worried I'm going to eat you?"

She brushed her fingers up and down the forearms resting on her waist. *Hairless? How weird.* The vibration against her back increased. He must've liked that. "You keep looking at my neck and licking your chops. What else am I supposed to think?"

He grunted, and his hot breath fanned over the skin below her ear. Goosebumps erupted on her arms, and she burrowed deeper into the warmth of his chest. "We do. During marriages. Or with mates." She jumped when he playfully snapped his teeth together at her ear and rasped, "Or enemies."

Lily shivered. "Does it hurt?"

Verakko settled behind her and released a contented exhale. "Only if you're an enemy."

Don't ask. Don't ask. Don't ask. "Verakko?"

"Hmm?" he murmured into her hair.

191

"You're touching me and...and we kissed. Isn't that breaking the rules?"

She felt him stiffen and cursed herself for ruining the moment.

He let out a defeated sigh and relaxed against her again. "It is, but I couldn't help it. I've wanted to kiss you since the first time I saw you. And the rest of this touching? Well..." He gently rocked his hips into her ass. She gasped at the semi-firm erection trapped between their bodies. "This is for survival. No way around it."

"Oh really?" she chuckled, arching her bottom toward him and making him hiss. "I think our clothes might be dry by now."

His arm around her waist tightened. "Definitely not."

Lily giggled and gazed into the crackling flames. An old memory played through her mind again, and she smiled. "When I was younger," she began, stroking his arm, "my family went on a trek through Turkey. I met a boy on our way. He was my first kiss."

Verakko's other arm, crossed in front of her shoulders, pulling her against his chest even more. "Why are you telling me this?" His voice was almost a growl.

Lily flushed at the thought he might be jealous. "In that part of Turkey, a lot of the wood you use for campfires is cedar. The one and only time we kissed, I remember it felt like every part of my body was tied in a knot. I couldn't catch my breath or slow down my heartbeat. My stomach was hollow and full at the same time. It was wonderful. I'd never felt so alive or nervous or excited." Verakko's muscles tensed under her hands. If she listened closely, she thought she might even hear his molars being ground into dust, but he remained silent. "And the one thing I remember from that night," she continued, "other than the kiss itself—which was terrible by the way—was the smell of burning cedar. Whenever I smell that scent, I instantly remember how I felt that night. It makes me happy and nervous in the best way."

Lily turned her upper body so she could look at Verakko. His lips were thinned, and his jaw was set in a harsh clench.

She took a chance and leaned in. To her delight, he didn't move away. She pressed a soft kiss to his firm lips. "That's what you smell like to me. Cedar."

Verakko's eyes widened for a moment, the bright green irises darkening until they almost looked black. The corner of his mouth slowly lifted, the tension in his body evaporating. He kissed her again, and a sudden purr vibrated through his lips, tickling her.

Heat rose on her cheeks at the intimacy of the moment. She rolled to her side, grinning privately. She'd never told another living soul about that night or about how she'd been searching for that feeling every day of her life since. "I just thought you should know."

"Thank you for telling me, mivassi."

Lily frowned as the word rang through her translator again. He'd said it earlier as well, but she'd been distracted to say the least. It was one of the words that didn't have a direct translation, which meant the voice that echoed in her ear stuttered its closest approximation, out of time with the speaker.

Mivassi. My alternative.

12

lternative? Alternative. Freaking alternative! The word kept replaying in Lily's mind over and over like a broken record. What did it mean?

She'd attempted to cool the immediate hurt and anger she'd felt when the meaning of Verakko's pet name had settled in her mind. After lying awake for hours, sour and confused, she'd finally drifted to sleep, only to have one unpleasant dream after another rouse her.

A dream of Verakko marrying someone else while she watched from the sidelines had been first. Then had come a dream of her on her knees, begging a faceless, statuesque woman for a marriage contract. The woman had cackled in Lily's face for what seemed like hours before Verakko had joined her, pointing and laughing at her ridiculous request.

Her last dream had involved a spiky-headed purple alien sitting down in her chair and asking for the usual cut and color. She'd stood frozen, gazing at its glimmering black spikes and wondering what to do until finally, it'd sneezed, shooting its head spikes into her face.

She'd bolted awake, naked, alone, and feeling vulnerable in far too many ways.

Verakko had returned soon after with a stick he'd guessed she could use to make a new toothbrush. All she could see when she looked at it was an image of him marrying another woman.

While brushing her teeth, she'd pondered whether the translator could be malfunctioning. As they'd bushwhacked their way through dense forest clinging to the edge of the river for hours, she'd decided *alternative* must be an odd phrase for someone not from his city.

Then, as the first drops of rain had begun to fall on their heads, she'd nervously wondered if it meant how it sounded. He would never marry her, so she was known as an alternative. An alternative to his wife. A second choice. Maybe even a mistress.

Her stomach remained tight and hollow, a shaky, timid urgency to shut down her emotional attachment before it was too late kept gnawing at her every time she caught Verakko's gorgeous gaze.

It wasn't really his fault. She'd made it clear she didn't want to participate in a typical marriage. But she'd had every intention of asking Verakko whether they could agree to fake it. They could date by getting married but would only pretend to try for a child so he wouldn't be looked down upon if they didn't work out. After hearing that nickname, though, she wondered again if marriage was even an option. How hard would she have to work in order to be considered by his mother? Would she always be thought of as an alternative because she wasn't "marriage material" or maybe because she was human?

Verakko had noticed her shift in mood and, after a few rocky attempts at conversation earlier in the day, had stopped attempting to speak with her. His eyes had been alight that morning when he'd presented her with her new toothbrush, but every time she'd avoided eye contact or had given him a forced smile or one-word answer, the light had dimmed a little more. After the trail had morphed into an overgrown mess and walking side by side became impossible, Verakko had taken the lead.

Lily winced as another tiny green insect nipped at her ankle. The slick, muddy ground was bringing out the creatures in droves. She wrapped her arms around herself for warmth and worried her lip while staring at Verakko's back. His black shirt was soaking and clung to his broad shoulders as he sawed through vines and hanging saplings with his small knife, occasionally becoming frustrated and ripping apart the dense flora with his bare hands.

Alternative. Her heart clenched.

Not even the discovery of another flimsy flag and carved message from Alex had worked to lift her spirits.

"I hate nature" was all it had said. Lily agreed.

Verakko stopped abruptly and cursed, shaking his hand as though he'd hurt it. Lily tried to catch a glimpse of what had happened, but he continued on almost as quickly as he'd stopped. A few bloody drops on fallen leaves was the only evidence that he'd hurt himself.

A pang of guilt hit her. He was working so hard, trying to clear a path for her to traverse through, and all she could do was stew about something that was really her fault in the first place. He'd told her he couldn't be with her. Told her how relationships in his city worked. She was the one who'd pushed for more, not him.

It scared her how close she felt to him. She'd only known him for a few days, after all. She could understand it if she'd been a little put out at the idea that they could never date. But this gut-wrenching sadness that made her want to tie him to a tree and never return to civilization? That was a reaction she'd never expected.

"Hold up," she called over the sound of slowly building rain.

Verakko spun to her, second lid in place to guard his eyes from the rain. His hair fell to one side, and small droplets of water trailed from the pointed tips of his ears to his lobes and then down onto his slick biceps.

She pursed her lips. *What right do you have to look so damn good! This isn't a photoshoot.*

"Did you hurt yourself?"

"It's nothing," he said automatically, balling his left hand into a fist.

Lily let out a defeated sigh and walked toward him, her soaking flats squeaking and squelching in the mud. She grabbed his hand and sent him a stern look until he uncurled his fingers, then winced. A deep gash ran through the center of his bright-green palm, leaking dark blood. "We should stop and find shelter until the rain lets up."

"It'll heal quickly. Don't worry." Verakko studied her, his shielded green eyes glowing faintly through his second lid. He looked as frustrated as she felt, except underneath it all she could also see longing and something that looked suspiciously like sadness.

Lily had never let the word *impossible* stop her. It was just a word. Nothing was impossible. But what if this truly was? What if she was giving her heart to a man who could never be with her?

A loud crash of thunder overhead made her jump and throw her hand over her chest.

Verakko's lips curled inward as though he were smothering a grin.

The corners of her mouth twitched. "That wasn't funny."

He transformed his features into a comical display of serious agreement.

Lily released a quick chuckle then sighed. She stared up into Verakko's eyes and smothered the nasty urge to lift onto her toes and press a kiss to his smirking lips.

My alternative.

Verakko's smile faltered, and his dark brows drew together, the silence between them heavy.

"I think we should keep going if you're able." Verakko slipped his shirt off and shoved it over her head before she could protest. The fabric was soaking, just like her own clothing, but the heat from his body still clung to the wet shirt.

Warmth spread through Lily's chest despite the icy rain.

"I'm confident this river leads to my home city. I'll ask my mother to send a group of her soldiers out to search for Alex if she isn't already there." He gave a weak smile. "I don't know about you, but I'm sick of living out here."

"Your mother's soldiers?" Lily asked, unnerved. "Why does your mother have soldiers?"

Verakko licked a fang with his tongue, and his gaze darted. "She's the queen of my city."

Lily blinked. *The queen?* "You're a...a prince?"

A crease formed on his forehead, and he scanned her face. Was she as pale as she felt? "I suppose."

"You'll be king someday?"

Verakko scrunched his brows together in confusion. "No. The people will choose her successor with her input. As her child, I'm excluded from consideration."

Alternative, a voice whispered in her ear, making her stomach flip. No wonder he'd told her it would never work! Her breathing hitched, and she turned away from him, then back. This would be all they could ever have. Stolen moments in a forest, away from prying eyes. Alien planet or not, a queen was a queen. Lily deflated. She'd never had a shot.

I asked him if he'd like to date. A hysterical laugh burst out of her at the thought, earning a perplexed look from Verakko.

"We should cover as much ground as we can in this weather. The Strigi won't fly through a storm like this." His lips thinned for a moment, then he said, "I can carry you."

"No," Lily blurted, taking a step back.

The skin around his eyes tightened, and a muscle ticked in his jaw.

Her heart thumped against her chest in protest. He was hurting; she could see it in his eyes. His confusion and sadness. Guilt swamped her. She'd pushed for this with her idiotic positivity. Thinking she could win over his mother and it'd all work out. She'd made a man from a planet low on females care for a female he could never have.

"What happened, Lily?" His voice was strong, forceful even. He didn't need to elaborate—they both knew what he was referring to.

"Last night, that name you called me," she began, knowing she had to hear it from him in order to truly move on. "It translated as *alternative*. Does that mean alternative to your wife?"

As his shoulders bunched and the muscles in his jaw worked, her hopes sputtered out. He nodded. "Technically, yes. But it means more than that to me. It means I'd never feel for anyone else what I feel for you."

"I think..." She gulped. "I think you were right. We should keep our distance from each other."

"Why?" he asked as if he knew it was the right thing to do but needed to be convinced of it himself.

"Because—" she looked around wildly, "—it seems like that nickname is more special than it sounds, but it's still a term for someone who isn't your wife, and I can't be in that type of relationship. Seeing you with someone else, even if it's just a temporary arrangement…it would hurt me. It'd be better for both of us if we stopped this now." Was she already past the point of no return? Lily felt like she'd be sick. She took a deep breath in and out, then pushed past him and muttered, "I'm sorry."

***

Verakko trudged after Lily, feeling lower than the mud beneath her flimsy soles.

He'd gone too far last night. She'd trusted him, let him in her mind, slept in his arms. She'd whispered sweet words to him, and all the while he'd been wondering how to get out of his tangle of lies.

Alternative. His translator had taken a moment to choose the word, reciting *mivassi*, then *alternative*, indicating it wasn't a direct translation. But it was close enough. *Mivassi* was a word that referred to a claimed alternative to your chosen spouse while under contract. Only used in the rarest of instances when a person recognized their mate while married to another.

Lids sliding shut, he hung his head. Her glassy eyes had made it clear she thought he was referring to her as a female second to his wife. Should he clarify? What would be the point?

He couldn't claim her as his mivassi. He had no evidence. If his eyes had changed or if his marks had appeared, he could claim her and his contract would be void, but without any evidence that she was his, the claim would be rejected and he'd have to honor his contract to Ziritha. Explaining the name may only give her false hope that he could get out of his marriage.

An equally upsetting outcome of him clarifying the true meaning of mivassi was that it may scare her. Claiming someone as a mivassi was the equivalent of announcing you'd unintentionally found your mate. Lily would be expected to stay with him forever. Knowing the physical and mental ramifications of being apart from one's mate, his mother would no doubt ensure she remained with him. By force if necessary. Verakko was almost one hundred percent certain Lily wasn't ready for that kind of commitment.

Either way, he shouldn't have used the name. It had been accidental, springing to his lips so readily. Likely because he'd grown up hearing it used as a term of endearment. He'd have to make an effort to not use it again. The depressing truth was, when all was said and done, he hadn't recognized her and had no right to call her mivassi.

Another bolt of lightning lit the gray sky. Verakko glared into the pouring rain. When he focused on his path again, he found Lily had disappeared around a corner.

He sprinted forward, an unreasonable panic clogging his lungs. He'd just rounded the corner when he skidded to a halt. She stood on the edge of the river, gazing into the distance.

They'd reached the fork.

13

Lily's shoulders stiffened as he approached. His fingers itched to reach out and pull her in close, but he held them back. Maybe she was right and it'd be better if he kept his distance. There was no way out of his contract that he could see. He needed to either let her go or explain everything and ask if she'd be willing to wait for him.

Suddenly she faced him. He couldn't be sure if the streaks on her face had been caused by raindrops or tears, but her swollen lids gave him a heart-wrenching clue.

"So, we should follow this one, right?" She sniffed, pointing at the smaller branch of the river nearest them. It led downhill toward jagged black mountains.

He stepped closer. "Lily—"

"I know, this sucks," she said with a raised hand. "Maybe we can talk more and see if we can figure it out, but right now, I just want to pick a direction and get out of this storm."

Verakko finally took a moment to register her appearance. She was soaked to the bone, stained with mud, and shivering. The normally tan color of her skin was pallid, and the tops of her feet were dotted with angry red bites.

Verakko's heart sank even further. She was miserable, and he hadn't even noticed. Too wrapped up in his own thoughts and fears. "If we head this way, I can take us through a shortcut in the mountains. We could make it to my city in a few days and get help."

Lily nodded resolutely and tromped forward. Her pitiful shoes flopped off her heels with every step, sticking in the mud.

"Please, Lily, let me carry you," Verakko said, accidentally infusing the words with *sway*.

She gave her head a little shake, then huffed out a breath and eyed him sidelong. She opened her mouth once, then closed it. When she spoke again, a bright bolt of lightning, followed by booming thunder, drowned out her words. She glared at the sky, then back to him. "Verakko, just for right now, I need you to not be so nice to me. It's making me crazy."

Frustration flared white hot in him. He flung his arms to the side. "What would you have me do, Lily? I can't stand seeing you this way."

Her shoulders slumped, and she stared at him a moment longer before mumbling, "Fine."

He didn't wait for her to change her mind; instead, he scooped her up so quickly her weathered shoes remained stuck in the mud. He bent at the knees, waiting until she plucked them from the muck, then sprinted down the hill, sliding and jumping along the shoreline expertly.

A small, vain, desperate part of him hoped she'd be impressed. When he peered at her face, though, he only saw resigned misery.

***

Lily clutched Verakko's neck, trying to breathe through her mouth so as not to become confused by his increasingly smoky scent. After a few remarkable leaps and bounds, he landed near the base of the mountain, skidding smoothly to a stop. He set her on the soft ground.

"I don't remember exactly where the entrance is. Can you wait here while I look for it?"

"Could I use the knife to leave Alex a message?" She avoided eye contact, but after he failed to reply, she glanced up at him, gritting her teeth against the sight of rainwater streaming down his bare chest. "In case she comes back this way for some reason."

His vivid eyes stayed glued to hers, then after a long, silent moment, he held out the knife. With a final inscrutable look, he stomped off toward the mountain, glowing eyes running over the vine-encrusted rocky base. The rain had calmed a fraction, but Lily's head was in more turmoil than ever.

She made her way to a smooth log a few feet away from the river and began to carve a note to Alex.

Back and forth, back and forth her brain went on. *There must be a way. There is no way. But surely there could be a way.* It was no use! How could she even consider being a side chick? Was this half-minded simpering woman chasing after a man, truly who she wanted to be? She'd never felt so out of control or reliant on another person. Not even her parents.

They'd always made sure she'd pulled her weight. Looking back at the last few days, Lily realized she'd become dependent on Verakko. She'd boil the water, he'd start the fire and gather the wood. Rough terrain? No problem, he'd carry her. A little cold? She'd expect him to give her his warmth. Before, if she'd been cold on a hike, she'd have erected a trash mound of leaves and branches and burrowed into the insulated mess until morning.

Was this how it'd be with a true partner? With him? Would she always feel this sense of fat, lazy, safety and stability? God, she wanted that. She wanted it more than she'd ever dreamed she could. That damned balloon of emotion expanded in her chest again, pushing against her ribs angrily.

Tears welled in her eyes as she gazed down at the weird note she'd scraped into the smooth bark. "Getting help. Stay put. P.S. Boyfriend trouble." She chuckled humorlessly and wondered how insensitive the note might seem to a starving, cold Alex if she happened to come across it. Jabbing a thin stick into a leaf, she erected a flag and stood back.

"I think I'm close," Verakko yelled over the sound of the rain.

She waved him on, not sure her voice was strong enough at the moment. Instead, she slipped the knife into her sagging pocket, peered down at her bare toes, and flexed them in and out of the soft, wet sand. A fleck of pink polish on her pinky toe caught her eye.

Less than a month ago, she'd been seated in her coworker Maisy's chair. When Maisy had asked what color she'd wanted, Lily had said she'd felt girly and adventurous that day.

"Hot pink, please," she whispered sadly, recalling the conversation. It felt like it'd happened a lifetime ago. She thought back to that week, running through the days in her mind. She remembered she'd begun to get the itch she always got after being in one place for too long.

Lily glanced over her shoulder, chin down and shoulders slumped like a child pouting in the rain, and watched Verakko knock on the stone, pointed ear angled close by. All this work. All this heartache. Maybe it was better to stay away from him. If Verakko somehow was able to convince his mother to let them be together, how long would it be before she felt that itch again?

She inhaled shakily and bent to rinse her muddy shoes in the river. She squinted up to the sky, thankful the lightning seemed to be lessening at least.

A faint shout of triumph echoed from far away. She saw Verakko grinning near an ominous black opening in the rock face. Spiders seemed to crawl up her spine. She hadn't been lying before when she'd admitted to being nervous in small spaces.

"How far is it?" Lily called while grimacing toward the dark tunnel. He shrugged, looking a little annoyed and more than a little exasperated. Lily shuffled her feet uncomfortably, then tried again. "How—"

Verakko's gaze shot to the sky, and a deafening, pulsating roar tore from his throat. He sprinted toward her just as a gust of wind hit her back. A scream built in her throat, but two strong arms slammed around her chest and knocked the air from her lungs.

Massive wings flapped on either side of her, lifting her into the air. Verakko roared again while bolting across the sandy shores of the river.

The ground raced by under her, and she screamed. Her mind finally latched on to the reality of the situation. She was being carried into the sky.

Fuck no. She would not be abducted by another asshole alien.

Lily swung out a leg and wrapped it around the man's thigh, hooking her foot behind his knee to keep herself stable. She lined up her other leg between his legs and swung her heel up as hard as she could.

With a howl of pain, he doubled over, diving toward the ground. She kicked again and again, landing a few more shots with her heel. He gripped her wrist and let go of the rest of her, holding her in the air by one arm and clutching himself between his legs with the other hand.

Her shoulder screamed in protest. The Strigi circled lower into the trees and dropped her a few feet from the ground.

"Get over here, you feguid female," he cursed through gritted teeth.

Lily scrambled away on her stomach, but a strong hand clutched the hem of Verakko's shirt and dragged her back. She rolled until she was facing the sky and shot her legs out, kicking any appendage she could reach while fumbling in her pocket for the knife.

A deadly sharp talon-tipped wing rested on her neck. "Stop, or I slash your throat," the winged male wheezed, still clutching his crotch with one hand.

She froze, cold metal meeting the tips of her fingers.

He leaned forward and bared his teeth. "You're gonna come with me nice and easy, or I'm going to use this wing to slice off a finger." He sent her a crooked grin. "I don't need you whole, after all."

Lily tried to keep the fear off her face. A familiar bellow sounded, making the birds in the trees take flight. Her heart leapt.

"Stay down while I take care of the Swadaeth scum." The pressure on her neck increased, the sharp talon cutting into her flesh. She remained still but peered up and saw Verakko burst into the clearing, then freeze.

Verakko's eyes shot from her to her throat to the winged male. Inky black spread from the corners of his eyes, enveloping the whites and irises. He'd said blackening eyes revealed something about his health, hadn't he? She frantically scanned his body but couldn't see any injuries.

The winged man chuckled and spat, straightening. "Oh, no. Don't tell me you think she's yours. This'll be fun."

Lily studied the man. Sickly green slashes marred his left arm, and he held it awkwardly. Dark circles stood out under his eyes, and there was a yellow cast to his skin. He wasn't at full strength yet. *Still stronger than me, though.*

She stretched her fingers in her pocket and gripped the hilt of the knife. The asshole above her smirked at Verakko, ignoring the threat under his wing entirely. "No marks yet, I see."

"You want to release her," Lily heard Verakko *sway*.

The sharp point of the talon at her neck dug in, and she let out a cry. "Try it again and she's dead." The Strigi barked out a laugh. "That won't work on me anyway. All my thoughts revolve around causing pain. The type of pain I've been in for the past three days."

"Lily, you'll be okay," Verakko called.

"You killed two of my kin!" the winged alien snarled. "I should rip her to shreds in front of you just to see your face." His mouth contorted into a disgusted sneer. "But I won't. My orders were only to bring you in." He tossed something toward Verakko. "Spray yourself, and I vow I won't hurt her."

Lily angled her head so she could see Verakko. He held a small silver cylinder in his hand. His eyes were furious and wild, flashing between her and the Strigi, but they'd returned to their normal shade of green.

He lifted the cylinder a few inches, and recognition hit. A silver object like that had been the last thing she'd seen before passing out on Earth. The purple alien who'd barged into her backyard without warning had sprayed her with one of those.

His brows drew together. "You vow you'll leave her behind?"

He's going to sacrifice himself? For me? Terror and worry and anger hit her all at once. *What the fuck is he doing?* She tried to call out, to tell him to drop the bottle, but the pressure on her throat was too great. There was no way she'd let him be taken. Not if there was any way for her to stop it.

***

A trickle of blood slid down Lily's pale neck and onto the dirt. A savage rattle tore through his chest. This male might not die today, but he'd die soon. And painfully. If only Verakko could focus his mind enough to *sway*. His gaze flew to Lily, sprawled on the ground under the male's deadly wing. Fear shot through his veins like ice, muddling his thoughts.

The Strigi placed more pressure on Lily's neck and shouted, "Choose!"

All of the air seemed to fly from Verakko's lungs at Lily's first gasp. He raised the spray to his face.

A flash of silver near Lily streaked through the air and disappeared into the Strigi's wing. He stumbled back, roaring in pain as she crawled away, coughing and inhaling deep, ragged breaths. Verakko clutched the bottle and grinned evilly.

He leapt, clearing the few feet between him and the sputtering male.

The Strigi's eyes grew wide. He attempted to shoot into the sky. But Verakko leapt again, catching his legs and wrenching him down so hard the male's face smashed into the leaf-strewn ground. Settling his weight on the Strigi's back, Verakko wrapped his arms around the base of the male's wings, binding them together, then savagely wrenched downward.

The Strigi screamed and flailed under him.

"You think you can hurt my female? Make her bleed?" He rotated his arms, twisting the shattered bones of the once-powerful wings. "The pain is unbearable. You want to pass out, but you can't," Verakko *swayed*, a vicious bloodlust pulsing through him. The male shrieked again, releasing a throaty sob.

He could hear his name in the distance. Someone was yelling. Asking him to stop. He twisted again. *My Lily. My mivassi. My mate. No mercy.*

Then she was kneeling in front of them.

"Get back!" he roared as the Strigi reached for her wildly.

"Please!" the male screamed.

Bitter fear hit his nostrils, and his grip tightened.

Her hands shot forward and clutched both sides of his face. A loud ringing sounded in his ears, but he focused on her. Her eyes streamed with tears and she mouthed, *Stop.*

Confusion hit first, but gradually, his sense returned. "Look away," he snarled.

Her eyes widened before she spun and stumbled away. *Away from me.*

Without a second thought, he released the male's wings. With a quick jerk of his hands, he snapped the Strigi's neck and sprinted after Lily.

She slipped and fell, her bare feet sliding on wet leaves. He came to a halt in front of her and reached out to pull her close, his eyes running over every inch of her he could see for evidence of injuries.

She rolled to face him, her eyes flashing to his as she hastily scooted away. The pungent scent of fear spiked.

Is she afraid of me? Verakko's breathing hitched. He reached a hand toward her, then stilled, noticing the knife still clutched in her fingers.

Her hand was shaking where she gripped the hilt, her eyes wide, pupils dilated. *She must be in shock.*

In one swift movement, he snatched her wrist, making her cry out. He squeezed until she dropped her weapon, then pulled her into his arms. Her body remained stiff for a moment before she finally shuddered and threw her arms around his neck.

"Lily, it's okay. It's me. You're safe," he *swayed.*

She nodded into his shoulder, digging her nails into his back.

His heart was still racing, matching the beat of her heart thumping against his chest. For the first time in his life, he didn't regret the pain he'd caused.

He leaned down and whispered into her hair. "I'm going to take you somewhere safe. Alright?"

Without waiting for her reply, he stashed the fallen knife in his pocket, cradled her against his chest, and sprinted for the tunnel. His eyes kept darting to the sky as he ran even though, logically, he understood no other Strigi would know where they were. He stooped to collect her wet shoes and the discarded bag from the shore, barely slowing his pace.

He scanned the sky again and tried to convince himself that the threat had passed.

Even so, the dark confines of the tunnel route to Mithrandir was the most secure place Verakko knew of in the unlikely event another Strigi lurked close by. No individual from any of the winged races would choose a black tunnel over the open sky.

Lily shook in his arms, clutching at him desperately. When he found the hidden entry pad again, he dripped a bit of venom onto his thumb and pressed it onto the concealed scanner. The door swung open with a soft whoosh, and he slid inside.

14

~

The Swadaeth tunnel, built to transport precious goods from Mithrandir to the forest city of Sauven, had very little light. Partially because lighting the rarely used winding passage through the underbelly of the mountain would've been expensive and difficult, but mostly because only a Swadaeth could access the tunnels using a drop of their venom—and Swadaeth didn't need light.

He'd only been walking with Lily clasped in his arms for a few minutes, yet it concerned him that the bitter scent of her fear had not abated.

"Don't worry, I can see. I've got you."

Lily's body stiffened. "Let me down."

Reluctantly, he did.

Once her feet hit the floor, she hissed. "Shit, it's cold. Where are my shoes?" She reached out in the dark, her hands landing on his bare torso. Her fingers flexed before she removed them. Gripping her wrist, he guided her shoes into her hand, then held her steady while she slipped them on. Her skin was as cold as ice.

"There are rooms with hot springs along this route. I visited one a long time ago when I joined my mother's convoy to Sauven."

Lily remained quiet, but he could see her eyes darting around, unseeing and wide. She was shaking again. He made to wrap his arms around her, but she pushed away, shaking her head. "Let's just get to somewhere we can stay the night."

They spent the next hour walking in silence. He tugged Lily behind him, her hand clasped in his. His insides twisted at the contact, knowing she was only allowing the touch because she couldn't see on her own.

Something had clicked in him back there during the attack. Lily was his. He had no doubts. But just because he was certain didn't mean she would want him, and even if she did, he couldn't ensure they'd be able to be together, at least not right now. He had to convince her to wait for him. He couldn't see another way.

A dim blue glow illuminated the path ahead of them, and he pulled her in front of him. "Do you see that light? The spring is there."

She tugged her hand out of his and walked away. Had he already lost his chance? Every instinct in him urged him to run after her, take her into his arms, and hold her until she softened against him the way she'd done before. But things felt different now. She was quiet and introspective and, if her scent was any indication, scared.

Normally, a mass of emotions played over her face whenever he looked at her, but now, her eyes appeared almost vacant, devoid of all feeling. Verakko jabbed his fingers through his hair and shuffled after her. Goddess, he'd never wanted to know a person's innermost thoughts more than he did right now.

She reached the sealed entrance to the spring and stared up at the moss growing along the ceiling. It glowed a warm electric blue and could be found in the tunnel near any damp, warm, dark place.

Verakko activated the entry pad with another drop of venom and pushed the door inward. A blast of thick, steamy air burst out, and Lily released a small sigh of pleasure. She rushed inside and stared at the large glowing pool of steaming water.

He should wait outside, give her time to herself to collect her thoughts, but he couldn't. He followed her in and shut the door, drawn to her like a magnet. The idea of letting her out of his sight after seeing her almost get taken away from him for good was unthinkable.

Verakko scanned the vaguely familiar room. The luminous moss grew in the cracks and corners of the stone walls and up into its high, domed ceilings. The light from it pulsed like glimmering veins and cast the hazy room in soft blue light. He bent to unlatch his boots, then toed them off, resolved to spend the night in the warmth.

Lily turned to him and ran her gaze over his bare chest. Verakko straightened, never as uncomfortable with a female's assessment of him as he was now. Her jaw was clenched tightly in an inscrutable expression. She leveled her impassive gaze on his and swallowed.

"You…" She blinked and swallowed again. "You have blood on you," she said, her voice no more than a whisper.

Verakko's attention shot downward, and he found streaks, almost black in the dim light, across his forearms and chest. Was that why she was acting so strangely, because he'd killed that soulless Strigi?

He rushed to the edge of the pool and rinsed himself, but he kept his eyes trained on Lily. She didn't turn to watch him, just stood rooted in place like a statue. Then she peered down at her shirt—his shirt—and, as though roused from a bad dream, began to struggle, trying to remove the wet fabric clinging to her skin.

Verakko crossed to her in an instant and helped her pull both his shirt and hers over her head, trying to keep his eyes averted from the thin scrap of see-through fabric covering her breasts. He threw the shirts out of sight while she splashed water on her neck and chest, ridding it of the blood that wasn't there.

"Are you still hurt?" she asked over her shoulder.

"Hurt?" He scanned his own body, wondering if he'd been injured and hadn't realized it. *No injuries,* he concluded. Was she asking out of concern for him? "No. I feel fine."

She nodded, mollified, yet the look of barely contained anger on her face remained.

He reached out to her when she stood, but she slapped his hand away, then glared up into his eyes.

His heart picked up speed, and a small spike of anger went through him. Was she really upset with him for killing that male? A growl rumbled in his chest before he could contain it. "I had no choice, Lily," he said with deadly calm.

Her face morphed into one of outraged disbelief. "No choice?" She took a step toward him. He took a step back. "No choice?" she repeated, taking another step.

"I had to kill him. He would've hurt you." Verakko retreated a step again.

"I don't care about that!" Lily's hands flashed out, her small fists slamming into his chest in a loud thump. "You were going to leave me!" she snapped.

Verakko stepped back again, lost. "I would never leave you," he argued, searching his mind to understand what she was talking about.

Her gaze grew fiery, enraged, and she pounded on his chest again. Pushing him farther back and against the door. "You were going to let him take you!" Tears streamed out from her furious eyes, and her scent of fear intensified.

Verakko's heart thudded out of control in his chest. *This fear is for me?*

She slapped his shoulder hard, stinging his skin.

"Stop it, Lily," he warned.

"He would've killed you!" She slapped again. "Or worse!"

He rattled another warning, then when she began to pound repeatedly on his chest, he snatched her wrists and spun her around, pressing her back into the smooth metal door and bracing her hands above her head. "Stop! Calm down!" he boomed, trying and failing to *sway*.

Lily stopped struggling and gazed up at him, face etched with anger. Her breath came and went in shallow gasps, her chest rising and falling in time with his. "You were going to let him take you away." Her voice broke.

He inhaled deeply and bent so his gaze was level with hers. "You have to know I would've come back."

"Your eyes were black. I don't know how, but you were hurt in some way. And you were going to let him take you. What if you couldn't get free?"

"I would've found a...a way to..." Verakko's words stuttered out as her words finally registered. "My eyes?" The world around him slammed to a halt, the thunderous pounding in his chest freezing as though even his heart feared he'd misheard her.

I recognized her? She's mine.

He peered down at her, his dry throat working soundlessly.

Her brows drew together. Then, without warning, she leaned toward him as far as she could with her hands still pinned above her and kissed him.

All thought fled. His mate was in his arms, safe, and she was kissing him. He released her wrists and ran his hands over her slippery body as though he'd never get another chance. Her hands flew to remove the scrap of fabric at her chest, then down to his pants. He palmed her breasts roughly as she fumbled with the fastenings on his pants. He groaned at the touch of her tongue to his and felt rare antivenom fork an icy path through the roof of his mouth, filling his fangs.

He slipped his hands beneath the loose fabric of her wet, thin pants, and they slid to the floor. Then, he palmed her ass, pulling her in close. *Not close enough.*

Lily slid a chilled palm onto the overheated length of his cock and whimpered sweetly into his mouth. He released her lips with a groan and descended on her neck, nipping and licking his way along the sensitive skin while she ran her hand up and down his shaft and scraped her nails across his scalp.

The scent of her arousal hung heavy in the air, driving him wild. He slipped his hands along the underside of her thighs, then gripped her ass, lifting her up and crushing her between his chest and the cool door. Lifting her higher, he sucked and swirled her dusky nipple until it pebbled.

Lily arched her back toward him and moaned softly as she dug her nails into his shoulder in the most delightful way. He lowered her again and touched her mouth with his, marveling at the sensations the new act created. Kissing felt more intimate than anything else he'd ever done, and he couldn't imagine sharing it with anyone else.

She panted his name in between wet kisses and wrapped her legs around his waist, rolling her hips and gliding her slick folds against him. Anchoring herself with one arm around his neck, she reached between their bodies, pressed tightly together, and gripped his shaft.

Lily jostled him with her hips, trying to put a little space between them, but he remained unmoving. He pulled his head back and stared into her eyes. Using his body weight to pin her in place, he placed his palms on either side of her face.

Her cheeks, forehead, and the top of her nose were all flushed. Long, shaky breaths were sucked in between her red lips, swollen from his kisses. She rocked her hips against him again. Whenever the small nub at her entrance slid across the head of his shaft, she let out a little gasp.

It was becoming harder and harder to hold himself back.

"Are you sure?" he croaked in a husky voice, looking deeply into her gold-flecked eyes. "If we start, I'm not going to be able to hold back. I'll have all of you tonight." He let his eyes drift to her neck so she knew what he meant. "In all ways."

Her brows furrowed, and she nibbled her lip.

He waited, his breath trapped in his throat, for her response. Finally, she gave a small nod.

"Yes?" he growled, his cock pulsing white hot in anticipation.

"Yes," she said breathlessly. Her hand snaked between them again. He eased his hips back but kept his eyes locked on hers. One of his hands cupped the base of her skull firmly while his thumb rested under her ear, holding her head in place. The other slid under her ass, hiking her higher up his body.

When the head of his shaft was lined up with her entrance, pushing lightly, Lily panted and ran her hand back up his body slowly before stopping to grip his shoulder.

Verakko pushed into her only a little; electricity seemed to crackle along every nerve. They both let out a low moan. He rested his chest against her breasts and inched in farther. He felt her belly tremble and held still, letting her adjust to his size.

Lily released a frustrated groan and used her legs' grip on his hips to bury his cock deeper inside her. He hissed, and his rattling growl resounded low in his throat.

He pulled out, then pumped into her again. Hard. Lily let out a high-pitched cry, her eyes widening. He watched her face for signs of pain or pleasure or both and when he only saw pleasure, pumped into her again and again. Each time he was buried deep, she made little mewls of pleasure.

Her core was slick and hot around his shaft, squeezing tightly. He took her mouth with his, moving his hand to cup her ass. She tore her mouth away and pulled herself closer, wrapping her arms behind his neck, one hand tangling in his hair. Cries escaping her on every exhale.

Sweat poured off them, making his hands slip over her smooth skin. He stopped, hooking an arm below each knee, and flattened his palms against the wall. Forcing her legs to spread farther apart. He entered her again.

From this position, the hard, flat area of his pelvis, just above his shaft, rested flush with the small nub she'd toyed with to reach her orgasm the night before. He seated himself inside her and ground his hips against the area experimentally.

Lily moaned and nodded wordlessly, shuddering and grinding her hips in time with him. He rocked into her at a steady pace, making sure he rubbed the small area on each upward thrust. Her eyes fluttered closed, her body growing stiff, until she screamed, "Verakko! Yes, don't stop."

She threw her head forward, biting down on his shoulder, and then her sheath convulsed and she came, moaning and whimpering into his neck.

He withdrew and set her on her unsteady feet. "Can you keep going?" he rasped, hoping the rumor that human females didn't need any downtime between orgasms was true.

Her dazed eyes grew confused, but she nodded. Without wasting any more time, he spun her around and pushed her front into the door. She was still panting, coming down from her orgasm when he slid his arm in front of her hips and flicked the small nub again. She cried out and bucked back toward him. He bent at the knees and slowly guided his length into her slick channel from behind, his muscles shaking with the effort not to grip her too firmly. The throbbing in his fangs grew almost unbearable.

Lily let out a low moan and sank against the door. He set a steady rhythm, rocking in and out of her while keeping his fingers curled around her small pleasure center.

Verakko brushed the hair from her shoulder and rumbled into her ear. "Lily, I'm going to bite you," he ground out, barely able to utter the words.

Lily gasped and peered over her shoulder at him, gaze bleary with pleasure.

"I need to *sway* you first."

A heartbeat passed and he thought she might deny him, but then she breathed "Okay" on a moan.

Verakko let loose his rattling purr, knowing he was going to mark his mate for the first time.

Lily's breaths hitched, and she scratched against the door as if she didn't know what to do with her hands.

"Open yourself up to me." The percussion of his rattling purr drummed through his voice as he *swayed* breathlessly. "My fangs sinking into your neck will feel as good as my shaft sinking into your cunt."

Verakko wanted to roar with pride when Lily frantically pulled her hair aside. He licked his fangs eagerly and ratcheted up the speed of his thrusts. He used the hand cupping her sex to urge her up and onto her toes, then slipped the other arm under her shoulder, between her breasts, and latched his fingers onto the opposite shoulder, binding her to his chest.

"I'm close," Lily cried, rocking against his hand in time with his thrusts.

With a roar, Verakko sank his fangs into her, and she screamed.

He smashed her against the wall with rough, erratic pumps of his hips. The antivenom from his fangs leaked into her, and his eyes rolled back at the feeling of release. He inhaled deep, shaky breaths through his nostrils, the blood in his veins pumping with renewed purpose. He'd finally recognized her, and now he was marking her.

Her body stiffened once again, and she quietly chanted, "Yes, yes, yes."

She choked out a high cry, and her walls clenched around him again, forcing his own orgasm to overtake him. He released her neck and bit the inside of his cheek to keep from bellowing and hurting her ears. Pushing into her as far as he could go and gripping her tightly, he groaned as his shaft pulsed jets of his seed into her.

They stood, plastered together, breathing hard until he noticed her legs shaking. He lifted her off the ground and kicked away their pants while gently kissing the puncture marks on her neck. Carefully, he waded backward into the warm water and dipped until their still-connected bodies were shoulder deep.

"Oh my God," Lily moaned, resting her head back against his shoulder and running her palms over his arms, still banded across her front. "That was amazing."

His purr rattled through him again, and pride expanded his chest. He licked and kissed the slowly healing punctures on her neck, marveling at how right they looked. "Did I hurt you?" He didn't think he had, but he needed to be sure.

Lily chuckled. "Only in the best way. I should've known you'd be a little rough."

He gently slipped out of her and nipped her lobe. "I'll be anything you want me to be."

***

The words replayed in Lily's mind, and she wanted to believe them. Really, she did. But how could they be true? She squirmed to be released. Verakko rumbled a deep sound of disapproval but gently pressed a wet kiss to her ear that made her shiver, and opened his arms.

She faced him. He looked so happy and relaxed. His bright-green eyes watched her with such contentment. A wistful grin transformed his features as his gaze settled on the part of her neck he'd bitten.

Lily thought back to the night before and recalled he'd mentioned bites were reserved for mates and wives. If he bit her, that must mean he had hope she'd become one of those things. Right? Or was she just fooling herself again?

When they'd first met, he'd told her mates were a couple married for life. It was the type of relationship Alice was in now. Could she see herself staying with Verakko for life? She didn't know.

If this afternoon had taught her anything, though, it was that losing him had scared her more than anything she'd ever experienced. The thought of not seeing him, arguing with him, laughing with him, threatened to level her even now.

Lily smiled to herself as Verakko waded to the edge of the pool, his devastating teal body glowing brighter in the neon-blue light from the bioluminescent moss. If an emotion like that wasn't enough to give a lifelong commitment a shot, she didn't know what was. Still, if they could start with something less permanent and go from there, she'd feel more comfortable.

He rummaged through a large trunk mounted onto the floor near the edge of the pool and produced a small bottle, grinning brightly. "Soap," he said, raising one dark brow at her.

Lily gasped and splashed over to him, uncaring of how desperate she must look.

"What'll you give me for it?" He chuckled, holding the bottle out of reach.

She stood back with her hands on her hips and tried to be annoyed. Her scowl cracked. The boyish look of delight on his face was enough to break any woman's resolve.

She gave him a sly smile and straightened her shoulders, pushing out her breasts. His gaze snapped to attention. She sauntered over to him through the water, reveling in the hungry way he eyed her movements. "Well, maybe if we get really clean all over," she purred, running her hand slowly down his rock-hard chest, then beneath the water and over his firm stomach, "I might be willing to kiss you in some other places." He jerked when she gripped his still-hard shaft, making her intention clear.

His eyes widened in disbelief. "You'd do that?"

Lily snaked her arms around his neck, pressing her breasts into his chest and grinning. "I think you're vastly underestimating how much I enjoy being clean."

He lowered the tube, and she snatched it. Then he dipped his head, a deep chuckle rumbling through him, and placed a soft kiss on her lips.

Lily let out an embarrassingly loud moan and leaned into the touch of her alien.

15

∞

Today is the day. I need to tell her everything. Verakko scrunched his chin and peered down at Lily, sleeping deeply, sprawled on his chest.

He ground his teeth. The haze of unprecedented joy that had overcome him the night before had worn off as the night had stretched on. After she'd fallen asleep in his arms, he'd finally searched his hands, frustrated to find them still mark-free.

But it didn't matter. His eyes had changed, which meant he'd recognized her as a potential mate. *Potential.* He scoffed, knowing deep in his bones that it was only a matter of time before his stubborn marks appeared.

His marriage contract with Ziritha no longer bothered him either, now that he could get out of it easily by claiming Lily as his mivassi. No, the worry that had slowly seeped into his mind during the night concerned her acceptance of the bond.

How would she take the news that she was unequivocally his and he hers? That neither of them would ever be with anyone else? That the longer they were together from the time his marks appeared onward, the harder it would be for him to survive on his own?

He could keep his distance from her for a while, give her time to adjust. But once his marks appeared, it would be incredibly difficult to give her space, or so he assumed based on all the accounts of mating he'd ever heard. No individual lived happily once their mate was gone. Not a single one. There was no way of knowing how the mating bond would affect him, seeing as Lily was human. Would the bond be weaker? If his feelings for her now were any indication, no. Would he have the strength to stay away from her if she refused to accept the bond?

A slice of anxiety, different from the constant worry that had plagued him all night, hit as a thought occurred. *What will my mother do if my marks do show up, but Lily refuses to make a commitment to me?* Verakko swallowed. Would she force Lily to remain with him? And if she did, would Lily come to resent him?

Maybe I shouldn't bring her to Mithrandir. He ground his molars and clutched Lily to him a little more tightly.

Lily made a small sound of discomfort, and he loosened his grip. She roused, yawning and stretching against him in a way that felt indescribably right. She gazed up at him, sleep still clouding her eyes, and smiled.

Fuck! Verakko inwardly cursed over and over as he looked at her. Couldn't they just stay here? Pretend like the rest of the world didn't exist?

Her eyes grew instantly worried. "Is everything okay?"

Verakko forced a smile and nodded. "Yes. I'm not looking forward to the rest of the journey, that's all."

Her gaze turned confused. "Wait." She took in their position on the ground near the pool, and a crooked smile spread across her face. "Did I fall asleep?"

Verakko grinned despite himself. "You did."

"Oh no." She chuckled, releasing a sigh and propping her chin on his chest. "Well, I guess us both getting some sleep for once is a good thing."

Verakko gave a noncommittal grunt. He hadn't slept at all.

She tried to lift off his chest, but he hauled her back down.

She laughed again. "Don't want to get moving?"

"Don't want to go back to the world," he said quietly.

Her fingers, which had been brushing up and down his stomach, paused, and she stared at him again with a sad smile. "We should talk, shouldn't we?"

His stomach turned sour. *More than you know, mivassi.*

Lily released a sound of resignation and planted a soft kiss on his chest. "We'd better start moving soon, or I'm never going to be able to get myself to leave." She ran her lips up the column of his throat, eliciting a low purr from him.

"Why?" he asked when she finally stopped.

She yawned again. "Anxiety-spiking pitch-black tunnels, or warm, well-lit room with a hot spring and a handsome, naked man? I need to force myself to leave now before I fully wake up and my sense returns." Lily draped an arm over her breasts and peered around her.

Verakko nodded toward the far side of the room. "While you were sleeping, I washed and laid out our clothes, but they're likely still damp from this air."

As she rose to inspect the clothes, he studied the flare of her waist and the delicious curve of her ass. How long would it be until he'd see this again?

A lump formed in his throat as he watched her hop awkwardly from one foot to the next, trying to drag the damp fabric of her pants up her body. *What if she doesn't want me for a mate?*

Lily brushed her hair off her shoulder and tipped her head in an attempt to see the marks from his bite. A piece of him seemed to crack, and he released a sharp exhale.

"What's the biting about anyway?" Lily grinned at him as he dressed. "I'm not saying I didn't enjoy it..." She padded over to him and curled her fingers around his neck, scraping her nails through his hair.

"I'll explain on the way," he said stiffly. Before he pulled away, he brought one of her soft palms to his mouth and kissed it.

"Are you sure you're okay?" Lily looked at him quizzically. "Your eyes are black again."

He covered up the strangled sound that burst from his throat with a cough. Instead of answering, he gripped her nape and pulled her in for a deep kiss. Could he ever live without this?

It took Lily a moment to open her eyes after he pulled away. He finished dressing, helped clean the small room, and waited by the door. She made a face of disgust as she slipped on her shoes.

At his questioning look, she explained, "Still wet."

A smile tugged at his lips, and he opened the door. Lily frowned, shivering as a blast of cold air flooded through the opening, then rushed out of the room with balled fists. "Alright, let's get this over with."

They walked in silence for a few minutes. The mellow scent of fear wafted from Lily and scraped against Verakko's senses like sandpaper. As the mating bond strengthened, her unrest became his. How much worse would it be once his marks showed up? He now understood why his aunt Yerew was always in such a bad mood whenever she fought with her mate, and also why their fights never seemed to last very long. It made him physically uncomfortable to know she was anything less than happy.

He studied Lily and watched her eyes continue to dart around the black tunnel, unseeing. She curled her arms into her body and hunched her shoulders, leaning into his side as he guided her through the passage.

Realization dawned on him. "Is it the size of the tunnel?"

"Is what the size of the tunnel?"

"I can smell your fear."

She let out a small sound of agreement. "Well, yes and no. I can't really see how big the tunnel is, but I keep imagining it's small, and that apparently is enough to make me claustrophobic."

"How can I help? he asked, voice tight.

"You're helping. Just keep talking to me." She scanned the space in front of her again. "Tell me about the biting."

Verakko couldn't suppress the flood of happiness he felt at her mention of his bite. "It's something we do to make sure the female has our antivenom."

"Antivenom?" Lily blurted, appearing startled. When he only stared at her, unsure what to say, she continued, "You put...injected me with antivenom? Why? Are you planning on biting me with venom at some point?"

Verakko chuckled and guided her forward again. "It's for procreation. Each Swadaeth's venom is a little different. All are deadly, but they aren't all exactly the same. We can be harmed by one another's venom if bitten, although the reaction would be more akin to a severe cold than death, as it would be in a non-Swadaeth. Since a child will have half the male's genes and half the female's, we inject antivenom to make sure the female doesn't become ill from the child's developing venom as it grows in her."

He knew they were getting close to the exit because it was becoming warm, the dry heat from the Dakuun desert permeating the tunnel. Lily gripped his forearm as she shuffled through the dark and wiped sweat from her brow. How much of her current state was because of the heat and how much was a reaction to the meaning of his bite?

"So, you could get me pregnant?" she asked with an odd look of confusion mixed with something unreadable.

Verakko shrugged, feeling brief joy at the idea before a nervous fear settled in. Hadn't she known that? "I thought you knew it was a possibility."

An awkward twitch of her shoulders was the only response Lily gave for a moment. Then, she worried her bottom lip and said, "I guess on some level I know we're the same species, but I never put two and two together. You're just so different from me. It's baffling that I might be able to have a…blue?—I don't even know what color—baby." Lily shook her head in disbelief and wiped her forehead with her shirt again. "It's a good thing I have an IUD."

Verakko scanned her body, not recalling any superficial device. "Where is it?"

She chuckled, her eyes still a bit wider than normal. "It's inside me. A type of birth control."

Verakko remembered Jade had been sure of her Earth-given birth control as well. Should he tell Lily her IUD might not be as effective as she thinks? "One of the humans, Jade, became pregnant while on a form of Earth birth control. I didn't look into it, but it may be that your IUD is…ineffective."

Lily's steps faltered. She stared into the darkness for a moment, then gave a deep sigh and shrugged. "Well, shit." She laughed. She threw her hand in the air in a gesture that said the new information was just a grain of sand on an ever-growing dune. "I guess we'll see what happens. I can't imagine it won't work, though. It isn't like the pill." She pointed, or attempted to point, accusingly at him and grinned. "But you're wrapping it next time."

Wrapping it? Verakko mulled over the odd phrase before the words *next time* registered, and his shaft twitched. The end of the tunnel came into view ahead. She'd taken the news that she could become pregnant pretty well. Maybe she'd take the news that she was his mate well too?

As soon as they got outside and she could look him in the eyes. He'd tell her then. His heart jumped in his chest with every step closer to the exit they got. Neither of them had eaten last night, and he was thankful for it, knowing his stomach was ready to turn at any moment.

When they finally reached the exit and stepped out, Verakko expelled a large pent-up breath. He pulled Lily through the door and watched her take in the first sight of his homeland.

Her eyes were wide, and her mouth hung slightly open. He peered at the scenery and tried to see it through her eyes. They were standing a few hundred feet away from the base of the black mountains. The tunnel had deposited them far from the mountains to ensure the crumbling sides, which often collapsed after heavy sandstorms, didn't block the tunnel.

The blazing sun was high overhead, shining down on a sea of glittering black sand. Towering dunes formed farther away from the mountains, barely blocking out the view to his city, only a day's walk away.

"It's beautiful," Lily whispered. She gulped and gave him a forced smile. "And a little bit terrifying, to be honest." She reached out and clasped his hand in hers, tugging him along as she trudged forward up the nearest dune. The small gesture was so natural and affectionate, it made his breath hitch.

"It can be quite dangerous if you don't know what you're doing." He stared back over the rolling hills of sand, recalling the days and nights he'd spent out here while serving in his city's infantry. "It may not look like it, but the desert is alive. Watching where you step is the most important thing to keep in mind. If the sand looks anything other than smooth, tell me immediately."

Lily raised her brows and scanned the ground anxiously. "Yep, that's gonna give me all sorts of nightmares."

As they came to the top of the dune, a glint in the distance caught his eye, and he pointed toward it. She spun, shielding her eyes.

There it was. Mithrandir. The new city, with its towering buildings, was visible from a great distance.

"Wow," she breathed. "It almost looks like a forest. The buildings are weird. Why are they so wide and flat on top?"

With a resigned sigh, Verakko slid behind her, twining his arms around her waist and breathing into her hair. "They only look flat. They're actually sloped inward and lined with solar panels. The mist and rain collect on the roof and are guided down through the center of the building and into large filtering systems underground. Then the water is pumped up to the top, where it falls back down again."

She scrunched her brows. "Why? Isn't that wasteful?"

Verakko chuckled. "No, not wasteful. The water is used as needed, and if there's a shortage, the water is managed better. It's an unnecessary luxury. The architect designed the building to be self-sustaining, but he also took into account my people's penchant for extravagance." He gestured grandly to the buildings, pretending to speak as though enraptured. "When visitors come to our desert city, they're awed by our lush gardens and never-ending waterfalls in the center of every building."

Lily chuckled. He shook his head, having always found the feature to be pointless and ridiculously opulent. Although the water was all used, he felt it could've been utilized more efficiently. A flash of excitement raced through him again. If he wasn't marrying Ziritha, that meant he wouldn't need to move back to Mithrandir either. He could stay in Tremanta with Lily, where technology was prized above gaudy displays.

She rested her head against his chest. "I can't wait to see the city."

With great effort, Verakko slipped his hands from around Lily and turned her until she was facing him. "We need to talk before we go to the city." He ran a hand over the back of his neck.

Lily nodded slowly and glanced to him with worried eyes. "I agree."

"I'm not sure you should go to Mithrandir. I think Tremanta would be a better place for you right now." This thought had come to him repeatedly last night, but he'd ignored it, knowing it would mean he'd have to be apart from Lily for a short while. But the more he thought about it, the more honorable a decision it appeared to be. "I don't know how my city will react to humans. They may not even be aware of your existence yet, and the Queen of Tremanta is giving humans certain liberties that my mother may not." *Like the right to choose not to be with me,* he thought, wincing as though a knife had sliced into his gut.

Lily's eyes shot back and forth, digesting the information, before landing back on him. A shy smile lit her face. "But what about you? Will you go to Tremanta with me?"

Verakko could feel his pulse thrumming through his body. "Yes. Eventually. I just need to settle something with my mother first."

Her eyes brightened. "You would go with me? Does that mean we could date?" Lily's gaze turned quizzical. "But I thought your mother had to choose a wife for you from your city." Her shoulders slumped, but then that determined look returned to her eyes. "Do you think it would ever be possible for me to negotiate a contract with your mom? I'd only want to pretend we were trying to get pregnant, obviously, and we could keep extending the contract if that's allowed, but it could be a way of dating." Lily looked at him, embarrassment clear in her features. "I know we've already been over this…

I just thought...after last night, maybe you'd thought of a different solution?" She lifted her brows at him hopefully.

"What if I told you we could be together forever, as mates?" he said hesitantly, tracking every expression that crossed Lily's face.

Her brows shot up momentarily, then drew together. Her expression turned distant as she thought, muttering "mates" under her breath.

Verakko could heart his heart pumping in his ears as he waited with bated breath for her reply.

"Uh..." She bit her lower lip. "A week ago, I would've said you were crazy, but..." She nodded uncertainly, tipping her head from side to side. "Maybe if we could date a while first."

Fuck. "There's something I need to tell you, Lily."

She narrowed her eyes at him. "What?"

"I lied before, about what my eyes changing means." She remained silent, so he reluctantly continued. "When a Clecanian's eyes change, it means they've recognized a potential mate."

"It doesn't have to do with your health?" She shook her head in confusion. "Then why did you tell me it did?"

"Well, at the time, I didn't want to scare you away. You were already so wary of me."

"Scare me off?" Lily studied him and crossed her arms over her chest, her confused expression becoming more suspicious by the second. "Verakko, tell me whatever it is you're trying to say. I'm not following. You think I'm your mate?

What does that mean? I thought it meant married for life. But we aren't married, so how could we be mated?"

"When a Clecanian recognizes a potential mate, *potentially* the one person in the universe meant for them, their eyes will change," he explained, trying to mentally force her to understand what they were to each other. "Then later on, when they've recognized them fully, marks appear on their hands."

"One person in the universe…?" Lily blinked at him, then her lips parted. "*Soul*-mate." She said the words calmly, but her eyes were alight with some unknown emotion. "You think I could be your *soulmate* because your eyes turned black?"

He let out an exasperated breath. "I felt you were my mate from the first day, but I was so confused, because my eyes hadn't changed."

"But you made me think you couldn't be with me for some reason. If you thought I could possibly be your mate, why wouldn't you just tell me?"

His muscles tensed at the accusation in her tone, and he began pacing. "At first, I didn't tell you because I didn't think it mattered. You didn't like me very much and I didn't recognize you, so I decided I must've been imagining the pull I felt toward you. But then things between us changed."

Verakko's gaze darted around wildly. He wanted her to understand the chaos that had been brewing in his mind. His reasons for keeping all this from her had seemed sensible at the time, but now, saying them out loud, he knew what they'd all been. Cowardly excuses. He hadn't told her because he hadn't wanted her to know about his engagement and treat him differently. That was the truth of it.

"I thought that maybe if my marks showed up and I knew you were my mate, everything would resolve itself, and my contract would've never mattered. But then they didn't show up, yet my feelings for you only got stronger, and—"

She held up a hand. "Wait, what?" She licked her lips, and her chest started to rise and fall more quickly. She scrunched her lids closed in thought and shook her head. "You...you mean you're married?" Her eyes flashed open at the last word, and Verakko recoiled at the anger flaring in their depths.

His skin broke out in a rare cold sweat. "No. Not married. Betrothed. But," he added quickly as her breathing started to become more labored, "that contract will be void as soon as I announce that I've recognized you."

Despite the scorching heat of the desert, ice sluiced down his back as he waited for her reaction.

Lily paced, eyes wide with furious disbelief. "This whole time? You've been lying to me this whole time?"

"I never technically lied..." Verakko's words died in his mouth at the glare she suddenly leveled on him.

"Technically?" Lily spat. "*Technically!* You've let me go on believing I wasn't good enough to be with you."

"I never said that. You—" Verakko tried to reach out to her. She all but leapt away. Was that what she had in her mind? That they couldn't be together because of some fault on her part? Verakko flushed with shame.

"You may not have said it, but that's the conclusion I came to based on what you did and *didn't* tell me! You said your mom, *the Queen*, would negotiate your marriage. You said I wasn't an option for you and you can't date. What else was I supposed to think? And this whole time you've been cheating on your girlfriend?" Lily yelled and began pacing again. Her arms whipped around wildly as she spoke. Her brows raised in brief surprise as though a thought had just occurred to her. She turned to him, seething. "You made me a part of it. Last night... I never would have... Why didn't you just tell me?"

Verakko searched for an explanation, unsure how to make her understand that nothing but the fact that they were mated mattered anymore, but came up empty. He studied her face and winced. She was furious, spitting mad, but deep in her gaze he could see the hurt. It hadn't registered in her at first, her initial reaction of anger overpowering, but the pain from his betrayal was rising now and settling itself alongside her anger.

"I've only met Ziritha a few times. That contract doesn't matter anymore," he pushed desperately. How to make her understand?

She paused her pacing and took a few steps away from him, a stray tear running down her cheek and scalding his insides. "Okay, tell me this. What if your eyes hadn't changed? What would've happened then?"

"I..." Verakko snapped his mouth shut, clenching his jaw. Wasn't that the problem he'd been working through for the past three days? Up until learning about his eyes changing, he hadn't known what he was going to do.

Lily nodded, her chin trembling. "That's what I thought. You would've married her, wouldn't you? When would you have told me the truth, huh? When we walked into the city? Right before your actual wedding? Would you have strung me along until the last possible second to give yourself time to recognize me?" She shook her head and backed away from him down the side of the dune. "I know one thing. If that's what soulmates on this planet do, I don't want one."

She was distancing herself from him both physically and mentally. He could see the emotion written plainly on her face vanish. Verakko cracked; he was losing her. "I didn't know what else to do, mivassi!" he shouted, gripping his head with both hands.

"That name!" Fury flared to life on her face again. Her steps became clumsy as she backed away from him more quickly, heading down the opposite side of the dune. He followed. "Because you're engaged! I'm the alternative."

Lily stumbled, and Verakko's eyes shot down to her feet. Cold terror sliced through him at the sight of rippling ground. He raised his hands. "Lily, stay still, you're—"

"No! You..." A large purple bulb rose behind her, its thick stem slithering out of the sand and its petals swirling open. Another tear leaked out, and she focused on his eyes. "Your eyes. They changed again."

He sprinted toward her as fast as he could, but he'd let her venture too far away. Her eyes widened, and she spun around just as the petals parted to reveal a long, deadly thorn. There was a flash of movement, then Lily was crumpling to her knees.

"No!" Verakko roared, catching her before she hit the ground. "Lily? Lily?" he yelled as he wrenched her away from the hidden curling vine-like base of the vonilace plant, now reaching out from below the sand to drag her under and siphon the moisture from her body.

"What was that?" she breathed, her eyes going in and out of focus.

"Stay awake, Lily," he *swayed* with everything he had. Pain sliced through him as though someone had ripped his heart out of his chest.

Her eyes widened briefly, then grew hazy again.

"Fuck!" Verakko lifted her into his arms and ran. He needed to get her to the city. To the doctor. Lily's lids slid closed, and she grew limp.

"Stay alive. Stay alive. Stay alive," he *swayed* over and over, putting all the force he could muster into the demand.

As though the universe sensed the importance of speed, his pace suddenly increased. His feet carried him across the desert faster than he'd ever gone before. Without stopping, he peered down at his hands and saw his marks. Bright blue and taunting.

16

"Just a little farther."

Broken words and phrases clanged through her head, trying to settle themselves. Lily attempted to think past the fire burning its way through her veins. Verakko? Was that his voice?

"Stay alive, mivassi."

Am I dying? She wanted to cry and sweat the burning sensation out of her veins, but there was nothing left. Every part of her felt shriveled and weathered. A bitter taste lingered on her tongue, and acid burned in her throat.

"I need you here with me, Lily. I don't want to be anywhere you aren't."

I'm here.

Stabbing waves of nausea sliced through her belly. Then it all faded to black.

***

"Help her!" A bellow pounded against her ear drums and cut into the soft parts of her brain.

Muffled conversation surfaced around her, but she couldn't make out much of it. The blistering heat inside had dulled and left her insides brittle. With each breath, it felt like another rib snapped in two until she didn't want to breathe anymore.

"Stay alive." The command rang through her mind again, and she held on to it.

Something stabbed into her neck, and she screamed in agony. On the verge of consciousness again, she tried to open her mouth to plead for it to stop but only tasted blood.

***

Cold. It was so cold here. Her whole body shuddered, violent tremors jostling her aching bones. She opened her eyes, but it was like looking through amber. Everything was distorted and tinted an awful orange.

She reached out her hands, pushing past the flare of pain and unrelenting nausea, and felt a cold, solid surface a few inches to her right. She reached to the left and found another surface.

"Verakko," she tried to call, but it came out as little more than a rasp.

She reached above her and found she was encased on all sides. Her heart began to pound faster and with each beat, shards of glass cut at her insides. Panic took over, and she thrashed through the pain. *I'm trapped. Is this a coffin? Why can't I see?*

Burning sobs tore up her throat. The tears building in her eyes felt like acid. Her breathing came in short gasps. *Not enough air!*

"Verakko!" she screamed as loudly as she could and slammed her hands on the coffin.

A thunderous banging sounded from all around her, along with the groan of metal and the tinkling of shattering glass. He was coming for her, she knew it.

A cool mist gathered around her suddenly, and her limbs fell limp.

17

〜

"I can't leave!" Verakko shouted, stabbing his fingers through his hair. He stared at Lily, lying peacefully in the medbay bed.

"You need to go speak with the Queen. You have marks! She needs to be notified," Desy countered. "She's stable. I'm only keeping her under for a little while longer to ensure her blood has been fully cleansed."

He stepped toward the door, but a knot twisted in his gut, halting him. "I can't reveal them to my mother, Desy. She'll force Lily to stay with me."

Desy, the doctor assigned to work in his building, scanned the room with wide eyes as though searching for someone who'd talk sensibly. "As well she should! This human is your mate. The whole city should be alerted. Don't you understand how momentous this is?"

Verakko barked out a laugh and felt a muscle in his eye twitch. "Obviously I do! I want to carry her through the streets and tell everyone who'll listen that she's my mate, but it isn't that simple." Verakko rubbed a hand over his neck again and stared at Lily. "You didn't see the way she looked at me. She isn't ready to be mated. Humans don't feel the bond the way we do. I'm not sure they feel it at all. To her, I'm just a male. One who kept things from her." He studied the blue marks crisscrossing over his wrists and hands. "She doesn't understand the significance of these, and if my mother forces her to remain with me before I have time to ease her into the idea, she'll resent me."

Desy crossed his arms over his chest. "And what if she never wants to be your mate? What will you do then?"

Verakko's throat worked past the painful lump forming. *What will I do?* He didn't know. "I won't force her to be with me. It wouldn't be right." He said the words without conviction, a hiss in his mind telling him he wasn't selfless enough or strong enough to ever let her go.

"Oh really? What then? Live your life without your mate? You'll grow more and more ill. You won't ever be able to be with anyone else. No children. No marriages." He stepped toward Verakko and gripped his shoulders. "Your mind will rot, Verakko. It's unnatural. I can't think of any instance in recorded history where a mated pair willingly remained apart for more than a few years. Not while both of them lived. It can't be done. There will come a point where you won't be able to stay away."

"Maybe not," Verakko argued, though he knew Desy's words were true. He could feel the intensity of the pull even now. "The fact is, we aren't a mated pair. I'm mated; she isn't. Maybe the effects won't be so bad for me because of that."

Desy stared into Verakko's resolute gaze for a long time before his hands dropped, and he let out a huff of frustration. "Fine. But you still need to go see her. You need to tell your mother…something. You know how much the people love Ziritha. If you and Lily are seen together in a way that appears at all improper, they'll take it as an offense against their future queen. You'll be reported for breach of contract, and then you'll be forced to reveal your marks to avoid punishment."

"No," Verakko countered. "I'd take the punishment instead." When Desy only shook his head in disbelief, Verakko held out his hands. "Do you have any paint?"

Grumbling, Desy crossed to a high compartment on his wall. He stopped in front of Verakko, holding an ancient-looking bottle of hand paint. "I'll keep your marks a secret for now. Even though it goes against everything I believe. But I can't keep her existence secret. As a new citizen, I'm required to report her existence to the Queen."

"I'll go speak with her now and ask to be assigned as Lily's guardian." Verakko inhaled deeply. "At least that will allow her to stay with me until I can convince her to accept the bond."

Desy painted Verakko's hands, the thick substance melding to his skin and changing color until it was indiscernible from his own complexion. "I'm somehow both envious of you and glad I'm not in your position."

Verakko could only muster an insincere half grin. He shuffled to the door after his paint had dried, shooting furtive glances over his shoulder at Lily. Before leaving, he said, "Don't wake her up before I get back unless you have to. I don't want her thinking I left her with a stranger."

Desy sank into the chair near his desk and waved him away.

Only a few steps from the medbay, Verakko froze, his feet unwilling to carry him any farther. He ground his teeth and forced his body to move forward.

Once outside the tower, he climbed into a cruiser, directing it toward the palace, and rehearsed what he was going to say. He'd spoken to the Queen of Tremanta once while Lily was being healed by Desy, and now knew that his mother was aware of the humans but had decided to wait to announce their existence to her people. He didn't know why, though. The Tremantian Queen had also acknowledged that his mother didn't feel the humans should be granted the same right to decline their mate if they were recognized. That meant if she learned about his marks, or even that his eyes had changed in recognition, she would force Lily to stay with him.

Verakko groaned and fidgeted in his seat. Asking to be assigned as her guardian, the citizen who'd slowly introduce her to the culture and customs of this world, would be a stretch. A male on the verge of his marriage wouldn't have time to be anyone's guardian. How could he convince his mother to allow it? If Ziritha found out about his request, she may even take offense that he'd put another female's needs above his own. If she saw it as a breach of contract, not even his mother could stop him from being shipped off-world.

He dropped his head into his hands and let out a bellow, injecting all his frustration into it.

The cruiser door slid open, revealing the colossal staircase leading up to the palace entry. He'd always hated climbing these stairs as a boy, never failing to become winded by the time he reached the top. All the stairways in Tremanta moved, carrying their passengers to their destination. Even the spiral stairways in the antiquated bunker Lily had been held in were mechanical. But not the Mithrandirian palace.

Verakko's mood soured further as he climbed the steps, baking in the sun. No, in his hometown, they wanted a grand entrance that tired its visitors so when they finally arrived at the top, they had to pause for a breath. Their strength symbolically leeching into the queen's domain to remind them of who was truly powerful here.

Two guards, armed with razor-sharp shade spears and magnetic shackles, guided him out to a balcony and instructed him to wait.

Verakko stood on under a canopy and stared into the distance at the crystal mountains to the west. The glimmering crags of crystal the mountains were known for glittered in the setting sun. He tipped his head, a sign of respect for them and for his father, now buried at the base of the mountain alongside his ancestors. He rarely thought of his father anymore, but when he did, it always made him smile.

His mother had been elected Queen when he was very young, but he still had memories of him and his father visiting her here. Verakko would always marvel at how powerful and stoic she appeared, towering over him in her glittering frocks. But his father would chuckle and comment on how nervous she'd seemed.

Verakko had never understood it, but his father had always had a way of reading her like no one else could. And as he'd grown older, Verakko had come to realize that she'd let him. Even though they hadn't been married for years, they had still shared a bond. He tried to think about how his father had acted with her. The type of words he'd used to get her to agree to let Verakko focus on technology instead of politics. What gifts he'd brought her to convince her Verakko didn't need to be monitored after his accidental fall from the vacant new city building. He couldn't recall anything specific.

Then how had he persuaded her so often? Verakko thought about Lily and realized what it must've been. They'd cared for each other in their own way. Maybe his mother wasn't as heartless as he thought, after all.

"Verakko," a light voice called from behind him.

He turned, and his blood ran cold. Ziritha glided toward him, a polite smile curling her lips. "Ziritha," he choked out.

"Ziri will be just fine. We're about to be married, after all."

Verakko licked a fang and wondered if it would be wise to explain why he was there before speaking with his mother. She was wearing a dazzling dress of pale pink that complemented her deep navy complexion beautifully. A gauzy bright peach fabric mokti draped over her throat and down her shoulders, morphing into the sleeves of her dress.

"Your mother should be along shortly. She asked me to greet you while she finishes her meeting." Ziritha looked him up and down with a raised brow. "I was going to say how happy I am that you're home and well, but you look rather ill. Is everything alright?"

Did Ziritha know about the humans as well? Verakko studied her silently. His mother did trust her. Would she have told her? "I've had a difficult few days," he hedged.

The delicate clicking of shoes made them both turn.

"Son," said his mother from the doorway, appearing as regal and reserved as always. Her deep teal skin, so like his own, was covered completely by a chin-to-toe vibrant purple cape. Verakko's dread deepened. His father had always claimed he could asses her mood based on her clothing. Shapeless capes, no matter how fine the embroidery and ornamentation, meant she was struggling with something.

"Mother." He dipped his head.

"I'm very glad you're alright. After the Queen of Tremanta notified me of your abduction, I was unsettled." She said the words, but her expression revealed no evidence of any emotion of the sort.

No use dragging this out longer than necessary. "I need to speak with you privately, Mother," Verakko said, shooting an apologetic glance toward Ziritha, who appeared to take no offense.

"Anything you need to discuss, you may do so in front of Ziritha," said the Queen with a lift of her chin.

Arguing wouldn't help his case, but if he was to have any success, he'd need to get his mother alone. "It's a sensitive topic, and I'd feel more comfortable speaking to you privately about certain information I've been entrusted to keep confidential."

"Are you referring to the human in your care?" Ziritha interjected.

Verakko froze, and all the blood seemed to rush from his face. He turned to Ziritha, eyes wide. *Had it been Desy?*

"No need to look so upset, son. I was alerted as soon as her doctor began administering care. I programmed an alert based on the Tremantian Queen's suggestion. The humans have been through so much already. But I can understand why you felt the need to keep her out of sight until speaking with me. I'll have her transported here as soon as she awakens." Ziritha nodded along as his mother spoke. "She can stay here until she settles in and finds a husband. You needn't be responsible for her any longer."

"A husband or a mate! This is all so exciting." Ziritha beamed. "A new race of Clecanians who can be mated and conceive children. This may change our whole world. Your mother and I have been discussing the repercussions since we first learned of their existence, and now one of them is here, a Swadaeth citizen. Remarkable." Ziritha tipped her head and added, with a stern look, "The way they were obtained is despicable, to be sure, but I'm confident we can provide a good life for her and convince her to stay after her one-year transition period is up. Unless, of course, she meets her mate." She grinned.

Verakko swallowed and forced a mask of calm back onto his features. His mother hadn't talked to Desy personally. She still didn't know about his marks, or this would have been a very different conversation. Verakko clasped his hands behind his back and fidgeted. His paint was still in place, but the instinct to hide his marks from view remained.

He studied Ziritha with renewed curiosity. He'd only met her a handful of times before, and this conversation was the most he'd ever spoken to her. She had a lightness to her that surprised him. When his mother had selected Ziritha as her protégé, he'd assumed she'd be distant and aloof just like his mother was. Their personalities couldn't be more dissimilar.

"That is very kind of you," Verakko began, choosing his words carefully, "but I'd like to continue to watch over her myself, as her guardian."

"Her guardian? But you won't have time. You need to take these few weeks to prepare for your marriage, do you not?"

Verakko stared and tried to mentally explain to his mother that this conversation would best be had without his betrothed present.

The Queen's eyes bore into his, and he feared she might just be able to read his thoughts. She lifted a brow, as though understanding something distasteful. His mother aimed her unblinking gaze at Ziritha, and they seemed to have a silent conversation all their own.

To his surprise, the first to speak was Ziritha. "Have you recognized her, then?"

Verakko faced her, readying to stifle a wince at the emotion he'd surely see. Outrage or offense or possibly disgust. But all he could see was curiosity. He swallowed. "No." Gaze darting between the two powerful females who held his future in their hands, he quickly added, "But I believe I will if I had a bit of time where we aren't struggling to survive."

He needed to win back Lily's trust and convince her they were meant to be together. And for that, he needed time.

"You're under contract, Verakko," his mother said, a chilling severity ringing in her voice. "Are you asking to break it?"

"No," he lied. "I'm asking to delay it. I don't know how much you're aware of, but humans don't recognize mates, and many believe their isolated evolution has affected their ability to be recognized in a timely manner. It took Theo months for his marks to appear."

"Yes, but from the reports I've received, he recognized her as a potential mate long before then. He himself admits it may have happened during the Testing, though there's no way to be sure," his mother argued reasonably.

Verakko ground his teeth. He'd hoped she hadn't learned that yet.

"If you haven't recognized her as a potential mate by now, then how is it fair of me to give you this advantage? You don't even have enough evidence to claim her as a mivassi. Why should I take the chance of finding a mate away from my other citizens who may very well recognize her immediately?"

"I feel she's mine," Verakko said numbly, his instincts screaming to claim her and end this once and for all.

Ziritha and the Queen frowned at each other silently.

Verakko's heart thudded in his chest. His mother would never allow something like this. What had he been thinking? He should return at once, steal Lily away, and hope his mother still cared about him enough to not send her guards after them.

He thought about his father again and wondered. He'd always told Verakko his mother wasn't as hard as she presented herself to be, but was that true?

"Mother," Verakko said, letting his desperation and ache show on his face. The Queen held his stare, and he could've sworn he'd seen the ghost of worry in her eyes at his tone. "I know this in my soul."

She studied him for what seemed like forever, her expression unreadable. "Our world will be changing very soon. Wars may start. Our people will call for the humans to be gathered. Our laws and our traditions are sacred, Verakko. And they need to remain so. I cannot break them for anyone."

Nausea roiled in his stomach, and he had to quell the answering snarl that rose in his throat. He shot his gaze to the ground. *We have to leave.*

His mother continued, raising her voice above what must be his obvious anger. "In three days, I'll be announcing the existence of the humans and their unique traits to our people. If you can make your eyes change or your marks appear before then, you will have legal cause to break your contract."

Verakko's eyes shot up, not trusting his own ears. His gaze darted between the two females before him, and he saw a gentle smile curving Ziritha's lips.

"Hear me, son." Verakko blinked as his mother's *sway* demanded entry. He looked at her, breath caught in his throat. "I cannot make you her guardian, so in public, you'll treat her as a betrothed male would any female who wasn't his future wife. If it's reported to me that you're in violation of the exclusivity clause in your contract, I'll have no choice but to send you off-world. Do you hear me? I will not have the public's respect for Ziritha or myself affected because of this, not now when we need their support and loyalty more than ever."

Verakko grinned, nodding. "I understand. Thank you. Thank you both."

"And if you don't recognize her—"

"I'll honor the terms of our contract," Verakko finished for her.

His mother peered at him for a moment longer. Before spinning and walking away, she said, "Return in three days."

When she was out of sight, Verakko glanced nervously at Ziritha.

"I hope you know what you're doing." She reached out and gripped his shoulder. "I'd hate to see you throw your future away on a female who may not deserve you."

"I think it's more likely I don't deserve her." Verakko's brows furrowed. "I'm sorry, Ziritha. I see now I don't deserve you, either. You should be angry with me. I've dishonored you, yet you seem so willing to violate our laws to help me."

"It's Ziri." Ziritha smiled and gave a delicate shrug. "What can I say? If you have even the slightest chance to find a real mate, I'm not going to take that away from you." She leaned in close and whispered seriously, "Don't mess it up."

Ziritha strode away through the same door his mother had.

Verakko's smile drooped lower and lower until it wasn't a smile at all. Three days?

Fuck, I'm gonna mess it up.

18

∽

L ily was floating. No, that didn't make sense. Her head was floating? She laughed. Yeah, that was it. Her head was cloudy, lighter than air.

"She's waking up," a melodic voice said from near her elbow.

Lily stretched, reveling in the satisfying zing of pleasure that coursed through her with the movement. Suddenly, hands were gripping the sides of her face.

"Lily, are you alright? Talk to me."

A solid train of thought was hard to hold on to at the moment, but she noticed the *sway* tickling her senses and pushed it away. "Stop that," she slurred, swiping clumsily at the hands holding her cheeks. "Verakkoooo's the only one can do that." She giggled as her own droopy voice played in her ears. "The. Only. One. Who. Can. Do. That," she amended, pausing on each word to ensure she had in fact included them all this time.

"Oh, thank the Goddess." The hands moved from around her cheeks and gently glided over her forehead. "It's me, love. It's Verakko. I'm here. Will you look at me?"

"Verakko!" she said excitedly, forcing her eyes open.

Verakko's face, a paler shade of teal than she'd ever seen it, loomed above her.

"Hey!" she exclaimed, grinning like a fool. Whatever drugs they'd given her were most certainly working. Lily tilted her head, examining her alien's beautiful worried face, and pouted. "I never wanna go outside again."

A toothy grin transformed his features. "Then we won't."

Memories returned to her slowly, and the haze began to lift. "Wait a minute," Lily said, furrowing her brows. "I'm supposed to be mad at you." Her mind was still feeling a little goofy, but the argument they'd gotten into before she'd been attacked by that flower thing replayed in her ears.

Verakko's grin faded, and he licked his lips.

Lily shook her head, trying to clear the fog a little faster. She pushed at his hands and struggled to sit up. "What happened?" She scanned the room and found another man settled in a corner glowering in Verakko's direction.

"You were stung by a vonilace," Verakko choked out.

Lily stared around the small white room. A metal object that may have once been a couch or maybe a cot lay mangled in a corner. A large glass tube along a wall caught her attention, and she wordlessly pointed at it. A coffin—she remembered being in a coffin.

She looked back at Verakko. The lightness had worn off, and now her mind was too full. Fear and anger, hurt and betrayal all roared to the forefront until the tight lump in her throat choked her. He'd lied to her. He was getting married.

Verakko reached for her, but she pulled away. Her eyes landed on the man in the corner again, and she clamped her mouth shut. They really needed to finish this argument in private.

He let out a small, pained exhalation as if someone had punched him in the stomach.

"Is there somewhere we can go?" she whispered.

"Yes. I wanted to be here when you woke up, but I need to go for a few minutes to get you some clothes before we can leave. Then I can take you somewhere else. You'll be safe in the medbay with Desy until I get back, I promise."

A medbay. Was that where she was? Her fingers itched to reach out and beg him not to leave her alone, but the anger and betrayal she was still feeling pushed her prideful side to remain still. "Fine," she grumbled, not meeting his eyes. "Wait!" she blurted, suddenly alert. "Alex. We need to find help for Alex." Lily flung her blanket off and made to stand, but Verakko pushed her back down.

"I already sent a team," he assured. "It was the first thing I did after I got you here." He peered over to the man in the corner, who returned the glance with a raised brow. "I'll tell you more about it later, okay?"

Lily nodded, momentary relief clouding her thoughts. She peered at the comforting hand still resting on her shoulder and shrugged it off. Verakko winced, lingering. After a long moment of charged silence, he stomped away.

"Don't let her go anywhere," he hissed at the annoyed-looking man in the corner.

The man frowned and quickly slid a forefinger and thumb up the point of his ear in a gesture Lily had never seen before, but somehow still looked rude. The equivalent of a middle finger, perhaps?

Verakko pressed his hand to the surface of the knobless door, and it whizzed open. He remained still for a moment, shoulders bunched and fists clenched, but then finally walked through without looking at her again. A curious pain tugged in her chest as the door slid closed behind him. Not a familiar ache of longing but a real, physical tug, as if something inside her was urging her to follow him.

After he was gone, Lily studied her doctor-turned-jailor—at least she assumed he was a doctor. His clothes were monochromatic and simple in a way that made her think it wasn't the style, but a uniform of sorts. His close-cropped grass-green hair and green skin, a darker forest green than Verakko's teal coloring, told her he was Swadaeth as well.

"Hello," she began tentatively. "Can you tell me what happened to me?"

The man assessed her in silence. When his gaze paused at her neck, she had to stop herself from pulling at the collar of her pale yellow, shapeless gown. "As he said—" he nodded toward the closed door, "—you were stung by a vonilace."

"And what exactly is a vonilace?" Lily asked, trying to keep the annoyance from her voice.

The man stood and began walking around the room, cleaning up spilled bottles and askew pieces of cabinetry. "Vonilace is a type of vining plant that hides under the sand in the Dakuun Desert. It spreads below the surface and produces one bulb at a time. If a stray creature happens to walk too close, the bulb will rise and inject the animal, or in your case, *human*." He said the word slowly, like it was odd to him. "The toxin paralyzes then poisons its victim while the buried vines pull its immobilized prey under the sand."

Lily's gut churned anew.

Unaware of the effect he was having on her, the doctor continued, "Then, small suckers along the vine will latch on to the animal and drain all the moisture from its body. Quite a fascinating plant, in fact."

A small grunt of agreement was all she could muster. A killer plant had almost drained her dry.

The doctor lifted a corner of the crumpled metal cot with a finger and made a sound of annoyance. "Your..." He dropped the cot with a clang and eyed her. "I mean, Verakko, dragged you away and carried you here just in time. Most would've died within minutes." His look of indifference suddenly changed to one of curiosity. "It must be something to do with your race. Tell me, are you immune to many toxins?"

Lily raised her brows, not sure how to answer. "I haven't tried many."

The doctor gave her a disappointed look, then finished righting his office and returned to his chair. "Well, you're very lucky. Verakko told me you vomited and convulsed the whole time he ran."

Lily's stomach gave a flutter, and she ignored it. "He ran the whole way?" He'd saved her life? Had she even thanked him?

"He did." The doctor's scowl returned. "Ran all the way to my door and demanded I heal you, then destroyed my office while I did as he asked."

"Thank you for helping me, and I'm sorry about your office." Lily didn't know what else to say. Part of her clung to the image of Verakko as her hero, running through the scorching desert and passionately crumpling metal in his worry for her. But the other part continued to remind her she was out of her depth. He'd lied repeatedly, and she couldn't help but feel he'd allowed her to be ignorant of other important things, as well.

How much did she really know about these people and this city? How much of what he'd told her could she even trust?

The doctor released a sigh. "I'll survive. I guess I shouldn't be surprised." He shrugged and lifted the corner of his mouth. "I mean if you really are...someone he cares for, I can see why he'd be upset."

Lily clenched her jaw and tried to rise from the bed. Vague memories of him whispering to her while pain sliced through her body came to her. Echoed words she thought she'd imagined replayed in her mind, and she pushed them away. "What's your name again? Desy?" she asked, wobbling on her feet but feeling no noticeable areas of pain.

"Yes."

"It's nice to meet you, Desy. I'm Lily. Mind if I ask you a few questions?"

***

"This isn't working. Please take it off."

Lily sighed and lifted the bulky helmet off her head.

"I need to go for a few minutes," my ass. For the last hour, Desy had been running test after test for something he referred to as an off-worlder health clearance. She'd learned she had an allergy to something called Ripsli and that besides being understandably underweight, she was perfectly healthy.

After many reassurances, annoyed arguing, and a failed *sway*, which she'd promptly scolded him for, Desy had convinced her to get back into the glass tube. Once in, he'd given her the elixir. Lily's heart had clenched, recalling Verakko's story of his father and how he'd refused the treatment.

Whatever it was, the elixir had certainly worked to revitalize her. For a moment, she'd felt like she was at her physical peak. Toned, tight skin, clear mind, and not an ache or pain to be found. The immediate urge to tell Verakko about her renewed vitality had hit her, then her mood had darkened once again.

A scan meant to identify her taste and scent preferences had been next, but every time an image or scent flashed through the large helmet, Desy would grunt and remind her to keep her thoughts clear and neutral.

Image of a pink fruit. *Verakko.* Smell of cooking meat. *Hougap with Verakko.* Bright, minty scent. *Lying near a campfire wrapped in Verakko's arms.* An unfamiliar image of a group of orbs that could've been made of some type of jelly hadn't even distracted her. Though she'd never seen or tasted the food before, her mind immediately wondered if Verakko enjoyed them.

"I'm sorry," she said, handing the helmet to Desy and peering at the floor gloomily.

"We can try again another time," he said, giving her a rare sympathetic look. "For the time being, you'll just have to taste it all and find out what you like in a more natural, time-consuming way."

"Will do, doc. Now tell me more about Ziritha."

Desy groaned and replaced the helmet in a hidden compartment positioned low on the far wall. "I've told you, it's not my place."

Lily clenched her jaw. Finally she had someone else to get her information from, yet he refused to answer her questions. His eyes kept darting whenever she asked anything, making her believe he was choosing to withhold information for some reason. "Then tell me about how someone gets out of a contract."

"They don't," he said flatly. His brows drew together. "Unless…"

Lily held her breath.

"They don't," he repeated more firmly.

"Unless what?" she wanted to shout, but kept her tone even.

"Are you sure you don't want me to take that antiquated device out?" Desy asked while pretending to straighten an impeccably organized cart.

"For the last time, no," Lily snapped. Ever since noticing her IUD during a scan, he'd been urging her to let him remove it. But when she'd asked about what replacement would work with human anatomy and what the side effects of their birth control might be, he couldn't give her an answer. Just because everyone else on this planet wanted to get pregnant didn't mean she wanted to.

He grunted and mumbled to himself about how it was unfair the Tremantians were keeping the humans to themselves and how he wasn't able to properly do his job without adequate data.

The door suddenly whizzed open, and Lily had to quell the warmth that spread through her chest at the sight of Verakko. She forced herself to remember their argument, and the answering spike of hollow pain in her gut helped to keep her emotions in check.

In. Out.

His bright-green gaze remained glued to hers. "I'm sorry it took so long," he said, ignoring Desy completely. He held up a long bag, then draped it over a chair.

Lily bit her lip, her body and mind in a sort of heightened emotional stasis, like a shaken bottle of soda waiting to explode. Everything she'd been feeling from before being stung was still there. Her shoulders seemed permanently tensed. Her breaths wouldn't remain even without constant focus, and the urge to either smack Verakko or kiss him still itched.

"Leave, Desy," Verakko hissed, still not looking in the doctor's direction.

Annoyance flaring, Lily planted her hands on her hips and narrowed her eyes at Verakko. "Both of you leave." She shot an apologetic glance at Desy. "Please. I'm capable of changing by myself." She lowered her voice and addressed Verakko in an admonishing tone. "Are you always so rude to people who help you?"

"Yes," Desy grumbled as he left the room.

A muscle twitched in Verakko's jaw.

"Not here," Lily said quietly when it looked like he'd argue. She didn't want to fight here. She wanted to get to a quiet private area and then...she didn't know.

A clear look of hurt and frustration flashed over his features, but he nodded and retreated through the door yet again.

19

Lily opened the oddly warm garment bag and let out an annoyed sigh at the gorgeous frock Verakko had picked for her. *Of course he has great taste. Why am I not surprised?*

Bright orange fabric the color of a sunset and rich maroon fabric slid through her hands. Lily studied it, enchanted and perplexed. The style of the beautiful garment was so odd that she couldn't figure out how exactly she was supposed to wear it.

After a few minutes of studying and toying with the golden clasps placed randomly throughout the garment, Lily attempted to slide into what she now believed to be a jumpsuit. The whole outfit began on her upper arms, baring her shoulders. The orange fabric shimmered and bunched behind her back, forming a sort of cape, while the maroon portions dipped low between her breasts and cinched at her waist. Beautiful curling patterns, the same color as the orange of her odd cape, twisted along the bodice.

Slits ran all the way from the hem of the pants to the cinch at her waist, revealing a good deal of leg and hip and leaving her feeling exposed. If it wasn't for the thin gold chains holding the slits together just above her knees, she'd worry the fabric would billow and give anyone watching a show.

Although it wasn't the most comfortable or modest thing she'd ever worn, Lily had a small, vain idea that she looked great in it. She took a few steps around the room, searching for a mirror, and cursed, halting. It was incredibly difficult to walk, the cinched cape restricting her movements and making her believe she'd tear something at any moment.

Lily stared hard at the door. Should she take the whole frock off and try again or suck it up and ask Verakko for help? After spending a few petulant moments arguing with herself, she carefully padded to the door and knocked twice.

As if he'd been waiting only a breath away, the door whizzed open. Verakko allowed his gaze to roam over her body hungrily. *Dammit,* Lily thought as her cheeks and chest grew hot.

It appeared he'd taken the downtime to change as well. His iridescent black shirt was short-sleeved and dipped low on his broad chest. It was held together in the front by thick leather laces. Loose black pants sat low on his hips and were stuffed into the tops of his well-worn boots. Lily hated how incredible he looked.

His heated gaze paused at her waist and was replaced with a look of confusion, confirming she had in fact put her outfit on incorrectly.

"I've never worn anything like this," she said defensively, pursing her lips.

Verakko gave her a lopsided grin, and she stifled a curse. God, she loved that smile.

He walked toward her, and Lily forced herself to remain still and impassive. It became harder and harder to do, though, as Verakko continued moving closer. He stopped right in front of her, only a few inches away. Heart thrumming furiously in her chest, she focused her eyes on the floor.

Although she couldn't bring herself to meet his eyes, she could feel his insistent gaze boring into her. Then, without a word, he slid his hands around her waist. Her breath caught at the sensation of his palms on her back, and she had to stop herself from ardently wishing he'd pull her in close. He fiddled with something as she held her arms out stiffly.

He's just a guy. You met him a week ago. He's a liar. Burning cedar hit her senses, and she barely contained a sigh.

A small click sounded, and suddenly the restrictive tightness of the jumpsuit lessened. Lily peered down and saw Verakko's hands emerge from behind her, holding two sides of a gold clasp attached to either side of her cape. He pulled the clasp under her elbows and locked it around her waist. Rather than trailing down her back as it did before, the orange fabric now draped over the side of her body and, to her relief, partially shielded the bare skin of her thighs.

Verakko remained in place, one hand still resting at her waist. She refused to look up at him. "Thank you," she said, stepping away. He let her.

"I brought you a mokti too," Verakko said, retrieving a small box from the chair.

"A what?"

"It's an accessory that many females wear. It covers your neck."

"Why?" Lily eyed the small golden item in his hand and waited breathlessly as he stepped behind her.

"Fashion, I suppose. Lift your hair." Lily piled her hair on her head and waited. The heat from Verakko's body seeped into her back, and his breath on her neck made goose-bumps break out over her bare shoulders. "A long time ago, moktis were used to completely cover the neck for modesty's sake, but now they've become more of a fashion statement and highlight the neck rather than hide it."

"Is that why Desy kept looking at my neck?" Lily asked, embarrassment flaring. "Do I look naked or something with-out a mokti on?"

A low growl tore from Verakko, but he quickly stifled it. "Most females choose to wear one, but some don't. Either way, he shouldn't have been looking." He wrapped some-thing large around her neck. The mokti must've been made of metal because when it touched her skin it was cold, and she hopped backward, surprised.

Lily hit Verakko's chest and like lightning, his arms shot down and wrapped around her waist, pulling her to him. A rattling purr immediately started in his chest and vibrated against her back. He dipped his head to her neck and inhaled deeply, squeezing her waist.

Her throat grew tight. She wanted to relax and accept Verakko's touch, but she couldn't. She felt so far away from him yet so close at the same time. Without saying a word, she attempted to step forward, showing him she wanted to be let go.

His purr stuttered out, and he slowly released her. He laid the cool metal over her neck again, and she felt a tug in her hair near the base of her skull as if he'd clipped something there. The mokti was like an over-large choker or a turtleneck of sorts.

Verakko smoothed the metal and let a longer piece drape down her front and between her cleavage. She examined it and found the metal formed small delicate golden flowers that grew progressively smaller as they trailed in between her breasts. The rest of the metal flared out and followed the curve of her shoulders.

She moved away and faced him.

"You look beautiful," Verakko said in a hushed tone.

Mental exhaustion suddenly overtook her. She was still so confused. He'd said his marriage was over because his eyes had changed and she was his mate. But he'd also said that mates stayed together for life. How could he just assume she'd agree to that? Was he so sure she wanted to be with him that she'd simply forget he'd been lying about being engaged this whole time?

"Let's go," he said, motioning to the door.

"Go where?" she asked weakly, following him out of the medbay and into a narrow hallway.

"To my home. You need food and sleep."

Lily's immediate reaction was happiness, her heart fluttering to think he wanted her to stay in his home with him, but she forced herself to ignore it. If they were going to have any shot at all, she needed to start thinking with her head instead of her heart. "No." She forced the words out. "I need you to take me to the government housing you mentioned so I can be on my own for a while. I want you to explain yourself to me on the way, and then I want to spend some time alone to think."

He licked a fang and narrowed his eyes on her. "No," he said simply. He peered down the hallway, then abruptly changed direction.

When she finally hurried after him, she found herself stopped in front of a double-wide metal door. "No? You don't have the right to tell me no, Verakko. I'm going to live wherever I want to live."

Verakko shot her a nervous glance and removed a small black device from his pocket. "There are things I need to explain to you first. I'm taking us on a roundabout route so we can talk without anyone listening."

Lily balled her fists. "Can't take a chance that your *betrothed* will hear about us?"

"She's no longer my betrothed." Verakko grimaced and pulled the two edges of the small square he held apart until a holographic screen flickered to life in the center. Then he placed the screen on the door and typed on it using symbols she'd never seen before.

Her brows shot up in question. "Does she know that? Or are you still *technically* engaged?" He remained silent, giving Lily her answer. "That's what I thought. I don't even know where to start. There are other things you kept from me, aren't there?" Lily ground her teeth and poked Verakko in the shoulder when he didn't answer.

She glared at his back. *How could I have just ignored all my instincts that told me he was keeping something from me?* Lily thought back to her first few days with him in the woods and recalled thinking he'd been explaining around something. How could she have ignored that?

A low pinging sounded, and she tensed. The noise was awfully similar to an alarm, yet Verakko seemed unperturbed. "Are we supposed to be here?"

"No," he said simply. "The alarm's new. Just give me a second."

Lily glanced up and down the pale blue hallway and took an instinctive step closer to Verakko. She realized then that although she was beyond angry with him, she still trusted him to keep her safe. Lily couldn't recall ever trusting anyone else as much as she did Verakko. Maybe that was why his betrayal hurt so deeply.

The pinging stopped, and the doors whizzed apart just as Verakko removed the screen and slid the device closed.

"Let's go," he said, motioning into a small room as wide and deep as the doors themselves.

"Go where?" Lily peered into the dark room, unable to see any outlet.

"It's a service lift. We're going to travel through the storage floors."

Lily tentatively stepped inside, only to have Verakko move in beside her, too close for comfort.

"Ready?" he asked.

Before she could question him, the floor beneath their feet moved, propelling them upward. Lily squeaked and gripped Verakko's hand without thinking. The rattling sound of a purr and a squeeze of his fingers brought her back to the present.

She peered up to find his gaze fixed on her. The hope and warmth in his eyes as he beamed down at her and gently ran his thumb over her hand tore at her chest. She quickly tugged her hand out of his and looked away. "You could've warned me," Lily grumbled, crossing her arms over her chest to prevent herself from reaching out to him again.

The platform stopped, and a new set of doors hissed open to reveal the oddest-looking warehouse she'd ever seen. For one thing, the items stored in the expansive area were on the ceiling instead of the floor. Beds, shelving units, and all manners of furniture were positioned on floating stands hovering near the ceiling.

Lily watched as a short table flew across the room and then disappeared through a dark opening in the ceiling.

"How...?" She was lost for words. All she'd seen of this planet was the inside of a cell in a bunker and the forest. It was only now hitting her that she was on an advanced planet full of wonders she couldn't even begin to imagine. A sudden wave of excitement rolled through her. What did the city really look like? Where was all the furniture going? Were there floors like this in between every floor of the building? When would she be able to explore out in the open?

"Lily," Verakko said gently, rousing her from her transfixed stare. His fingers fidgeted as he spoke. "I went to see my mother while you were unconscious, and she refused my request to be your guardian."

Guardian? Lily pinched the bridge of her nose, not following in the slightest. "You said I'm your mate."

"Yes. You are. But I didn't tell her that. She still thinks I'll be marrying Ziritha in a few weeks."

A frustrated sob built in her throat, and she wanted to stamp her foot in irritation. "Have you changed your mind about me being your mate?"

"No! Never. I just... If my mother learned the truth, she'd force us to be together." Verakko pressed a hand to the small of her back, urging her forward.

"What?" Lily halted in her tracks and stared at him in horror. "And what if I say no?"

"Then," he said slowly, the corners of his eyes crinkled as if he were stifling a wince, "I'll have to marry Ziritha, and you'll be forced to marry someone else."

Lily scanned the room around her, unseeing. "What?" she yelled.

"I'd better start at the beginning. There is a law on this planet," Verakko began.

She tried to listen past the ringing in her ears.

"I didn't mention the law when we met because I didn't want to alarm you," he added quickly, leading her through the gently curving room to a lone door identical to the one they'd emerged from. "The city that comes across a Class 4 being is the one obligated to take care of them and integrate them into society as they see fit. Many cities have decided they'll force their new human citizens to marry, the same way they do with their Clecanian citizens."

Lily tried and failed to form words until she finally latched on to something he'd said in the desert. "You told me Tremanta was giving more rights to humans than other cities. Is this what you meant?"

He nodded.

"But you were leading me here long before that. You knew this would happen? That I'd be forced to get married?"

Verakko urged her forward again, darting nervous glances over his shoulder. "I didn't know for sure that that would be my mother's decision, but I suspected."

Lily shrugged off his hand. "So you decided that instead of explaining things to me, you'd take the chance of me possibly being forced into a marriage by your people?"

"Well..." The guilty look on Verakko's face told her everything she needed to know.

"This is my life. How dare you decide something like that for me!"

Verakko's hand shot out to grip her wrist. "But it doesn't matter anymore because you're my mate."

"Let me go," Lily grated.

When he only stared at her, she lifted her palm to her face, twisting his wrist, then snatched his wrist with her free hand and wrenched it away. Verakko stepped back and circled his wrist, breathing deeply. Lily stomped toward the closed door and waited with crossed arms.

Verakko followed, removing the small square from his pocket again and planting it on the metal doors.

"You only just learned I'm your mate! You were leading me to this city before your eyes changed. You were going to bring me here, knowing I'd likely be forced into marriage. Even after I told you specifically that I didn't want to get married on this planet." Her nostrils flared at the heady scent of cedar wafting from him. "And on top of all that, you were engaged! So you brought me here, thinking I'd be forced into marriage and knowing it would be to some other man! How could you keep that from me?"

"If I had told you, you would've never come with me. I tried to get you to go back to Tremanta that first day, and you refused."

"You *tried*," she scoffed. "Did you *try* by telling me that if I went to any other city but Tremanta, my freedom would be taken away and I'd be forced to marry some stranger? Or did you *try* by simply demanding we go to Tremanta? A city that was an unknown distance away in the opposite direction from Alex?" She placed her hands on her hips and studied his bunched shoulders.

"Would you have gone the other way and abandoned Alex if I had explained it all to you?" he shot back.

Lily ground her jaw, knowing he was right. She would've continued down that river either way.

Verakko leaned down until they were at eye level. "Exactly my point." He returned to his screen and started typing into it again. "What was I supposed to do? Allow you to live in the forest until you eventually died? How much longer do you think you could've survived out there?"

Lily reared back. "That's not the point. You took away my choices. If you had explained this right from the beginning, I might've decided to return to Tremanta with you. Or maybe I would've stayed in the forest. It doesn't matter. Even if every option presented to me was shitty, I had the right to make my own shitty decisions!"

The door whizzed open, and another platform stood waiting. Lily stepped onto it, too focused on Verakko's tight expression to worry about the sudden jolt of upward motion.

"You're right. I should've told you about everything. At the time, my reasoning all made sense. I was just trying to keep you safe."

Lily's argument died in her throat as emotion swelled. She'd trusted Verakko more than she'd ever trusted anyone. She understood why he'd lied about the laws of his city. Even if she didn't agree, she understood that he'd been attempting to keep her safe. Frustrated tears blurred her vision, but she continued to blink them away. She didn't feel safe. She felt exposed and vulnerable and powerless. And the person she thought she could count on to navigate this terrifying new world had kept so much from her. Was her life even her own anymore? Or would these aliens decide everything for her?

The platform stopped again, but the doors didn't immediately open like before. Verakko peered down at his screen, which was displaying an opulently decorated hallway occupied by a thin, bright-blue man and child. They walked slowly, chatting about something she couldn't hear.

When they'd disappeared from view, Verakko covered his lips, miming for her to remain silent. He opened the doors and guided her out. The hallway, like the odd warehouse level, was curved, and circled an incredible sight. A tower of water pouring through the center of the building, just as Verakko had described, visible through a wall of glass.

They reached one of the few doors on their left, and Verakko released her, planting his hand on the surface. Whirring and buzzing sounded, and the door swung open.

As they entered the dark space, small floating balls of light began illuminating near the ceiling, like silver bubbles. The room was large and dominated by a collection of cream-colored pillows and cushioned couches as wide and deep as king-sized beds. Clacking from her right suddenly sounded, making her jump, and she watched in awe as a stairway comprised of glass and glimmering metal dropped from the ceiling. Her eyes followed the stairs to a second story high above.

The home was beautiful and well appointed. The furnishings immaculate. Silver finishes glinted everywhere, and odd pieces of sculpted art were scattered about.

Lily frowned; this house was beautiful, but it didn't feel like Verakko. It was too...perfect. Staged, like a gallery display of the ideal futuristic living room. "I thought you lived in Tremanta. You have a house here too?"

Verakko stared at the floor for a moment, licking a fang, and then leveled a miserable look on her.

"Oh," she choked out as realization hit. "This is for her, isn't it?"

He shrugged. "I purchased the home weeks ago after signing the contract. I had to make sure it was ready in time for..."

"Your wedding," she finished numbly as his voice trailed off. She shook her head. "I really don't think I should stay here. I want to go to the other housing."

He released a deep breath through his nose and stared at her. "I understand you're angry with me, but you aren't ready to be on your own yet, I need to help acclimate you to our city."

"Oh, you mean acclimate me by picking and choosing the information you deem is important and lying about the rest?" Lily reproached with her hands on her hips and her brows raised.

"The city doesn't know about humans yet. You wouldn't even be able to converse with anyone if you needed help because no one has your language uploaded on their translators." He pulled her down the hall and into what she could only assume was a kitchen of some sort, then strode around the room, pulling various odd foods and tools from different compartments.

"And what about your fiancée?" she shot at him. "How do you think she'll feel when she finds another woman in *her* house? I know you may not be connected romantically, but she's obviously put a lot of work into decorating this place, only to have me come and use it all first."

Gripping a deep purple bottle, he paused and said, "I told you. In my mind, she's no longer my betrothed." He took a long swig of the beverage, then pushed it into her hands.

Lily tilted her head at him, indignation at his matter-of-fact tone scratching against her nerves. "Your contract is still intact, yes? That means you're still engaged. It doesn't matter what's in *your* mind. It matters what's in everyone's minds."

Verakko plucked the bottle from her hands and took another swig before replacing it; his hard stare bore into her. "Whether or not I marry her is entirely up to you."

"Up to me?" she repeated, confusion setting in again. She laughed, raising her bottle in the air sarcastically. "Well, why didn't you say so?"

"I'm set to be married in a couple weeks. There are only one of two ways to break my contract." Unlatching a large pocket on his thigh, Verakko produced two bottles, both visibly old and dusty. "One, I announce that my eyes have changed, meaning I've recognized someone who could potentially be my mate." He poured liquid from the smaller of the two bottles onto his hands, uncaring of the drips that fell to the floor, and wrung his hands together. "Two, I announce that my mating marks have appeared, proving you're my mate beyond a shadow of a doubt."

Verakko lifted his hands. She stared at the bright-blue designs curling across his wrists and hands that hadn't been there a moment ago. Her breath caught in her throat. How could marks like that have appeared out of nowhere? Was there some kind of magic on this planet? When he said *mate*, was he being serious? Not just a fancy phrase for a wife, but a real-life honest-to-goodness soulmate. And she was his?

"I signed a contract before I ever met you," he spoke quietly, the melodic tone of his voice gone. "There are consequences to breaking it. If I did, I'd never be able to marry anyone else in any city, and I'd be sent away. Recognizing a mate hasn't happened in centuries. Not until Jade showed up earlier this year. You don't understand how special it is. How rare these are," he said, lifting his hands again.

Lily swallowed and tried to ignore the pangs of longing shooting through her.

"I felt that you could be mine when I first laid eyes on you. But I didn't recognize you right away. I kept putting off telling you about Ziritha because I wanted to recognize you so badly, and I worried you'd treat me differently if you knew. It was selfish, but...I didn't know what else to do. I thought maybe if I explained my situation, that perhaps we could be together after our marriages were through. But now that I've recognized you, you won't be forced to be with anyone else."

"I'll only be forced to be with you." Lily recalled what he'd said about mates and how it was for life. Cold fear made her stomach flip. She began pacing, a weak attempt to control her chaotic emotions. "You're telling me this is my choice, but what kind of choice is it? Be with a stranger and watch you get married to someone else, or be with you forever? How am I supposed to make that kind of decision in two weeks?" She froze and faced him, fury and longing and fear all clamoring for acknowledgment. "You want me to make a lifelong commitment after you've done nothing but lie to me? How do you expect me to do that, Verakko? How do I know there isn't more you've been holding back?"

Verakko lifted his hands and opened his mouth, but all that came out was a frustrated breath.

"You know how I feel about marriage. I told you I want to know my partner inside and out before committing my whole life to them. And you knew how I felt about Clecanian marriages, yet you led me here. You might've changed your mind at the last minute, but you were planning on bringing me here before that. Was this all some kind of game to you?" Tears burned at her eyes and blurred her vision. She tensed her muscles to keep a sob from escaping. "Humans have become a valuable commodity on your planet, so you make me depend on you. Care about you. Open up to you. So that if you recognized me, I'd be forced to agree or else watch you marry someone else? It's only been a few days!" Lily shouted and lifted her hands protectively in front of her. "I won't be trapped."

"I never wanted to make you feel trapped, Lily." His gaze darted around, and he clutched at his hair with both hands. "I'm not explaining this right."

"You've explained it fine. I'm angry, but I understand why you did what you did. If you'd told me about your fiancée, I would have treated you differently. If you'd told me about what might happen to me here, I would've never agreed to come. And now, I can see you want me, want us to be together, but…" She took a deep breath, then continued. "I understand, but it doesn't change how I feel. I feel hurt and betrayed and stupid. And I feel like I don't know you anymore." Lily swiped a tear off her cheek. "And that makes me feel even more stupid, because I only met you a week ago. I *don't* know you." Verakko's chest shakily rose and fell, and the look of misery and pain in his eyes cut through her like glass. "If you're asking me to make a lifelong commitment to you right now…I can't." Lily recalled Verakko saying the exact same thing to her, and a sob tore from her throat.

Verakko crossed to her before she had a chance to blink. She tripped back a step, and a blast of smoky cedar hit her nostrils, but instead of the calming effect it normally had, she only felt angrier.

"Do you care about me?" He cupped her cheek, and she wanted to melt. "Be honest," he added. His voice rang through her mind, and fire seemed to shoot through her veins.

"Don't you dare try to *sway* me!" Lily shoved at him with all her strength.

Verakko gazed into her eyes, the intensity of his bright-green stare sending chills down her spine. "If I show anyone these marks, it'll get back to my mother, and she'll force you to be with me. If I don't make that announcement, I'll have to marry Ziritha to avoid punishment, and you'll have to negotiate a contract with some other male. If it were up to me, I'd have claimed you as my mate already. But I acknowledge I've already kept too many things from you, and I also realize you don't feel the mating pull the way I do. So, I lied—to my mother, *the Queen*—in order to give you time to decide what you want to do. It's up to you."

"I need a minute alone. Where can I go?" Lily asked quietly, biting the inside of her cheek to keep the tears threatening to fall at bay.

Verakko pointed to the stairs, and she silently followed him up. She barely took in the second seating area overlooking an expansive view or the framed screens playing a short movie on the walls, what she assumed was their version of art. Lily didn't want to acknowledge the mystery woman's impeccable tastes. She just wanted to be alone.

Verakko led her into a large, bright bedroom dominated by a tall bed, and her eyes locked onto the soft mountain of blankets and pillows. She felt Verakko lingering behind her and inhaled deeply.

She didn't want to look at him or his handsome, grief-stricken expression anymore. It wasn't fair. He'd been lying to her from the start, yet every time she looked at him, she wanted to forget she'd ever learned about his betrayal. She wanted to run into his arms and pretend everything would be okay.

The pull to forgive and forget angered and terrified her. Would she always forgive him this quickly? Always brush any indiscretion under the rug because she couldn't bear the thought of life without him?

She crossed her arms over her chest and glanced toward the ceiling covered in silver glowing orbs before turning to face him. His dark brows lifted in the center with worry and pain. He ran his gaze over her body not with lust but with barely contained longing. He stared at her like she was on the other side of thick glass. As if he wanted to touch her with every fiber of his being but could only look.

"I'm going to make us some food. Come down when you're ready."

Lily swallowed and nodded, not trusting her own shaky voice. When he silently left, she sank to the ground, pulling her knees into her chest. She didn't know what to do. A part of her wanted to drag him back in the room and agree to be with him, but the other part was scared. How could she promise to be with a man who'd already betrayed her trust so thoroughly?

How could she be with someone who made her feel so dependent and helpless? She never wanted to need anybody, yet here she was, sleeping in his house, wearing the clothes he'd bought for her, and relying on him for almost every aspect of her future. She'd put all her eggs in Verakko's basket and now remembered why she'd never done it before. Trusting someone wholly and completely was terrifying.

She allowed a few quiet sobs to escape her, then attempted to focus her mind. *In. Out. In. Out.*

20

After Verakko had left, Lily had crawled into bed and replayed everything she'd learned. Verakko had lied, but a reasonable part of her understood why he'd done it. If he thought she was really his mate and he had no emotional attachment to his future wife yet couldn't break off his engagement, she could see the difficult spot he must've been in. Had it been right for him to lie and keep so much from her? No. Did she understand why he'd done it? Unfortunately, yes.

More than anything, Lily was upset with herself. She hadn't listened when he'd pushed her away; instead, she'd initiated most of their romantic encounters. She'd been the one to brush off his objections with false optimism, believing she understood the culture well enough. *You will never understand a culture you haven't been fully immersed in.*

However, there was something she didn't know if she could look past. He'd made decisions for her. Taken her choices away from her. Important choices that would affect her life in immeasurable ways. Could she forgive that?

She flipped onto her stomach and tried to clear her mind. The bed was the softest she'd ever laid in, and the room smelled more fragrant than seemed normal. It was almost like someone was burning a lilac candle that never dissipated.

It wasn't unpleasant, but floral aromas weren't her favorite, and all she could think about was how much better Verakko smelled. After staring unblinkingly at the inside of the blanket she'd cocooned around herself, she finally rose.

Quietly, she padded around the beautiful bedroom, feeling like an intruder. A small bathroom connected to her room presented a host of new questions. What should she use to brush her teeth? Where was the faucet for running water? And what the hell kind of mirror made her look so good, and where could she get one for herself?

As Lily examined herself, she realized something had happened to her body. Something not entirely unwelcome but felt like a violation nonetheless.

Desy had explained to her the elixir would rejuvenate her down to the cellular level and repair any damage present, but she'd just assumed it was the alien equivalent to a B12 shot. That it'd make her feel great but would ultimately not work any miracles.

As she looked in the mirror at her perfectly unblemished skin, strong, shiny nails, and thick lashes, she realized it hadn't been an exaggeration. If they could do all that at a doctor's office, then what the hell did they need a spa for?

She tugged at her shiny, dark hair in the mirror and tsked angrily. "I've spent years perfecting my highlights, and now they're just gone!" She muttered a curse, swinging her locks behind her back.

While her appearance was radiant, her insides were a dark, jumbled mess. As soon as Verakko had left, she'd yearned for him to come back. It was so odd, this feeling that she wanted him to be in her eyeline, but also to not say a single goddamn word to him. How could such conflicting emotions all be directed toward one person?

She sighed and stared at herself in the mirror. "What are we gonna do?" Could she even stomach the idea of marrying someone else?

Just say it out loud and see how it feels.

Lily nibbled on her lip, afraid to listen to even herself. Finally, she leaned in closer to the mirror and said, "He's my soulmate." She frowned at the thrill that shot through her. "If that's true, you ridiculous universe you, send me a sign."

"Lily!"

She jumped as Verakko's voice rang out from the first floor. She straightened and shot a sidelong glare at the mirror. "That wasn't a sign; he probably heard me," she hissed before leaving the bathroom.

When she reached the first floor, she didn't immediately see him, then the familiar scent of cedar hit her nose. She fought to remain rigid as he stepped in front of her.

His eyes scanned her face as though he hadn't seen her in weeks. Skin prickling with heat, she internally shook herself. He handed her another dark purple bottle—the first bottle lay untouched in her room. She stared at it but didn't really see it, still too wrapped up in her own thoughts.

"Mott," he said, drawing her attention. He aimed a pointed glance at the bottle she held loosely in her hand. "It's alcohol. It isn't a favorite among most females, but I didn't have time to stock the kitchen while you were being healed. Dinner's ready, I just have to bring it out."

She tried to focus on what she needed to say. "Verakko, I appreciate the effort, but I need some time away from you to process how I'm feeling."

Verakko rocked back on his heels, studying her. "I disagree."

She blinked at him, making sure she'd heard the tone of finality in his voice correctly. "Excuse me?"

"I think that if you go off by yourself while still angry, you'll start to second guess what we have and you'll convince yourself everything must've been a lie, even though we both know that isn't true." The words were uttered calmly, but Lily saw the determination in his eyes. "You don't have to decide anything this minute. You'll need to learn from someone in the meantime anyway. You don't know how to use any of our technology. You don't even know how to stay away from Ripsli products, which I know you're allergic to. And I can help you figure out what you need to do to pursue the career you want." He stepped toward her and gripped her shoulders. "You helped me survive out in the forest when I knew so little. Let me help you survive here."

Lily blinked, furious that he was right. He briefly squeezed her shoulders, then dropped his hands. Unsure what else to say, she looked down at her bottle and took a sip. The liquid stung as it slid down her throat.

"Just a few days," she confirmed, weakly clutching the bottle against her chest.

"Yes, miv—Lily," he amended and disappeared through the door to the odd kitchen.

Sparks of static electricity crackled over her scalp at the almost-uttered pet name. Scowling, she wondered if she should question him about the name again. Taking another long pull from the bottle, she retreated into the living room, deciding against it. She was far too susceptible to Verakko's particular brand of sweet talk as it was. She settled herself on the odd half bed, half couch.

How did I get here? Lily shook her head in exasperation and watched the silver glowing orbs bob around the ceiling. It wasn't as if she'd had much say in the matter; this was an alien planet, after all. Verakko was right, she didn't know how to do anything for herself, but with a flare of irritation, she realized she was allowing that to be true.

Lily stood again, intent to ask the right questions this time. Questions about each and every device in the house and what it did. Questions about the food being prepared. How it was being prepared. Where she could buy it. How it needed to be stored. But she only made it a few determined steps before bumping into Verakko exiting the kitchen. "Can you show me how the appliances in the kitchen work?"

He smiled and moved past her to a small shining panel on the wall. "Yes, but not right now. The food is ready." Skating his fingers across the screen without looking at her, he programmed something.

Lily took an instinctive step back as the large couches began to move, sinking into the floor. A small table and chairs, made completely of a clear material that looked like glass, rose to the center of the room.

"Tomorrow, then," Lily said, her attention divided as the dark tint on the enormous windows faded and a gorgeous view of the glittering black desert came into view.

Verakko stopped fiddling with the control and faced her.

Lily forced her focus back to him. "Then tonight, I want you to answer all of my questions, and I mean all of them. Truthfully. No more leaving upsetting information out. I have the right to know what I'm in for."

He stepped toward her. She could feel the heat radiating off his body, and from this close, she could also see that beneath his calm, strong demeanor was a hint of anguish. "I'll tell you everything." He turned and walked back toward the kitchen. "Over dinner. You need to eat."

Lily rolled her eyes and stomped toward the windows, mott in hand. "Impossible man," she muttered under her breath. Only one crescent moon was visible at the moment, but the sky was clear and sparkling—the portion of sky she could see anyway. The large flat roofs of the other buildings crowded nearby blocked the full view overhead. She looked down and guessed the house was at least fifty stories up. She pressed her hand to the glass, angling her head to squint toward the ground.

"Do you need another drink?" Verakko intoned from behind her, making her jump.

She spun and found him standing near the table, now set with food and cutlery. She glanced down to her mostly untouched bottle and shook her head. Lily studied him and noticed his body language was off. His shoulders were tensed, fists clenched, and he forced his eyes to remain on hers, not as though he wanted to look at her, but as if he were trying to not look anywhere else.

He cleared his throat, and for the briefest moment his eyes slid to her palm, still flattened against the window, then back to her. As realization hit, a sudden impulse to run over and soothe him forced her feet to take an involuntary step in his direction.

"It's the windows, isn't it? Why in the world would you buy a house this high up if you're afraid of heights?"

"It isn't normally a problem, but I'd prefer it if you didn't stand so close to them." He puffed out his chest and sat down, avoiding eye contact. "It was the floor Ziritha suggested."

Lily came to join him at the table, brows drawn. "She made you buy this place even after you told her how uncomfortable heights make you?"

"Why would I have told her?" He scowled, reclining in his chair.

"Seems like something important to talk about before buying a house in a skyscraper." Lily shrugged. "You told me."

His gaze turned serious. "You're different." Verakko looked at his food and added in a mumble, "You're the only one I've told the story of my fall to."

Lily's heart squeezed in her chest. *The only one?*

She gave herself a mental shake and studied her food. Odd gray cubes were covered in a charcoal-colored sauce that smelled savory and a little familiar.

"I kept it simple. I didn't know how much you'd want to eat, and I didn't know if you'd prefer to remain a vegetarian now that you have the choice once again."

Of course he'd been thoughtful enough to think about that. He couldn't have made this easy, could he? Been a lying ass through and through? No, he had to have just enough reasonable explanations and sweet gestures to make her question everything.

Lily scooped up a small amount of food with the odd flat spoon he'd provided. She wasn't particularly hungry, though she couldn't recall the last time she'd eaten, but she was curious to try the unappealing gray slop that smelled so much better than it looked.

The sauce was bright and citrusy while the gray cubes underneath were savory with a slight crunch. She chewed thoughtfully and decided she liked it. The motionless alien across from her drew her eyes. He hadn't touched his food but was watching her intensely, a muscle ticking in his jaw.

Lily sighed and set down her odd utensil, then took a long pull from the bottle, wincing as it burned a path down her throat.

Time to get some clarity.

***

Verakko flexed his hands, now free of the paint. It had felt beyond wrong to have them hidden, but Lily's continuous nervous glances toward them made him wonder if he should paint them again to make her more comfortable.

He took a swig from his own bottle, having already downed an entire one in preparation, but every bit of him, from his toes to the tips of his ears, felt shaky and nervous. How did one convince the other half of their soul to accept them?

"Alright, first," she said, peering at his hands again, "when did those appear?"

"After you were stung," he answered, shifting in his seat.

Lily's jaw clenched, and she crossed her arms over her chest. "Why didn't I see them before, when I woke up?"

"Because I made Desy cover them."

She lifted a brow. "Were you planning on hiding them from me?"

"No. I didn't want anyone else to see them and report them to my mother."

"And she would force us to be together because...?"

"We're mates," he said shortly.

She bobbed her head with wide eyes and studied the marks again. Wordlessly she rose and began pacing back and forth in front of the windows. He had to quell the instinct to pull her away to a less anxiety-spiking area.

What are you feeling? His throat worked, and he clamped his mouth shut to prevent the *sway* building in his throat.

She pinched the bridge of her nose and squeezed her eyes shut. "You're telling me that marks you've never had before magically appeared on your wrists because we have some kind of connection you can't have with anyone else?" She leveled her disbelieving gaze at him.

A corner of his mouth turned down at the simplicity of her explanation. Was it even possible to describe the magnitude of what marks meant to someone who came from a world without them? "Yes, I suppose."

"Well, why don't I have any then? I'm your mate, but you're not mine?"

Verakko shot to his feet, unable to contain a growl. Lily leveled a furious glare on him that, without words, settled him.

He took a deep, calming breath before answering. "No. I am your mate and you're mine, but humans apparently don't get them. Maybe you've evolved past them, or maybe it's a malfunction unique to humans. I don't have that answer, but what I do know from the other mated humans I've met is that there is some sense of recognition lingering inside."

"Because I'm half Clecanian, or descended from Clecanians or..." She threw her arms in the air, a wild look lighting her eyes. "Or whatever the hell humans are." Her gaze turned desperate. "I don't understand. How could those just appear out of nowhere? Why didn't they appear sooner?"

"Something happened to me when I saw you collapse. I don't know how else to explain it, but every obstacle that'd been weighing on me since I met you just went away. All I could think about was that I might lose you." He ached to reach out and grab her but forced himself not to. "It was the most afraid I've ever been in my life. I never doubted I could protect you. I knew I could fight a Strigi or a sefa to keep you safe, but..." He swallowed, ice sliding down his spine at the mere memory, "I can't fight poison."

Lily shifted her shoulders and nibbled her lip but remained silent.

He crossed to her, ignoring the spike of fear at the view through the windows. "I won't force you, though. If you tell me you don't want to be with me, I'll do my best to stay away."

"Can't you convince your mom to—"

"I can convince my mother of very little. She already granted me the favor of allowing me to reside with you for three days before she announces your existence to the city. She won't do more."

"What will happen then? After her announcement?"

Verakko stifled another growl rising in his throat. He knew what would happen, and he wondered if he had the strength to weather it. "Males and their family matriarchs will visit. See if they recognize you or see if you'll open negotiations with them."

"What if I say no?"

"If you don't choose, I'm afraid whoever is assigned as your guardian at that time will choose for you." At Lily's look of disgust, Verakko explained, "The only thing required from you during a marriage is cohabitation. You won't even have to speak to the male if you don't want to, as long as it's part of your contract."

Lily stared out the window silently for a moment, then her gaze shot back to Verakko's. "Wait...what's in your contract? What will you have to do?"

His stomach roiled. "I had to buy this house and stock it according to her preferences. I need to prepare her dinner unless asked not to, and I'm required to dine with her once per week." He balled his fists. "And the contract states that we'll attempt a pregnancy."

Lily's hand covered her mouth, and she stepped back.

"I won't, though! I can't." When she remained unconvinced, he added, "You are my mate. I won't be able to be with anyone else."

"As in physically?" She took a few steps toward him. "Are there physical side effects?"

"Yes. I'm faster, stronger, and my *sway* should be more powerful as well."

Please don't ask. Please don't ask.

"What about if I say no? Would anything happen to you, physically?"

She asked. Verakko inwardly groaned. Lily was strong and wouldn't be pushed into anything easily, but one of her weaknesses was her compassion. If he told her about what would happen to him if she chose to deny their bond, she'd feel pressure to remain with him whether she wanted him or not. But he'd agreed to tell her everything. The good and the bad. "I'd rather not say."

She titled her head at him and crossed her arms, waiting.

"I don't know how severe the effects would be, but all accounts of Clecanians being separated from their mates seem to indicate varying levels of illness over time."

Lily's shoulders fell, and her brows drew together. She stared up at him, worry clear in her eyes. If the situation was different, that look would've melted every bone in his body. Concern for her mate shining in her eyes. He never would've dreamed he'd see it.

"You'd get sick?" she whispered, searching his gaze. "How long would it take? Are you feeling sick now?" Her gaze roamed over his body again, more slowly this time.

"No, I'm fine. I'm with you now. Separation for extended periods of time is what would affect me. It isn't the same for all Clecanians, but I'd grow incrementally weaker. Be more prone to illness. From the accounts I've heard, my mental state would suffer more than anything else. Depression. Fits of rage. But, again, this has never happened before. The mating bond has always been reciprocated equally. There was never a question of whether two people would be together. I do know that the longer we remain together, the worse it'd be if we were separated. It could be that if you decided you didn't want to be with me, I wouldn't feel as many effects. We haven't been together long. I've only had my marks for a day, after all." Verakko shushed the voice in his head screaming that what he said was a lie. It wasn't. He didn't know what would happen if she left him. He only knew that every fiber of him revolted against the notion, but he couldn't say one way or the other what being away from her would do.

Lily's eyes watered, and she hid her face from him. All he wanted to do was touch her, but he didn't know whether it would do more harm than good, so he stood there with muscles clenched, waiting for her to say something, anything.

When she finally faced him, he saw the evidence of wetness around her eyes. "What if in a year I choose to leave this planet? What if the laws change and I can go back to Earth? You want to be with me, forever? Monogamously?"

For every second of every day I'm alive. He took a step toward her and tried to work out what he should say. She was already so wary of him and skittish of relationships in general. Would she want to hear the truth? "I'd follow you anywhere, mivassi. If your face is the only one I see for the rest of my life, I'll die a happy male."

Her chin trembled, and she sniffed. "What happens if you break your contract but don't reveal your marks?"

"Eventually, once I do reveal them, we'd be allowed to be together as mates, but otherwise I'd never be allowed to get married again. And I'd be sent away. For years. Unless the

309

laws change, you'd be forced to marry once per year while I'm away."

His throat tightened. To not see her for years? To know she'd be forced to marry at least two other males and be powerless to do anything about it? What if he returned to find her smitten with someone else? Or worse...gone. She'd pointed out something to him he hadn't yet considered. Lily wasn't required to remain on Clecania after her year was over. Would she leave? "If that's what you need, I'll do it."

Her features softened. She crossed her arms around her waist. "You'd do that for me? Even though you could force me to be with you by revealing your marks?"

Verakko let out a rough bark of laughter. "It's not like I haven't thought about it. I have arguments with myself every few minutes about doing just that. It's unnatural for me to hold back. It's not what's supposed to happen. Mates have always felt the pull equally. There *is* no doubt." He closed the distance between them, relieved she didn't step away, and rested his hands on her upper arms. "Every part of me knows you're mine. But I want all of you, and I know that if I force you into it, a part of you will always resent me."

"And if I agree to be with you, there's no going back? Even if we become unhappy?"

"Never," he said truthfully. "I'm barely holding myself back from you even now. If you tell me you'll be mine, that'll be it for me. I'll never be able to let you go. But I will do everything in my power to make sure you never become unhappy."

"And I only have two weeks to decide," she whispered to herself.

"I'm set to be *married* in two weeks, but it'd be best if we didn't live together after my mother announces your existence to the city. If I saw other males trying to court you, I..." Verakko let his hands drop, worried he'd accidentally squeeze her too tight at the thought. "It'd be better for everyone if I wasn't there to see it."

Lily stared at the ground and nodded silently. Her brows were drawn, and she nibbled her lip, the way she always did whenever she was thinking hard about something, but there was such miserable conflict on her face as well. He lifted her chin until she met his eyes, and his chest constricted. She'd had an elixir while at the medbay, yet she looked more exhausted than ever.

"Why don't I take you to your room and let you get some sleep?"

Lily let out a sigh. "I doubt I'm gonna be sleeping anytime soon."

Verakko pushed his luck and swept her long hair off her face, then cupped her cheek. A purr lit in his chest when her eyes slowly shut at the contact. *I still have a chance.* "Let me help. I can *sway* you to fall asleep."

"Verakko, I..." she began to argue, her gaze becoming stern, but then her face fell and she groaned. "Actually, maybe that wouldn't be such a bad idea."

He led her up the stairs to his room. He should've led her to the room he'd prepared for Ziri, but something about putting her into his bed had felt right. Verakko frowned as they reached the door. Did that mean he'd have to sleep in the other room?

In the forest, he and Lily had slept close together. He'd held her in his arms the last two nights, something he'd never imagined he'd be able to do with a female. Lily hadn't indicated it was odd for her. Did human couples share beds the way he knew some other alien cultures did?

When they reached the darkened room, she turned to him and her cheeks pinkened. "Do you have anything else I can wear?"

His shoulders slumped a little. Why would she pick him if he couldn't show her he'd provide for her? The damn clothiers of this city insisted on selling clothes the ancient way, in physical stores rather than virtually, and he'd only had time to pick one outfit for each of them before returning to her. "My shirt?" he offered, whipping it off just in case. "I haven't moved any clothes in yet. I'll make sure to get more tomorrow. You can pick them out if you'd like."

Lily eyed his shirt, then took it. "Thanks."

She fiddled with the clasp at her waist. He should leave now, give her some privacy, but he couldn't bring himself to do it.

The clasp remained locked in place and she let out a huff, tossing his shirt on the bed to get a better grip on the small piece of gold metal. She peered up at him, cheeks now red. "I got it off earlier, but the damn thing won't—Ow!"

He sped toward her. She lifted her finger to her mouth and sucked on it while glaring at her own waist.

He bit his lip to keep from grinning. "Can I?" he said, gesturing at her waist.

She crinkled her brows and studied him while still sucking on her injured finger. Slowly, she nodded.

The metal of the clasp had caught in an odd way, forcing him to snap it in two. He swept the fabric behind her back and gazed down at her. She was so close. He could wrap an arm around her waist and pull her in for a kiss so easily.

She peered up into his eyes when he didn't move away, and he saw her breathing deepen. With slow movements, he ran his hands up to the clasp on her left arm, then let the fabric fall open.

He held her gaze and moved to unhook the clasp on her other arm, then the one on her back. He let his hands linger on the small of her back and tugged her in close. Her hands came up to rest on his shoulders. Verakko tried to shake himself. He couldn't imagine how overwhelmed and emotional Lily might be feeling right now, and he was taking advantage. He rolled the fabric down over her waist and let it pool on the ground at her feet.

He kept his eyes on hers and stifled a groan when her gaze flicked toward his mouth.

But dammit, he was feeling the same way she was, except he also had the added frustration of experiencing the ache of not claiming his mate.

Her lips parted on an exhale. He let out a defeated growl and pulled her flush against him. The feel of her soft breasts on his bare chest had his cock shooting hard in an instant. He gripped her around the back of her neck and slanted his mouth over hers. A groan tore from him at the ecstasy of her small tongue swiping against his. She slid her arms around his neck, lifting to her toes and driving him crazy with the slow, lusty swipes of her tongue. The faint scent of her arousal was masked under the thick underwear he'd given her. His fingers itched to rip them off.

He let his rattling purr rumble against their connected bodies and smirked at her answering gasp. He forced her backward while deepening the kiss until her backside hit the edge of the bed. His large bed had been crafted especially for his frame and rose to Lily's waist. Gripping her hips, he lifted her onto the bed, then hooked an arm around her lower back and pulled her hips against his.

When he ground his hard length against the sensitive spot at the apex of her thighs, she released a moan so sweet he might've come right there. But then she pulled away.

Breathing hard, she stared up into his eyes. He had her hips pinned open against his and leaned his upper body over her, so she propped her arms behind her and leaned away. He exhaled a growl at what he saw in her stare. Clarity.

"Before, you said this wasn't allowed. I'm assuming that has something to do with your engagement."

Verakko forced himself to answer honestly, though his contractual obligations to another female were the last thing he wanted to talk about at that particular moment. "Before I knew you were my *mate*..." He emphasized the word and forced his gaze to remain on her face and not slither down to see her exposed body now open to view. "Ziritha knows I'm here with you. This is technically a violation, but—"

Lily shook her head and interrupted. "I don't want to hurt any woman by doing this with you right now, in her house no less."

Verakko scowled. "This isn't hurting anyone. Ziri doesn't see me or this place like that." How to make her understand that the betrayal Lily thought Ziritha may feel was so far from the truth.

Lily stared at his mouth for a moment, and he thought she may reconsider, but then her brows drew together and she plucked his shirt from where he'd thrown it. "I hear what you're telling me logically, but I still have a lifetime of Earth experience making me feel shitty about this. Until I see for myself that people who are married don't have bonds like I'm used to, I don't think we should do this."

He growled and snatched the shirt out of her hands.

"Verakko," she said in a warning tone. She reached for the shirt and missed, jiggling her breasts in a devastating way in the process.

Frown securely in place and balls aching with unrelieved lust already, he righted the shirt and held it above her head. He sent her a frustrated look and saw a small smile playing at her lips before she lifted her arms and allowed him to slide the shirt down. He'd committed a few crimes in the past week, but covering up her glorious body felt like the worst one yet.

He took his time pulling the fabric down to her hips, making sure to brush his knuckles against her nipples as he did. She shivered at the contact. When his shirt was on, he rested his balled fists on either side of her hips and focused on her face, letting her see his frustration. To be fair, he supposed he deserved it.

They remained silent for a while, just staring, the air between them tense.

"May I sleep here with you, Lily?"

She bit the inside of her cheek and considered him.

She neither agreed nor refused when she said, "I'm still mad at you."

The small uttered statement stung more than it should've. Her words lacked venom, but he could hear the truth behind them. Mad wasn't the right emotion. It was a mask for hurt. The type of hurt that would be the biggest obstacle against him. What he'd done to her for the past week might not have cut her deeply enough to sever ties with him, but it would seed doubt. The kind of doubt that would take longer than he had to squash.

To his mivassi, with all her considerable know-how and abiding confidence, doubt in her own feelings toward him would hurt his cause more than anything.

"I'll spend the rest of my life making it up to you if you let me."

Lily swallowed but said nothing.

"I'll start now by helping you fall asleep." He straightened and watched as she buried herself under a mound of blankets. Removing his pants, he slipped into bed beside her and programmed the lights to dim.

Hoping beyond hope she'd allow it, he pulled her in close to his chest and swept the hair from her neck. If she minded his shaft, now fully erect again and cradled against her bottom, she didn't say. He ran his nose along the column of her neck and felt goosebumps erupt over her arms.

"Ready?"

She hesitated a moment, each millisecond of doubt in him another blow to the gut. One day they'd get to a place where she trusted him implicitly again, and until then, he'd need to be patient. At length, she nodded.

"Sleep deeply, mivassi, and have only pleasant dreams. You'll wake in the morning renewed and ready for a long day." He continued to *sway* the last words after her body had grown limp and her breathing even.

Verakko remained in place, petting her hair and running his knuckles over her cheek, all while thinking of ways he could expedite her decision.

A thought struck him and he disregarded it, but it continued to flicker to the forefront of his thoughts, demanding to be considered. It may not go over well at first, but it could end up being just the thing she needed to understand. She might not believe him about the position he was in, yet there was one person she would believe.

Verakko slipped his arm from under Lily's head and retrieved his communicator from the kitchen.

After a few moments, the call connected. "I need a favor."

21

Lily pulled a fluffy pillow into her chest and squeezed. The cool fabric felt heavenly against her warm chest, and she snuggled farther into her covers. *Covers?*

Her eyes flew open, and she bolted upright. As her vision cleared and she saw the large bed, shining stone floor, and blue-gray walls, she recalled where she was. She flopped back down onto the mattress and took a few deep breaths to relax her racing heart.

The scent of flowers hung heavy. Lily scanned the room but couldn't find any discernible source. Did it get vented in or something?

When she was sure Verakko was in fact gone, she pulled his shirt, which she was still wearing, over her nose and inhaled deeply. It was more faint than normal, but the smoky scent she loved so much clung to the fabric and soothed her.

She laid there gazing up at the ceiling with her shirt over her nose and mentally scanned her body. No soreness in her back, no lingering aches or pains from the forest. On the whole, she was deliciously comfortable and relaxed. Verakko's *sway* was better than her ambient noise machine. Or Ambien, for that matter.

If I stay with him, I bet I could get him to do it every night.

Lily thought about everything that'd happened yesterday. All of their fighting, his revelations, and the unexpected moment of intimacy they'd shared last night. Although they'd argued for most of the day, the heated conversations between her and Verakko almost felt right. Like they were working toward something by fighting rather than tearing each other down with their words. Discontent trickled into her thoughts. Why did it feel so natural to forgive him and move on? *Do I feel the bond like he said?*

She and Verakko had something special; she wasn't blind to it. Could that be enough to be happy forever? If this were a familiar type of Earth relationship, she'd probably have decided to let him suffer for a few more days before ultimately forgiving him, but the stakes were higher here. If she opened herself up to him again, there would be no going back. No breaking up. No divorce. Not if she cared at all about his well-being.

Am I ready for that?

Lily almost didn't notice the room growing brighter and brighter. When it finally was bright enough to make her squint, she looked toward the source in confusion and saw a glorious sight. What she'd thought was a solid wall had transitioned into one large, transparent window.

Lily slid off the bed and took in the view. It was so unearthly. She'd seen black sand beaches before, but she'd never seen anything like the utterly bare, rolling black sand desert before her. The sky was cloudless and bright blue, yet it still didn't quite look like a sunny day. Something about the bleakness of the glittering sand, stretching as far as the eye could see, made the day appear menacing.

Another whiff of a mishmash of floral scents hit her nose, and she grimaced. *It must be coming from somewhere.*

Lily padded down to the first floor and found Verakko huddled over a pile of what she guessed were some kind of electronics parts. He glanced over his shoulder when he heard her come in, and she couldn't stop the grin that spread over her face.

He wore a very odd set of glasses that doubled as small screens. Every time he shifted his focus, the lens would zoom toward his face then away, trying to magnify whatever he was looking at. Small symbols could be seen flying across one of the small lenses, while the other remained blank. The combination of the eccentric glasses and his heavily muscled, shirtless torso was a gorgeous sight.

Verakko flipped off the glasses and leapt over the back of the couch. His hands reached out as though to grab her, but then he pulled them back and awkwardly placed them on his hips before dropping them to his sides. He beamed at her without speaking until she felt her cheeks grow hot and had to look away.

"What are you doing?" she asked, waving to the small fragments, one of which was now smoking slightly.

"I, uh…" Verakko glanced to his work area, then did a double take and rushed over to smother the burning piece with a small cloth nearby. "It's a surprise. For you."

"Oh, you don't have to do that." As soon as the words came out, a chorus of little voices in her head berated her. She loved presents, no matter the size or cost. Growing up, her parents had rarely exchanged gifts. Especially not ones that had no use.

Verakko chuckled and backed toward the small table they'd dined at the night before, now sharing the space with one large couch. "Well, I still might not. Those parts are very outdated. I went to rummage through my old storage cube, and that's all I had, so…" He shrugged and motioned to a plate on the table.

Lily's stomach gave a rumble in answer. She sat at the table and tried to keep her emotions on an even keel, though all she wanted to do was be happy, give in.

This is how all relationships start. I can't decide anything during the honeymoon phase. What happens when that wears off or I get antsy or he does something unforgivable?

Lily glanced down and confirmed that her plate was empty.

Verakko handed her a tall, thin glass of pink liquid and gave her a lopsided smile. "It's wanget." When she raised a brow in question, he explained, "The pink fruit from the forest."

Despite herself, Lily frowned, and her stomach gave an angry gurgle. "I'm sorry," she apologized, not wanting to seem ungrateful. "I don't know if I can eat another one of those so long as I live."

Instead of being disappointed or offended, Verakko laughed and circled behind her chair. He leaned down, and she thought she felt him smell her hair before speaking into her ear. "I know, I know. Just trust me. There's a beverage made from the fruit. This is the type without alcohol."

Lily took a long breath to settle her stomach, then took a small sip. The fruit she'd eaten for weeks on end had always been just a little too bitter to be deemed enjoyable. The sparkling juice she drank now was what that fruit had always been meant to be. Sweet and light with a hint of tartness.

Verakko rumbled a chuckle and stood, running his hands down her arms as she greedily took a longer gulp. "You can try the alcoholic version when you're out today."

Lily craned her head up to look at him. "When *I'm* out?"

Without warning, he wrapped his hands under her chin, holding her head securely in place, and kissed her. It only took her a half second of deliberation before she returned his upside-down kiss.

Lily was relieved when he moved away. Her willpower dwindled each time he did something like that.

"I'm having someone else show you around for a while, and then I'll meet you later," he said, disappearing into the enclosed kitchen then reappearing with a stemmed bowl. He set it down in front of her, and she noted the frost building on the outside of the glass. Not exactly a nice, warm cup of tea.

Lily angled her head this way and that, trying to understand what type of food she might be about to eat. A solid layer of pale blue…something rose halfway up the bowl, and a variety of fruits and nuts topped it.

Noticing her reticence, Verakko sat across from her and scooped a bit of the concoction onto his flat spoon. To Lily's surprise, the solid blue layer cracked. "Mishun bowl. It's a common first meal for Mithrandirians. The cool temperature of the mishun is supposed to help wake you up." He ate the blue food and held it in his mouth for a moment before swallowing. "The nuts the mishun is made from also help boost energy."

Lily took a small bite and grinned. "It's like ice cream, only…harder, maybe?" She scooped out a larger spoonful and savored the burst of flavor and texture created by the mix of sweet and salty toppings accompanying the minty mishun.

"Do you like it?"

"What's not to like? You guys eat ice cream for breakfast." Lily eyed him as he watched her eat. "You weren't lying about being a good cook, then."

His mouth twitched downward briefly. "I'll take that as a compliment."

The glass orbs hovering near the ceiling flickered just before a small chime sounded.

Lily glanced at Verakko questioningly, her mouth too full of the delicious breakfast to use words.

"Your escort for the day," he explained, rising.

Lily realized he was heading toward the door, and she hastily tugged her shirt farther down over her thighs. Choking on her mouthful, she wheezed, "Hold on!"

Verakko paused, turning to her with raised brows.

"Who is it? I thought no one was supposed to know about me. Shouldn't I change first or something?"

"She brought something for you to wear, seeing as I broke part of your outfit yesterday."

Lily flushed, thinking about his strong hands undressing her. Then with a start, his words registered. "She?"

Verakko was already opening the door by the time she stood. "Thank you for coming, Ziri," he said, blocking Lily's view of the woman.

Ziri? Lily searched her mind. She knew she'd heard the name before. The cold mishun curdled in her stomach, and her whole body crackled with electricity.

Lily shot mental daggers toward the back of Verakko's head. How could he do this without warning her? Shame and guilt tore at her. She was the homewrecker, and now she'd have to come face to face with the woman whose life she'd screwed with.

In a fleeting moment of cowardice, Lily bolted toward the stairs. When her foot was on the top step, she halted. *You need to face her. You slept with her fiancé. She deserves a little more respect than this.*

"Lily?" she heard Verakko call from the doorway.

She kept her eyes trained on the ground and took a deep breath. *In. Out. In—Dammit!* She realized she was still wearing nothing but underwear and Verakko's shirt.

She smoothed her wrinkled top and forced herself to look toward the person Verakko would marry if she didn't accept him.

Her heart stuttered. The woman before her was stunning. Half of her mass of tight, icy-silver curls was pulled back, while the rest fell down her back and over her shoulder. Her light-blue skin and gauzy white dress made her look like a goddess who might spend her time sculpting the clouds.

Ziritha regarded her with sparkling blue eyes, and Lily felt like crawling into a hole and dying. She glanced between the two of them, their eyes watching her warily. How could Verakko really want *her* instead of the creature standing next to him? They looked so perfect together.

"Hello." Ziri held out a white dress identical to her own and smiled gently. "I brought you a change of clothes. It's a spa gown and mokti."

Lily's body thrummed with apprehension as well as annoyance directed toward Verakko. Although the word *spa* registered in her consciousness, she was still too taken aback to comment on it. She crossed to them both and took the dress and small bag Ziri held out for her, while berating Verakko with her lack of eye contact. "Thank you. You shouldn't have… I mean, I should've…"

"Yes, I know it's quite odd." Ziri eyed Verakko disapprovingly. "He really should've fetched these things for you himself, but seeing as these circumstances are quite unusual, I offered to do it so he could be here when you awoke."

She needed to get away to mentally prepare for what would be an unquestionably awkward day. Wiggling the dress in front of her, she sputtered, "I'm gonna go put this on. Be back in two shakes." Only just preventing her eyes from rolling, she wanted to shrivel in mortification. Two shakes? She'd never used that phrase once in her life.

Both aliens peered at her with a look of concern. Lily spun and fled up the stairs, desperate to be out of sight before they saw her cheeks turn bright red.

***

Verakko watched as Lily practically cleared the steps in her attempt to get away. Maybe he'd made a mistake asking Ziritha to come.

"She's a little skittish, isn't she?" Ziri said from next to him.

"Not for many things, but when it comes to me, I suppose so." He frowned at her. "You're too early. I didn't have the chance to tell her you were coming."

Ziri tsked. "It's a wonder your mother was able to negotiate a contract with any female if this is how you speak to them."

Verakko bit his tongue. He'd forgotten how proper he was expected to be when it came to Clecanian females. He'd relaxed with Lily. Spoken to her honestly and without the restrained politeness he'd learned in school. "My apologies.

Humans are different. My way of speaking changed while we were in the Sauven Forest."

She nodded, concealing a smirk.

"I'm going to go make sure she's alright," he said while continuing to back away. "I'll meet you back here at twenty-eight b.h."

Ziri waved him away, gaze already scanning the room, assessing his choices.

When Verakko reached Lily's room, he heard a barrage of angry whispering. He slid the door open, and she spun. Before he had a chance to tell her how beautiful she looked in her spa gown, she was hissing at him. "How could you not tell me she was coming!"

"I—"

"Why is she even here?"

"Last—"

"Oh my God, she saw me in your shirt, and I feel so bad and—"

"Lily!"

"What?" she yelled, advancing on him.

"I was going to tell you this morning, but she got here earlier than expected."

Lily huffed, crossing her arms over her chest and turning away from him.

He stepped closer to her, but she refused to meet his eyes. "I knew I'd never be able to convince you she feels nothing for me. I also thought you might doubt whatever I tell you because I'm biased. The only person you'd trust is her."

Lily's lips pursed, a sign she was coming around. He gripped her chin and angled her head to face him.

"Ziri's the only person in this city, besides my mother, who knows about you and knows that we're closer than is allowed."

"I thought I wasn't supposed to be wandering around. Isn't that why we snuck up here in the first place?"

Verakko didn't want to explain, knowing it would once again remind her he wasn't technically single in the eyes of the law, but he did anyway. "*We* shouldn't be seen together. You and I alone, entering my home. But if you're with Ziri, no one will think twice. We get many visitors from different cities. And no one knows about humans. They'll assume you're an off-worlder being shown around by our future queen."

Lily yanked her head out of his grasp and stepped back. Her eyes remained fiery. "How much can I ask her? What does she know?"

"I assume she suspects we've been intimate, but she doesn't know for sure. And she doesn't know about my marks. Ask her anything you wish, but be careful not to reveal that we're mated. I don't know her well enough to say how she'd react to that news."

"Fine," Lily grumbled. "I don't know how to put the—" she motioned to her neck with aggravated swipes of her hand, "—on."

"The mokti?" Verakko made quick work of attaching the mokti to her hair again. "This dress is a traditional spa gown."

He caught her eye and saw a glimmer of interest spark to life. Tentatively, he ran his hands down her tense shoulders. "I've arranged a full trip to my favorite spa and basin."

Her gaze flicked to him again, and she bit the inside of her cheek.

Verakko recalled the similar spark of joy in her expression when he'd revealed he had a gift for her. Mentally, he filed away the information. His mate enjoyed gifts. "Remember when we were in the woods and I promised you a trip, on me?" She met his eyes, and he grinned down at her. "Maybe after, I could take you to a bed as you requested."

Her mouth contorted as she tried to smother her smile. Verakko stepped toward her and pressed a kiss to her unresponsive lips.

"But what if someone calls about Alex? Maybe I should stay."

"Ziri has a communicator. If I hear anything, I'll contact you immediately."

When he looked back down at her, she sighed. "Alright. Let's get this over with."

She'd already begun heading to the door when Verakko stopped her with a hand on her arm. "Oh, and Lily, when you're at the spa, make sure to not book a full-body massage."

Her brows drew together. "Why?"

Verakko smothered a growl. "Do you have full-body massages on Earth?"

She shrugged. "Yeah."

He raised a brow and looked pointedly down her body, letting his gaze linger in certain areas. "*Full* body?"

"Wha—" she sputtered, her eyes growing wide.

22

"First, I want to introduce you to some hairstylists on the upper level, and then I think we can go down to the basins. After a soak, we'll work our way back up through the floors. I'll stick close by since no one will have your language uploaded yet."

Lily walked alongside Ziri, but every time she thought of something to say, Ziri started on a new topic. They'd left the building Verakko's house was in and were now waiting under an oddly lush crop of plants. Lily craned her neck and guessed that the shade provided by the overlapping flat roofs of the buildings allowed for a sort of oasis to exist in the sand below.

The air outside the temperature-controlled building was hot and dry. Although she began to sweat, the moisture from her skin evaporated almost immediately.

"Do you know what services you want done?" Ziri asked.

A large silver ball floated toward them, drawing Lily's undivided attention. When it didn't seem like it would veer off course, she hastily stepped away.

"It's alright, Lily. That cruiser is our ride."

"Ride?" She cocked her head, legs still tensed.

"All the spas are in the old city." Ziri pointed off into the distance to a grouping of small buildings. Lily had assumed they were storage facilities of some kind. How could it be a whole city?

The large silver sphere stopped in front of them, and a panel slid open, revealing seating. Once they were both in and seated, she felt a slight lurch. Ziri smiled at her from across the cruiser.

Lily's gut churned at the kindness she saw seeping from the pretty alien's gaze. "Ziritha, I need to say something to you."

She arched a delicate silver brow in response.

Lily was momentarily distracted by the faint shimmer glinting from her lifted brow. She studied Ziri's hair again now that they were in close proximity and saw that it too shimmered as though a spray bottle of glitter had somehow attached itself to the follicles of her hair.

"How do..." Lily stopped herself and forced her mind back to the task at hand. "Verakko told me you know about me and him, and I have to say how sorry I am. I didn't know he was engaged—Er—I mean, under contract."

Ziritha grinned at her like she'd just said something adorable. "You don't have anything to be sorry for. Verakko is the one who crossed a line. But if what they say about humans is true, I can't blame him."

Lily thought she saw a brief flash of jealousy light Ziri's eyes. "So, you're really not upset?"

Ziri sighed and leaned back in her seat, twirling a lock of her hair around a long finger. "Another female might've taken more offense and exposed the breach, but I don't feel that way. In all honesty, I'm curious."

Curious? The door to the pod suddenly slid open, preventing Lily from questioning her further.

She followed Ziritha out of the floating ball and froze in place. Until that moment, she'd forgotten how Verakko had described the old city as being located in a pit. Before her was a massive, sheer drop-off circling a tall cylinder of land, like a waterless moat around a medieval city.

She imagined that long ago the city would've been carved directly into the rock, but now the addition of stained-glass windows many stories high, jutting lavish balconies, and sprawling vines made the column of a city an *Architectural Digest*'s wet dream.

Colossal ornamental mirrors placed on each side of the divide acted as sun catchers, directing the light from above down into the shaded lower levels of the city. Lily squinted, trying to see the bottom of the perfectly round trench, but could only see layers upon layers of draped fabric extending from a sprawling green balcony that circled the whole base of the column.

"Are you ready?" Ziri said, rousing her.

Lily could only nod with wide eyes.

A single bridge connecting the two pieces of land was bordered on either side by large statues of stern, fanged men and women. As she walked with Ziritha along the bridge, she felt their eyes on her. She focused on the other people crossing the bridge, more out of her depth than ever. A large majority were men, mostly Swadaeth, but many were other races. A few, with their overlarge heads and four arms, looked different enough that she assumed they weren't Clecanian at all. Any lingering worry that she'd stand out as the only "alien" vanished.

The people on the bridge walked in silence for the most part or chatted seriously to one another. Lily glanced toward Ziri and saw that her expression had changed. The chatty, bubbly woman she'd shared a ride with was now impassive.

A man and woman walking by dipped their heads toward Ziritha and tapped their left shoulders with a thumb. A sign of respect perhaps? As Ziri returned the gesture, then tilted her chin upward imperiously, Lily saw it. A queen in the making. Ziri looked as regal as anyone she'd ever seen.

From the way Verakko had spoken, Ziri would become queen whether or not she married him. How long had she been training for her role?

A few of the people walking in their direction wore clothing similar to her own. White billowy fabric with relatively few accessories compared to the decked-out, fully dressed majority. Lily rejoiced as she examined the odd, intricate makeup and hairstyles sported by not only the women but men. A short woman with a sunflower-yellow structured suit and matching lace mokti caught her attention. Her lids were painted a bright purple, and small objects that looked like pearls dotted her eyes from the inner corner up to and above the brow. Her bright blue hair had a faint shimmer as well.

Alex would have a field day here. Lily smiled, forcing herself to remain positive, and daydreamed about the day when she and Alex could walk side by side, gossiping about all the crazy fashion and alien species they saw in the city.

Lily started to ask Ziri about the treatment she'd need to make her hair sparkle, but then scanned the quiet crowd again and thought better of it. Was it rude to speak in public spaces like this the way it was in some countries on Earth?

Deciding she should take her cues from Ziri for the time being, she remained silent.

After walking through a towering archway, they entered a large public square of sorts. Vendors milled about, projecting holographic signs advertising their wares, which were nowhere in sight. Lily decided they must be the equivalent of those arrow holders on city corners directing customers to shops located somewhere else.

Still silent, Ziri guided them to a long line of large glass tubes. As she approached, a portion of glass slid open, and Ziri stepped in, indicating Lily should do the same. Willing her nerves about entering the small space to dissipate, she stepped in.

"Floor twenty," Ziri said to the space at large.

A soothing male voice repeated, "Floor twenty," and they moved downward.

All at once, Ziri's stoic expression morphed. She faced Lily, smiling, and pointed out through the glass. "You'll be able to see each floor as we pass them. Tell me if there are any you'd be interested in visiting later."

Lily's brows drew together, and she stared at Ziri for a moment longer before looking back out through the glass. The elevator was moving quickly, and she barely had time to register one incredible view before another replaced it. A whole floor of colored glass windows shone a dazzling display of jewel-toned light on a crowded market. A shining black stone restaurant with thick black columns and millions of tiny glittering orbs floating around the ceiling like stars cast the room in a soft glow.

"What's on those floors?" Lily asked after seeing at least four floors go by that were blocked from view.

"Those are our schools. Early education for all young Swadaeth is near the top, then trade schools are next, and the secondary schools are below."

Husbandry school, Lily recalled. "What did you learn in your school?" she asked while studying a recreation floor with a gym, a large portion of which was dedicated to people hurling spears at distant targets.

They reached their floor, and Ziri stepped into a large conservatory filled with exotic flowers, bushy trees, and familiar hanging saplings. Lily felt an odd sense of joy at finally recognizing something.

"Emotional professionalism, sexual education, advanced reproductive education, things of that nature."

Small birds flitted around the towering light-filled space, but Lily's attention was drawn back to Ziri. Her voice had shifted, becoming tighter and reserved. Her features had hardened once again as well. Was that what she meant by emotional professionalism? Why? What was the point in hiding her sweet personality?

Lily became momentarily distracted when a handsome man clothed in a translucent fitted shirt approached them.

"Hello. Which floor is your appointment on today?"

"We've reserved pool seven and have rooms booked on each floor, but we may not be using them all. My companion would like to see a menu. She's a newly immigrated off-worlder."

The man grinned at Lily and bowed. "It's my honor to assist such a lovely off-worlder. Welcome to Mithrandir."

Lily smiled back. "Thank you."

The man's green brows rose.

"Her language is rare and not among the typical uploads."

"Ah." The man produced a small white pad from behind him and handed it to Ziri.

He eyed Lily up and down with more interest than she was comfortable with after learning about some of the *services* provided at the spa.

"Lead on," Ziri demanded.

The man glanced to Ziri. His grin remained in place, but Lily could tell it had transformed from something genuine to something forced. She'd used smiles like that many times over when speaking to unhappy customers.

He nodded and led them through the artfully planted garden to the large green balcony she'd seen from above, only now Lily realized it wasn't just *green*—it was in fact soft, spongy moss. This city sure liked to show off how much plant life it could grow in the desert. She remembered what Verakko had said about his people having a penchant for extravagance.

The man leading them opened his mouth to speak, but Ziri spoke first. "Two turys, please. Also, can you see if Hetta is available? Tell her Ziritha is asking for her."

A surge of annoyance at the way Ziritha was treating this guy flared. Sure, he'd made her a little uncomfortable before when he'd ogled her, but he didn't deserve the blunt tone. She shot him an apologetic smile, thinking he'd return it and leave, but he lingered, eyes glued to her.

Ziri looked over her shoulder and caught his stare. She stepped between them while Lily tried to work out what exactly was happening. "She's new to this city, and her home culture is very different. She's not interested in you."

Lily held in a gasp, her cheeks growing hot. Was that what she'd made him think?

Disappointment dimmed his bright gaze as he nodded and turned to leave.

"What did I do? I don't understand?"

Ziri motioned to a set of chairs, and her features softened into a smile. "You'll learn. Smiling like that at an unfamiliar unmarried male, as an unmarried female, will give the impression you're interested in him opening negotiations with you."

Lily sunk into her chair, weighing her next words carefully so as not to offend. "The way you spoke to him seemed so cold. I was just trying to be nice." She scrutinized Ziri's warm, unguarded gaze. "Is that why you...change...when we're not alone? Your personality, I mean?"

Ziri frowned in thought for a moment. "It's how most females are taught to act with unfamiliar males. I'm more relaxed around males who know me, but when it comes to strangers, it's better to be reserved. Lessens the chances of giving anyone false hope."

Lily studied Ziri's pinched expression and wondered if she didn't dislike being "reserved."

After the spa attendant had returned with two glasses of what Lily learned was the alcoholic wanget beverage Verakko had told her about, Ziri explained all the treatments she could choose from.

When their spa schedule was settled and full of couple's treatments, since thankfully Ziri didn't want to stray too far from her side, Lily began her interrogation. Questioning Ziri about marriage contracts, laws concerning broken contracts, the humans already found in Tremanta, and what Ziri expected to happen during her marriage to Verakko, if it occurred.

Lily made sure to keep her queries curious, as if she simply wanted to know what would happen *if* Verakko recognized her. Ziri's enthusiastic responses made it clear to Lily that if she found out Verakko had already recognized her, Ziri would report his marks herself. Lily got the feeling Ziri would even consider revealing Verakko's marks without their permission a favor.

Whenever Lily had hinted that not all humans would find the idea of being bound to a person they barely knew favorable, Ziri had repeated some variation of the phrase "But they'd be mated." The idea of a human denying the bond appeared to be unthinkable to the future queen.

They talked until Lily had run out of questions to ask. As it turned out, Verakko had told her the truth about everything, including that he and Ziri barely knew each other. To Lily's frustration, every question about Verakko she asked was met with uncertainty. Ziritha knew off the top of her head what grades he had and how willing he'd been to concede on certain things during their negotiation, but she hardly knew anything about his personality. His fears. The things he enjoyed. His sense of humor. How he could be a little bit cranky in the morning.

This woman, who'd be his wife, didn't know Verakko at all. A smug heat radiated through Lily's chest as she realized Verakko had let her see him in a way he hadn't even let his future wife. It could very well be that Lily knew him better than anyone.

After an hour of conversation and many glasses of tury shared on the reflected, sunlit balcony, Ziri's friend Hetta had also stopped by. Ziri explained that Lily was a hairstylist back on her home planet and was considering becoming one again.

The rest of the hour or so before their pool reservation was spent with Lily excitedly learning all she could about the glitter treatment from an enthusiastic Hetta, while Ziri sat sullenly translating.

"Can we please speak about something else? At this rate, I'll never want a glitter coat again," Ziri complained, a hint of a playful whine in her voice.

Hetta pursed her pouty maroon lips at Ziri. "Alright." She focused on Lily again. "Think about which color you want for when I see you later, okay?"

Lily nodded with a wide grin, but she already knew what she wanted—her highlights returned and a gold glitter coat.

"Ziritha?" a deep male voice said from behind Hetta.

Lily noticed both women instinctively stiffen, their masks of indifference sliding into place. Lily tried and failed to do the same.

Hetta moved out of the way and revealed a muscled, tanned man who, with only a devilish grin and dark, piercing eyes, oozed charm. He wore a long white garment unbuttoned at the chest. On any other man, the getup might've looked feminine, but on his large frame it appeared fashionable and utterly masculine. The attendant leading him down to the pools peered between them. The handsome man quietly said something to the attendant and changed course, walking over to them instead.

Ziri turned, and Lily was surprised to see her features soften. "Fejo," she exclaimed warmly. "I thought you'd already left yesterday."

"The ship is ready and waiting in orbit, but you know I couldn't join the crew until I visited the famed basins one more time. I'll be hopping on a jumper tonight." Fejo's eyes slid to Lily, and he cocked his head, narrowing his eyes.

Lily smiled, then awkwardly scrunched her lips downward and turned away, recalling what Ziritha had said about interacting with men you weren't familiar with.

"May I join you?" The curiosity in his voice made Lily stiffen.

Before she'd heard Ziri agree, a chair had been plopped down in front of them, and Fejo sat with one hand on his knee, staring curiously at her.

"Fejo," Ziri warned. "She's not available."

Lily glanced up to him, forcing her gaze to remain stern.

He shot her a dashing crooked grin and lifted a dark brow. "Too bad. I'm fascinated by Earthlings."

Lily's head snapped to attention, and out of the corner of her eye, she saw Ziri's do the same. "You know what I am?" She turned to Ziri, waiting for her to translate, but to her shock the man answered her.

"I do. I'm a Tremantian, you see. I met a delightful human earlier this year." He donned an expression of utter misery and shook his head at her. "Alas, she was also unavailable. But tell me, gorgeous—" his roguish smile returned in a flash, and he leaned further toward her, "—who has snapped you up? Have you elicited some kind of special response in someone?" His eyebrows lifted suggestively. "I mean other than the obvious."

Lily blushed and gave a *what the fuck* look to Ziri.

"Behave, Fejo," she said while hiding her own grin. "What do you know about the humans?"

He reclined back into his chair with a mock sigh of resignation. "You know me, Ziri." He slid his eyes toward her. "I know everything."

"I'm sure." Ziritha pursed her lips and took a small sip of her wine. "Wait!" she said, her eyes lighting up. She glanced over to Lily, lips pursed as though trying to think of how to say what she wanted to say. "Fejo knows him," she said, not using Verakko's name.

"Intriguing," Fejo remarked, crossing an ankle over his knee.

"Your pool is ready," came a voice from behind them.

Ziri held up a hand, indicating she'd heard the attendant who was now peering at Fejo with a frown. She leaned toward Lily. "He knows him well. He may be able to answer those questions that I couldn't."

Lily scrutinized Fejo. He lifted his brows, amused curiosity shining in his eyes.

"Will the male be joining you?" the attendant called from the edge of the balcony.

"Possibly," Ziri replied without looking.

"I can only stay for a short while, but I'd be delighted to answer all your questions about..." he leaned forward with a lopsided grin, "Uzad? Bostu? Ooh, or maybe Matten? I know them all well."

Lily glanced between them. "How do you two know each other?"

Ziri and Fejo exchanged meaningful looks, and Ziri gave a sad smile. "There's a male I care about who's worked with Fejo for a long time now."

A tense moment of silence passed before Fejo said in a voice free of bravado or humor, "He's doing well, Ziri. He wanted to visit, but…it wasn't his turn. There wasn't anything I could do."

Ziritha nodded, schooling her features and taking a long drink.

"I'm a trader," Fejo explained. "I travel between the planets that are a part of the alliance and transport goods. I just finished my Clecanian deliveries and am heading back out for short trip tonight." He glanced sidelong at Ziri. "But then we'll be back."

"And you trust him?" Lily whispered to Ziri.

"Very much," she said seriously.

Lily narrowed her eyes and stared hard, trying to see past his swagger. She'd let him hang around, but she'd make sure to be the one asking questions.

23

"Verakko!" Fejo barked, the deep rumble of his chuckle vibrating the water around his chest.

After Lily had agreed to let Fejo join them, they'd traveled to the lowest level of the old city, changed into their bathing clothes—which were really just stretchy opaque slips—and headed outside to the natural hot spring pools dotting the floor of the Well.

Each pool had swathes of colorful fabric draped over them, creating private tents. Their pool, number seven, was positioned far away from the rest, ensuring a modicum more privacy.

"Why are you laughing?" Lily asked, sipping on her tury.

"Just the idea of that morose, unfriendly male being lucky enough to be engaged to you and potentially mated to you." He laughed, shaking his head incredulously and gesturing between Ziri and Lily. "Am I missing something, or have females all of a sudden started to prefer males with low communications scores?" To himself, he muttered, "Gotta remember that at the next Ceremony."

Lily and Ziritha looked at each other, then back to him, their confusion clear.

"Jade," he said, gulping his dark-green beverage so unlike the bubbly pink liquid in their glasses. "Jade is mated to one of the most temperamental males I've ever met. And I believe she loves the brute." He lifted his shoulders in exasperation. "I can't get a female to marry me, but two sullen Clecanians have humans fawning over them?"

Fejo's relentless charm faded, and Lily thought she saw true envy etched in his features.

Ziri must've seen the same because she said, "Maybe you'll have more luck this year. You're participating in a few months, right?"

"My happy ceremony day will be upon me again in three short months, not that anything will come of it other than some fun during the testing phase. I have that cross-universe trip scheduled right afterward. No female is going to choose to marry me knowing that."

"Humans might choose to partake in the Ceremony. You never know. There could be a human interested in space travel." She glanced at Lily. "Do you think humans would view Fejo as attractive?"

Lily snorted at the ridiculousness of the question. "Yes," she quickly confirmed, seeing the uncertainty that suddenly glinted in his eyes.

"See?" Ziri said.

Fejo grunted and focused on Lily, changing the subject. "What do you want to know about him?"

"Does he lie a lot? He failed to mention Ziri to me in the forest, and I can't decide if it was an abnormality or if he lies often." Lily had made sure to describe only the bare minimum about the time she'd spent with Verakko, and she'd also chosen to keep Alex's existence private.

"Yes and no." He smiled. "It's in character for him to only say what he must to the people around him. Always thinking he's the smartest person in the room and everyone else is just there to mess things up. I could see him thinking he knew best. But he isn't a dishonorable male."

"How do you know him so well?"

Fejo shrugged. "Well, I know him, but we aren't close. My father used to bring me to Mithrandir often. He was friends with Verakko's father. They'd force us to play together." Fejo rolled his eyes. "All Verakko would ever do was tinker with these little electronics."

Lily smiled to herself as the image of Verakko doing the exact same thing that morning popped into her head.

"Has he recognized you as a potential mate?" Fejo questioned, draping his large arms over the edge of the pool.

"No," she lied, making sure to school her features. She'd never been the best liar.

Fejo tilted his head and narrowed his eyes on her. Lily's heart pounded furiously, waiting to see if he'd caught on. His gaze slid to Ziri, who was distracted by a small piece of moss floating in the water, then back to her. Her nerves calmed when his features relaxed once again, and he took another sip of his drink.

"Too bad," Ziri said, flicking the moss out of their pool. "It would've been easy to claim you as his mivassi if the initial recognition had happened."

An electric zing shot through her body, now at full attention. "What do you mean 'claim me as his mivassi'?" She leaned forward in the water, eagerly glancing between her two pool mates. "He calls me that. Mivassi."

Ziri's lips curled into a knowing smile. "He does?"

Lily grunted impatiently. "What does it mean? In my ear it translates as *alternative*, but he told me that's not right."

Fejo and Ziri glanced at each other, both smiling. "Technically the translation is 'my alternative,'" Ziri explained. "It's a very common, but also very outdated, clause in most marriage contracts."

Lily slid forward in the steaming water, perched at the edge of her bench.

"The mivassi clause is meant for those times when someone already under contract recognizes a mate. Although it hasn't happened in...I don't even know how long. You were supposed to go to the queen or king at that time with your prospective partner and claim them as your mivassi, your alternative to your current wife or husband. If there was enough evidence to show that you could be mated, either marks or an account that your eyes had changed, your contract was voided without penalty."

Lily took in what she heard and recalled when he'd first called her the name. He'd told her from the beginning he'd thought she could be his mate. Did the use of that pet name confirm it? Her heart hammered in her chest. "Is it a common term of endearment here in Mithrandir?" she asked, wondering if it could be the equivalent of "baby" or "honey," although their surprised expressions told her differently.

"No." Ziri laughed. "It's a legalese term. I've never heard it used like that before. No wonder you found it strange." She raised her delicate brows high, creating deep lines in her normally perfect forehead. "And after you learned about me? Ooh, that translation must've been infuriating, especially if he didn't take the time to explain it."

Fejo shot them both an odd look. "I know why he used it."

"You do?" Ziri said, puzzled.

"You remember Yerew and Vik?" he asked Ziri, making Lily's irritation spike. *I'm the one who needs to hear about it. Focus!*

Ziri shrugged noncommittally. "I remember stories about them. Did you know them?"

"I met them once or twice when—"

"I don't mean to be rude," Lily interrupted rudely, "but who are they?"

Fejo grinned at her brusque tone. "They were his aunts. Great aunts, I think."

Ziri peered up to the pale fabric of their tent ceiling thoughtfully. "People used to tell stories about them; I don't really remember them, though. Only that they were mated. The last couple to get marks in Mithrandir, right?"

"Yes." Fejo nodded. "Yerew was Verakko's father's aunt. She was a clothier in the garment district. One day she met Vik, and they recognized each other. They knew immediately that they were mates, but their marks didn't appear, and Vik was in the middle of her marriage. She pored over her contract for days, looking for a loophole, until finally she found the old mivassi clause."

"Usually marks don't take long to appear after the initial recognition, you see," Ziri added. "So the mivassi clause was really just a relic. Thrown in for the rarest of scenarios."

"Good thing it was." Fejo grinned. "Vik took Yerew to the Queen at that time and claimed her as her mivassi. The Queen agreed and voided her contract, but even after that their marks didn't appear for a full year after the initial recognition. I only met them twice near the end of their lives—they were ancient at that point, hundreds of years old. But I remember it. As a loving joke, Vik always called Yerew her pesky mivassi."

Lily's throat constricted, and tears welled. "Why wouldn't he tell me that?" she choked out.

"I don't know."

Lily thought about it, and her heart pinched. She knew why. If he'd explained the name in the woods, he would've had to admit he was engaged. How else would he have been able to explain the application of such a specific word to her?

351

Although it seemed like ages ago, it'd been less than a day since he'd taken her back to his home. He'd had so many other things to explain. When would he have had the time to explain the nickname?

"Couldn't he claim me as his mivassi now to get out of his contract?" Lily asked, glancing between Ziri and Fejo.

"Not without evidence. That's why I said it's too bad his eyes haven't changed." Giving her a sympathetic grin, Ziri shrugged. "If that happened, you'd be considered mates, and this would all be resolved."

Lily's shoulders slumped. Not a loophole for her. She still needed to give Verakko an answer. She sipped her drink in silence.

"Well, I hope he recognizes you soon." Fejo winked. "It's clear how much you love him."

Lily froze, mouthing at Fejo like a fish. *Love?*

"That's crazy. I've only known him for a few days. I don't... I mean, I can't already... I don't love him." Lily's voice rose progressively higher as she babbled.

Do I?

24

"Twenty-eight b.h. That was clearly what I said." Verakko examined the clock near his door again and frowned. *Twenty-seven.* An hour late.

Verakko had spent the day building what he hoped would be a meaningful gift for Lily. If it had been any other female, he would've thought the gesture too personal, but he gathered from his time in Tremanta and his knowledge of the other Earthling named Alice that humans were generally eager to feel close to their partners. If he could just remind Lily of their time together before doubts had settled in, maybe she'd decide to accept his marks.

If Lily continued to be torn, would he really have the strength to keep his marks a secret and allow her to venture off on her own? He let out a shaky breath. *I have to be willing to.*

It wasn't as if either of them would be getting married tomorrow. Verakko was confident Lily wouldn't be interested in being courted by any other males. Even if she went to live on her own, he'd still have time before his marriage began to try to win her over. The deadline his mother had given him was merely a chance to avoid competition. Still, the idea of her being so far away from him, even if it was just a few floors, was literally sickening. Verakko absently ran a hand over his stomach. *Must be a symptom of the mating bond.*

He squared his shoulders and continued pacing near the front door, pausing at every small sound. This was ridiculous, he decided after quelling the instinct to begin a search of the hallway. Retrieving a mott, he leaned back against the cool wall and tried to calm himself. When the doors finally swooshed open, he turned away and painfully swallowed the overlarge gulp he'd taken.

"Sorry we're late."

Verakko shot his head around, trying to bite his tongue to keep from scolding Ziritha, but his words died in his throat.

Lily was there, looking more beautiful than ever. The pale-gold dress she wore was simple yet somehow more impactful than the intricate designs of normal Mithrandir attire. The unadorned fabric shined faintly and flowed over her curves like water. A delicate collection of chains weaved through her glittering hair, once again highlighted with gold the way it had been when he'd met her.

She'd chosen not to wear a mokti. Instead, shimmering, deep golden paint coated her neck, bright near her chin, then fading until it blended in with her natural skin near her delicate collar bones. He stepped toward her, every bit of him feeling undeserving of the vision before him. His throat remained tight, so he just stared at her.

"I advised against the dress, thinking it too simple," Ziri chimed in, reminding him she was still there. "But I'm glad to say I was wrong."

Lily smiled at him with painted lips.

Ziri cleared her throat. "I need to be getting back to the Queen." She turned to Lily, who smiled warmly at her. "It was wonderful to spend the day with you. I hope we'll see each other again very soon."

Lily wrapped her arms around a perplexed Ziritha. "Thank you so much for everything."

Ziri furrowed her brows at Verakko, not used to receiving hugs from near strangers. He shrugged in response. She smiled and patted Lily awkwardly on the back.

After Ziri left, Verakko had to shake himself out of his daze. "You look... I don't know if there's a word strong enough to do you justice."

Lily lowered her chin and grinned, a pretty pink tinting her cheeks.

"Did you have a good time?"

She gave an unsure smile. "It was...enlightening."

He studied her face, trying to see whether "enlightening" was a bad thing or a good thing and decided from the lack of worry in her gaze that Ziritha must've helped him. He released a low breath he hadn't realized he'd been holding. "Are you ready for your present?"

Lily tried to contain a wide grin and failed. "Yes." She peered around him, clearly thinking it was here.

"I actually have two gifts for you."

Her brows lifted in surprise. "Two?"

Verakko's chest expanded in anticipation. "My mother called. Alex has been found."

Her relaxed grin faded for a moment, and she searched his eyes, seeming dazed. "Really?" she said on a breath.

"Yes. She's safe."

Lily's face broke into a glorious smile, and then she let out a soft sob, all of her anxiety seeming to go with it. Her eyes turned glassy. "She's okay. Can we go see her? I need to talk to her."

"She's waiting for your call." Verakko lifted his communicator.

Lily soundlessly held out her hands. Verakko connected the call and spoke to the male on the other end, then handed the communicator over to Lily when the male left to retrieve Alex.

Lily clutched the communicator and silently ran an apologetic hand down Verakko's arm before dashing upstairs.

He gazed after her for long moments, his skin tingling from where she'd touched him and his heart full.

***

Lily vaulted onto the bed and held her breath, straining to listen. *Come on, Alex.*

"Hey there, Lilypad!" came Alex's smooth voice.

"Al—" Lily began crying from happiness, her words strangled and incomprehensible.

"Oh, hey, don't cry. I'm good."

"What happened to you?" Lily choked out.

Alex let out a whistle. "Oh, dude, so much. You really need to get over here, or I need to get over there. I'm in Sauven right now, but I'm supposed to go to some other city pretty soon. Trema…Tremeada…I can't remember what it's called. I don't even know where to start. I woke up on the shore of that river with a major headache. Pretty sure I had a concussion, and I spent I don't know how many days just vomiting and sleeping. But that's not the craziest thing that's happened."

"Tell me about it." Lily chuckled, reminded of her current predicament with Verakko. "What else happened?"

"Lilypad…" Alex paused dramatically. "I'm freaking getting married!"

"What? When?" Lily was shocked, both at the news as well as the stab of envy she felt. But then a simmering anger set in. "Wait, are you being forced into a marriage?"

"Well…"

"Tell. Me. Everything."

***

"Where are we going?" Lily asked for the third time.

He grinned down at her. The exuberant smile on her face had been immovable ever since she'd come downstairs. And it was contagious. "You'll see."

They walked down the hall to the restricted service elevator, and Verakko called it up, circumventing the alarm this time. It'd taken careful planning to make sure he'd be the only person able to access the one-hundredth floor, but a simple rescheduling of personnel in the buildings system would be enough to grant him a few hours without anyone being the wiser.

They stood waiting. Verakko felt a mixture of trepidation and hope at the furtive glances Lily kept leveling on him. His chest expanded at the thought that she may be coming around. A darker part of his mind reeled to think she may even let him touch her again today.

Her nostrils flared, and she turned toward him. "I missed that smell."

"Am I doing it again?"

Lily only smiled. She moved in closer and lifted on her toes, then buried her face in the crook of his neck and inhaled. Verakko's heart thundered, stomach growing tight and hands fisting at his sides to keep from pulling her to him. He should push her away until they were out of sight and in the elevator, but he couldn't bring himself to do it.

She sighed on an exhale. "That house smells like super-strong flowers all the time. I don't like it."

He began to explain that it'd been Ziritha's scent preference, when the faint sound of footsteps hit his ears. Lily gasped as he quickly pushed her away and urged her to walk down the hall, but it may have been too late.

A short female with long braided hair and a formal gown paused in the middle of the hallway, staring at them.

Lily stiffened, her intelligent eyes taking in the scene, and wisely put more space between them as they walked. The female began walking down the hall again. Maybe she'd wanted to make sure she didn't intrude on a private moment. As they passed one another, the female cocked her head and craned her neck to follow their progress. Perhaps she'd just been surprised to see them waiting at a service elevator.

Verakko exhaled a relieved breath when she passed, but said nothing. It wasn't as if he knew the female.

He guided Lily to another service elevator on the opposite side of the building and called it. Luckily this one was closer, only taking a few moments to arrive. They stepped in, and when the doors slid closed before them, Lily spoke.

"Do you know her?"

"No," Verakko breathed.

She placed a soft palm on his forearm, erasing all thought from his mind. "She didn't see us doing anything wrong. Only walking together. I mean, Ziri and I were literally in a hot tub with Fejo today. That must've been worse than us standing a little too close together."

Verakko's head snapped back as though he'd been slapped. He replayed her words in his mind, making sure he'd heard her right. "Fejo?" he growled.

Lily arched a brow at him, letting him know he needed to tread carefully. "Yes. We saw him at the spa, and he knew what I was. Ziri explained that you two were old friends, and

I decided I wanted to ask him more questions in private, so he joined us. Is that a problem?"

Verakko faced forward and cracked his neck before rolling his shoulder and taking a calming breath. "No," he grated.

Lily pursed her lips.

He peered at her sidelong as they approached their floor. "What did he tell you?"

Her annoyed expression shifted and was replaced with a sly smile. "He told me where the name mivassi came from."

Verakko grunted and checked the feed to make sure the floor was clear, then opened the doors. Fejo would have known about his aunts, but he still didn't like the idea of the charming male speaking with his mate. Not when they were still in such a precarious position and he was still so uncertain whether she'd decide to stay with him or not.

Lily gasped as the doors opened, and Verakko's chest puffed out a little. *Fejo could've never brought her here.*

Although this floor always made him uncomfortable, as it was the highest accessible floor of the building, he could admit it was beautiful. The water that was constantly recirculated from the lower floor's gardens was pumped up here and then cascaded down through the center of the building. Lily gazed at the torrential falling water in awe.

But the impressive sight of the water wasn't the reason he'd brought her here. He rolled his shoulders again, shaking off the flare of jealousy and anger at the idea of her spending time with Fejo, and placed a hand on the small of her back. "Do you remember the story I told you about Daera?"

Lily nodded, allowing herself to be guided to the far side of the room while her eyes remained riveted on the funnel of falling water.

His skin tingled in protest as they drew nearer to a large window. He gripped her hips, instinctively not wanting to take his hands off her at this height, and nodded out the window into the distance. "Those are the mountains I told you about."

Lily smiled up to him with brows drawn, rather than looking out the window. She ran her eyes over his face as if trying to work something out. Then, slowly, she covered the backs of his hands with her own and gazed out the window.

A purr started in Verakko's chest at the contact. Far off in the distance, the towering blue crystals that dotted the dark mountains glowed in the moonlight.

"They're beautiful." She ran a thumb over his hand. The paint covering his marks didn't deaden sensation, yet something in him ached for the paint to be removed, to feel her soft fingers caress his marks without any barriers.

He guided her away from the window and pulled his controller out of a pocket. "Do you remember what we were doing when I told you about them?"

Lily grinned. "Yeah, I remember I was kicking your ass at checkers."

Kicking ass? Verakko chuckled inwardly at the odd saying.

"Yes, well…" He typed in a few commands, and twenty-four flying objects rose from their hiding spot.

Lily stared wide-eyed and open-mouthed as the pieces settled into their programmed locations. "What is this?"

A larger object than the rest floated high above and projected an enormous checker board onto the floor. The gold and teal pieces, each as wide as dinner plates, remained hovering above their designated spaces.

"Did I get this dressed up to play checkers, Verakko?" she asked, tilting her head at him.

Doubt roared to life, exaggerating the hollow dread in his belly. With a clenched jaw, he uncertainly said, "Yes?"

Muscles primed to wince, he waited for her response.

The corner of her mouth lifted, and she pressed a soft kiss to his cheek. "I love it."

Verakko's breath whooshed out of him.

"I'm teal," she said, walking to the other side of the board.

He held in a frown as she moved away. Well, obviously she couldn't stand next to him and play, but her distance still made him anxious.

"Do I tell you which piece I want to move?" Lily stared down at the pieces hovering inches off the projected board.

He nodded.

***

Lily couldn't remember ever receiving a gift even halfway as thoughtful as this one. She stared at her pieces, trying to think of what move to make first, but her mind couldn't seem to focus. Had he built all of this today? While she'd been at the spa? He must've. Checkers didn't exist on this planet, which meant he couldn't have had the pieces already. What an incredibly impressive man.

She gazed at him across the room and nibbled on her lip to hide the goofy grin threatening to spread. If someone walking by could see into her brain at that moment, all they'd see was scribbled hearts with the initials *V* and *L*. It was becoming harder and harder to listen to her own reason. *How long have I known him? Less than a month. Hell, a week. It's only been a week. Do I know his last name? No. Do I know his favorite type of music? No.*

Lily and Verakko both took a few preliminary turns while she attempted to argue with her own eyes to remain focused on the board and not on the way his streaked blue hair curled gorgeously over one eyebrow. An intimate image of them together on a sun-streaked patio, him sitting in a chair and her standing in front of him trimming his hair, sprang to her mind and expanded her chest with warmth. When the image shifted into a much-naughtier scene, wherein her shears had been abandoned and the chair toppled, the heat traveled from her chest and pooled in her core.

"How is Alex?" he called from across the room.

Her cheeks heated, as if she'd been caught doing something rather than just daydreaming. "She's...not great but not bad either, I guess. I told her we'd come visit as soon as we could. Would that be alright?" She raised a brow.

Verakko paused for a moment before answering. "I'll make sure you get to see her. Yes."

Lily's chest deflated. He'd phrased it that way because the person taking her to Sauven would depend on her decision about him, she realized. If she chose not to stay with him, whomever her guardian turned out to be would take her. She pushed those worries from her mind and focused on him again.

Verakko made his move, and Lily noticed the piece he was floating across the board was colored a different shade of gold than the rest. It looked older, more rudimentary, if it was possible to say such a thing about a flying object that had seemingly no wings or propellers.

She spotted an opening and jumped one of his pieces, then clapped her hands together.

Verakko grimaced, eyes roving over the board in frustration. "You enjoyed the spa?"

"Very much. Thank you again for setting it up." She chuckled. "No massages for me, though. I was too nervous about it."

A flash of fang accompanied his grin. "I can't say I'm upset. If you need to be massaged *anywhere*, I'd be happy to oblige."

Lily shivered, feeling her nipples harden under the silky material of her dress. Before she could stop herself, throaty words were spilling out of her. "I suppose I do have a few kinks you could work out."

Verakko's gaze darkened, and he licked a fang.

His lost piece that she'd just jumped drifted toward her, and she stepped away, thinking it was heading behind her to land somewhere. Instead, it hovered in front of her hands as though expecting something.

"I forgot to mention. These pieces are special. For each one you win—" Verakko grinned and tapped a finger against his controller, "—you get a prize."

Lily squealed in delight as a compartment on the top of the round object emerged, revealing what was unmistakably a piece of candy. "Candy?" she asked, wanting to make sure, even though it was already halfway to her lips.

Verakko's shoulders shot back triumphantly, and he nodded.

Over the next few minutes, they joked and flirted and played checkers, each earning themselves delicious sweets. Lily made her final move with an exaggerated frown directed toward a joyous-looking Verakko.

He jumped her remaining pieces, then punched the air, reveling in his victory.

Lily giggled and chewed on the last of the unfamiliar fruit-flavored candy that was somehow both chewy and juicy. While Verakko did the same, she peered down at the pile of checkers and studied the odd-looking one.

Along the top of the round object were sloppy vertical symbols.

"The Super Bandit version two," Verakko intoned from the other side of the room. "I found it in the storage cube my father had packed my things into."

Her chest grew tight.

He pocketed his controller and crossed to her. Smile fading, eyes growing serious. Looking at her with drawn brows that urged her to believe him, he said, "I wanted to show you that the things we shared…what I shared with you…they *were* real."

Lily swallowed and gazed up at him, knowing in her heart what he said was true.

A half laugh, half sob escaped her, and she nodded, throat too tight for words. She twined her arms around his neck and kissed him. Strong arms wrapped around her waist. He lifted her, drawing her chest flush with his, and slanted his mouth against hers to deepen the kiss. The sudden purr that erupted from his chest vibrated through him, tickling her tongue and lips as she clung to him.

One week, her mind hissed in the background. *Do I know what side of the bed he sleeps on? No. Do I know the name of his first pet? No.*

Her grip around his neck tightened. With an answering groan, his hand rose to fist her hair.

I know what he's like in a bad mood. I know he'll sacrifice himself to protect me. I know he loves tinkering and hates heights. I know he can be shortsighted and pompous and rude.

Do I know he's mine? Yes. Lily sighed, melting against his warm, rumbling chest.

Do I know that I love him? Yes. Deep down, she felt it. Somehow, someway, the bond was real, and despite everything she'd been through, she could feel it pulling them together inextricably.

This man was hers. It'd come as a shock earlier to have someone else point out the feelings she'd so viciously denied, but there was no doubt left. She'd been falling in love with his infuriating personality and hidden gooey center since they'd first met.

"Let's go back to the house," she panted after breaking off the kiss.

He gifted her a glorious, fanged smile and made a deep groan of approval. Dropping her to her feet, he programmed his floating checkerboard to clean itself up and led her to the door.

She needed to figure out a good way to tell him. He'd done so many romantic things for her, and now it was her turn to do the same. She'd plan something for tomorrow. She inwardly grinned, thinking of a few things she'd like to do with him in bed, but decided that telling him she loved him and agreeing to be his mate in full required a little more romance and a little less lust.

They climbed into the lift, and she continued to brainstorm. Maybe she could build him a fire in the apartment? No, stupid. Get a private natural pool at the spa like they had in the tunnel? Maybe.

Her thoughts were interrupted when he pushed her into the wall of the lift. His mouth descended onto hers, his tongue gliding against hers in slow, languid strokes. Lily whimpered into his mouth, and her sex clenched.

Verakko ran his hands down to grip her ass and let out an approving hiss. They stayed locked together, breathing hard for long moments after the lift stopped moving.

When he finally tore away, he gazed down at her, his eyes a beautiful glowing emerald in the dim space.

"How about you take me to that bed now?"

The most gorgeous, heat-inducing, wolfish grin spread over his face. In a voice gone deep with lust, he rasped, "Yes, mivassi."

25

They pulled away from each other and tried their best to smooth their rumpled clothes and calm their breathing before leaving the service lift, but Verakko couldn't force the evidence of his arousal to abate.

This night had gone better than he could've ever hoped. Lily had kissed him. She'd gazed at him with tenderness in her eyes instead of the cold hurt she'd been sporting for the last few days.

All they had to do now was make it a few steps to his temporary home, which he'd be selling and exchanging for whatever Lily preferred as soon as she consented to be his. Checking to see that the hallway was clear, he tugged her out and down the hall.

The faint scent of her arousal through her underwear toyed with his senses, and he had to fight the urge to simply throw her over his shoulder and leap the remaining distance to his home.

A sharp trill sounded from his pocket, tugging at his thoughts, but he ignored it. Whoever it was could call back.

Pressing his palm to the scanner on his door, he waited for it to open, then whirled Lily through the doorway. As soon as the door closed, he advanced. She smiled deviously at him and backed away. Icy veins of antivenom traveled along the roof of his mouth and filled his fangs in preparation.

The trilling continued, and Lily frowned. "Shouldn't you get that?"

"Fuck no." He leapt toward her, landing inches away.

She laughed and rested her fists on his chest. "They keep calling. You should at least see who it is." She bit her lip. "Once I get you up there," she said, nodding toward the ceiling, "you won't be leaving for a while. Better check it now."

Lily slid her hand down his back, making him shiver, then reached into his pocket, producing his communicator.

His eyes flashed down to the screen, meaning only to assure her it was of no importance, but then he looked again. He grunted in frustration and took the device. "It's a formal summons from my mother. She requests I go to her right now."

"Why?" Her expression grew worried.

He shrugged, not wanting his own sudden anxiety to affect her mood. "This is usually how she summons me. Could be anything." He pressed a soft kiss to her upturned mouth and gathered the strength to step away. "I'll be back as soon as I can."

There was still a note of concern in her eyes, but she smiled shyly and nodded. "I'll be waiting."

Verakko backed away from her, releasing a miserable groan at her seductive tone. Before he decided to ignore the Queen's request altogether, he turned and stomped out the door.

The whole ride to the palace, Verakko tried to predict what his mother might need from him. The female from hours before kept popping into his mind. Had she reported him? He shook his head at the idea. If she had any evidence against him, guards would've escorted him to the palace. He wouldn't have been summoned.

It was more likely that his mother wanted a report on his progress with Lily. Perhaps to properly plan her speech. The back of his neck prickled as he realized Lily hadn't given him a definitive answer one way or another.

He reached the palace and jogged up the steps at lightning speed, coming to a halt in the entryway. As he waited to be announced and led in, dread settled like a weight in his stomach. One of the guards shot him a sour look, and he returned it tenfold.

"Follow me."

Verakko followed one of the armed guards through the sprawling foyer and froze.

"I said follow me," the guard demanded from near an archway.

That was the way to the trial room.

His legs tensed to run while his mind raced to find another escape. He'd never make it anywhere if he ran. Definitely wouldn't make it back to Lily.

He forced his feet to move, following the guard, and heaved out a deep sigh of relief when the guard continued through the large trial room and into a private office situated near the rear. The office was large but devoid of windows, making the sparsely furnished room feel smaller than it was.

His mother stood on the far side of the room, hands clasped behind her back, staring at a large screen mounted to the wall. Laws and contracts and communications were all organized on the screen, ready to be reviewed.

"Verakko." Ziritha walked into the room, closing the door behind her. Once they were alone, the look of pity on the female's face had his insides turning to liquid. Something was wrong.

"What's happened?" he barked a little more harshly than he should've, fear and anxiety getting the better of him.

"Baeo and her son have reported you," his mother intoned, facing him with a tight expression.

All of the air seemed to leave his body. Blood rushing in his ears, he thought about Lily, in his home and waiting.

"Her son apparently met Lily at the spa today and was interested enough in her to ask his mother to inquire about negotiating a contract, but when she came to speak with Lily, she saw you touching inappropriately in the hallway of your building and she scented you on the female as she passed by."

Verakko threw his hands up, his shock morphing into fury. "That isn't a breach of contract! How did she even know where Lily was staying?"

Ziri peered between them with drawn brows and sympathetic eyes. "He said he couldn't find her registered guardian listed anywhere, so he looked up the name of the person paying for her services and figured you'd been assigned."

"That's not enough evidence," he hissed, balling his fists so as not to punch anything.

"No, it's not. But it's enough for a trial, and you won't be able to lie. Can you truthfully claim you haven't breached your contract with that female?" His mother gave him a hard look, already knowing the answer to her question.

Think! How to get out of this? If he was brought to court and claimed innocence, he'd be subjected to an examiner's *sway*, forced to allow it to permeate his mind and answer all questions honestly. He might reveal everything down to his marks. If he pled guilty and admitted to a breach in his contract, he'd be questioned and sentenced, but not *swayed*.

He shouldn't have left Lily. He should've seen this coming. Why hadn't he taken her and run? A thought occurred to him, and he narrowed his eyes at the females before him. "Why did you ask me to come here? It's normally guards who retrieve citizens for questioning. Did you want to make me feel at ease so I wouldn't fight back?" His words grew progressively louder and more hostile as the realization that he may not see Lily for years settled in.

"Control yourself!" his mother boomed over him, a brief flicker of anger flitting over her features before powerful control reigned once more. "I asked you here to give us the opportunity to speak before the council arrives." Another flash of anger lit her eyes. "I told you to stay out of sight. To treat her like you would any other female who wasn't your betrothed. You didn't." Her voice grew quiet. "And now there's nothing I can do to help you."

He needed to reveal his marks; it was the only way. Show them Lily was his mate, and this would all be over. The contract would be void. She would be his.

"I won't be trapped." Lily's words played through his mind. The pain on her face and the tears in her eyes when she'd said it cut him like a knife even now. He couldn't do that to her again. Not for this. It wasn't as if it'd be forever. He'd serve his time and return to her. She was his mate, after all. He didn't need to be eligible for a marriage to be with her. When he did finally reveal his marks, whenever that day came, it would be because she was ready and because she knew without a shadow of a doubt that they belonged together.

A sharp buzz sounded at the door.

"I'll have my guards retrieve Lily while you plead your case. She'll be given the opportunity to speak on your behalf."

"No!" he blurted. "She'll be frightened. They don't even speak her language. And..." He needed to find a way to warn her not to make a claim of innocence. Warn her she'd be *swayed* to tell the truth and she wouldn't legally be allowed to brush off the *sway*.

"I'll get her," Ziri said, stepping forward and finally speaking. Her voice was croaky, almost as if tight with restrained emotion. She gazed at the Queen. "She knows me."

The Queen studied Ziri for a moment before nodding.

When Ziri had fled from the room, Verakko and his mother stood staring at each other. She opened her mouth to speak, but shut it again.

Another knock echoed around the room.

She took a step toward him, her brows creasing in something that resembled concern. "Can you give me any reason…" She swallowed and let out a long exhale. "Any at all, that would keep me from sending you away?"

Verakko studied his mother. Her features were tight, her mouth thinned. But her eyes glimmered with sadness. Was he finally seeing what his father had always said was there under the surface? Was she allowing him to see vulnerability? His chest constricted.

"I appreciate what you've done for me already, Mother. I won't reveal that you gave me time with her. But there's nothing I can say." Verakko saw a muscles tick in her jaw at his words, and he couldn't help but smile. "It's alright. I'll be fine. You'll see."

She stared at him for a moment longer before straightening and donning a mask of indifference. Head held high, she crossed to the door and stepped into the trial room, where her council was already waiting.

In an ornamental chair placed along the side of the long room sat the smug female from the hall, along with an uncomfortable-looking male.

26

Lily grinned and let out a deep sigh after the door closed behind Verakko. She spun in place, then scanned the room. "Hopefully he'll be back soon," she said to no one in particular.

Running her hands over her hips, she luxuriated in the incredible softness of the odd fabric. She wandered to the kitchen and examined the tips of her hair. The glitter coat was so fine it almost looked like shine from a distance.

Once in the kitchen, she stood in the center and peered around, not sure what to do with herself until Verakko returned. Deciding she had an opportunity to examine an alien house that most scientists would kill for, she began looking in every nook and cranny of the two-story home.

The two bedrooms seemed typical enough. Lily frowned at the cream and silver bedroom on the first floor, obviously meant for Ziritha, then a grin tugged at her lips. That meant Verakko had wanted to squirrel her away in his room.

A separate room with only a small pool of hot water made her stop. Did she have time for a quick dip before Verakko returned? With a last longing look at the steaming tub, she pulled herself away.

Lily searched every unlocked cabinet, squinted under every piece of furniture, and rifled through every drawer she could find. Most of the objects she came across were recognizable. Or at least she believed she could deduce what they were for. Some of the others items she found confounded her.

Currently she was standing in front of the gleaming control panel for the furniture, wondering if she felt brave enough to press a few alien symbols and see what would happen.

The front door whooshed open, and Lily whirled around, her heart ramping up to a frantic beat at Verakko's return. How could she have ever doubted she loved him?

When she found Ziritha panting in the doorway, her smile faded. Her hair was no longer immaculate, frizz haloing her scalp, and she was winded. Quite unlike the graceful, poised pre-queen she'd been with all day.

"Are you alright?" she asked, wishing she knew how to get Ziri a glass of water.

Between pants, Ziri breathed, "He's been reported..." Deep breath. "They're at the palace now... The council will vote..."

Lily rushed forward, her heart thundering in her chest for an entirely different reason. "What? Who?"

Ziri shook her head and tugged on Lily's arm. "They can't make a decision about anything until all members of the council are there. They'll wait for me. I wanted to get here as fast as I could to explain. Let's go."

"But—" Lily began, insides growing cold.

The woman pulled her roughly through the doorway and leveled a serious stare on her. "We need to go," she *swayed*.

Lily grunted and brushed the *sway* away. "That doesn't work on me."

Ziri let out a huff of frustration and eyed her for a moment longer before heading down the hallway, Lily in tow. "He's going to be sent away. You need to plead in favor of his character, and hopefully the sentence will be reduced. Tell them you initiated the pairing and make sure to play up the differences in your culture, and if you care for him at all, do not tell them he lied about being under contract."

This was all moving too fast. One minute she was smitten and awaiting her mate's return, and now she was getting pointers about how to get him a reduced sentence. Unlawful pointers, if Ziri's hushed tone and nervous glances around them were any indication. "What'll happen to him?" Lily tried to recall what he'd told her. "He said he'll be sent away? To where? Tremanta?"

"Tremanta?" Ziri halted and turned on her. Her eyes were fiery and full of emotion, but Lily sensed it wasn't anger directed specifically at her. "Off-world, Lily. He'll be sent to serve on a barge in space, far, far away from here. You'll go years without seeing him, and you'll have to marry other males in the meantime." She shot an angry glare behind her. "When he finally returns, he'll no longer be eligible for marriage, but you still will be. Do you understand me?"

"He'll be sent where?" Lily breathed, an iron band tightening around her chest. *Sent away for years? Because I was too scared to realize what he means to me in time?*

They stepped onto a lift, and Ziri tried to smooth her hair and clothes.

Lily pressed a hand to her belly as it roiled in protest, her mind racing but unable to follow any one train of thought. She slid her eyes shut. *In. Out. In. Out.*

Before she'd realized it, they were exiting the lift and walking toward a cruiser.

They climbed in and sat in silence, both working through their own thoughts. A mirror appeared on the wall with a touch of Ziri's hand, and she examined her appearance, dabbing here and there to perfect her makeup.

"Why are you helping me?" Lily thought back to what Verakko had told her about his mother, the Queen. What he'd mentioned about the women of this planet overall. It seemed as though the people would lose respect for Ziritha as a ruler if she didn't punish a breached contract. It would serve her better to push for a severe sentence. It'd make it clear to everyone that she wasn't the type to be fucked with or disrespected.

"I know what it's like to not be able to be with the male you want."

"Fejo's friend." Lily recalled their brief and personal conversation at the spa.

Ziri smiled sadly. "If there's even the slightest chance that Verakko's marks could appear for you, I want to see that through. It's selfish, really." She swallowed. "If humans are found to consistently call forth marks, then maybe the pressure to marry and procreate will be taken off the females of this world." Ziri shrugged, and the hope in her eyes just about broke Lily's heart. "Maybe no one would care if he and I were together."

Lily swallowed hard. His marks had already appeared, but she'd asked him to hide them. It was clear that this world was suffering, that people were placing their species' needs above their own, yet she'd only been concerned with the ways in which this society might be unfair to her.

"The Queen has commanded the council to update their translators so they'll all be able to understand you," Ziri said, her serious expression back in place.

The door slid open again, and Lily saw they were stopped on the top of a massive entryway. She stepped out and turned in place. The buildings of the old city could be seen to the right, the towering skyscrapers of the new city behind them.

With a deep breath, she followed Ziri into the cool interior of the entryway. Guards on either side tilted their heads toward Ziri and tapped their thumbs to their shoulder as she walked while studying Lily curiously. The hall they traveled through was gorgeous, lined with shining stone and thick columns, but she couldn't seem to pay attention to any of it.

Over and over in her head, she rehearsed what she should say. Trying to decide what approach would work best with a group of reigning aliens. Emotional outcry for the man she loved? Lily glanced sidelong at Ziri's stern expression and thought not. The only foolproof way to ensure Verakko's freedom was clear.

It was decision time. A small part of her remained fearful of the world knowing about Verakko's marks, but it was an irrational fear, cemented by decades of lackluster experiences. She loved Verakko, so why did it still terrify her to agree to be bound to him forever?

Ziritha rounded a corner, and Lily's steps faltered as she followed the woman into a severe, vaulted room. The floors were tiled with black stone, imitating the glittering black sand of the desert. Or maybe it was the sand from the desert, treated in some way to make it hard. The dark blue of the walls did nothing to relieve Lily's growing dread. The soft lighting provided by extra-large glowing orbs near the ceiling worked to make the space feel foreboding rather than romantic. At the foot of the room, a group of silent, dour individuals stood.

On a raised platform stood the Queen. Lily snapped her jaw shut, her immediate response to seeing the intimidating woman; awe. She wore a deep blue robe almost the same color as her navy skin. It covered her from neck to floor, yet her arms peeked out through slits in the fabric and rested, clasped in front of her.

The Queen's critical eyes bore into hers before running down her body. Lily forced herself not to hunch her shoulders.

Ziri halted Lily with a hand and whispered, "Wait until you're asked to speak," then continued forward alone to take her place at the foot of the Queen's platform, along with four other individuals.

One stern woman wore a pale blue robe. Another wore a purple, two-piece formfitting outfit and openly frowned, showing her mood more readily than the two remaining men, whose expressions were impassive.

Movement from the corner caught Lily's eye, and she saw the same woman who'd passed them in the hall before she and Verakko had gone on their date. Standing next to the woman was the attendant from the spa, the one who'd flirted with her, his head hung low as though he were embarrassed to be here. He refused to meet Lily's eyes. Had they reported them? Based on what?

She tried to calm her initial reaction of fury, reminding herself that in their minds, they'd witnessed the husband to their future queen carousing with an unknown woman. She couldn't blame them for reporting the infraction, especially if it was as much of a slap in the face as Verakko had made it out to be.

The sound of heavy footsteps behind her made her turn. Her breath hitched at the sight of Verakko and a guard. Although he wasn't restrained, he walked alongside the guard without complaint. His eyes stayed glued to Lily as he passed and headed for the platform in front of her. He gave her what was meant to be a comforting smile and nod, but the smile didn't reach his eyes, and the stiffness of his body made the nod more of a jerk of his head. Her eyes flashed to his hands, but they were still covered.

When he reached the front, the Queen spoke into the cavernous space, her voice bouncing forcefully off the cold stone walls. "Verakko Ye'vet has been found to be in breach of his marriage contract. Baeo saw him with Lily of Earth. She witnessed them pulling away from an embrace in the hallway outside of his home."

Lily stepped forward, ready to explain that Baeo hadn't seen what she thought she'd seen, even knowing it was a lie, but Ziritha shook her head in warning, and Lily slammed her mouth shut. She locked eyes with Verakko and saw a muscle twitch in his jaw.

He didn't look particularly perturbed by the proceedings. He stared at her intensely, as though attempting to take a mental picture of her. Tears welled behind her eyes.

The Queen continued, "The accused was questioned, as is customary after a report of a breach is made. Verakko has admitted guilt. Therefore, I'll decide his punishment, and the council will decide the severity."

Lily's stomach flipped. He'd told them he was guilty? Why not tell them the truth about the marks? Claim her as his mivassi? Something?

The Queen addressed Lily directly. "Since you're not familiar with our laws, I will tell you the typical punishments for breach of contract are the loss of all future marriage eligi-bility as well as an off-world work assignment, allowing a post in the city for a hardworking male more appreciative of the gift of having a wife. My council will decide on the length of the assignment after hearing statements from the accused and from the abettor."

Lily tried to calm her racing heart. They'd both get to speak. He wasn't going to be sent away if she had any say in it.

The Queen looked at her son with thinned lips. "Do you have any claims to make for this female? And if not, would you like to say anything for the council to take into consider-ation while deciding on the severity of my ruling?"

Lily shot her panicked eyes to meet his. *Tell them! Show them your marks!*

Verakko remained silent for a moment, his brows drawn. He gazed down at the floor and licked a fang. Then he looked back up at her and smiled weakly.

Verakko raised his head to his mother and squared his shoulders. "I do not."

Lily stared at him, and a surge of love heated her insides. He was trying to keep his word to not force her into anything. He was allowing himself to be sent away for who knew how long, even knowing she'd be forced to marry other men. All because he thought she needed more time. The balloon of emotion always expanding in her chest finally burst, and she released a throaty sob.

She quickly tried to school her features, but their audience had noticed. Verakko took a step toward her, his hands flexing, but stopped when the guard behind him cleared his throat, reminding him he wasn't really free.

"Do you not wish to claim her as your mivassi?" asked Ziritha suddenly.

All eyes turned toward her. Lily saw the briefest flash of surprise pass over the Queen's face as she looked at her protégé. She then turned to a scowling Verakko with brows raised.

Verakko lifted his chin, the resolution to do what he thought Lily wanted clearer than it had been before. "I do not wish to make such a claim."

The Queen's apathetic mask faded, and she looked between Lily, Verakko, and Ziritha with narrowed eyes. Her gaze finally settled on Lily. "Do you have anything you'd like to say to the council on behalf of Verakko?"

Another strangled sob broke free, and she nodded.

"Lily, it'll be alright. It won't feel like long," Verakko rasped from his place near the council.

Another tear slid free, and she grinned. She raised her head to the Queen and in a strong, sure voice, declared, "Verakko is my mate. He'll be staying here with me."

A frenzied murmuring broke out in the room, echoing off the walls. Excited and disbelieving glances shot from Lily to Verakko. A few of the guards frowned down at his covered wrists and shook their heads in disapproval.

All Lily could do was watch Verakko's wide-eyed face. He held her gaze with such a defeated, worried look that she knew he must be thinking she'd revealed their bond out of guilt or pity.

"He covered his marks," she continued, "because I asked him to. I was uncomfortable with the idea of matehood. If you take the paint off, you'll see."

"Hute, fetch remover, now!" Ziri shouted excitedly to a guard, who scurried away. Lily could see the restrained joy in the woman's masked expression.

"When did the marks appear?" the Queen asked.

Lily peered at Verakko, his head hung low. Her skin tingled, needing to get to him and explain that this was what she wanted. That she'd been an idiot for thinking differently and she was so sorry for putting him in this position. "Just before we arrived in the city." Lily paused, unsure what to call the woman. "Majesty," she tried.

"And you've made him hide the bond since then? Why are you suddenly revealing it now?" She saw a flare of anger in the Queen's eyes and could've sworn it was outrage on Verakko's behalf.

Verakko's head raised as well, his worried eyes begging for an explanation.

"I didn't fully understand what it meant or what was at stake. We don't have matehood on Earth, and I was scared. I started having feelings for him after only a few days, and when he told me he was under contract with another woman, I didn't know how to handle it. But none of that matters anymore." Lily had to stop, her throat clogging with emotion. Another tear slipped free. She held Verakko's gaze, hoping he took the words she said to heart. "I love him. I love how impatient and snarky and intelligent he is. And how he softens when he's around me. I've been traveling the world since I was young, and I've never felt like I fit anywhere." Verakko's brows relaxed, and his chest expanded. Lily sniffed. "But I fit with him. And I don't want to be anywhere he isn't."

Verakko shuddered out a breath and beamed at her. His loud, rattling purr reverberated around the room as the guard who'd left to find remover rushed over to Verakko's extended hands with a cloth. They held each other's grinning gazes as if no one else existed.

Small gasps broke out around the room again when Verakko's marks were finally revealed. Everyone's eyes fell on the Queen. Lily held her breath.

With a small, almost undetectable smile, she said, "The contract is void."

Lily's stomach somersaulted as Verakko dashed toward her at a preternatural speed. Vaulting into his arms, she twined her hands through his hair and kissed him. Tearing away, she whispered, "I'm so sorry it took me this long to see it."

"That you love me?" Verakko said, grinning.

"Yes." Lily chuckled, keeping her voice low.

Verakko blew a breath out through his nose and shook his head in wonderment. "Mivassi, I would've waited my whole life for you."

Lily kissed him again, the tidal wave of happiness suffusing her being more intense than she could've ever imagined.

Epilogue

Two months later

"You're heading out tomorrow, right?" Alice said, while tickling the foot of Laura, Jade's chubby baby girl.

Lily smiled as Laura squealed with delight. "Yeah, it's been a while since I've seen Alex. Time to catch up."

Alice leaned back in her seat, draping her shining brown hair over one shoulder and crossing her long legs. "Well, thanks for meeting with us. We need more volunteers to contribute to the human database." She huffed out a breath. "There's only so much I know, you know? I've already detailed everything I can remember about animals and everything I remember learning in school, but more people means more info. I hope if enough Clecanians read up on us, it'll help smooth the transition for the next time someone finds a human."

"It might've helped for me and Verakko if he'd known more about Earth going in."

"Did someone say my name?" Verakko strolled in through the front door, Jade, Theo, and Luka at his heels.

Lily stood and crossed through their living room to greet him with a quick kiss. He deepened it at first, then reluctantly pulled away when she swatted at his chest. The past month had been the best Lily could remember. She and Verakko had chosen to leave Mithrandir and purchase a home in Tremanta. She had decided that being closer to the vast majority of humans would be beneficial, and Verakko had been eager to return to his beloved job.

They'd purchased a house on the edge of the city, close enough for Lily to enjoy the many amenities of city life, but far enough away that their trendy one-story home overlooked the woods. Every morning, Verakko would walk her to beauty school before taking a cruiser to whichever site needed a technologist. He often tried to explain what he'd done that day when he got home, but Lily understood very little of it.

"How was the tour?" Lily asked, peeking around Verakko's large frame to the other three closing the door behind them. He'd taken them out to his workshop, where he built all kinds of gadgets.

"I didn't understand technology at home, and I'm not going to understand it here," Jade said, bending over to greet Laura, who giggled and produced an impressively sized snot bubble. The little girl had faint pearlescent markings running all over her skin as well as bright red hair, just like Jade.

Theo, Jade's large husband whose frown was in place remarkably more often than Verakko's, nodded unconvincingly. "It was...impressive."

"Why are you asking them?" Verakko groused. "No one here appreciates the beauty of my work."

"I do," Luka, Theo's brother, argued. "I'd love to talk with you more about collaborating on tech for the reserve." He kissed a blushing Alice on the lips and continued. "Since I've started working fewer hours, I'm worried I'm missing critical observational breakthroughs. I need a piece of tech that can follow specific animals and record, but that isn't discernible to them. I haven't been able to find one that works yet. They all scurry as soon as it comes near."

Verakko and Luka then launched into a heated discussion about what types of materials would put off the least amount of scent, while the rest of them sat and watched, trying to follow along quickly enough to add to the conversation and failing.

The first one to break and beg for the barrage of technology jargon to end was Laura. Fat tears fell from her eyes as she cried. In a matter of seconds, her cries became ear-splitting wails.

"Sorry. She's just tired. We missed naptime today," Jade said. She caught Theo's raised brow and added, "Okay, okay, I made her miss naptime." Jade smiled at the other women. "She just started laughing, and for some reason, the funniest thing in the world is Cebo. I think he knows it too because he comes over and tickles her with his whiskers, and it's the cutest thing. I couldn't interrupt!"

"I still can't believe how fast she's growing," Alice said.

Jade lifted Laura into her arms and bounced on the balls of her feet. "I know! It's happening so much faster than a full-human baby. Too fast for me." They all winced as Laura let out another ear-splitting shriek.

"Maybe Verakko could *sway* her to go to sleep?" Lily asked, peering up at Verakko, who was looming over her chair.

He shook his head. "I can't begin to know what she's thinking."

"It's okay." Jade grinned mischievously. "Wanna see a magic trick?"

Theo, who'd been quietly sipping on a mott in a far chair, stifled a grin and set his drink down. He gazed at Jade and Laura with a staggering amount of love as they approached.

The rest of the room watched as Jade handed Laura off to Theo. He curled his baby girl against his chest and kissed the top of her head.

Lily didn't notice anything extraordinary as Laura continued to wail. But then suddenly another sound rumbled through the room. As Laura's cries stuttered out and her eyelids grew heavy, Lily realized Theo had started purring, the relaxing rumble against his chest lulling Laura to sleep almost instantly.

"Isn't that the greatest thing you've ever seen!" Jade whispered.

She and Alice both nodded enthusiastically. Verakko wrapped an arm around her waist from behind, and she leaned into his warm chest.

"We'd better head out now before she wakes up," Jade whispered, careful to pick up their things without making any sound.

Theo kept his hold tight on Laura and followed his mate, nodding to them with an unbidden grin.

"We'll get out of your hair too. I'm sure you need to pack," Alice said, moving to give Lily a hug. "Will you be back in time for the meeting?"

Lily sobered and nodded. "Any more news on PRIC?"

Alice shook her head, a concerned look entering her eyes. "We haven't heard anymore from them, but the idea of them hiding in plain sight is terrifying. Every city has made announcements about the humans, and the ones who've been found are safe for now, but what happens when a rescued woman comes across one of her jailors masquerading as a simple chef or something?"

Lily shook her head, worry making her throat dry. How many more women were still out there? How many, like her, were choosing not to make themselves known? How many hadn't made it?

As if sensing her sudden upheaval, Verakko's grip around her waist tightened, and he rubbed a palm on her shoulder.

Alice smiled at the gesture and waved her hand in the air. "Forget about it for right now. We'll have hours to talk about it when you get back. Just enjoy your trip."

Lily sighed, not sure it was possible to wipe it from her mind completely, but smiled anyway and bid the last of their visitors farewell.

When the door finally closed, she let out a long breath and plopped onto her soft green couch, sipping the last of her tury.

"Don't worry, mivassi. It may sound callous, but now that the world knows how important humans are, they'll be very well protected. I'm confident that if any Insurgents make any attempt to harm them, they'll be caught."

Lily nodded, but remained unconvinced.

Verakko rounded the couch and sat next to her. "Also keep in mind what impulsive creatures human females are," he said, gazing out the window with mock sincerity.

A laugh broke from Lily's belly. He always knew just how to make her feel better. She angled her body on the couch so her head rest against the arm, then raised her foot and playfully kicked his thigh. "Shut up." She giggled.

"I mean, their actions will be so inconsistent and illogical..." Verakko shook his head, then raised his eyes to the heavens. He snatched both her feet and sprung onto his knees. "Any active PRIC members left won't be able to keep up with their unfathomable thought processes long enough to catch them anyway."

She laughed at the outrageous claims and tugged at her feet.

In one swift motion, Verakko pulled her legs until she was lying fully on the couch and then crawled over her.

Lily tried to smother her grin as he lowered onto his elbows and hovered above her. "You know none of that is true."

With one hand, he gripped the collar of his shirt and tugged it over his head.

Lily's pulse picked up at the sight of his naked chest. He gazed down at her, and his eyes locked onto her neck, making a jolt of liquid heat pool in her core.

Wedging his hips between hers, he ground against her, shaft already hard. Verakko lowered his mouth to the sensitive spot on the curve of her shoulder and tsked. "Ruled by emotions. That's what you are."

"Oh yeah?" Lily purred while running a hand down his firm stomach.

Verakko groaned into her neck in approval.

While he was distracted, she hooked her ankle around his leg, gripped the back of his pants, and shoved as hard as she could against the side of the couch. They rolled, and Verakko landed with a thud on the ground, Lily straddling him.

He growled low but grinned and raised his arms behind his head, looking pleased as punch at the change of positions.

Lily chuckled and rocked her hips, eliciting another rattling growl. "I guess we are a little unpredictable," she joked.

Like a flash, Verakko sat up and slid her skirt up to her hips. With one quick tug, he ripped her underwear off. She arched into his hold as he lavished her neck with sharp nips from his fangs, followed by soothing kisses and swipes of his tongue. Despite their playful repartee, her mind muddled until nothing else in the world seemed to matter. She rocked her now-naked sex against him and frowned at the barrier still between them.

She sat back, but Verakko's arm immediately wrapped around her waist to hold her in place. When she made her intentions known by reaching between their bodies and fumbling with the fastenings on his pants, he made a sound of approval and loosened his hold.

She eased back until he released her completely. His rapt gaze was hungry as he watched her move down his body and kneel between his legs. After Lily's emotional declaration of love in Mithrandir, she and Verakko had barricaded themselves in the bedroom for days, exploring each other's bodies. The first time she'd run her tongue along his shaft, a seemingly unheard-of thing for a Clecanian woman to do, he'd cursed, and every muscle had tensed in the most erotic way.

He reclined on his elbows, his glowing eyes now a darker shade of emerald, watching her every move.

***

Verakko stared in awe as his mate slid his pants down his hips, allowing his cock to spring free. She gave him one of her devastating grins and lowered her mouth until she was a breath away from the head of his shaft. When she wrapped a firm hand around the base of his cock, he hissed.

"Tell me again about humans," she said in a false tone of confusion. "You said they were unpredictable?" She released his cock and lifted a brow at him.

He barked out a laugh. "Did I say that?"

With a smile, she licked a bead of precum off the head of his shaft. He barely prevented his eyes from rolling back.

"I misspoke," he breathed, trying not to thrust into her soft palm.

"I thought so," she agreed seriously, licking her way up the side of his shaft while working her hand up and down.

Verakko's body felt like it was on fire. That was how it always was with her. Their spark, which he was confident would never die, transformed into an inferno whenever they made love.

Verakko balled his fists and cursed when her hot mouth covered the head of his cock. She took him deeper into her mouth, matching the motion of her pumping hand. The scent of her growing arousal hit his nose, and he couldn't stand it anymore. He'd never let her ache, not while there was something he could do to ease it.

He tugged at her hair, and she released his shaft with a wet pop. "Fuck, you're sexy."

Her pink-flushed cheeks pulled into a grin. Verakko sat on his knees and gripped her hips. With a modicum of effort, he tossed her onto the couch, feet still on the ground. Still kneeling on the floor, he hooked his arms under her knees and pulled them apart.

Lily gasped, and the scent of her arousal grew. He ducked and, without teasing, swiped his pointed tongue against her sex, lapping up the sweet taste of her arousal. She jumped at the sudden contact, but he held her firm, clutching the tops of her thighs with his large palms.

He swiped his tongue against the sensitive nub at her opening, the way he'd learned she liked, and waited for her telltale moans to quicken. When her breaths started coming in small gasps, he slid one finger inside her core and pumped in time with his tongue. Lily's hips jerked against his mouth, and he growled.

She shoved her hands into his hair and squeezed, sending the most delicious prickle of pain along his scalp. Her moans stopped, and instead she only sucked in little gasps of air. His mate was about to come.

He shoved two fingers inside her slick entrance and pulsed in time with the small flicks of his tongue. Her body stiffened, but he continued to work his mouth on her. As her thighs began to tremble around his ears, his shaft gave an angry throb.

A high-pitched cry tore from her throat just as he felt her body shudder. He slowed his movements, letting her come down. Each of the small whimpers she made as he nipped the inside of her thighs ratcheted his own arousal higher and higher. When her breathing evened out, he gripped her around the waist and dragged her off the edge of the couch until she straddled him once again.

"Hi." She smiled with a dazed grin on her face. She wrapped her arms around his neck, but he snatched her wrists and brought them above her. He flung her shirt up and over her arms, revealing her small breasts and pebbled nipples. She let out a small gasp as he rocked his hips against hers and licked her nipple. He let his fangs brush the underside of her breast before swirling his tongue around her nipple in the way he knew drove her crazy.

Slowly she began to rock her hips more fervently, the scent of her wet heat spiking once again. She tugged on his hair, and he tilted his head up.

Love shone in her eyes as she leaned down to kiss him. "Hi." He grinned, a breath away from her mouth. She smiled and slid her tongue over a fang, already filled with antivenom.

Verakko wrapped his arms around her back, pressing her flush to his chest and deepened their kiss with a slant of his head. Her slick entrance gliding over his shaft and her soft whimpers into his mouth told him she was ready. He palmed her ass and lifted her, aligning their bodies, then lowered her slowly onto his cock.

Lily moaned, breaking away from the kiss to stare into his eyes as he worked himself deeper into her until fully seated. She rested her forehead against his for a moment and nibbled on her lower lip, then rocked forward. They both released a low groan when she lifted off him and surged back down.

Verakko gripped her ass, pushing and pulling her body, creating a steady rhythm. The velvet heat of her tight sheath gloved his cock as he pumped into her.

"Look at me, mivassi," he demanded as her moans grew breathy again.

She peered down at him in that heavy-lidded pleasure-filled way that almost undid him every time.

"Are you ready?"

A brief grin spread over her face, quickly replaced by a low moan as he forcefully ground his hips against her entrance. When she looked at him again, she said, "I'm ready."

Verakko pressed a soft kiss to her jaw. "I love you, Lily."

"I—" Her nails dug into his shoulders, and she gasped as he flipped her onto her back and settled between her legs.

He slid in and out of her in slow, smooth strokes that made her shake and claw at his chest. "Did you say something?" he cooed in her ear.

She let out a breathy laugh between moans and opened her mouth to speak again, but her words died in her throat as he pumped into her more quickly, curling his hips to rub her clit on each thrust.

"Open up," he grated, loving the way she nodded breathlessly and drew her brows in concentration. "My fangs sinking into your neck will feel so good, you'll be on the verge of coming, hard."

His mate whimpered and tilted her head to the side, exposing her neck for him. He licked a fang, and his hips picked up speed.

With a snarl, he buried his fangs in the soft flesh of her neck while bucking into her.

Lily moaned and locked her ankles around his hips, urging him on faster. He felt her body tense on the verge of orgasm. As soon as her walls started spasming around him, he came. He bellowed into her shoulder, her prolonged orgasm milking him on each thrust. Still languidly rocking against her and making her shiver and moan, he collapsed onto his elbows.

When his racing pulse slowed and the lightheaded ecstasy faded, he beamed down and pressed his palms to either side of her face. Eyes still closed, she grinned.

Verakko planted a soft kiss to one eyelid, then the other, then her nose, and finally to her lips.

"I was going to say I love you," she panted, her face still flushed with exertion.

"I know." He nuzzled against her neck again, grinning like a fool at the mark visible on her tanned flesh. His insides always roared in argument whenever he healed the dark marks.

She placed her palms over his and smirked. "Oh, you know, do you?"

He withdrew from her and collapsed onto his back, pulling her to rest atop him as he did.

He rolled his eyes. "Yes, you're always telling me. On and on. 'I love you' this, 'I can't live without you' that…"

Lily giggled and sprinkled soft kisses along his jaw.

"I suppose…" He sighed. "If you really wanted to, you could tell me again."

She laughed and braced his face in her hands the same way he had. "Verakko, look at me," she said, imitating his deep voice.

The corners of his mouth twitched.

"Now, open up to me," she continued in that deep tone.

"I sound nothing like that."

She raised her brows at him until he nodded, pretending to open his mind up to her nonexistent *sway*.

She shuffled up his body until her face was directly above his, her glittering hair falling in waves over her shoulder. Her eyes grew serious. "Verakko, I love you more every single day."

Despite his jesting, his heart swelled, making his chest tight. He nodded, throat too clogged to voice the right words. She grinned wickedly, knowing just how deeply her words affected him.

She tsked, shaking her head in mock dismay, even while tenderly running her thumbs along his jawline. "Ruled by emotions. That's what you are."

His rumbling chuckle was replaced by a rattling purr as his life, his mate, his mivassi, leaned down and kissed him again.

About the Author

Victoria Aveline has always enjoyed immersing herself in a good romance. Alpha males are her weakness but, while possessive dominating heroes have always been titillating, she craved something more. So she decided to create a world in which devastatingly sexy men could be aggressive and domineering but still bow down before the matriarchy.

Victoria lives with her husband, dogs, and about sixty thousand badass honey-making ladies. When not writing or fantasizing about future characters, she enjoys traveling, reading, and sipping overpriced hipster cocktails.

victoriaaveline.com

Made in the USA
Middletown, DE
23 October 2021

50866421R00243